Ruin of the Soul

Jean Dorricott

For Brian and Pippa, Keith and Becky, Susan and Matthew
and their children with love and thanks.

Science without conscience is the ruin of the soul
Francois Rabelais

Chapter 1

The robobus lurched over a pothole and Rachel's shoulder banged against the window, waking her from her doze. In the gloom she reached out for Ben but her son was missing from the seat next to her. As she jumped up in a panic the coach swayed to a stop and she hit her head on the overhead lockers. Rubbing the bruise, she squirmed her way over their bags to the central aisle. The robobus lights were dimmed but she made out four dark figures at the front fumbling with the override.

Ben's shrill voice instructed the male adults on procedure.

They ignored him.

He used his Coventry school autobus regularly and Rachel thought, I bet he understands it better than they do.

Seeing her he said, 'Some idiot keyed in the wrong co-ordinates. We're on the M6 to Manchester, not the M54 to Wales.'

When the robobus was finally started on the correct route he snuggled close to her, complaining his feet were cold. So were hers. Heating was defunct and January cold swirled through gaps under the doors and round windows.

Behind them a woman was complaining she'd been robbed earlier in Rugby. 'Just got on the bus when they took my suitcase. Hijacked right in the centre, in North Street. Guns. Scared stiff, I can tell you. Police – what do they care?'

'Should be armed guards on all these buses,' said her companion.

'We might be hijacked again,' Ben whispered excitedly.

'Hope not. It isn't *fun.*'

She stared out of the window nervously. Robobus headlights fought the blackness ahead bravely but were soon swallowed up by night. No other lights as far as she could see, though they were travelling through one of the planet's largest conurbations. Built in the 'teens, housing, factories, roads and public buildings stretched continuously from Northampton and Kettering in the east to Shrewsbury in the west. A magnet for thieves and criminals across the world.

And dark tonight. National Grid overload yet again.

Everything she and Ben possessed was in the luggage compartment. Arrival in North Wales couldn't come soon enough.

Yes, in spite of earlier doubts, she was right to accept this job. In the Welsh mountains there would be peace for both her and her son. Ben would flourish in the small village school where bullying was under control and no thugs lay in wait outside the school gates. He was struggling to learn Welsh since all lessons were conducted in that language, but that was a small price to pay for safe village streets and kind people. Nothing more savage than the bitter winds and rain of mid January and the rampant wilderness of the Snowdonia Reserve. Dead winter, but spring not far away.

She was woken from her doze by searchlights and Ben scrambling across her to get a better view out of the window.

'It's the border,' she said as the robobus halted and two police came aboard.

'ID,' they demanded and passengers shuffled through bags, wallets and pockets for the essential card.

Ben asked why they'd been stopped.

'Smuggling. We're searching the baggage now.' The policeman pointed to the opposite window where they could see the raised doors of the luggage compartments.

'Smuggling what?' Ben asked Rachel.

'All our food and clothes are rationed. You *know* that. Some people get hold of them illegally. Sell them and make a mint.'

After an hour they were cleared and off again. And now there were more potholes and the road zigzagged between stone walls so the robobus lurched dangerously from side to side. It staggered up steep turns for mile after weary mile and then grumbled and whined as the road turned sharply downhill and the brakes struggled to hold the vehicle.

It was impossible to sleep. Not that Rachel wanted to, tormented as she was so often by nightmares of losing her son. She tried to reason away her fear that they predicted the future. They were surely only due to the major emotional losses she'd suffered recently. But they persisted nevertheless.

She fingered the necklace she kept hidden under her clothes between her breasts. She never removed her talisman. Four years ago her husband Dan had given her the pendant on a simple chain, insisting she wear it always and take the greatest care of it. 'It's token of our love,' he said as she hugged him. 'No matter what comes, remember I love you.' It turned out to be their last evening together. Did he have a premonition?

At the time she was so happy, relieved that his strange withdrawal during the past months was over at last. For a long while it had been impossible to penetrate his reserve, a deep frustration with life that included her. 'There's nothing wrong,' he always said angrily if she asked.

6

Her happiness was brief. He left to lecture at the university the following day, but collapsed at a lunch time dental appointment. He was pronounced DOA at Liverpool University hospital. Cardiac arrhythmia, said the coroner. Could have happened at any time. Everyone was sympathetic. She was devastated.

Shortly after that her mother was diagnosed with terminal cancer and Rachel had to resign her research post at the university and take Ben with her to Coventry. Who else could care for the sick woman since Rachel's father and brother had walked out years ago? She taught for four years, in a science post where student misbehaviour caused more and more frustration. At the same time the quality of life was deteriorating rapidly everywhere. Goods became ever more expensive. As unemployment increased those still in work went on strike for higher pay. Street markets sprang up where people sold or bartered family treasures. Second hand electronic goods sold particularly well as firms had long since transferred their manufacture to the Far East, and now their import price had rocketed far beyond the pocket of the average middle class purchaser. Street theft became ever more violent. Food was short and queues long. Only last month she'd been shopping in a supermarket when a mob with guns stripped the shelves.

After her mother's death the nursing carers encouraged her to apply for a post with Eckstazia, a world-wide Christian organisation they supported enthusiastically. It had a strong commitment to welfare and social improvements through research and development and had also part funded her previous research work at Liverpool University. The post was that of field research officer at a hill farm in North Wales, but she didn't expect to be successful as she'd been out of the field for so long. The application was difficult because she became gadget poor after she left the university and had to rely on her school's antiquated computer system.

Still, she applied and was amazed to be offered an online interview with Dr Shuji Akimoto, leader of the team at Eckstazia's Penybwlch Research Facility. She read up his web profile on Eckstazia's site, and learnt he was in his late fifties, American born of Japanese and French/American Indian parentage. His intimidating degrees and qualifications were listed, including senior positions held over the years. He was a world citizen, educated in Canada and the UK, a linguist, a poet (four slim volumes, a website dedicated to spiritual themes of love and beauty) and an artist who modestly called himself a dauber (paintings hung in important art collections – including the Tate Modern and those of the Emir of Kuwait, Yeo Lili of Shanghai, Professor Hilary Barron the European Union's advisor on ethics and religion and the British Secretary of State for Health. The latter had donated his painting to the prestigious Great Ormond Street Hospital where seriously sick children would be uplifted by its depiction of heavenly joys.)

She found a slot on the computer's timetable and completed a mock interview program that recorded the interviewee's responses. The replayed video shocked her. She thought of herself as attractive, young, active. A thirty-year-old well up in the teaching profession. She saw a run down woman with straggly dull brown hair. A spotty face from poor diet, tired green grey eyes with a furrow between them, a broken incisor from a mugging as she walked home from work.

She attempted to spruce herself up for the online interview. She paid good money for a decent haircut. Bought cheap makeup to hide skin blemishes, eye bags and lines, using it with caution. Eckstazia considered female camouflage to be unscriptural and unnecessary.

Shuji Akimoto was flat faced with heavy lidded eyes. Luxuriant black hair, temples well covered, and not a fleck of grey. In spite of his awesome profile he was gentle and encouraging.

She stuttered, repeating herself. But to her amazement she was offered the post at Penybwlch, a farm rented from the huge Snowdonia Reserve. Pay was less than her teacher's salary, but board and lodging were included for herself and Ben. Dr Akimoto also appointed an online pastor, Emmanuel Rappen, to guide her spiritual path. Three months ago she signed her contract. She checked the box declaring her faith and commitment to the Lord Jesus Christ and her belief in his imminent return to judge the earth.

*

At last the robobus stopped at their destination, a small town on the North Wales coast, and Rachel and Ben were met by a young woman about the same height as Rachel. She wore a brown padded jacket and trousers. Her face was shadowed by the only bright thing about her, a gaudily striped knitted hat dragged almost over her eyes against the chill.

She said briskly, 'You're late. I'll be lucky if I don't get a parking fine and *that* won't please the boss. Should've mobiled.'

'Don't have one.'

Rachel and Ben collected their luggage while the woman took Rachel's small day bag, and hurried her across the bus bays towards an old and dirty Skoda. Ben followed, trying to be grownup and only snivelling quietly as he dragged the case on wheels with his little rucksack on his shoulders.

'Brought the whole house, yeh?' the woman said as Rachel shoved her holdall into the boot, then Ben's case and finally her own large rucksack that felt weighty as Atlas's heaven.

'It's all we have.' Everything in the world.

As the Skoda coughed into life the woman said, 'I'm Alyson Gunnarsson. From Iceland. Obviously. How old's the boy?'

'I'm nearly ten,' Ben said loudly from the back seat.

'You'll be taking him to the junior school tomorrow?'

'Yes. Appointment with the head at nine thirty.'

'Then you'll take Freya to the comp for eight thirty. Thanks.'

'Freya?'

'My daughter.' Alyson swerved to avoid a pothole as the road became steeper and narrower. 'Martin's booked the car for ten thirty so you must rearrange schedules with him. He's our analyst. Pleasant enough, you shouldn't have trouble.'

'I've been promised my own car.'

Alyson made a gravelly noise that Rachel interpreted as a laugh. 'Lady muck are we? You're only a teacher.' She paused. 'I mean teaching's a fine profession in its own way, but you're only a beginner in *this* job. What d'you know about research?'

'I've a masters degree in entomology. Research in the Wirral Reserve, part funded by Eckstazia, while I was at Liverpool University. Lyme disease in humans. I studied diseases of the ticks that carry the sickness so we could prepare strategies for reducing the numbers of carrier insects.'

'Eric – my husband - and I were told you're just a widowed teacher from Coventry.'

'That as well. I went back there after Dan died because my mother was ill.'

'Better now?'

'Dead too.'

'I'm sorry.'

Rachel swallowed hard and turned round to Ben. He was sleeping lightly, head drooping on his rucksack. She persisted, 'Pastor Emmanuel promised me a car with the job.'

'Oh, Emmanuel. *He* wouldn't know. And you *have* got a car. You share it with five of us. Me and Eric, Martin and two technicians.' Alyson swung the car expertly into a driveway 'This is the top of the pass and the road ends here. There's only a track down the other side back to the coast.'

Their way was blocked by a pair of large black metal gates. In the car headlights they shone plain and functional, barricading the Eckstazia scientists in their quarters.

'A bit Gothic.' Alyson opened the window and held her hand out. The gates swung open. 'Sometimes the mechanism doesn't recognise the car. So you open the window and flash your key card at it. That usually works. If it doesn't – contact one of us. You don't want to be left on the wrong side, especially at night.' She drove up a long gravel drive and parked the car alongside three others. Three top of the range hydrogen fuelled cars.

'I'm in the cottage behind us. You're in the main house. With the top brass. Shuji, Jennifer and James. And canny Annie Davies.'

All Rachel could see of the house was an immense bulk of blackness with lights in a few upstairs windows. The stately door was opened to them by an old woman with a twisted mouth who was less than pleased to see them. They dumped their bags in a grand entrance hall and followed Annie into a dismal kitchen. Here they struggled to eat stale bread, jam and meat flavoured paste, all washed down with stewed tea and served by a peeved Annie. She muttered in a strong Welsh accent that people should arrive at the time expected and cursed the estate's tenant farmer who hadn't delivered enough milk. No sign of Dr Akimoto or the other two scientists who lived in the house.

*

'Mummy!'

Ben was screaming in terror behind Rachel, but she struggled in vain to turn round and clutch him. The steady stare of the judge pinned her down like a beetle in a display cabinet. An old woman judge with heavy glasses wearing a shoulder length wig.

That in itself was odd. Surely wigs had been abolished years ago.

'Mummy! Mummy!'

A treacly inertia pervaded Rachel's whole body. She gaped with open mouth at the old woman.

The judge said, 'Your son is forfeit.' She put a black cap on her head. 'And he will be taken away from you and reared by persons unknown and . . . '

'Mummy! Wake up!' Ben was shaking her and squealing like a pig, and suddenly she was awake in the strange bed.

'Wha's matter?'

'Mum, listen.'

Real shrieking. Distant but clear. Piercing through the wind that growled round the corners of the unknown house. Vibrating with terror through the night.

She leapt out of bed, knocking her head on the low ceiling of the unfamiliar room. Swearing, she rubbed the hurt, then put her arms round her son.

'Shh, deary.'

His trembling subsided as the sound died away.

The room was grey and ghostly in the moonlight and she'd forgotten where the light tap was. Then she remembered this huge Victorian house was so outdated it still had switches like the ones she'd used when she was Ben's age. She fumbled across the wall near the door, flicked the light on and pulled on jacket, trousers and trainers.

'Don't go, Mum.'

Still half in her nightmare she dared not leave him alone. 'OK, come too. Here's your gear.'

The screaming began again, a different tone of agony and despair. It faded. Then a final tortured screech made them both jump. Rachel located its direction to the left of the house.

'Torch,' she muttered, rummaging through her untidy bags for her light stick. Nothing. And where in this unknown house would she find one?

She opened the door onto darkness. No one was up and about. Four other people, all sleeping through such a racket. How likely was that? Did no one care?

Briefly she thought of waking Annie. But where did the old housekeeper sleep? And what if she should barge into one of the scientists' rooms by mistake? She hadn't met any of them yet. As for the tenant farmer Annie had spoken of so scathingly, she only knew that he lived alone in the Ty Bach, wherever that might be on this vast Welsh estate.

She searched in vain for the hall light switch. Remembering the stairs went up to a landing before turning downstairs again she hunted cautiously with her foot. Which way did they turn? She'd been so exhausted yesterday evening after their long journey and the meagre meal with Annie, that she could barely remember how to reach the hall. The wooden stairs creaked and her sweaty hand slipped on the polished banister. She held out her other hand to Ben as he followed her. His fears had faded into a delicious excitement at this adventure, safe with Mum.

'Look, Mum.' He picked up a light stick from the hall cupboard and waved it till it shone, illuminating their troubled faces. 'I saw it there last night.'

'Well done.'

'It's not a very good one.'

'It'll do. There's moonlight outside.' They smiled at each other and her heart lurched. He looked so like his father sometimes. Large brown eyes with long lashes, dark hair with the same rebellious lock that always fell over his forehead and a quick impatience with anything that displeased him.

The front door was locked, and she was unsure of the safety number. Ben shone the light on her keypad as she fumbled with it, and she found the combination on the second try and opened the door onto pitch darkness.

The moon was occasionally obscured by rushing clouds and the wind was bitter as black ice. She heard rather than saw the tall pines soughing and clattering in the gale. Bare branches of oak and beech scraped twigs together. Evergreen shrubs obstructed the pair, the spiky holly and berberis pulled at their clothes. Damp dead leaves whipped round their ankles.

Blessing her good sense of direction and Ben's torch, she shortly found a gravel path leading through the garden. A few granite steps down, then a small gate and they were standing in the covered car park filled by the scientists' cars.

'Over there,' Ben said, waving his torch towards the farm buildings, all in darkness. He clutched at her hand, his little fingers cold as stone. 'He's gone quiet. D'you think he's *dead?*'

'Hope not.' She suddenly felt isolated and stupid. Why on earth had she come without backup? Why had she brought her young son? She stood irresolute but he pulled her on as the moon came out briefly and lit up a gap between the sheds. Cautiously they approached, Ben tiptoeing dramatically at Rachel's side as they turned into a yard. In the far corner light from a window shone a deformed rectangle on the concrete.

'That's it,' Ben stage-whispered. 'He's in there.'

The wind tore at them, needling them with frost. Around the yard the trees clamoured high above her head, immense giants guarding the hillside behind the farm. She had never heard so much noise from woodland, never imagined mere trees could make more racket than city traffic outside their old flat in Coventry.

Yet nothing moved in the shelter of the yard except a steamy smokiness swirling from cracks in the closed door beside the window.

It wreathed around a yard brush and upturned barrow silent as mist in a graveyard.

'You stay here,' she ordered and took the light stick. 'Scarper if I shout.'

She approached the light stealthily, shining her torch along the open sheds on her left. A van. Implements whose use she couldn't guess. And something hanging on the wall that looked like a prohibited gun.

The lit window was filthy. A dark human figure moved across the room but dirt prevented any sight of the corpse.

She shivered. No one could expect her to confront the murderer or murderers alone. Now a hasty retreat, a wake up call to the people in the house. . .

Splashing. A disgusting stirring sound, liquid sloshing and wood thudding on metal.

She retched, stumbling against the yard brush which fell with a noisy thud.

Angry barking from the room. The door was flung open showering light and billowing steam across the yard. A wild dog leapt towards her, then crouched, teeth bared and nose wrinkled in an evil snarl.

'Sy 'na?' A rough male voice. 'See 'm off, Toss.'

The dog's tail lashed and ears flattened. Its crouch became prelude to a spring.

Ben rushed to her, screaming, clutching at her wildly, trying to protect her. He shrieked still louder as a tall figure darkened the light. It gave an order the terrified pair couldn't understand, and the dog shuffled away, eyes fixed on the intruders and still growling. Then the silhouette turned to them.

'D'ma.'

A command that meant nothing.

'You. Come here.'

Reluctantly Rachel obeyed, shielding her son behind her.

Steam writhed round the man, issuing from the room behind like smoke from hell. His boots were big as stallion hooves. His hair stuck up like horns. He filled the doorway, his head brushing the lintel. He was rank with sweat and farmyard filth.

He looked her up and down. 'You're the latest nosy parker.'

'I'm Rachel Kerem, ecologist.' She couldn't control the tremble in her voice.

'Exactly.' His Welsh accent was harsh, lacking music and rhythm, his English impeccable. 'Snooper.'

'Screams,' Ben whispered. 'Woke me up.'

The man moved to one side allowing light to shine on the boy's white face. 'They didn't tell me . . . so there's a child as well.'

'I'm not a child. I'm Ben,' the boy protested as bravely as he dare.

'Double trouble.'

At this angle she could see his face, hard and narrow with twisted mouth, broken nose and one eye slightly askew. His age? So weather scarred was his face that he could have been any age from thirty to sixty. He wore a brown nondescript garment covered in stains that hid most of his body. Glancing down she saw the knife in his bloodied hand, and she gagged and jumped back.

Immediately the dog crept forward. It snarled and she felt its hot breath on her bare ankles.

The man had followed her gaze and now he played with his knife. passing it in front of his throat suggestively while he smirked at them both.

Ben, seeing the knife and feeling his mother shake, began to cry.

'Shut it,' ordered the murderer. He tossed the knife behind him and it clattered on the floor. 'Curse you, it's only a pig. Have you never heard one squeal before?' He turned back into the outhouse and Rachel followed him cautiously up a small ramp, the dog still creeping along behind. Now they were standing on the same level she realised the butcher was smaller and slighter than he'd appeared at first, about her own height and lean as a whippet.

The room was drowning in steam. Mistily the pair saw a pale pink body hanging naked and bristly, its hind legs roped and slung over a hook in the rafters. Blood dripped slowly down its snout from the red gash in its throat. As it swung gently it spattered the wet concrete floor with drops that mingled in the mud left by the butcher's filthy boots. Cursing, he steadied the corpse over a stainless steel bucket threequarters full of blood. With his other hand he stirred the thickening contents with a wooden spatula. Wood on metal. Rachel recognised the sound.

'Black puddings,' said the butcher. Then he grinned at Ben, his teeth white, uneven and sharp as a fox's. He held out the stick and blood from its tip plopped back into the bucket. 'Have a stir, bachgen?'

Ben moaned with fear and clutched his mother's arm.

The man made an exclamation of contempt and turned his attention to a metal bath of water bubbling merrily over a couple of gas rings. He picked up a scraping knife, washed it in the water and held out the handle to Rachel. 'Now you're here, make yourself useful.'

She gaped at him.

He ordered, 'I'll scald. You scrape off the bristles.'

'No way.' She put her arm round Ben, turning him to the door. The dog snarled. She said coldly, 'Keep your tyke under control.'

He sneered but whistled through his teeth and the cur trotted to him. Then he turned to the butchery tools laid out sharp and shining on a slate shelf and started to hone the knife on a steel, still whistling. The dog licked at the spots of blood and he cursed it, pushing it away with his broken boot.

Ben didn't cry until he and Rachel reached the front door. 'He's a thug. Why did he kill it?'

'Bacon. Sausages.' She put her arm round him.

'Poor pig.'

The hall light had been switched on and as Rachel fastened the door behind them a woman screeched, 'Where *have* you been at this time of night? Disturbing us all.' Annie the housekeeper shuffled towards them from the direction of the kitchen. She wore fluffy red slippers on her feet and a thick wool knitted robe in shades of brown and fawn that reached from her shoulders to her ankles. Her thin grey hair hung in night time disarray on her shoulders. The left side of her lip was distorted and dribbled spit which she dashed away angrily as she continued, 'You don't wander about at night. Ever. And taking the child. How disgraceful!'

Why should Rachel explain herself to this woman who was, after all, only the housekeeper for the research team? Even so, she felt the need to justify her prowling. 'We were woken by screaming. I'm surprised everyone else slept through it.' But even as she spoke she realised she was the only ignorant one in the house. *They* would all know it was just a pig. Yet did the farmer – she couldn't remember his name though Annie had told her earlier – did he always butcher his animals at this crazy hour? She glanced at her watch. After one o'clock. Friday already. And home slaughtering was totally illegal.

'You've been *down the yard?*' Annie's Welsh shriek was as unmusical as the farmer's. 'Don't you ever go there. You're not employed to nosy around.'

An upstairs door opened and a man's voice called angrily, 'What's the matter? How can I get to sleep with all this noise?'

'Just problems with the new employee, Doctor Akimoto.' Annie was cringingly polite.

'The woman's only just arrived and she's making trouble? Tell her to be quiet. Some of us have to work tomorrow.' His door banged shut.

'Now get yourself and the boy back to bed and no more wandering, Mrs Kerem.' Annie followed them upstairs and waited until they entered their room.

Ben was shivering as Rachel tucked his quilt round him. 'Story, Mum,' he whispered, but she was now so utterly weary that her brain couldn't retrieve any of his favourite space invader tales.

'A Jesus one,' he said.

She tried Jesus calling the little children, but he said, 'I want Dad.'

'He's in heaven with Granny, dear, where there isn't any unhappiness.'

'I want him *here*.'

'So do I, but Jesus wanted him too. Jesus knows best what's good for us all. One day we'll all be together again but you and I must wait and be patient.'

'Why does my other Granny not like me?'

'She does really.' How could she explain that Dan's parents had never accepted the daughter-in-law who wasn't a practising Jew? She felt sometimes they blamed her for Dan's early and sudden death four years ago.

Ben started to cry like a little child so she helped him into her own bed, and asked Jesus to take care of them both. He tossed for a while, but at last he slept, breathing nasally with little snorts.

*

Unable to sleep herself, Rachel lay on her back, eyes open. Cloud had thickened, rain started to patter and then to lash against the window. Trees groaned and the night was full of unexplained thuds and bangs. The old house itself creaked in time with the gusts of wind.

She hadn't exactly endeared herself to her new boss tonight. She fondled her pendant automatically, her protective charm. Apologies would be in order tomorrow – no, today. In a few hours. If only she didn't feel so tired, so confused.

She wondered about the box on the nearby table. 'Courtesy of Pastor Emmanuel' it said on the label, but she and Ben had been too tired to open it when they arrived. And she knew in advance what it would contain. An e-book full of dull homilies. As if she wasn't fully aware of Christian morals. She wasn't too fussed about this spiritual mentor Dr Akimoto had provided. A doddery old parson without a doubt. She'd received a few emails via the school computer but hadn't troubled to access his website. Alyson, the researcher from Iceland, had been pretty dismissive of him.

Ben muttered in his sleep, flung out his arms and whacked her on the chin. She grinned and moved his arm away. Her bed was a large single one, but he'd crept well into the centre in his sleep. As she rolled him back gently she heard a door beneath them open and shut stealthily. Footsteps. A door or cabinet lid creaking open and then slamming shut loudly. Some angry words, faintly, in a man's voice. The door opening and closing again, and footsteps on concrete fading among the noise of wind and rain.

That tenant farmer without a doubt, whose name she'd forgotten but whose ugly features were indelibly printed in her memory. Bringing in the pork joints.

The whole incident was bizarre. Killing pigs in a shed at midnight! When all animals had to be slaughtered at properly registered abattoirs. Humanely. In sterile conditions for fear of passing diseases to consumers. Every animal was electronically tagged, its provenance assured and for the past four years, all meat had been rationed. Diet control for an obese nation said the government posters. The usual weasel words. Everyone knew the failed euro could no longer buy cheap food abroad and idle British farmers failed to cover the shortfall.

Furthermore domesticated animals were forbidden within five miles of wildlife reserves. And this man kept pigs actually *on* Snowdonia Reserve property. He had an illegal dog as well.

The door below opened again, the cabinet lid squeaked but the man didn't leave. Where *was* the Ty Bach, the Little House where he lived? Tomorrow she'd find out what was going on.

The windows flexed and a loose slate complained to the gale as tree branches scraped across the roof.

'Penybwlch, head of the pass,' she said softly. 'Pen uh boolch.' No, she hadn't got it quite right yet in spite of studying Welsh these past three months. She had a good ear for the nuances of language, and was convinced she and Ben would soon master Welsh intricacies.

Light woke her, a pale crisp glow of winter dawn barely illuminating the walls and furniture. Ben slept peacefully beside her, his face innocent in the dim light. She crept from the bed, careful to dodge the beam that she'd struck last night in her hurry to get down the yard. The ceiling was low, quite different from the lofty hall and stairway. The windowsill was puddled with water and reached barely higher than her knees. Her fingers became wet as she traced them along the leaking wooden frames. She looked out and drew a deep breath. It was so beautiful.

The trees surrounding the house whispered and waved peacefully. A narrow valley extended down from the house between steep crags silhouetted against the slow dawn. It was full of rhododendrons, the scourge of these wild valleys. But how imperial they'd be in their spring purple in a few months. The hillsides were covered in dead bracken on their lower slopes and heather clad to their tops. Far beyond was a silver glimpse of river with rounded hills on its further bank. The winter sun was just rising above them, still orange and pearl. She would love the mornings in this mysterious land so full of hidden histories and ancient superstitions. A bewitching land that could captivate the heart.

Immediately beneath her a concrete path led from a back door down past bushes to the hidden yard. She glimpsed slate roofs among the trees. Those must be the farm buildings of last night's adventure.

She shivered, hoping they would have little further contact with the uncouth butcher.

To her right the main part of the mansion jutted forward into a garden of high tangled shrubs. The door she and Ben had used was in that section, but she couldn't see the path, steps or carpark from here. Now she realised there were two distinct parts to the house. The larger part was an add-on, far more splendid than the original farmhouse. She and Ben were housed in the old section with its low ceilings and small windows.

They'd been too exhausted last night to do more than give the room a cursory glance before tumbling into the beds. Now she noted the fitted cupboard along one wall, two upright chairs pushed under the table and two easy chairs. No pictures, but a wall computer screen above the table old as the one she'd had as a child, in the happy days before the family break-up. The carpet was threadbare in patches, and covered with a mothy sheepskin beside the larger bed. A bed almost as old as the house. She'd seen a similar one in Coventry. A young woman was selling up family treasures on the street, anxiously polishing the high leather headboard with its painted flowers and studded edges. Who, she wondered at the time, would buy such a monster? Yet here in Penybwlch the old bed looked homely.

She rummaged in her holdall for some clothes. The bathroom was across a narrow hallway and by the time she returned Ben was up and fiddling with the box on the table.

'What's this, Mum?'

'How exciting!' she encouraged with false enthusiasm. 'Open it up.'

He pulled back the cardboard flaps and packaging. First he found a pair of binocular glasses.

Rachel inspected them. 'High lens diameter. Wide angle. *And* night vision.' She fitted them on and stared through the window, testing the magnification.

Ben opened another box. 'A mobile.'

'No, it's a yapp!' his mother exclaimed.

'What's that?'

'Smartphone. The name's a corruption of i-apps. I haven't had one since we left Liverpool.' My god, this was an improvement on the expected homilies! she thought as she fiddled with it, unable at first to access the information she wanted. 'Listen. It pronounces Welsh words and phrases. Oh, and it can ID plants and animals. It magnifies too. I can get any information I need.' She'd check out Reserve regulations concerning the keeping of domestic animals among other things. She turned its screen on her son. 'If you'd been chipped it'd tell me all about your life. As it is I get limited info about your name and age.'

He snatched it and tried it on his mother. Laughing they played with the gadget until it suddenly rang out a brief tune. The screen image flickered and Penybwlch buildings appeared, sunlight shimmering over roofs and trees waving in spring breezes. She transferred the little image to the wallscreen above the table and together they watched and listened as music played. An orchestral piece by the modern composer Podolski, soothing and spiritual. A piece Rachel had always loved but had rarely had time or opportunity to listen to in her frenetic and gadget-poor life.

As the image and music faded a young man's face appeared, an open face with honest eyes and full mouth. Pastor Emmanuel Rappen, present in realtime.

'Good morning, Rachel and Ben.' His eyes were deep blue and enticing as the sea on a summer's day. Behind him the sun shone across sand dunes and shingle.

'Good morning,' they replied in unison. And Rachel stammered, 'Thank you. For everything . . . all these.'

'You're welcome. I hope your stay at Penybwlch'll be happy and fruitful.' His shoulder length hair shone gold and copper in the sunlight, an aureole encircling his face. 'Remember how precious you both are to us all. Partly because you are widow and orphan, in need of comfort and a home, but mostly for what you are in yourselves. You'll enrich our work for the betterment of human lives everywhere. And remember, I have *your* interests at heart specially. You may contact me by yapp at any time, and I'm available directly every Friday evening so we may discuss the past week and look forward to the next.'

The picture faded. Beautifully inscribed words claimed, 'No one who trusts God will be brought to ruin. Psalm 34, verse 22.'

'Who's that?' whispered Ben, awestruck.

'Emmanuel, our friend and guide. I didn't know . . . never realised . . .'

'What, Mum?'

'He looks so *young*.'

Ben shrugged and turned back to playing with the binocular glasses, but Rachel pointed at the screen. 'That's true. Trust, and we'll be safe.'

'That guy with the pig was scary.'

'And his dog. But God'll keep us.'

But there was a big problem ahead. Her angry supervisor, disturbed from righteous sleep at the end of a hard day, Dr Shuji Akimoto.

When she and Ben entered the dining room she recognised his distinctive smooth black hair as he stooped over containers of fruit juices, cereals, milk and fresh fruit arranged on a magnificent oak sideboard. A feast indeed.

He was taller than she'd expected and his face was severely lined unlike his enhanced screen image. He said solemnly, 'Good morning, Rachel and Ben Kerem,' and gave them a slight bow. 'I hope you slept well after your night excursion.'

She couldn't tell whether he was angry or forgiving. 'I'm sorry we disturbed you. I . . .'

'Did you see the pig?' Ben asked. 'The man killed it. It screamed. Just like a human. There was blood . . .'

'Quite so,' Shuji interrupted. 'You're an observant young man, I see.'

'And it . . .'

Shuji said amicably, 'I think it's best if we all forget about that incident.'

But she was not sure it would be forgotten. Still, breakfast was inviting; she hadn't seen such a spread for years. She and Ben helped themselves with gusto.

The dining room was far more attractive than the kitchen. Round the top of high white walls was a frieze of swagged ivy picked out in pale green, and a bronze-finish chandelier hung from a central boss. The windows had thick stone mullions giving distinction to the room. A few easy chairs were arranged by the window with an occasional table covered with neat rows of research magazines and a vase of silk flowers. The carpet was thick and dark green, the table a polished oak matching the sideboard. The table's centrepiece was a Chinese bowl containing more silk flowers among gold centred ivy leaves and trailing periwinkles.

As Rachel and Ben sat down, Annie entered, in long black dress with white apron, her hair scraped back into a wispy roll. She pushed a heated trolley with canteens of porridge and scrambled eggs. She served Shuji with the eggs, ignoring Rachel and Ben, and returned to the kitchen as silently as she'd come.

Shuji said as he wiped his mouth on a crisp white serviette, 'I'm busy today, but I hope you'll both join us all for dinner tonight. Tomorrow you and I will discuss your work here, Rachel. Ten o'clock. In my study.' Again that slight bow as he rose from table. No smile, no frown.

The other two scientists were still absent when Rachel and Ben finished. As they returned to their room Annie met them in the hall, her currant black eyes staring malevolently at them. 'You've got the car. You pick up my parcel from the store on the quay.'

'Can't the farmer collect it in his van?'

'Out of action. No fuel.' Annie's hair roll dropped a couple of pins as she shook her head.

It had looked roadworthy last night, and surely every farmer had privileged fuel tokens, unlike most of the population. But there was no reason for Annie to lie.

Annie unfolded a paper sketch map of the farm buildings and surrounding land. 'This part is farmland and you're barred from it . . . ' She stabbed at it with a crooked arthritic finger. 'Unless Dr Akimoto gives permission. Or,' and she gave a derisive snort, 'William Parry.'

Of course. That was the name of the lout in the yard. Rachel placed the map carefully in her pocket.

Chapter 2

'I hate it here,' Freya said sulkily, scrambling out of the car with a pile of ancient books. She didn't look at all like her mother. She was tall with a narrow nose, long fair hair and blue eyes. The trousers of her prim school uniform were too tight while her grey jacket was worn and baggy and Rachel wondered why Alyson dressed her only child so badly.

Her comprehensive school was at the edge of the nearby town on the river estuary, the same river Rachel had seen earlier that morning from her window. In the schoolyard students milled round shouting unintelligibly at one another.

'Welsh, Welsh, Welsh,' Freya said, as sure of her opinions as only a young teenager can be. '*Bor*-ing Cymraeg. Why should I have to learn everything in the stupid language?'

Ben took off his head phones, saying, 'I'm learning Welsh, aren't I, Mum?'

'We both are,' Rachel said.

Freya dropped a book and some of the pages drifted into the gutter. She picked up the book but let the pages flutter away. 'So . . . oo rubbish. No smartphones. Ten year old laptops. All bust. Kids think it's *fun* to smash 'em. There's a flat screen outside the maths department playing drivel on infantile Pythagoras, can you believe? And the English one's Shakespeare for dummies, and we're told to watch them in break times.' She stalked off towards the school buildings.

The estate car engine sputtered and coughed its ancient way into life and Rachel drove through dilapidated housing till they arrived at the medieval town wall enclosing the town centre. Graffitied signs directed them to the quay along a rough tarmac road where weeds forced their way through cracks and potholes. Beyond a stone archway they parked on a broad dockside, bright in the low winter sun.

Above them a great grey castle menaced the little town. Strong and compact as a grizzled lion guarding its kill, it crouched on a massive rocky outcrop. It squinted balefully at the surrounding countryside through vertical window slits. Out of each corner tower four smaller ones pointed to the sky like threatening fingers. There were two flagpoles.

'What's the flags?' Ben asked.

'The dragon's Welsh. The other's the new Independent England and Northern Ireland flag. It's the Union Jack without the St Andrew cross of Scotland, though it's still got blue in it.'

'Why no Wales?'

'Wales has been part of England for years so it's included in St George's red cross.'

A few small fishing boats were tied to gull-spattered bollards. The gulls themselves were swooping and cackling across the water of the estuary, robbing one another of food scraps. Buildings lining the quay were in substantial need of repair, their missing slates covered by cracked tarpaulin. Denatured wooden walls hadn't seen protective paint or tar for years.

Two old sailors sat side by side on a large box. They stared at the lapping water, mouths half open, eyes half shut. One wore a cap, the other a woolly hat, both dirty. Their worn trousers were tied at the ankle with string and their jackets were streaked with filth.

Ben whispered, 'The gulls've shitted on them. D'you think they're dead?'

Rachel giggled. 'No, they've turned into stone statues. No use asking them which is Annie's store.'

Without turning, one of the sailors said, 'That's the place you want.' He spat in the direction of a brick building with dark windows, felt roof and two bolted doors large enough to take a vessel. A smaller door was inserted in one of these, and this stood open.

After the sunlight it was dungeon dark inside. Ben staggered against a clattering pile of buckets. Voices, both male and female, exclaimed loudly in Welsh. As the newcomers became accustomed to the one dusty electric light, they made out coiled ropes, rusty cans and tins of all shapes containing food, engine oil and paint, along with piles of nondescript boxes unopened and unmoved since they'd arrived here aeons ago. Shelves sagged with hammers, spanners and chains, heavy containers of nuts and bolts, nails and screws. The place smelt of rusting metal, stale food, grease and paraffin while an indefinable maritime odour wove through the whole.

At the far end a trestle table served as counter and support for a drunken cabinet. A man and woman lolled against it. Two other men and a second woman slumped on wooden stools. All were middle-aged, and so roughly dressed that even Rachel's charity clothes looked trendy. Ten unfriendly eyes stared at the newcomers.

The seated women stated in English, 'You've come for Annie Davies's order.' She didn't move. She didn't smile. Her tightly tied hair shone brown under the dim light and her clothes were grey and dull as Annie's dressing gown.

Rachel replied, 'That's right.'

Ben picked up the metal buckets.

'Stop messing around,' said one of the men.

'*Mess?*' Ben stared round at the general shambles. 'I'm only helping.'

'Don't.'

The tallest of the men was rummaging under the table. He dropped a tightly tied cardboard box on the top. 'All there, Missus.'

'And tell Annie,' said the woman aggressively, and now Rachel was close to her she could smell bad breath and see rotten teeth, 'tell Annie to sort that Will Parry of hers. Fencing, tell her. Along the top road. There's been a wolf.'

'Two,' said a man who had been silent. 'Evan's Mary was attacked. Can't walk.'

'Someone's dog,' Rachel said coldly, angered by their hostility.

'We're stupid? Don't know the difference?'

Rachel replied robustly, 'All reports of wolf-savaging incidents in the national parks have proved to be false identification of dogs. The wolves are far more frightened of us than we are of them.'

'Wrrr,' the man growled deep in his throat. 'That's Welsh Assembly speak.'

The woman added, 'Roebuck finished Jones Bron Edda. Alan Griffiths' right arm is useless. Red deer.'

The tall man said, 'And *we* can't afford hospital treatment. Or bionic replacements. Not like you English.'

'Saesn'g,' hissed the woman leaning on the bench, her long nose pointing at Rachel like a snake's snout.

Rachel's grasp of politics was hazy, her knowledge of differences between the English Government and Welsh Assembly nonexistent. She refused to be drawn into a political argument and said firmly, 'Stags never come near towns and wolves run away unless you corner them. So anyone who gets hurt has only themselves to blame.'

The tall man menaced her, 'You keep your cursed wolves under control. You may think you're well protected at Penybwlch, but . . . .' He stepped towards her.

One of the women caught his sleeve. She spoke rapidly in Welsh, too rapidly for Rachel's limited understanding.

Frightened and puzzled by their belligerence, she picked up the heavy box, almost overwhelmed by its fishy stench, and hustled Ben out into the sunlight.

Ben asked, 'Why were they so nasty?'

'I don't know. We haven't done anything to deserve it.'

As they returned to the car the two old sailors turned their heads in unison, watching them, expressionless.

They drove along narrow streets passing chapels with highly decorated brick fronts named Sion or Carmel or Bethel. Between them were rows of fishing cottages, little town houses opening directly onto the streets, municipal buildings and medieval frontages, all roofed with the ubiquitous slate, all poorly repaired. A few shoppers turned to watch them, their faces blank, their clothes drab and worn. Coventry folk couldn't afford to dress well, but they hadn't sunk to such depths of indifference as these dull creatures. On the high street shop windows stared blankly at them, the empty spaces behind them carpeted with dusty letters and fliers. Ar Wrth was scrawled in white across numerous glass doors.

Ben consulted the yapp's Welsh. 'For Sale,' he translated triumphantly.

'*All* of them?'

'Sure.'

They arrived at the junior school where the headmistress was supervising a small group of six year olds replacing last term's pictures on the entrance hall walls with new vibrant splodges. She at least was smart. Polished shoes of soft leather, orange and grey cotton blouse with a bow at the neck. A grey suit in fine wool, barely worn. Next to her Rachel felt shabby.

'Good morning, Mrs Kerem.' The Head shook Rachel's hand introducing herself as Mrs Lloyd. 'And Ben.' Solemnly she shook his hand as well, and they stared at each other. Then to his confusion she spoke to him in Welsh, and his finger went into his mouth.

'Take that out,' the Head said in English. She turned to Rachel. 'What is his academic level? I'll put him into a lower group until his Welsh improves.' She turned to the boy again. 'I'll introduce you to your new class while your mother waits here. Start on Monday.'

Rachel compared it with the primary school her son had enjoyed in Coventry. Noisy, boisterous kids. A bit lively, said the staff ironically. But here? The group of unsupervised children was still working hard, barely speaking to one another. Come to that, the whole school was quiet.

'Did you like it?' she asked hopefully as he returned to the car.

'Poof. Stinks in here.'

'Fish in Annie's parcel. Your new teacher, what's she like?'

'OK.'

She parked the car at Penybwlch spot on the new time she'd negotiated with Martin the analyst. He jumped in, thrust his young round face out of the window to ask her what dead animal she'd hidden in the car and bumped away down the drive in a cloud of dust.

Rachel held the fishy parcel well away from her clothes as she stared up at the house. The newer part was ostentatious Victorian gothic with two square towers projecting either side of a monumental arched doorway. False battlements surmounted them. The roofs had decorative metal strips running along their apexes and were covered with lichen dotted slate. A stunted silver birch struggled out of the side of a massive chimney. Three storeys of solid stone walls. No damp course. Heating expenses must be enormous. No wonder they needed that large wind turbine on the hill behind.

The original farmhouse was attached to the right of the main house. It was very old, consisting of two squat storeys and rampant with ivy. Its slate roof was chipped and green with mosses and the chimney was small. Like a child's drawing it had four windows, two up, two down and a low central door with a path leading down to the yard.

Ben walked towards the old house but a gate now shut off the entrance to both yard and house. He rattled it, but it was padlocked. 'Wasn't shut last night.'

Beyond the gate they saw Annie's gaunt figure in a long drab coat, gesticulating fiercely at Parry who lounged against a shed wall, woolly hat pulled well over his ears, dog at heel.

Annie's Will Parry, the woman in the town store had said. He was unlikely to be the housekeeper's employee. As Parry raised two contemptuous fingers at Annie Rachel suddenly saw the connection. Annie Davies and William Parry had the same twisted mouth. A genetic fault. His age was uncertain, but he looked younger then Annie. A brother or cousin?

The wind blew towards her so Rachel could hear Annie's words, but her Welsh wasn't up to the interpretation. The housekeeper was furious, barking hoarsely at the farmer. Suddenly he lunged forward and snatched her by the throat, his coarse words echoing round the buildings. Then he looked round and saw Rachel and Ben watching beyond the gate. He released his hold and strode away into the yard, whistling his dog to follow. Annie shook her fist at his back, then disappeared into the old house.

'Could you understand what they said, Mum?'

'No. Could you?'

'Dod-oo-ee. Laying eggs, I think. Could be wrong.'

'Why so angry about *eggs*?'

'Dunno.'

'Odd.'

*

'What's the singing?' Ben asked that evening as he and Rachel came downstairs for dinner. The front door was open and as they walked towards the well-lit carpark they saw Martin fitting a light to his bike. Another young man and woman sang robustly and tunelessly about the rapture of life, yeh.

They stopped as Ben approached and started giggling. 'Horrid noise,' admitted the girl.

'Cacophonous.' Martin rolled the word round his mouth with relish.

'Where're you going?' Ben asked.

'We only stay in the cottage during the week. Seconded from Bangor University. Back Sunday evening.'

The other man said, 'Twelve miles. Keeps us fit.'

'I came off in a pothole last month. Coast road's full of them.' The girl showed a bandaged wrist under her sleeve. She pushed her thick plait of fair hair over her shoulder as she smiled. 'You're Ben and Rachel, aren't you? And we're Martin, Tim who's part time sec to Shuji, and me, Ashley.'

Rachel asked, 'Rapture? You were singing about rapture. What's that?'

Ashley stared, her blue eyes wide in surprise, '*The* Rapture. You really don't know?' As Rachel shook her head, she continued, 'Eckstazia *means* the Rapture. Ecstasy. It's the wedding day of Jesus when all of us faithful believers'll be snatched up into heaven, saved from all the tribulation that's going to come. Those left behind will think it's UFOs have got us or rubbish like that, but we'll be rejoicing and worshipping for ever with the saints in glory.'

'Up into the sky? Like a rocket? ' Ben goggled.

'Sure. Thousands of us. Taken from our cars, our trains, our homes, wherever we may be. God's indisputable sign that Jesus is his son.'

Ben persisted, 'Going to the moon? Or Mars?'

'No, to heaven. It's invisible. Where God lives with all his angels.'

Ben stared into the immensity of the darkening frosty sky and the single eye of Venus gazed steadily back. 'If you don't go up, what happens?'

'You're the Left Behind. Not at all nice for you. I worry for my Dad. He doesn't believe, so he'll miss the Rapture.' Her pretty face was downcast.

Tim broke in, 'There'll be big trouble for seven years. That's *the* Tribulation. Muggings, murders, bombings, immorality everywhere. Worse even than today. And at last God will show his anger with sin. He'll increase natural disasters like volcanoes and earthquakes . . .'

'Famines, wars, plagues like rinderpest. Then God and Jesus will come in power and throw all the wicked and the unbelievers into hell for ever and ever.' Ashley recited the phrases with pleasure, and Rachel wondered if she included her doubting father among the hell-bound.

Tim continued, 'If you're left behind you'll have to get hold of water purifying tablets because fresh water will turn to blood like Moses' miracles in ancient Egypt. And you must set up a hideout with food, blankets and guns to protect you from the vicious criminals roaming the earth unchecked.'

Martin finished fixing his light. 'The most dangerous man is the Antichrist. He'll be charismatic . . . '

'What's charis . . . whatever?' Ben looked up at his mother.

'Charming, attractive. Popular.'

'Yeh. And because money will be useless he'll offer everyone an electronic implant. On their forehead or arm. This'll control all your finance, so you won't be able to eat or live without it. But you mustn't accept it on any account. It's the mark of the Beast who hates God, and once you're implanted you'll never be able to remove it, and God will punish you for eternity.'

'Oh, come on, Martin,' Rachel said. 'All babies have been implanted at birth for ages. Is our government the Antichrist?'

'It comes close. How many Christians are there in Westminster? Real ones I mean, not just say-so ones.'

Rachel grinned. 'Where d'you get all this stuff?'

He said severely, without a flicker of a smile, 'Don't you read your Bible? It's all there. Jesus promises to come again and take us up into the heavenly mansions. Saint Paul says we'll be caught up in the clouds to join the Lord in the air, just like Enoch and Elijah in the Old Testament. Ezekiel tells us it'll happen during the great war when the armies of the north – that's the Russians – attack Israel, like they're threatening at this very moment. Surely you believe Jesus is coming again?'

'Why, yes. All Christians believe that.'

'Don't you believe the Bible is God's Word of salvation for sinners?'

'Of course. That's standard Christianity too.'

Ashley said, 'Then you read Revelations. Everyone in Eckstazia's waiting for the Rapture. It's close. The signs are all there. Haven't you got an online spiritual mentor? He'll record the prophecies on his website.'

'Emmanuel's my mentor.'

'*Emmanuel?*' All three young scientists stared at her round-eyed. 'Pastor Emmanuel Rappen? He's tops.'

'Tops?'

Martin continued, 'He's Eckstazia's Supreme Pastor in Britain.'

Ashley interrupted, 'So many people want to meet him that he lives in a private retreat, a solitary monk. He's only accessible via his website. He's such a spiritual man, quiet, caring, full of love for anyone in trouble.'

'He's never messaged me about this Rapture. But I don't communicate often. We couldn't afford web access at home, so I had to book time at the school where I taught. As other staff were in a similar position there weren't many free slots. And it was always crashing.'

'We can look now,' Ben reminded her. 'He's given us a touch-screen yapp. Talkie talkie, no keypad.'

Tim whistled. 'State of the art, eh? He must think very highly of you.'

Ashley's pixie face was solemn. 'You know about his miracles? He cured my friend's dad's cancer. It was inoperable but he stretched out his hand and said, "Be clean."'

Tim said in an awed voice, 'Just like Jesus and his disciples. And did you hear of. . . . '

'C'm on.' Martin slapped on his helmet and put his boot on the pedal. 'See you Monday, Rachel and Ben.'

Ashley felt her front tyre. 'Hope William repaired the puncture properly this time.'

'How likely is that,' Tim said with contempt.

How young they were, Rachel thought as she watched their red tail lights bounce down the uneven drive. Their happy voices, laughing and joshing, echoed back to her with memories of her younger days. She was only a few years older, and yet there was a lifetime of experiences separating her from them. As for Rapture, the thought of rising suddenly into the air seemed ludicrous, if not downright scary.

'What's that noise?' Ben asked, hearing a bell-like sound from the hallway behind them.

'A gong,' she said. 'How quaint. Calling us for dinner. Let's go and meet the rest of them.'

They were last to arrive for dinner and the three scientists had already said grace. Unwittingly, Rachel sat down without making the proper thanksgiving, Ben beside her. Beautifully cooked portions of fish had been placed on their plates by Shuji, who was sitting at the head of the table.

'I want fish fingers. Mum, I *really* want fish fingers.' Ben spoke softly in his moany voice.

'This is *fresh*, Ben. Try it.' They hadn't had fresh fish for years. Rachel popped a chunk in her own mouth, relishing flavour and texture.

'Don't care. I want them.' His voice rose to a squeal.

The other diners smiled wanly and continued eating. Only James Restall, a roundfaced molecular biologist, took time out to talk to the despondent child.

'Fish fingers is only left over bits mashed together, Ben. With lots of fish flavoured fungus added. This is real. Out of the sea.'

Ben tried a piece again. 'Aw right. But I like. . .'

James grinned and a cheerful dimple deepened near his mouth. 'Fish fingers. I know. But you might get to like this in time. We have it every week, and Annie's an excellent cook.'

Every week, Rachel thought in delight. And then she hesitated. It had come in that parcel from the town store. Fishy in more ways than one, because European fishing fleets had long since expired with the collapse of fish stocks. And food coupons certainly couldn't support farmed fish. Didn't anyone else find it unusual?

She glanced round the table. It was obvious from their smart clothes that they'd all changed for dinner and she was ashamed of her pilled red sweatshirt and patched jeans.

James sat on Shuji's right. He was barely older than herself, a chunky young man with a good humoured face. Most noticeable were two regrown fingers on his left hand. Not quite the right shape. Stiff. Some ten years ago researchers came to understand limb regrowth in the limbs of amphibians such as salamanders and treatment was permitted in humans a few years later. They weren't wholly successful at first, so she deduced James' injury was an old one as today's repairs were invisible with full movement restored. But only for those with plenty of money. His brown hair was receding and she wondered why he hadn't had trichosis therapy as Shuji certainly had.

Just then James looked up and smiled at her. His large brown eyes were fringed with lashes dark as his hair. They twinkled at her in such a friendly way that she felt immediately at home. She smiled back. He was so completely different from Shuji.

And from Jennifer Beard, the other member of the trio who lived in the main house. She sat on the other side of Shuji, a mousy haired woman in her late forties with a scattering of grey threads showing she didn't bother to colour. Her oval face was void of smile lines and a dark crease showed between her eyes. She ate with fierce concentration but all her bodily movements were supple and elegant.

None of them seemed at all interested in the provenance of the fish as they munched their way through each succulent morsel and sipped their wine. So why should she be concerned how their food coupons were spent? It was a long time since she or Ben had eaten this well, certainly not since Dan died four years ago. Would they also be eating William Parry's pork and bacon soon? She hoped so.

The chandelier lights flickered and Jennifer complained, 'That faulty turbine again. You Poms should've worked out electricity storage strategies by now. We Aussies developed vanadium flow batteries to overcome these momentary hiccups last century. Failure proof technology.'

The lights failed altogether.

'Great!' Shuji exclaimed. 'And what about the lab?'

'We're linked into the spare generator at nights,' James said. 'We had this problem last winter before you came, Shuji, so I always make sure everything's safe and sound.'

In the confusion Ben brought out the light stick he'd found previously and set it upright on the table so the glow lit their worried faces.

'Well done, young man,' Shuji said. 'And here comes the redoubtable Annie with candles. How long do you suppose we'll be without light, Annie?'

'Hard to say, Dr Akimoto. Electric's been bad all day. Wind turbine sabotaged, isn't it?' She sounded almost pleased.

James said anxiously, 'That's what you told us last winter. Who's behind it?'

'Couldn't say, Dr Restall.' She spoke so correctly and politely that Rachel found it difficult to connect her with the aloof woman who'd been so unwelcoming the previous evening.

Shuji inspected the fruit bowl. 'No bananas, Annie?'

'No, sir. Housekeeping won't run to it.'

'Well, well. We must sort that out,' he said jovially.

Bananas! Rachel thought. When had she or Ben last shared one? Could he even remember?

Ben was about to comment, so she nudged him, shaking her head. Shuji knew she was in financial difficulties but she didn't want the others to know how poor they both were.

James said, 'I was just about to explain to you, Rachel, that our weekends are al fresco. Most of us leave and Annie goes home Saturday morning till Monday. So if we stay over and want meals, we have to let her know and she'll leave food in the kitchen fridges. I've taken the liberty of ordering meals for you and Ben for this weekend, on the assumption you'll be staying around.' Shadows passed eerily across his face in the flickering candlelight. His cheerful smile seemed strangely sinister.

Rachel shivered, told herself not to be stupid and thanked him.

'We'll be back Sunday evening for church,' James said. 'We hope you'll join us then.'

The meal over, they all retired to the lounge, a fine high room twice the size of the dining room and with a deeper frieze and three chandeliers. Candles were already placed on tables, mantelpiece and the grand piano. Ben wandered over to the piano, lifted the lid and played a note.

Jennifer said immediately. 'Stop that noise.'

He let the lid slam and turned to a mahogany display cabinet full of unusual curios. A shrunken head with long hair took his fancy, but the door was locked. He pressed his face and fingers against the glass and polished wood as Annie entered with a tray of coffee.

'Get off,' she ordered him. 'Who d'you think has to clean up after you've left dirty marks all over?'

He stared back at her rebelliously, but joined his mother when she called him.

'Look, Annie's brought you hot chocolate, just as you like it.'

'Don't want it.'

She patted the soft feather cushions on the leather settee and he sat beside her reluctantly. He looked exhausted, dark shadows under his eyes, his whole face pinched and grey with weariness and anxiety. He sipped the despised chocolate while staring blankly into the large wood fire crackling merrily in an open hearth.

As suddenly as they'd failed, the lights came on again and they all breathed sighs of relief.

Shuji poured himself coffee, said a brief 'Goodnight' accompanied by his customary bow and left the room, cup in hand.

Jennifer said to Rachel, 'We don't often talk shop in the evening but we'll make an exception for you.' Her voice was harsh but not unfriendly, its Australian accent marked. 'You aren't going to work with us in the lab, but you ought to know what we do. What's your take on rinderpest?'

'Not much more than what's on your web site.'

'Not a lot then.'

'It's cattle plague. A virus, spread by direct contact and in water and grazing contaminated by infected cattle dung. It used to infect large parts of the world. Dreaded scourge of Europe for centuries and still a notifiable disease, though it hasn't been seen in the UK for ages.'

'Mid nineteenth century, to be accurate,' James said. 'Compulsory slaughter of diseased stock was first introduced then, which helped reduce foot-and-mouth in the UK at the same time. Rinderpest's a ruinous disease, very virulent, causing death within a fortnight and considerable pain and distress to the animal.'

Rachel filled her cup again. 'Early this century there was a big push to wipe it out worldwide. Successful in . . . I forget.'

'Twenty eleven. Like smallpox in humans, completely eradicated. The Global Rinderpest Eradication Programme, GREP, was set up by the United Nations in nineteen ninety-four. There were three lineages of the virus that caused the disease, and two of these were eliminated by the turn of this century by strict segregation and co-ordinated vaccination. Vaccination's the best control method. The third lineage persisted in east Africa, chiefly Kenya and Tanzania due to the nomadic Somalian pastoral ecosystem. Wild animals in the national parks provided a reservoir of a mild form of disease. Buffalo, eland, giraffe, warthog. Occasionally the virus mutated into a more virulent form and spread out among nomadic domestic animals.'

Jennifer lent forward gracefully as she took a chocolate mint from a box on a marble inlaid table. 'Modern methods were eventually successful and research teams moved on to other problems. Eckstazia was pre-eminent in backing the eradication scheme financially and in forwarding the research. We at Penybwlch are one of two facilities in Britain who now store the virus. Pirbright's the other. We research possible mutations. Just as well because it reappeared in the Sudan eighteen months ago. A severe form of lineage one.'

'I didn't know,' Rachel exclaimed.

'No reason why you should. The media was preoccupied with the Coronation at the time,' James said. 'It spread like wildfire. People didn't recognise it at first. Cattle hadn't been vaccinated. A month later it arrived in South America and devastated their beef industry.'

Rachel carefully took Ben's half finished mug of chocolate from his hand as he slumped against her, eyes closed. She put her arm round him. 'But there's never been rinderpest in the Americas. How did it get there?'

James looked sharply at her. 'Er, yes. Odd, because it's only spread by discharges from infected animals and not by meat or humans. Difficult to explain.' He glanced swiftly at Jennifer and she took up the tale. 'There's been a clandestine trade of live cattle between east Africa and South America for years.'

James nodded. 'That's right.' He sounded relieved. 'Fortunately some companies still had stockpiles of vaccine. Once they rediscovered them the major crisis was over. We think it's been contained though it may well be hiding in wild animals.'

Jennifer stood up, stretched her shapely body and yawned. 'So that's why we're so important here. That's why I'm going to India, Pakistan and Afghanistan in April to discuss possible meat and milk problems arising in that area should rinderpest become endemic again. The trade routes from south east Africa go via Sudan through Egypt, Palestine, Iraq and then Iran so the whole area's highly vulnerable. Many farmers returned to using cattle as draft animals once the fuel restrictions to reduce global warming came into play. A return of plague would be disastrous for their economies. I'm also visiting home for the same reason, though Australia hasn't had rinderpest since the nineteen twenties.' She said, 'Goodnight,' as she left the room.

Rachel stared down at her son sleeping comfortably against her body in the crook of her arm. He should be in bed, but she was loath to disturb him. She looked across to James. 'Shuji hasn't been here very long has he?'

'Six months. He was seconded to us from the Food and Agriculture Organisation of the UN. Prior to that he worked for them in Argentina on foot-and-mouth. It's endemic in the Chaco region shared by Argentina, Brazil and Paraguay. Wild animals pass it on, and it's impossible to vaccinate all the cattle in such a remote area. Before that he was in Kenya, in the Ilemi triangle on the Sudan and Ethiopian border, dealing with foot-and-mouth in migrating Turkana cattle herds. So he knows how local societies function in both areas and how best to combat rinderpest, should it ever return.' He smiled at the sleeping boy. 'Worn out after all his adventures.'

'We're both very tired.'

There was a pause and then because James was so approachable she asked, 'Did you hear the pig being slaughtered last night?'

'No. My room faces towards the lab in the opposite direction from the yard. I heard from Shuji there'd been a commotion.'

'It's illegal to farm pigs so close to a wildlife reserve in case they spread disease to the wild boar. Five mile limit throughout the European Union for all domestic animals.'

'This is Wales. Their Assembly may apply different rules.'

'But surely even here farmers must have their animals slaughtered in a registered abattoir?'

'Don't worry about it, Rachel.' He smiled gently at the weary pair. 'It's not our business. Leave it to the agricultural inspectors. They come every few months.'

Ben stirred and muttered. He stretched, opened his eyes, closed them again and snuggled closer to his mother. Before he could settle down she gently pulled her arm away and woke him completely. 'C'm on. Bedtime.'

As she pulled the quilt over him he asked 'Why are you so quiet, Mum?'

'Just thinking. About pigs.'

*

Not just pigs.

She sat at the table and fiddled with her one photograph of Dan in its cheap wood frame, keeping quiet until Ben slept. Nine o'clock, and she was exhausted. Her loneliness hit her. No one left. Her father and brother were so estranged they didn't know about her mother's death. Or even her own marriage and its tragic end. Aunts, uncles, cousins had never been close. She'd lost touch with school and university friends after marriage and childbirth.

She had swingeing debts.

First the debt she'd incurred from student loans and never paid off after marriage, though she could have afforded it then. Instead she and Dan lived well and prepared for the baby without thinking of the future. As partner in his financial arrangements, her arrears became astronomical when he died. Interest on the loans went up and up. Fines were added for unpaid monthly bills. Lenders became increasingly unfriendly.

Her teaching job in Coventry should have provided enough to pay back some, but her mother's illness ate up any excess money because the financially strapped health service now charged for many medicines. Throughout the long winters heating was impossibly expensive, even for the sick. She and Ben shivered in their thin second hand clothes while her mother huddled under a mountain of duvets, for ever cold. State help for the needy had been reduced, and the complicated application forms for assistance covered thirty pages and were impossible to fill accurately. Her mother refused to sign them. 'We aren't poor,' she said. Or, 'I don't need drugs. I just want to go quickly.' She didn't.

Rachel's memories of her mother's final days tore her heart out. She rested her head on the table, sobbing quietly for fear of waking Ben and frightening him. She must be strong for him, both father and mother. Yet she'd already proved incapable of shielding him from life's tragedies.

Like Dan's loss. His dear face slipping from memory. 'Oh, God,' she said silently. 'Oh, Daniel, if only you were here and I was happy again. I didn't know until too late how really really happy I was with you. Now you're gone for ever. . .' and her whole body ached with desire for his arms and his love and for those dear idiosyncrasies that had niggled her when he was alive.

Why had she let go their digital pictures of marriage, Ben's early years and their holidays that he'd catalogued so carefully? She regretted the assistance given her by Eckstazia members when he died, though they were two of the kindest and dearest women. They met her after his funeral, offering their help. 'We're both trained bereavement counsellors, fully qualified to help you at this difficult time,' they said. They made sure she ate and rested. She played with little Ben while they packed up Daniel's clothes. She wanted to keep them all, burying her face in his jackets for the last fading smell of him. They weaned her of such crippling grief by sending his clothes to charity shops that supplied bankrupt citizens. 'Think of the help they'll give to the poor,' they said. They took away his computer and files, shredded any papers. 'We'll give the computer to someone needy. We'll make sure the hard drive is safely wiped.' She didn't realise until too late that most of her family records had been destroyed as well. She felt as though she'd thrown him away altogether.

But it had been for the best, hadn't it? Because when it became apparent she couldn't afford the university rent for their flat any more her new friends had found her a cheaper one. Far too small to take more than a few meagre mementoes of Dan and her marriage. They settled her into her new rooms sympathetically. 'You'll thank us, dear, once you get over your loss. Because you will in time. We don't mean you'll ever forget him or love him less, just that it won't be so painful.'

The week after she and Ben moved her mother rang to tell her the traumatic results of her latest hospital tests. Rachel had to uproot them both again, leaving Liverpool and memories of Dan for Coventry and her dying mother. Her two friends had comforted her and promised to contact Eckstazia members in Coventry on her behalf. As Rachel's mother became more frail, carers provided by Eckstazia looked after her at subsidized cost, so Rachel could continue to teach.

Yes, Eckstazia had provided her with help in her time of greatest need. Their actions had totally wiped out her initial feelings of unease, for before he died Dan had come to dislike Eckstazia intensely. It was a strange prejudice that had haunted the final weeks of their marriage when he'd been vitriolic about the new woman professor of his philosophy department who was a leading Eckstazia member.

But she'd only known kindness after his death from these sincere Christians.

Come on, she said to herself. Stop whingeing about the past. You can't change it. Look to the future. That interview with the boss tomorrow for instance.

She slept heavily, without dreams. And was woken early Saturday morning by Ben, pulling at her arm.

'Noises outside, Mum.'

'Only Annie,' she said dozily. 'She goes home first thing today and comes back Monday morning.'

He went to the window and stared out into the dark morning. Eventually Rachel rolled out of bed and joined him. Carlights shone across the forecourt and van doors opened and slammed. It wasn't the farm van, though it was equally dirty.

'There's that dodgy guy,' Ben said.

'William Parry.' She recognised the wool hat jammed on his head and his quick gait as he dumped a wooden crate into the rear of the van.

Annie came out of the house and spoke sharply to him.

Rachel opened the window a smidgen. They were arguing, using abusive words absent from her Welsh lessons.

Another man, oldest of the trio, tried to mollify them. In vain. He shrugged, shouldered his package and walked stiffly to the van. Then he ordered the pair to shut up, a term Rachel knew. He nodded towards her window and she pulled Ben down as they all stared upwards. William marched back through the door beneath her window while Annie and the older man got into the van and drove away. Probably the man was her husband, taking her home.

'Was that the pig?' Ben asked.

'And other stuff. *We're* not getting to eat it after all.' She was hugely disappointed in spite of her disapproval of the illegal operation.

'Where's it going?'

'Goodness knows. Something funny's going on. I'm pretty sure they're running a black market.'

'What's that?'

'Crooks dodging rationing and taxes. They get hold of essential goods like food, fuel and clothes at low prices from rubbish sources and sell high, but not as high as legitimate traders. That tempts people to buy from them. They use cash not cards so nothing's recorded. Don't pay taxes. So the government has less money to help the needy. And everyone honest has to pay more and there are fewer legal goods around for us. They make a mint out of everyone else's suffering. And they're linked to drug running and money laundering of profits from crime.'

His face wrinkled in displeasure. 'That's *wrong.*'

'Sure. Very.' Then she thought, what if he says something at school? 'Just keep that to ourselves, Ben.'

Chapter 3

'Come in, come in. Make yourself comfortable.' Shuji's mouth smiled as he indicated a leather backed chair. He sat at a wide mahogany desk with incorporated computer and three neat stacks of papers. Most of the polished Victorian wall panelling was hidden by books, mainly old leather-bound antiques. On the wall opposite his desk were three computer screens, one showing a Gordian tangle of graphs and formulae, the others blank.

Rachel watched him cautiously as he read the screen, made alterations, spoke icily to a distant scientist about leukocyte fraction and proper preservation in heparin, and condemned the transfer of frozen and therefore useless samples to his lab. He was quite oblivious to her, making her aware of her own insignificance.

The study was on the first floor of the outer tower. One window had the same view as her own down the valley and the second one looked over the woods. It was a cold room. Background heating was nonexistent, probably due to the turbine's intermittent failures. She shivered even though she'd become used to lack of heating in Coventry. Sitting there in her threadbare sweatshirt she envied Shuji his thick hand knitted jumper with complex designs in green and mustard, and woolly fingerless gloves. If only her mother had taught her to knit, but her youth was spent in those halcyon days of plenty when no one had bothered about life skills.

She sighed and raised her eyes to a startling canvas behind Shuji depicting a great fire of multicoloured flames rising into an azure sky.

Her boss rubbed his thin artistic hands together as he closed down the screen at last. He nodded towards the picture. 'Yes, one of my own. The Rapture of saints into heaven. The day of ecstasy, of joy everlasting.'

So the casual appearance was phoney. He missed very little.

'I hope you'll both be happy with us, Rachel.'

'I'm sure we shall.'

He stood up and beckoned her to the window. Standing beside this tall intelligent man she felt frumpish and even less important. When she looked out she saw among the trees and shrubs a tiled roof of a large one-storey building.

'Our lab,' he said, smoothing down his already sleek black hair. 'Not the most exciting of places, but we have plans in the pipeline. Eckstazia is committed to combating increasing world food shortages and our lab here is crucial to that policy. Prof Hilary Barron. . .'

Rachel started. Hilary Barron was the Professor of the Philosophy department at Liverpool University where Daniel had worked. The woman he'd been so prejudiced against.

Apparently unconscious of her surprise, Shuji continued smoothly, '. . . she is, as you must know. . .'

But she didn't.

'. . . the President of Eckstazia's Central Council in the UK. Our lab proposals have been expedited through her many contacts. Only the Welsh Assembly regulations hinder our rebuilding. The Chief Planning Officer of the Snowdonia Reserve has taken a most negative approach by having the lab designated a listed building. In fact it's a rather uninteresting structure dating from the nineteen twenties. Built as an indoor badminton court, I gather. Fortunately there are friends of Eckstazia on the relevant committees, though we still have a lot of hoops to jump through before we can put our plans for enlargement into operation.'

He pointed to her chair and she sat down obediently.

Still standing he continued, 'The necessarily high security ensures limited access, only to the rinderpest team. Your entrance is forbidden. Indeed impossible. No one can enter without the essential codes and the lobby is programmed to recognise specific personnel. Micro-robobugs fly to attack any unauthorised person, sending out alarm signals at the same time. Bioterrorism is my constant concern.'

'Bioterrorism!'

'Naturally. A group possessing the rinderpest virus could hold the world to ransom by threatening famine. No tillage across large areas of the world, no milk, meat or hides.'

She shuddered. 'And some organizations wouldn't bother to threaten. They hate our way of life so much that they'd release the virus into cattle without warning in order to cause mass destruction.'

Shuji looked at her sharply with an expression she couldn't understand. 'That *is* a possibility. Anyway, while I advertise widely the good work done by Eckstazia, no location is given for this research establishment. Only authorised personnel like yourself are permitted access to Penybwlch's website.'

'Where shall I work then?'

'In your room. Jennifer Beard assures me it can accommodate you, and Emmanuel's provided you with some necessary equipment. Ask Jenny for anything else you need.' He sighed. 'Recording the wildlife of Penybwlch is part of William Parry's remit, but sadly the man's proved quite incapable of collecting the simplest data over the two years he's worked for us. The appointment of a qualified field officer like yourself has become essential.

'Now. Penybwlch estate is roughly a hundred hectares and part of Snowdonia Reserve. Eckstazia doesn't own Penybwlch; we rent it from the Reserve and we have a statutory obligation to produce a detailed inventory of the wildlife for the Reserve records.'

'The effect of the recent introductions of wolves, deer, wild boar and so on, on community structure, dynamics and interactions, checking out possible reduction in global warming. . .'

'Precisely. You'll find a map and data on your yapp of sites that were recorded in the past. You're to update these. Records to be sent weekly to the Reserve's senior research officer. There'll be video-conferences to attend.'

She nodded enthusiastically.

'Keep your yapp with you at all times to check your position, as the estate is large and mountainous and until you're used to it you may get lost.'

Rachel pulled Annie's map out of her pocket. 'Are some areas forbidden?'

Shuji fingered the scrap with distaste before dropping it in the waste bin. 'Annie likes to think she's in charge of Penybwlch. Ignore her. There's a strange system here, something to do with the original compulsory purchase of the property by Snowdonia Reserve. Parry rents privately some fifty acres surrounding the outbuildings. The yapp will show you the boundary. You don't enter it. The rest of Penybwlch is Reserve land, Eckstazia's concern. And yours. Parry is employed to tend the full estate, both his farmland and the rest of Penybwlch, but he's an idle fellow.'

He sat down again, his heavy lidded eyes staring out of the window. He was silent so long she thought the interview was over. As she moved to stand up he said, 'You told me you're a born again Christian so you've been accepted as an associate member of Eckstazia. Currently your job probation expires after two months and then I'll assess your readiness to become a full member. For that you must acquire an awareness of your own sins and your absolute inability to attain godliness on your own.'

Irritated by his apparent denigration of her spiritual status she said sharply, 'Yes, I know Jesus' divine grace is my only source of redemption.'

He looked at her critically. 'You'll discuss this with Emmanuel, I trust?'

She said more carefully, 'Of course. I cherish his advice.'

'He'll guide you into full membership. I needn't tell you you're greatly privileged in having his interest. He's a confidant of the Archbishop of York and the Archbishop of Westminster, and he's advisor to the Councils of both Evangelical Christians and Hindus. The revered Buddhist nun, Venerable Josephine, praises his wisdom and integrity.'

His lips curved in that slight smile. 'We're not always so serious about our faith. Jesus' love brings joy to us all. We're on this earth to honour him, to cherish our fellow Christians and to work with heart, mind and soul to hasten the day of Jesus' return when all sorrow and sighing will cease. Then he will judge the nations, and those sinners who refuse his Lordship will perish eternally.' His eyes closed as if in deep prayer. When he opened them he stared straight at her till she dropped her gaze. 'However, Emmanuel mentioned to me he's concerned you're still tied to your memories of your husband.'

'I've kept very little. A photo. A few letters.'

'Nothing else? No computer records?'

'Nothing like that.'

'That's good.'

She wondered why he sounded relieved.

'It's over four years, Rachel. Time to move on. Leave him to the good mercies of Jesus and put away any mementoes you still have of him.'

She resisted the temptation to touch the necklace beneath her sweatshirt. No way would she put it aside.

'My daughter bought a chastity ring when she was sixteen to show she was dedicated to entering marriage as a virgin. I suggest you buy a widow ring. Suitable texts can be engraved on them. Paul's letter to Timothy springs to mind. Christian widows who have been faithful in marriage must set their hopes on God alone, perform good deeds, take care of children, be hospitable and help the distressed.'

'But surely Paul goes on to say young widows may marry again.'

He looked annoyed at her correction. 'Have you someone in mind?'

'No, Shuji, I haven't. I'll give some thought to your suggestion.' Widow ring indeed. She smiled to conceal her irritation, fully aware by now how perceptive he was.

He paused before continuing, 'Another matter. Eckstazia's finances are boosted by the commitment of our members. You realise ten percent of your salary is a gift to Eckstazia?'

Ten per cent? Why?'

'Your tithe. A tenth of all you earn as required by Moses, hallowed by custom down the centuries and essential giving for sincere Christians throughout the world.'

She was confounded. Quickly she calculated that the necessary tenth would make a very large hole in her intended debt repayments. 'I can't afford . . . ' she began.

Shuji said gently, 'I'm sure you wouldn't wish to stand apart from the rest of us.'

She was too choked to reply but she nodded, unable to refuse.

'Emmanuel is impressed by your courage and commitment over the past few years. But he also sees you as a young soul, somewhat rebellious and doubting.' He smiled again to soften his words. 'That will change as you grow in faith. So welcome to our little society, Rachel. I'm sure you'll be happy here. We're an accomplished group. I find these hills most inspirational for my painting and poetry. James alas lost the ability to follow his favoured career after a mountaineering accident in Scotland.'

'His fingers?'

'Precisely. He was a highly accomplished cello player and now he refuses to play at all. If you have any leanings that way, perhaps you could encourage him. . .?'

'I don't play anything now. Learnt piano when a child, tried violin in the school orchestra but couldn't make more than a screech.'

'A pity. Jennifer was a classical dancer in her younger days.'

'That's why she walks so beautifully.'

'And she's well versed in classical literature. Last year, before I came, she persuaded our younger scientists to act in Oedipus Rex, the Sophocles tragedy. I expect you're familiar with it?'

Rachel shook her head.

'Performed at Bangor University. Very well received. And your other interests? Your cv was a little sparse.'

What could she say? There was no point in invention; she'd be found out immediately. 'I haven't had much spare time.'

'My dear Rachel, one can always make time. Yes, motherhood is important, but remember Martha who busied herself so much with mere household chores that she missed out the better part, the spiritual conversation her sister Mary had with our Lord.' He rose to his feet and bowed slightly. 'Enjoy your weekend. I suggest you take time to walk through some of the reserve.'

As she quietly pushed the heavy door shut behind her she felt very inferior. Was that what Shuji had intended? Then her thoughts turned to Daniel. He would have said, 'Don't be so wet. Remember how faithfully you look after our son and how you cared for your poor mother in her last illness. That's better than producing a Greek play or strumming a cello any day. Why d'you always put yourself down?'

*

'Let's explore outside, Mum,' Ben was waiting impatiently for her in the hall.

'Lunch first. See what Annie's left us.'

Shuji came down the wide staircase followed by James swinging a couple of rucksacks. 'Have a good weekend, both of you,' James called, but Shuji ignored them. The two men drove away in James's car.

There was ham in the kitchen fridge.

'Is that our pig?' Ben asked.

Rachel laughed and shook her head.

'Was it a wild pig?'

She said, 'Quite possibly, because farmers are forbidden to rear domestic pigs close by the reserves.'

'Why?'

'For fear of spreading disease among the wild pigs. Or if one escapes, then it'll breed with the wild ones and contaminate their genome. Same for all domestic animals like goats and cats. They're planning to release aurochs here . . . '

'Or ox?'

'Wild oxen. So all cows are banned because they were domesticated from ancient aurochs.'

'Dogs?'

'Not permitted because of the wolf connection. And no, I don't know why William is allowed to keep his dog.'

As they ate it started to rain, and it rained as if the whole objective of the weather gods was to flood the earth again. Rain slashed against the windows obscuring the narrow valley, waterfalls fell from moss filled gutters, water seeped under the back door and puddled the pitted red tiles.

'Don't,' Rachel said as Ben splashed his foot in the puddle, spraying the cupboards and walls.

'More work for Annie,' he said.

'That's unkind.'

'So's Annie. Let's explore the house. Kitchen first because she's gone home.'

The back door led into a narrow yard behind the house. It was hardly wide enough to be called a yard. Rather it was a passageway between the house and the quarry wall into which the building was set. The wall was some fifteen feet high, cement rendered, cracking and bulging in one place.

'Will the hill fall down?' Ben asked anxiously.

'Course not,' Rachel said firmly. 'Shut the door, Ben, rain's coming in everywhere. We're in the oldest part of the house. They must have quarried out the mountainside when they built it. What a job in those days! Pick and shovel, no mechanical diggers.'

They browsed through the wooden cupboards. Shelves were scrubbed clean and white and utensils gleamed. Annie was proud of her kitchen.

'Haven't tried this one yet,' Ben said.

'Another store cupboard, probably.'

'No it isn't. It's a room. With chairs and a little table.'

She followed him into a dark room smelling of polish and clean linen. The view from the small window was blurred by rain torrents from an overflowing gutter, but they realised it must look out onto the passageway and retaining wall. In spite of the gloom it was cosy enough with a comfortable armchair and a bag of knitting beside it. A sewing machine on a black oak table was surrounded with patterns, dull grey cloth and cotton. Annie was an industrious woman.

The rest of the furniture was dark and heavy, old enough to be Victorian. A sideboard with elephantine legs bore a spotty mirror and a host of trinkets; a cut glass bowl containing sewing machine reels, buttons, elastic and safety pins, two pottery dogs staring disdainfully into the room, old salt and pepper mills, boxes of all shapes and sizes. Ben ached to open these, but his mother frowned at him. A faded cross-stitch 'Lord Thou Seest Me' and the date eighteen ninety six hung over a vast heavily ornamented carver chair. Its back was carved with climbing plants enriched with scallop shells.

Two popular video prints provided the only link with the present age. They recycled their short sequences of wild elephants charging and a leopard waving its tail lazily as it drooped over the branch of an African tree.

'No wall screen,' Ben said in wonderment. 'She must be as poor as us.' He tried another door. 'I bet this is Annie's bedroom.'

Rachel looked over his shoulder into another small gloomy room containing an iron bed and deal cupboards. To the right there was a further door with an old fashioned key in the lock. Ben turned it easily.

'We shouldn't,' Rachel said hesitantly. 'These are Annie's private rooms.'

Ben opened the door cautiously and peered through. Then he vanished.

Alarmed Rachel followed him into a dreary hallway lit by a low wattage bulb. On their right the hall ended in a blank wall. On their left it disappeared round a corner. No other doors. No tiles, no carpet. Just stone flags, uneven with centuries of use. And a right royal smell. Rachel was unused to farming odours and the combined stenches of dried bog, unwashed sweaty socks and welly boots, henshit, insanitary loo and wet dog hit her like a punch on the nose. From Ben's gasp she gathered he felt the same.

Three wooden crates were stacked along one wall. Rachel lifted the lid of the top one cautiously. Eggs. Lots of dirty eggs in card trays. Thirty to a tray and two trays side by side on the bottom of the crate. She reckoned it would take six layers altogether.

The lid slipped from her grasp and banged shut.

A dog scrabbled furiously at an invisible door round the corner, barking for it to be opened.

A man's voice. Angry. Welsh they couldn't understand. And a door handle being turned.

'Quick! It's the farmer!' Rachel whispered.

They jumped round, knocking into each other and almost toppling the pile of boxes. Rachel managed to steady them as a flood of light indicated the hall door was now open. The dog's claws scraped along the stone floor. It growled softly but with menace. Ben dragged his mother inside Annie's bedroom and shut the door quietly. The dog snuffled and snorted under it. It whined and scratched.

Footsteps. Firm, fast, recognisable. Rachel stealthily turned the key as William Parry shook the handle. He spoke fiercely to the dog. Swore in Welsh. Rachel and Ben held their breaths as his footsteps went back down the corridor and the far door slammed.

Rachel grasped Ben's hand and led him back to the kitchen.

'Gerroff, Mum,' he complained, pulling vainly at her grip.

'That was stupid of us,' she said as she let him go. 'What if he'd caught us spying? I guess he thought it was rats. But it's very interesting. The Ty Bach refers to this old farmhouse section and Annie and William live there.'

'So do we. We're over both Annie's and William's rooms.'

How unlikely it was that the pair should live so close. Their mutual hatred was so intense.

Ben said proudly, 'So I was right about them arguing about eggs in Welsh yesterday.'

'They loaded crates into Annie's van this morning. Where did those eggs come from? Three hundred and sixty to a box.'

'Are hens allowed near reserves?'

'No.'

Ben held up two fingers. 'Pig meat and egg crates. Two things that shouldn't be here.'

'Three. You've forgotten the fish. That was definitely under the counter.'

Continuing downpour kept them inside the house for the rest of the day.

Rachel said, 'There must be other ways into Ty Bach. It was all one house once.'

The corridor between kitchen and dining room looked as if it should lead there, but it was blocked by an inbuilt mahogany cupboard with fine china displayed behind its glass doors.

Ben opened it and tapped the back. 'Sounds hollow.'

'Once it must have opened onto the hallway where the eggs are. We'll try upstairs.'

'Is our bit of the house very old?'

'Must be three hundred years at least.'

'Ghosts.' His voice quavered.

'Of course!' she mocked.

'I *heard* them. Someone came upstairs. Then someone else. Three people. I peeked out the door but there wasn't anyone. *You* didn't wake up.'

As they went upstairs the treads creaked ominously.

'That's your ghosties and long leggety beasties and things that go bump in the night,' Rachel smiled. 'In an old house like this the stairs creak as they relax overnight.'

The rooms in the original farmhouse had lower ceilings than the Victorian section, so after they'd climbed to the first floor landing they had to go down eight steps to reach the passage that led to their room. On the other side of the passage was a boxroom and their shower room. This corridor too was blocked at the end.

Ben thumped it.

Rachel said, 'Plaster board. No way through. There must be separate stairs.'

'Annie said I can have the boxroom,' Ben said. He'd never had a room of his very own. 'Let's look.'

47

The boxroom smelt musty. It had a threadbare carpet and a collection of broken lamps, tennis rackets with snapped strings, two wooden chairs each missing a leg and an ancient dressing table with cracked mirror. A grimy cupboard set in one wall was full of rotting linen and cotton. Old curtains, towels, sheets, all flyspotted, moth-eaten and rust marked.

'I can put lots in here,' he said.

'Models galore,' she laughed, for making things was one of his passions.

He pulled the disintegrating material out onto the floor and they both coughed and spluttered with the dust.

He smeared his sweatshirt sleeve across the dirty window. 'Look, Mum. I'm over Annie's room and I can just see the top of that huge wall.'

Rachel peered out through the waterfall from the guttering. 'It's a really steep hillside. That strong wire netting on top of the retaining wall stops stones falling into the back of the house. And tree roots, grass and brambles help to consolidate it. It's quite safe.' She looked around her. 'It's a lot lighter than Annie's downstairs room.'

'I can't see much from the window.'

'D'you think you'll like it if we clean it up?'

He nodded, dancing. 'Yes, yes, let's do it now.'

*

Sunday afternoon was cold and cloudy but the rain had cleared, so Rachel winkled Ben out of his new room where he was fiddling with her yapp. Off they went to size up the lab. This was connected to the Victorian side of the house by a covered way. Ty Bach and the outbuildings were invisible from its doorway. It was set among the ubiquitous lanky rhododendrons whose huge leaves tipped water onto the explorers. Everywhere was silent except for the rustling of evergreen rhododendron leaves and wind in the high bare branches. No one worked here on a Sunday.

As Shuji had indicated, it was not an impressive building. True it was large, but the construction was substandard.

Ben jabbed at the foundation bricks with a stick and a section of mortar fell out.

Rachel took his hand firmly. 'Destructive little beast. They'll have to repair that now.'

He wrested his hand free and tapped more gently on the wooden construction above the bricks. 'It's not a *proper* building.'

'Wood's a perfectly adequate building material. Specially when well maintained and painted like this.'

The single door was impressively locked by a large keypad. She went to the nearest metal-framed window.

'Lift me up, Mum,' Ben demanded.

'You won't see anything. They're blocked up. It's all due for rebuilding.'

They wandered through overgrown gardens till they came to a ten foot high chain-link fence with strands of barbed wire at two foot intervals.

'Wow,' Ben said. 'That's *something*.'

Rachel traced it on the map on her yapp. 'See, it goes right round the farm, including the areas we can't go. It prevents wild animals wandering round house and outbuildings.'

'Then it just stops. They could come round the end.'

'Probably they don't bother. They're shy.' She adjusted the map scale. 'I can't see many fenced properties round here. Animals can wander right down to the town and the castle.'

'Those people in the store were cross about the fence.'

'Weren't they just. Wolves and stags. I guess teenagers went out chasing them.'

'Are they dangerous?'

'You'd be lucky to see a deer let alone a wolf. But wild sows can be nasty when they've got piglets. So don't go beyond the fence on your own.'

'You said the police would always know where to find me if I was hurt or lost.'

'True. They can see us all from the thermal imaging satellites but not so easily in these woods. You just press your wrist alarm and they'll home in on you and find you. And so will I. Straight away. But don't you go there without me.'

'*You'll* be going there alone.'

'I've got my yapp. And I shan't confront any animals, don't worry.'

Eventually they reached a gate into the reserve. They climbed through woodlands, both of them puffing a little at the steep gradient. Presently the trees thinned, impenetrable gorse took over and they had to dodge spiky branches.

'It's always in flower.' Rachel pointed to the occasional yellow blossom. 'There's an old saying, when the gorse is out of bloom then kissing's out of season.'

'What's that mean?'

She explained, smiling.

At last they came to open bracken and heather country and reached the top of a small bluff.

'We're nowhere near the very top,' Ben said, staring at the mountain that towered over them.

'But look at the view this way over our valley.'

Ben turned and whistled.

Even under cloud it was impressive. Their valley was full of trees, and nestling among them the main house brooded over its farm buildings like a hen with her chicks. The old quarry into which it was built was hidden among holly, pine, fir and bare branches of sycamore, beech and ash.

Rachel took her binocular glasses from their case.

'Let me see.' Ben tugged at her arm.

She showed him how to adjust them. 'Can you pick out Ty Bach all covered in ivy? That window left of the door is ours and the door's the front entrance to Ty Bach.'

'Downstairs is all William and Annie's.'

'Yes, and some rooms upstairs too. Can you see the farm buildings, the carport where Shuji and James and Jennifer keep their cars, and the semidetached cottage where Alyson and her family live?'

'And the Bangor crowd next door. Mum, it's all so scary dark.'

'Wait till spring. The larches'll grow bright green needles and the birches will have the daintiest of pale leaves. There's laburnum among the rhododendrons – together they'll flower in royal colours of gold and purple. The birds will start singing and nest building. It's just wearing its winter sleeping clothes for now.'

She tested her yapp by taking a shot of a dead bracken frond. 'Correct ID,' she told Ben. '*Pteridium aquilinum*, perennial with extensively branched underground rhizomes with maximum spread of 390 metres. And hey, this is interesting, Ben. It spreads by cloning, so some plants can be dated back to the end of the last ice age. That's *old!*'

He wasn't listening. 'I can see William and his dog walking across the hill. Just to the right of the turbine.'

Screwing up her eyes she made out two dots strolling through rough pasture on the far side of the valley. Beyond them woodland extended up the flanks of another range of hills. And, invisible beyond those, the sea.

'We can't go there, can we?'

'Not without William's permission.'

'He won't give us that.'

'But we can go through some of those woods and onto the rest of the reserve. All those hills behind William's farmland belong to it. Right down to the sea. And if you look to your right you'll see the river our stream flows into, and the town on the estuary with its castle and walls we visited two days ago.'

'Not many boats in the harbour.' He swung the glasses round again. 'What's that house, Mum?'

The next building down their valley was quite different from Penybwlch. It was equally splendid, twice as long but single storied and modern, with a glass atrium stretching the length of the front. It settled back comfortably into the hillside. There were no chimneys. The roof was sullen black.

Rachel set the yapp to telescope mode. As she'd suspected the mansion was covered with maximum efficient solar tiles. The shrubs and trees around it were a little higher than the low roof, tucking the house in like a blanket. In front stretched landscaped gardens with terraces curved along the contours of the hillside and a series of small fountains and waterfalls flowing gracefully across them. The tarmac drive zigzagged through trees down the steep hillside to meet the main road just below Penybwlch's high forbidding gates.

'It's very grand. The owner must be exceptionally wealthy.'

She compared the two buildings. Penybwlch's ostentatious towers grafted onto a humble farmhouse grated on the senses. This other house harmonised with its surroundings, subtly and skilfully making its statement of opulence.

'Hey! You-ooo!'

Ben and Rachel turned round sharply.

'It's Freya's lot.' Ben shouted in reply. Doing his stealth bomber impression he zoomed down into the hollow between the bluff and the mountain to greet the family. Rachel jogged after him, rustling through dead brown bracken fronds.

Alyson, her red and orange striped hat pulled well over her ears, introduced her husband Eric. He was as unlike her as it was possible to be. Tall, with a gingery beard and straw coloured hair poking from under his navy hat, he was all aging Viking. His eyes were slate blue, large and striking. He stared at Rachel as he shook her hand and greeted her with a strong Icelandic accent.

Freya had the same eyes and a similar narrow nose in a smaller version. She was busy ignoring bomber Ben. 'How are you, Mrs Kerem?' she asked with teenage dignity.

Rachel hid a smile. 'Enjoying our first walk in the reserve. So you don't go away weekends like everyone else?'

'How can we?' Alyson said angrily as they walked together along the grassy track. 'The Skoda's only for essentials like the school run and research projects. Nearest bus two miles away. Then the expense. Three tickets.'

'There's bikes,' Ben said, innocently adding fuel.

'Oh, bikes! We *have* ridden down to the town occasionally, but it's steep all the way back.'

Freya added, 'And William never mends the punctures. It's his *job,* isn't it, Dad?'

'It certainly is. You'll soon find, Rachel, that William is the laziest man on earth. Nothing like his mother.'

'So Annie's his mother?'

'Why yes. Hadn't you noticed how alike they look?'

Ben said, 'They're always fighting.'

'No love lost between them, for sure.' Eric smiled down at him and ruffled his hair, which annoyed the boy intensely. 'Annie's a hard worker, always pleasant and she keeps her promises to you.'

'She's an old witch.'

'Looks aren't everything. And William's no fashion model. He's also idle, rude and generally bloody minded. Thinks he owns the place. Dotes on his mongrel, Toss. Don't you roam on his farmland because he'll set the brute on you.'

They reached the top of the next hill and Rachel took a few deep breaths.

Alyson remarked, 'You aren't very fit, are you?'

'Too much city muck in my lungs.' Then she held up her hand for silence and pointed. The dead bracken heaved. Snuffling and snorting, a young wild boar hove into view, took one startled look at the humans, barked an alarm and crashed away towards the woods. They laughed as its brown rump flashed momentarily and Alyson said softly, 'The reserve's a beautiful place. All times of year.'

Ben said, 'That pig had better watch out for William.' He looked across the valley and exclaimed, 'The house has gone. And the hills.'

'Valley mist,' Eric said. 'It'll rain again soon. Most days you're lucky if you get a view at all.' He told Rachel, 'I don't envy you working outdoors. Cold, dreary and vast, that's Penybwlch in winter.'

Freya moaned, 'And tonight it's bloody church.'

'*Freya!* Language! Ben!' cried her parents together.

'*I* know that word,' Ben remarked scornfully.

'Yes, Ben,' said his mother. 'And don't let me hear you use it.'

Freya said stubbornly, '*You* used it, Dad. You said bloody-minded. Can't I be sick this evening?'

'No you can *not*,' said her father sternly.

As they walked back to the garden James' car returned. He and Shuji got out. Shuji put his arm round the smaller man's shoulder as they stood talking together.

'Just look at those two,' Alyson said sotto voce to Rachel. 'They should watch it. They may be high up in Eckstazia but they're vulnerable just the same. Expulsion straight away if anything's going on.'

'Why are Eckstazia against gays?'

Alyson looked at her pityingly. 'You check it out in your bible. Eckstazia website'll give you chapter and verse and explain why it's one of the most evil sins.'

Chapter 4

'Ouch!' Ben yelled as he banged into the front passenger seat.

Shuji swivelled round. 'Fasten your seatbelt properly.'

'Sort him for goodness sake, Rachel.' Jennifer swerved the car past another pothole. 'I can't concentrate with an idiot boy shouting down my neck.'

Rachel soothed her son's shoulder with one hand and jammed the other over his mouth as he shouted 'I'm not an idiot!' He tried to bite her but she pinched his mouth, and he sulked back into his seat.

Sunday night. The windscreen wipers full on against the rain Eric had predicted earlier. The car turned uphill as the road became ever more narrow and bumpy. The mountain church of Llanfechan was remote, its local congregation minuscule. Yet it had been chosen by the Penybwlch scientists for their weekly worship.

Jennifer swore as she scraped her car against a stone protruding from the high bank.

The car headlights shone on a metal gate.

'Open it, Rachel.'

Rachel gathered her second hand rabbit fur coat round her, squelched through mud, tripped on stones and reached the gate. Hinges had long since rusted away and both ends were tied with wire to the posts. She struggled with freezing fingers. The wind smelt cold with old sheep dung and another animal she couldn't identify. A bell tolled, sometimes loudly, sometimes faint as the gusts harassed its note. Her legs and feet were soaking and she wished Jennifer had warned her the church was on a mountainside.

Jennifer sounded the horn impatiently.

Rachel waved towards the headlights. She yanked the gate open bit by bit until she could rest it against the grass bank.

Jennifer's head appeared through the window. 'More. More.'

Rachel heaved at the recalcitrant bars and at last the car went through safely. The road deteriorated into two metalled strips either side of grass and tussocky reeds. Eventually it became a wet grass track where the wheels spun uselessly.

Shuji opened his door. 'We'll walk the rest of the way.'

They went through a tall gate under an arch of granite. A distant stone porch supported a light illuminating a path of sweet mountain grass between slate grave slabs. Everywhere the pungent animal smell.

'Phew,' said Ben. 'That's rank.'

Recognising it now, she replied, 'Wild ponies.'

Ben peered into the encompassing dark. 'There's a wind turbine.'

Eventually she distinguished its hum from the wind whistling between gaps in the stone walls and the clatter of branches. The bell had stopped clanging. Carlights swung across the hillside as two more cars skidded behind Jennifer's. All the Penybwlch contingent were here now.

Rachel followed her son inside the tiny porch. She passed her hand over its whitewashed stone and stepped into hollows made by centuries of other prayerful feet in its hallowed slate floor.

Inside was warm and brightly lit. A holy water scoop, heavily whitewashed, protruded from the wall by the door. It was dry. Opposite was a plain octagonal font with wooden lid. A young priest in long black garment stood by it, smiling at them. He was thin as a drainrod, his clothes patched and faded. His face was weather beaten, his ginger hair had receded to a small fringe round his bare crown. But it was his eyes that held her, grey eyes showing an independence as fierce as a buzzard over sunlit moors.

'I hope you'll both soon feel at home here, Rachel and Ben,' he said in a gentle Welsh voice.

'Funny seats.' Ben rubbed the back of an oak bench where it had been polished by the touch of many other fingers, long since dust.

The priest replied, 'Not as old as the church. Worshippers have found consolation here for over a millenium.'

The floor was warm to Rachel's frozen feet in their thin shoes. Modern heated tiles, granite grey, powered by the turbine. Luxury.

It was an unusual building with a large north transept, originally built for the male congregation and situated on the left of the chancel. The east window had been enlarged many years ago. It had three lights of plain glass. No soaring decorated arches or canopies. No grisaille lozenges, no saints or donors. Only the sloping sill and beyond that the rain and the night.

'What's that say?' Ben asked, pointing.

The wall to the right of the window was covered with strange faded words. Dog Latin? Old Welsh?

'I can't read it,' she said. 'The skull and three crossed bones underneath are a reminder we must all die.'

The benches were barely wide enough for four people. The Bangor crowd sat behind Shuji and James while Jennifer sat on the other side of the aisle. Alyson, Eric and a very sulky Freya were the last to enter and they stopped to say hello to Rachel before taking their places behind Jennifer.

As Rachel pointed Ben to a pew at the back, Ashley started some gospel music on her music maker. Ben banged his feet in time. The place became less solemn as the group chatted and laughed together.

Rachel showed Ben the construction of arched beams holding the slate roof over the nave and the rough boarded roof over the chancel.

'Look at the windows to see the thickness of the walls.' Their nearest window was tiny and simple. Holly twigs with brilliant berries stood in a plain glass vase on its broad sill.

'Why are they so thick?'

Before she could answer the priest silenced the music with a smile and said to them all, 'I am so happy to see you again. I thank you once more on behalf of the Welsh congregation for providing wind power and new flooring. Before you came Llanfechan could only boast two services a year. It was due to be deconsecrated and closed. Like so many small churches it would have disintegrated back into mere rubble with all its history lost. By setting up this weekly English service you've saved our heritage.'

The door latch clanked. Cold air whipped round the congregation.

The priest's face lit up. 'How pleased I am you've come,' he said to three newcomers.

A tall man with broad shoulders held the door open. Under his open raincoat he wore a smart grey suit with white shirt and pale blue tie. He bowed slightly towards the woman who entered after him.

She had the kind of presence that would arouse respect in anyone, Rachel thought. Not tall, but so dignified that she appeared to tower over them all. Her face was dispassionate, most discreetly made up and completely free of lines, though Rachel suspected she was in her forties. She was not merely beautiful as models and actresses are. She was stunning.

Behind her came a square-jawed female looking more like a minder than a servant who helped remove her coat. The night was wild with wind and rain, yet neither coat nor fashionable flat navy cap bore any trace of disturbance. Smart materials, rebuffing all weather and protecting the wearer from both excessive heat and cold. Underneath her coat her trouser suit was an impeccable dark blue; the silk scarf at her neck multicoloured but tasteful. Soft brown strands of hair escaped her cap, and the church lamps caught their glimmering gold highlights as she moved. She paused at the back of the church and surveyed the occupants, her gaze stopping momentarily on Rachel who shuddered involuntarily at the contact.

Shuji hurried towards her, holding out his hand. 'You honour us with your presence.'

She smiled and the church seemed brighter. 'Please, Shuji, none of that. We're all equal sinners in the sight of God.'

He led her to the front of the church where she sat in a separate dark wooden chair as intricately carved as Annie's. Her companions thumped down behind her next to Jennifer.

The priest spoke briefly to them of God's love and goodness to all that he had created. Yet God is neither he nor she, he reminded them, but far greater than our minds can reach. Reason is our guide to God while grief and sorrow, joy and friendship help dissolve the veils that obstruct our understanding. But in the end, only by love is Love known.

He spoke directly to her, Rachel felt, as she prayed her loss of Dan wouldn't turn her sour, but open her heart to compassion for the grief of others.

No human is ever beyond redemption in this life or the next, said the priest. Nothing good is lost; everything is held safely in Love's hand.

They sang spirituals and popular modern hymns recorded by Ashley. Ben danced with Tim and Ashley in the aisle. 'Hallelujah!' they sang, and the church was so full of music and light that Rachel felt a lump in her throat and praised God for his kindness in bringing her to this holy and restful sanctuary.

The atmosphere changed when James Restall gave the sermon. 'The news is bad. It's always bad because our world is full of problems. And they're getting worse all the time. Water for example. A new war between Turkey and Iraq over the failing waters of the Tigris and Euphrates. Terrorism endemic along the borders of China, Laos, Burma, Thailand and Vietnam as they squabble over the Mekong. Egypt's six year battle with the Sudan, Ethiopia and Uganda over the Nile.

'Global warming continues in spite of all our efforts and food production is in crisis. All of us here know that the task of feeding the world is Herculean. Here in Britain crime's on the increase. More muggings than ever in our cities, riots and murders are rife, even the new megaprisons are overcrowded.

'Many people are afraid and anxious. But not us. We know that these things are the sign that Jesus' return is imminent, when everything'll be put to rights.' He waved his left hand and the regrown fingers splayed out awkwardly. Quickly he hid his hand again, and Rachel noted his embarrassment at the minor deformity.

His listeners shouted, 'Hallelujah! Praise the Lord!'

'We're Eckstazia, the company of worldwide believers who put Jesus and his glory before everything else in life. We wait in faith to be raptured into the heavenly kingdom!'

'Praise him. Glory to his name!'

Ben said, 'I don't want to go up like a space probe, Mum.'

Tim turned round to look at him. He was giggling. 'It'll be great, Ben. Better than going to the moon any day.'

Across the aisle Freya took a sideways glance at Ben, shook her long hair scornfully at his interruption and straightened her back. She stared at James, pretending to listen.

Ben stuck his bottom lip out rebelliously.

Rachel thought, so everyone believes in this rapture, not just the youngsters from Bangor. She tried to imagine being sucked up into the sky. Like Ben, she failed.

James gave chapter and verse for the rapture. While she'd laughed at Martin and his friends, James convinced her by his sincerity. She felt afraid. What if Ben was not chosen when she was raised? Who would be left to care for him, doubly orphaned? Lord, please Lord, she begged in her heart, he's so small, so vulnerable.

James continued, 'We're finding life difficult now, but believe me, this is nothing compared with the great troubles on earth after we've left in the rapture. But when Jesus finally returns he'll call all nations before him, the good and the wicked alike. And as St Paul tells us, we who've been his faithful servants will judge them. Liars, thieves, fornicators, adulterers, corrupters of children and all those who tried to delay his return. We shall even judge the angels. As God commanded Joshua to destroy the inhabitants of Canaan, so he'll order us to thrust the evil ones, men and women, young and old into eternal hell.'

Ben nudged his mother. 'Will he stop soon?' His loud whisper carried round the tiny church and Rachel shook her head, placing her finger on her lips.

'I'm *bored*,' Ben persisted.

James frowned in their direction.

She took pens, a Christian colouring book and a toffee from her bag and bribed her son into silence.

'People today mock the idea of hell. Our ancestors knew better. They believed. And feared. Remember Hieronymus Bosch's great paintings, the Last Judgement of Michaelangelo, the great Requiem of Verdi.'

How hot it was, Rachel thought, but she dared not take off her rabbit coat because the lining was in shreds. She opened it as far as was decently possible.

Ben wriggled and dropped the book slap on the floor. Rachel put a firm arm round his shoulders and pulled him close.

'Clear off, Mum,' he said loudly and squirmed under her arm and into the aisle. 'See, I got away.'

'Come back,' she mouthed desperately, but he jiggled over to the font. The priest was sitting at the back of the church while James preached, and he got up softly, indicated to Rachel to remain seated and approached the boy.

Ben tried to lift the font cover but it was too heavy. As he dropped it the thud and squeak echoed round the church. Heads turned. Ben squealed.

'What is it?' asked the priest gently, leading him back to the pew behind his mother.

'That font's for burying babies, isn't it? They die too. My Dad and my granny are skulls and bones like *those*.' He sobbed as he pointed towards the painted wall by the altar.

The priest put his arm round him. 'No, no, my dear. That's only the part of them they don't need any more. They're in heaven where you'll see them again one day. Try not to be sad. They wouldn't want that.'

He smiled at Rachel as the boy slumped against him. 'Don't worry,' he mouthed.

James was finishing his talk. 'Remember Judas. The man who was one of the chosen twelve, dear companion of Jesus. Who betrayed the Son of God. Betrayal, most odious of all sins, reserved by Dante for the deepest circle of hell. Be on your guard, for we also can fall from grace and there is no second redemption. The Devil is no figment of the imagination. He is real, close to you and very evil. Remember Judas who went out, leaving the noble fellowship during that final supper. "And it was night," says St John. *For Judas it was eternal, horrendous night.*'

As the service ended the man in the grey suit beckoned Rachel and Ben forward. The handsome woman pointed Rachel to a seat beside her as she continued her conversation with the priest.

'I hope you'll consider these points prayerfully, Tomos.'

'Of course, Professor. But finally we shall have to disagree amicably. The Bible has been understood in many ways down the centuries, and modern textual criticism and archaeological discoveries have radically changed past interpretations.'

She smiled graciously. 'We must always be careful lest our individual prejudices and preferences hamper the salvation of others.'

'Naturally.'

'Thank you, Tomos,' she said in courteous dismissal. 'Now, Rachel. I'm glad you had a safe journey from Coventry in spite of the breakdowns. The buses are so unreliable these days. And I hope you're settling happily in your new situation.' Her calm demeanour was belied by the intensity of her gaze and Rachel dropped her eyes. 'School tomorrow is it, Ben?'

He mumbled a reply, scuffling his shoes on the floor.

How did this stranger know so much about them? Who on earth was she? Rachel was acutely aware of the bare patches in her fur coat and the worn trousers and sweatshirt she'd bought on Coventry's street market under the bronze eyes of Lady Godiva, proudly naked on her horse. She drew her muddy legs and shoes back under her seat, conscious that the woman's ankle boots were new, well polished soft calf, and hardly dirty at all.

'Now how can we best deal with this hyperactive young son of yours?' She smiled showing perfectly even white teeth. 'We have an excellent local doctor. A private one, not one of those poorly qualified Regional Health Service practitioners so underpaid and under resourced these days. He'll advise on medication to cure the boy's little problem. Now don't trouble yourself about finance, because it comes with the job. Eckstazia has its own medical services and hospitals. Essential now the old National Health Service has collapsed.' She sighed. 'Hard times for the poor, Rachel.'

Hard times indeed, Rachel thought, relieved she was slowly leaving poverty behind.

Ben stuck his finger in his mouth and Rachel pulled at his arm. He resisted.

'You're not a child any more, Ben,' said the woman gently.

He removed his finger.

The scent the woman wore wafted round them. The sheen on her suit was so beautiful that Rachel wanted to stroke the material. Manmade. Chinese quality job. When had she last seen something so grand? So well cut?

The woman rose, ignoring Rachel as she turned to Shuji who'd been fretting in the background.

Alyson tapped Rachel's shoulder. 'Don't worry,' she whispered, and they both looked at Ben where he stood despondently fingering a pew end. 'But you'll have to do what *she* says, Rach.' And she indicated the woman with her head. More loudly she said to Ben, 'Did you know there's a holy well here?'

His young face brightened. 'What's a holy well?'

'There's a little mountain spring bubbling up from the ground in a corner of the churchyard. Pure as pure. Long ago it was a pagan shrine to a water god. A Christian Celtic saint sanctified it fifteen hundred years ago and the converted fitted it into the new religion and built their church beside it. It's said to cure sick children. We've got sacred water in Iceland too. There's a great waterfall where one of the pagans threw his idols when he converted to Christianity.'

Rachel's attention wandered. The smart woman was saying to Shuji, 'And Tomos?'

'I've suggested an on-line Eckstazia training course, but he says he's too busy.'

'How can he be in a tiny parish like this? See to it, Shuji.'

'Of course. Of course. At once.' Shuji was apologetic. He bowed several times.

Who on earth was this woman?

She asked Jennifer as they returned to the car through the rain.

Jennifer snorted with laughter. 'Professor Hilary Barron, of course. Surely you've seen her on the website?'

'I didn't notice. . .didn't connect. . . I thought. . .supposed. . . she lived near the University of Liverpool, since she's on their staff.'

'Really, Rachel. How naïve! Hilary Barron owns Plas Du, the black house a mile down the valley. Or perhaps you haven't noticed that either?'

Rachel was glad the night hid her red face. So that was Hilary Barron, Daniel's senior. No wonder she'd been so knowledgeable. Now Rachel had met her she wondered why he'd disliked her so. She was appointed to the University a year before his death and was already advisor to the government on ethics and religious affairs. Within six months she was headhunted for a similar post with the European Union. Had he, so ambitious a man, been jealous at the contrast between his pedestrian career as senior lecturer and her swift climb up the ladder?

Dan had ground his teeth. 'Pulling power. Contacts everywhere. These days it's not what you are, it's who you know.'

Rachel reminded him, 'Always has been.'

He had glared at her and stormed off.

Or had he been subject to hatred masking suppressed sexual attraction? Hilary was certainly charming and magnetic, a combination some men found highly fascinating. She remembered Dan saying, 'The guys fall over her. Kiss her arse,' and giggled to herself as she recalled Shuji's obsequious behaviour.

She stared unseeing at the speeding wipers sloshing the rain either side of the windscreen steadily as a metronome. Dan had been mistaken. Though Hilary Barron was unable to attend his funeral as she was out of the country, she had sent a sympathetic message extolling Dan's qualities. Her department made a substantial donation to a heart charity on his behalf. In spite of her prestigious position, today she'd been sympathetic and generous to an unimportant new Eckstazia employee like herself.

Jennifer braked hard at Penybwlch gates and Ben was thrown against Rachel. He hit out at her, both arms flailing. 'Grr off.'

Yes, Hilary was right. Ben *was* becoming a handful. He'd done as he pleased while she'd been busy teaching and nursing his granny. They hadn't had enough quality time. She hadn't taken him places as Dan would have done. But she'd make up for it. Show him the wild animals on the hills, take him round the castle. Buy toy models in the little town, if they could find any shops selling kids' stuff.

*

Shuji handed Rachel a card as she came into the lounge. 'Company doctor. Contact him tomorrow for an appointment for Ben.'

She thanked him. She'd put Ben to bed after their return from church, and now she poured herself some tea.

Jennifer looked up from the sofa. 'Annie's best herbal. Excellent for relaxing you before bed.'

'That woman knows all there is to know about the wild plants,' James said. 'You could do worse than to consult her about the reserve, Rachel.'

Sure, she thought. Whatever.

Jennifer asked, 'Has Ben always been troublesome in church?'

'We didn't go in Coventry.'

Shocked silence.

Then Shuji said, 'I hope you'll be regular here.'

'Of course. In Coventry I had to care for my mother full-time at weekends.'

The tension in the room dissolved away as James asked amiably, 'And how did you enjoy the little service in our rustic church?'

She knew he expected a compliment on his contribution. 'I found your talk most helpful and interesting.'

'Good, good. I thought of you when drafting it. As I prayed before the Lord he gave me to understand that you as a new member of Eckstazia would appreciate a little explanation of our beliefs. Some people, even Christian people who claim to know their Bible, are unaware of God's timetable for the last days.'

'Tomos was most comforting.' She felt pinpricks of tears in her eyes thinking of his kindness to Ben.

Jennifer said, 'Oh, *Tomos*. He's really quite ignorant. Typical Welsh peasant. Unread and almost illiterate.'

James laughed. 'Come on, Jenny. That's unfair. He went to a Welsh college to study theology. Lampeter or somewhere.'

'His ideas are so antiquated. Not a mention of punishment for the wicked.'

Shuji broke in, 'You have to remember, Rachel, that until eight or nine years ago there was a strong so-called liberal movement in western churches that was successful in putting forward quite erroneous ideas. No hell. No devil. Gays had Church blessings or even spurious marriages. Our back to the Bible approach hasn't reached the Welsh proles yet. It will.'

Jennifer gave a mocking laugh. 'Beware the Welsh peasant. Gloomy unresponsive resentful hayseeds. But how can *you* judge, Rachel? You haven't met any except Annie Davies our own personal Welsh dragon – beware her poisonous bite! And William Parry, our shiftless tenant farmer. I made a small request of him a month ago. "Right," he says, sullen as ever. And has he done it? What *does* the fellow do all day?' She patted her mouth elegantly as she yawned. 'I've a good book on line to read. See you all tomorrow.'

A hard woman, Rachel thought. Now, James . . . he was both good-looking and kindly. She'd get on well with him. But it was time for her to check out her own work.

She stood up.

Shuji stopped her. 'A word of warning. The animals on the reserve mountains aren't dangerous. But you want to be aware of them when you're out classifying wildlife.'

'We had several large mammals in the Wirral Reserve where I did my research.' She smiled at him. 'I never had any trouble.'

James was unconsciously combing his fingers forwards through his hair to hide the receding patches. 'I was a student at Birmingham when the European Union directive set out their list of reintroductions for Britain. It was a great time. We hoped to re-establish walrus – the last one was shot in the middle of the nineteenth century. Bears haven't been seen here since Roman times. Both are still on the list but not yet introduced.'

How good that he felt her concern for wildlife. 'Dan and I always hoped they'd be brought back. Perhaps not bears on the Wirral. Too many humans. But here in this vast wilderness. . . One day.'

'We've got lynx and very shy they are too. I glimpsed one a year ago in one of the woods. They'll take a medium sized deer. As do the wolves of course.'

'We scared a wild boar today.'

His dimple deepened as he looked at her. 'There are beavers up the Conwy and Lledr valleys.'

'I'd love to see them. Is it far?'

'Our nearest ones are high above Dolgarrog on the river Ddu. Too far to walk from here unless you're very energetic. I'll take you and Ben in my car one day.'

'It's like the Middle Ages again. The greening of the countryside is one of the best things that's happened in my life time. Woodlands regenerated. Industrial agriculture substantially reduced. Fewer chemicals. A return to sustainable organic farming.'

James nodded. 'Good clean food. A bit more expensive . . .'

'Farmers are forever demanding a bigger cut.'

'Greed's endemic in our society I'm afraid. But rationing ensures everyone gets a fair share. And now the countryside's been opened up everyone can get out and enjoy it.'

'Except travel's hugely expensive. So are the family wildlife camps. Not many people in Coventry could afford country holidays. Ben's only introduction to wildlife has been online programmes and school films.'

Shuji said, 'So you jumped at the chance of bringing him here.'

'Yes indeed. But I've warned him not to go out onto the reserve without me. Especially in spring when mothers are protecting their young or at rutting time.'

James agreed. 'A labourer up valley was gutted by a roebuck's antler last year.'

So the grumblers in the store on the quay had told the truth. 'Do wolves go down to the town?'

James and Shuji glanced quickly at each other. James said, 'They're not a prob.'

'Some locals said. . .'

'Oh, *them*. They know you're a newcomer so they'll complain vociferously to you. They're *always* bleating. It's myth and moondust. Big bad wolf! We were all reared on that fairytale but it's untrue. Rule number one, never believe what the locals tell you.'

'I told them there are no valid reports of wolves harming people.'

'Well done,' said Shuji. 'But make sure you can keep contact at all times when you're on the hills alone.'

'Just in case,' James said sombrely. But he smiled into her eyes.

*

Ben's first week at school unsettled him. He wasn't sleeping well.

'I'm OK,' he said when Rachel fussed over him the following Sunday. 'Can we go look for the hens?'

'There aren't any.'

'There's cocks crowing early. I hear them from my room, like I hear the wolves in the woods at night.'

'Probably pheasants or pigeons,' she smiled. His knowledge of birds was very limited.

'There *are* hens. I saw William take food across the fields yesterday. I followed him.'

'On the farmland?' She was angry as well as frightened. 'You must never go there. He'll set the dog on you.'

'Toss didn't even smell me. I kept downwind.'

In spite of her anxiety she almost laughed at the serious little face of her budding scout. 'And did you see any hens?'

'Might've,' he sulked. Then he admitted. 'No, 'cos I came back. I was scared.'

'Just as well. Don't you snoop round the farm, young man.' She dropped soluble pills into a glass of water. 'Time for your medicine.' Once these drugs clocked in he'd become more amenable. The company doctor had been so kind, so understanding. He had demanding children of his own, he told her. This treatment had done them a world of good. Family peace at last. He'd smiled encouragingly.

When Ben was at school the following day and Rachel was pulling on boots before setting off to the woods, Annie came into the cloakroom.

'See here, Rachel Kerem. That boy of yours. You keep him off my land.' A lock of her thin grey hair escaped from its bun and quivered on her shoulder as she shook her head disapprovingly.

So the little wretch had been seen after all. Defensive anger rose up in her. 'He hasn't done anything wrong.'

'Oh hasn't he? He was seen all right. In the places I told you not to go. Seen by my *sson*,' and she hissed the word. 'You sent him spying round the farm, didn't you?'

'Of course I didn't. He's just a little boy. He's. . .' but what was the use of trying to explain to this ignorant old woman that young children are naturally inquisitive?

Annie said triumphantly, 'I've reported you both to Dr Akimoto. *He* says you're to keep him in order. *He* says the boy's unstable. On the medicine.' She stalked back to the kitchen and banged the door.

Surely Shuji wouldn't gossip with this woman? Yet how else would she know about the medication? Rachel was still trembling with anger as she fastened her jacket and set out into the reserve.

Chapter 5

The woodlands soothed Rachel. Frustrations melted away as she trampled through dead leaves and brambles checking plants. Her yapp indicated the survey sites and also pinpointed where actual plants had been reported three years ago when the last records had been taken. She was delighted to discover an ancient hawthorn with a six foot girth among the birches and oaks. Currently the woodland was bare of flowers, but her yapp charted the dormant plants too. In one area starry white windflowers, a ground hugging plant found in old woodlands, would make their appearance in a couple of months. In another bleak spot hidden bluebell bulbs waited the warmer weather as did cuckoo plant and stinking wild garlic. Animals, whether insect, mammal or bird, were few and well hidden as wet chilly January slipped into wet chilly February.

But she also noticed fallow deer had gnawed the bark on saplings and eaten away woodland scrub, so destroying nesting sites. When spring came she expected to find fewer beetles, woodland flies and butterflies. Perhaps the bluebells had also been eaten since the last survey. The estate wolves were not doing their job efficiently, and idle William Parry was ignoring management guidelines on culling.

Wild pigs constantly watched her through beady eyes, scuffling away when she came too near. She saw few birds except occasional blackbirds, crows and once a dunnock scurrying like a little feathered mouse into the nearest hideout. She watched it, wondering how she would identify the more difficult species, as it was hard to home in on quick moving birds with her yapp. Insects, she mused, were her forte, not birds. The list for this woodland included nuthatch, treecreepers and two species of woodpecker. She decided she'd contact one of the local bird trusts in the nesting season. They'd send a bird spotter to help her and it would be good to have a fellow wildlife enthusiast to chat to.

On one occasion she saw a lynx in a sycamore fork. It stared back, its eyes wide with apprehension. Its pointed ears flickered as she stood admiring it. Then it yawned showing pure white canines.

Rachel touched her broken tooth with her tongue. 'I wish mine were as good as yours. Do Eckstazia have free dentists as well as doctors? Worth asking.' And then she wondered what effect these hunters had on the woodland birds.

Another time she distinctly heard sheep. Not the occasional plaintive bleat of a grazer but the anxious calls of a moving flock. She dismissed it as fantasy. There were no sheep on the reserve. How could there be? Apart from the rigid ban they'd make easy prey for wolves.

Human animals were few and distant. Only William Parry, if he could be called human.She swung her binoculars on him whenever she saw him and the dog and watched him out of sight. If he seemed to be heading in her direction, she quietly moved away. But generally he would disappear over the tops, striding towards the hill range above the sea.

Occasionally she climbed out of the shelter of the woods through bracken dingles into heather country. Sooner rather than later she'd have to classify the wildlife up here where the rain slashed her face and the wind buffeted her until she could barely take a step against it. Once she climbed the mountain, *ffridd* as the Welsh called it. She stood at the very top, panting. Nothing except a bitter grey moor stretching away until it merged with the dismal heavens in a mist swirling with Ben's ghosts. Gulls hidden in the clouds gave banshee screeches. Two carrion crows croaked and carked to each other, wheeling out of low cloud and stretching black wing feathers like fingers clutching for her soul.

She shivered at the barren hostility. The devil's land, where old Satan himself went roaring like a lion seeking someone to devour, and Christians were his preferred option. Invisibly he attacked heart and spirit so she echoed her Lord as she said aloud, 'Get thee behind me, Satan.' She desired to love God more and to live a life committed to kindness and truth. Working with Eckstazia she'd have support to help her achieve these goals. It was a wonderful organisation with spiritual foundations and solicitude for the needy.

As the days went by she felt fitter. Good food, fresh air, continual exercise whatever the weather she had to confront. Four changeable weeks varying from mist to downpour via drizzle and sleet. But the struggle improved her complexion and her hair began to shine with renewed health. She couldn't yet run the hills like a deer, but at least she didn't bob about like a rabbit any more.

She bought clothes from the second hand shop in town on days when she did the school run. She also ordered a package from an internet store. None of them fitted well, and she regretted she'd had to sell her mother's old sewing machine because it had been far too heavy to carry from Coventry. She'd never been a good hand sewer, but now necessity taught her and eventually she was better kitted out for the evening meal. Ben was allotted school uniform from the thriving second hand store at school. She mended and altered that too.

She was almost completely happy. Only Ben worried her. He no longer joined them for dinner after Shuji requested courteously that he eat earlier. He intimated the boy was disruptive and that the scientists needed tranquillity after their day's work. They found his continual questions irritating. Shuji told her he'd arranged for Annie to provide an earlier meal that he could eat at a little table in the corner of the dining room. Then he could do his homework while the adults enjoyed a civilised repast.

At first Rachel hurried her own dinner to join him in her room. They'd sit at the table in quiet companionship as he used her yapp for his homework. Then they'd practise Welsh together. His improved more rapidly than hers due to its continual use at school. If he wasn't too tired he'd make up the latest model dinosaur she'd bought him from the odds and bits shop in town. But that was rare. School exhausted him; he went early to bed. As time went on she spent longer on her meals chatting with the others after her long day alone. When she finally went upstairs to his room he'd be asleep. Then she'd cover him over gently and pray for him.

'Oh God, help him to find true faith in you. Don't take me away in the Rapture if he's to be left behind alone in all the troubles that come after.'

So small and childish with his long flick of hair on the pillow and the dark lashes on his soft cheek. So innocent in his sleep that it broke her heart with love and concern.

He was happy enough to come round the reserve woodlands with her at weekends. She passed on Annie's warning that William had seen him spying and after this he didn't fuss her any more about looking for possible hens on the farmer's land. On the only fine dry Saturday James drove them both to see wild duck and geese on a distant inland lake. They picnicked in the lee of a huge boulder left by the Ice Age in the U-shaped valley. Either side of them mountains soared into the sky, their peaks jagged and black against the hazy blue. So steep were these and so mighty that the low winter sun barely reached into the valley and a raw wind blew steadily across the lake. They hurried back to the warmth of the car. When James learnt the boy liked model building he took them to a real toy shop in Llandudno further along the coast. It was full of wealthy parents with fractious children, and prices were horrendous, but James bought Ben a small model plane. When they returned to Penybwlch he showed Ben a ramshackle shed near the labs.

'Old workshop,' he told him. 'A very handy vice but the tools are rusty. When the weather's warmer you can clear the place out and try making something big. There's an old pram. You could make a go-cart.'

Ben thanked him without enthusiasm. He was quiet, too quiet. But hadn't she wanted him to be more amenable? To work hard at school? She was undecided, troubled, but grateful for James's help. His concern for her and Ben warmed her heart. It was so long since anyone had showed them so much kindness. Was it just his nature to be kind? Or something more?

She turned to Emmanuel's site frequently. Every day he left her a spoken message, a new biblical phrase or an encouraging thought. Sometimes praise for her humble mothering of her son. Occasionally a reminder that holy obedience entails full acceptance of God's word. She held his messages in her memory all day and meditated on them as she munched sandwiches in the sheltered woods. She began to live for Friday evenings when she could speak to him direct. His smile entranced her and his compassionate eyes saw into her heart. She was seduced by his gold-bronze hair drifting Christlike to his shoulders, by his gentleness and courtesy. So rarely had her troubled life known such solicitude by another, not even Dan. But she hid that betraying thought far from consciousness. Truly Emmanuel was a miracle worker bringing her peace and security. God had sent him to her, the God who was taking care of her and Ben, the mightiest force in the universe.

Though Dan would have said, 'What force? Classify it please. Physicists can measure forces from the very minute inside an atom to the ones that shape the universe, and they don't find any evidence that some magic god is playing with nature in an unlawful manner. If he did, the whole universe would suffer. One molecule reconfigured, say a water molecule turned into wine, and everything's out of kilter. The butterfly effect. Yes, long ago people thought gods controlled the weather, hardened human hearts and sent diseases and famines. *We* know different. We're heirs of a scientific tradition that's found physical causes for all events – climatology, psychology, epidemiology.

'So what can this god *do*? He's quite unnecessary. And if he does change the course of events in order to make things easier for Christians, how unfair! How unjust to heal one cancer patient and not another. How immoral to be all powerful and all loving and *then* create a world where the innocent suffer.'

'There's more to this world than you dreamt of, dearest,' she said as she sat on a mossy log among quiet grasses watching treetops wave fiercely high above.

Then one day she found her door unlocked.

Odd, because she always kept it safely shut against Annie's snooping. Nothing had been moved. Or had it? Dan's photo was crooked in its frame. And had she really left those papers on the desk in such a muddle?

She frowned and dismissed the matter.

It was mid February and sleet and a rampaging easterly wind had forced her back into the house to complete identification and collation of some recent specimens. As she inspected them car headlights flashed through the murk and she heard a vehicle drive up. She went to the side of the window and peered out cautiously. It didn't sound like William's van. She'd seen William driving it several times, though Annie had declared it was unroadworthy and without fuel. So much for the woman's honesty. How dumb to think her lie would remain undiscovered.

The sleet slanted across the headlight beams but in spite of the gloom she could just make out the letters on the side. ACCG and a Welsh dragon. The Assembly's Department of Environment, Planning and Countryside.

So this was the farm inspection day that James had spoken about. They'd find out what William Parry was up to. He couldn't hide traces of black market dealing from those eagle-eyed guys.

She recognised William's back as he bent to talk to the passenger. The headlights clicked off and two men walked up the path with him and into his house. Their voices came up to Rachel from the room beneath.

She strained to hear their words, but the sound was an obscure hum. She tiptoed round her room listening carefully. The conversation was loudest in one corner and she peeled back the thin carpet to find a narrow gap between wall and floorboards. With her ear to the crack she picked out Welsh words. *Moch*. Pig. William's voice and something about *gwlan*. Wool? Bwlch y Ddeufaen. Pass of the two stones. Was this a farm in the hills? A man called Parryboots. The name Elwyn Isallt.

The clinking of mugs obscured the words. Then one of the inspectors said the word eggs. They discussed the weather for a long time, English mingling with the Welsh words. Rubbish forecast. Said February would be mild and dry. Not this fierce icy wind. No fishing. An hour passed. The mugs clinked for a second time. More car lights swivelled across the ceiling as Alyson set off to collect the children from school. It would be evening soon. When would they actually inspect the farm?

71

Chairs scraped. Boots stamped. The door opened and the three men went down to the waiting van. They unloaded it, transferring empty crates and other heavier boxes to the house. Then they reloaded it with full crates and large cardboard cartons. One of the men slipped, dropped his carton and cursed. William wheeled a couple of drums from the yard and heaved them neatly into the van. The inspectors got in, the headlights went on and the van turned round and went back down the drive to the road. With her nose pressed to the window she watched the lights jump as the vehicle bounced over the potholes.

The door banged beneath her and there was William marching off towards the farm buildings. She drew back swiftly. Had he looked up and seen her?

Bribing inspectors. Illegal goods of all kinds for the local black market. Annie Davies and William Parry were running a nice little business by the look of things. And the farm inspectorate were in on the game. Corruption was rife in this corner of the Principality.

She inspected the crack in the floor. A little circumspect enlargement. A tube as an ear trumpet. More concentration on her Welsh lessons.

And perhaps a trip across William's fields after all?

*

After Friday school Mrs Lloyd, Ben's headmistress, requested an interview with Rachel.

She beckoned her into her office, pointing Ben to a chair outside the door. She indicated a nearby bookcase of Welsh early readers. Ben ignored them.

The Head showed Rachel to a low comfortable chair, and seated herself in a higher more commanding position behind her oak desk. She was as well dressed as before in considerable contrast to the Welsh people Rachel observed in town. This time Rachel herself was better clothed and felt at less of a disadvantage.

'We find Ben a very lethargic child, Mrs Kerem. Does he get enough sleep?'

'Plenty. Nine hours at least.'

The Head tutted disbelievingly. 'His teacher - I'm sorry she can't be here to discuss the matter. She has an important meeting to attend -'

More important than Ben's welfare?

'. . . his teacher says he spends much of the time dozing.'

Rachel said forcefully, 'I can assure you, Mrs Lloyd, that my child sleeps well. His health is of the utmost importance to me.' Yet he frequently woke with nightmares and came to her room for reassurance, often sleeping beside her till morning. She hesitated to break the habit. They were both lonely, still settling into this alien place.

'His reading level is well below his classmates and he struggles with both maths and science.'

'I find that hard to believe. In Coventry he was above his age bracket in all three subjects. Surely this is merely the disadvantage of having to learn everything in Welsh?'

The headmistress stared down at Rachel. 'Mrs Kerem. I hope you will not object if I put it to you that you're a stranger here. It is perhaps inappropriate to criticise our culture, which, I must point out, is more ancient than your own. The education system of this country is fully autonomous and no longer subject to a syllabus designed by colonising Anglo Saxons.'

Rachel mollified her tone for her son's sake. 'Naturally I wasn't disparaging your education system, Mrs Lloyd. I merely remarked that Ben is finding the extensive changes to his life difficult.'

The head smiled with her lips but her eyes were hard. 'We've decided to put him down a year. . .'

'*Another* year? He's already with eight year olds.'

'And struggling. Furthermore he's not an outgoing child, is he? He has a problem making friends. So with your permission I'll arrange for him to see the Education Authority's psychologist for a full assessment. Between us we can devise an educational plan more suited to his needs.' She pushed a form across her desk for Rachel to sign.

Rachel pushed it back. 'Thank you, but no. I'm convinced Ben will improve rapidly as his facility with the language increases.'

The head shook her head and its dark curls quivered. 'I'm sorry you refuse our offer, but it's your prerogative.'

Outside the door, Rachel touched Ben's shoulder. 'Come on, sleepy head. Let's pick up Freya and then home for the weekend.' He trailed behind her to the estate car.

She told him Mrs Lloyd was going to move him down another year. 'Just while you pick up on your Welsh.'

'I know,' he said dully and refused any further conversation on the matter.

Once he was asleep she turned to Emmanuel for her weekly meeting. Before he greeted her she started to recount her worries. She'd moved Ben away from his friends and his happy school in Coventry with its understanding staff and these Welsh teachers seemed unable to appreciate how difficult it was for him. How could he make friends when they all chatted away in Welsh? Playground Welsh, with all its hidden nuances and shades of meaning. Remembering his outburst in the little church she wondered whether he had a psychological problem stemming from the double loss of father and granny? Should she have taken up the offer of a psychologist's assessment?

Emmanuel reassured her. Offered prayers. Told her everything would work for good for those who love God. She remembered the Bangor students trumpeting the recluse's miracles and was comforted for a while.

That night Ben slept through without troubling his mother but she lay awake as new thoughts occurred to her. Could his medicine affect IQ? Was it turning him into a zombie? The doctor had said it would take a while to stabilise. As a precaution she'd reduce his dosage. Or was he affected by *her* continual worries, hard as she tried to hide them? Her fear of inadequacy as both mother and only wage earner, her inability to reduce her debts. Eckstazia's claim to ten percent of her income and her desire that she and Ben should live up to their new situation had reduced her loan repayments to zero. She could only just scrape enough to pay the interest. Worst of all, was some genetically based disease clocking in? One of Dan's brothers had died at the age of eleven, of some unmentionable disease. His family was estranged, so it would be impossible to find out.

*

Suddenly it was daylight and Ben was jumping on the bed. 'Come on, Mum. Let's go out. The sun – look!' He rushed to the window and drew back the curtains.

They hadn't seen more than a hazy gold sovereign in the sky for days, and now brilliant beams full of dancing dust shone across the room.

Rachel decided to forget Ben's medicine for the day. They'd go for a walk together. She'd find out what troubled him. She'd check for signs of mental or physical deterioration.

'The hens, Mum.' He pulled urgently her hand once breakfast was finished.

In spite of her secret enlargement of the hole in the floorboards, she warned, 'We mustn't snoop, Ben. It's quite wrong.' Do as I say, not as I do! Does child rearing make liars of us all?

He made a face. 'We won't damage anything.'

With anger she remembered the government inspectors' dishonesty. It was surely her public duty to discover any illegal animals. She didn't hesitate any further.

He led her down the drive.

'William might be around with his dog.'

'Silly. I checked, didn't I? He's gone out in his van.'

The fence guarding William's land had three foot of netting with another foot of barbed wire on top.

'Why's it so high?' Rachel mused. 'There aren't any wild animals in this area.'

'There used to be cows and sheep long ago, didn't there?'

'You're right, dear. The fence must've been put up for them. It's still in good condition though it's old.' She pointed out the slow growing lichen that encrusted the posts.

'It's broken down near the main gate. I climbed over by the gate post.'

They got over safely.

'Now we've got to keep out of sight of the buildings in case Annie sees us. So we go through the little trees and this boggy bit.'

She squelched across a rivulet.

'Keep on the tussocks, Mum, and then you won't sink over your boots.'

She'd told him that on previous walks and she smiled to herself as he repeated it so seriously. Ben was fine. He wasn't stupid at all.

'Watch out, Mum!'

She brushed a whippy goat willow branch out of the way of her face. 'Thank goodness you're here to warn me,' she grinned.

The ground rose and became drier. 'This bit's prickly,' Ben muttered. They struggled through gorse and bramble towards a stand of bracken where the going was easier among the dead fronds.

He stopped so suddenly that she almost knocked him over. 'Shh,' he said in a whisper, finger to lips like a character in an adventure film creeping up to the enemy's castle.

That's how he sees this exploit, she thought. Danger Man. Spy Master.

She looked round her. They'd come in a big circle and were a couple of hundred yards from the outbuildings but well hidden. The slate roofs glimmered black as moonless night skies. It had been many years since the mud-coloured walls saw a coat of whitewash and only one had a window facing the farmland. The rest must open onto the yard. Behind the buildings she could see the chimneys and roof of the main house.

Ben pulled at her jacket. 'Get down,' he hissed.

There was no one about that she could see, but she joined in his game and squatted beside him, still staring at the buildings.

'Don't tread on any twigs.' He was well into SAS mode as he steered her towards a fir covered hill with bare branched scrub in front of it.

'Keep low now. There isn't much cover.'

They crawled uphill on damp knees dodging spiky thistle pads until thorny branches of hawthorn blocked their way forward.

'Shh,' Ben ordered holding up a hand in warning as they heard a vehicle clattering along the distant drive. He raised his head cautiously. '*William,*' he hissed.

Rachel was about to insist on their immediate return but she caught a smell of confined birds and heard the low cackling of fowl. Having come so far she couldn't turn back now.

'Keep low and he won't spot us,' Ben whispered. He led her around the hawthorn barrier. 'You can stand up now.'

They were in a large circular grassy area slightly sloping up the hill. The hawthorn and bramble surrounding it hid it well from any prying eyes. At the far end a fir wood protected the clearing from north winds. Wooden stakes supported a corrugated iron roof covered with turf and under this rough shelter were piles of hay mixed with dead bracken. A stack of food sacks was covered with a green tarpaulin. Most puzzling were long strange excrescences erupting from the trampled grass. Ben crossed to one and beckoned her, and she realised with a shock they were three foot high sheds with turf roofs and walls of wire mesh. There were eight of them, at least a hundred feet long.

None of the reconnaissance satellites high in the sky would ever distinguish them from natural mounds.

She followed Ben down a slope to the door. Now she could see the building was dug another few feet into the ground, making it nearly six foot high from base to turf clad roof. Some job, she thought, digging out this unrelenting hillside.

Her son opened the top section of the split door and recoiled from the ammonia stench of hen droppings saturating rotting straw and bracken.

A white hen shot out through the open door squawking violently and disappeared in the direction of the fir wood. Ben slammed the door shut and said some Welsh words that Rachel didn't want to understand.

'We'll have to catch it,' she said, running into the darkness of the wood. The dead needles smelt pungent as she trod their soft rottenness. Ahead of her the bird rushed between the tree trunks, calling frantically. Panting, Rachel gave up the chase and at once the hen flapped nervously towards her shed, crying plaintively to her mates inside. They cackled back noisily.

Every time Ben bent to catch her she fluttered away among the sheds.

'Leave her,' Rachel said. 'Let's get back before William arrives. He's sure to have heard the noise.' She looked at the impressions her boots had made in the mud. 'Scuff your feet over the marks. Quick.'

But they were too late.

A low growl and William's sheepdog shimmied through a gap in the hawthorn. Its ears were flat against its head and its blood-red tongue hung out between its teeth. It dropped to its haunches, staring at them both, its eyes glinting green in the winter sun. Its tail brushed the dead grass seedheads from side to side. Then slowly, so slowly, still lying down, it shuffled one leg forward after the other, moving towards them like a monster black slug.

'Walk backwards slowly. Very slowly,' Rachel ordered, heart beating fast. In Coventry feral dogs had killed a woman and child . . . Eaten . . . oh god, she mustn't think of *that*.

Clutching hands they backed away towards the sheds.

The dog crept to one side of them and growled deep in its throat. Its teeth were sharper than a shark's.

They retreated further.

'Stick,' Ben whispered, snatching at a stake from a woodpile.

The dog sprang before Rachel could protect her son, but it merely grabbed the stick from his hand and dropped it on the ground.

It stood upright now, slavering at the mouth, the skin round its muzzle wrinkled in snarling anger.

They stood stockstill, waiting for a furious William to appear.

The dog's ears flickered.

'Listen. What's that?' Ben asked.

The dog's ears pricked up.

'What? I can't hear anything.'

Its ears flattened again.

'Nothing I guess,' Ben said.

The animal sighed and settled down to its slow crawl, forcing them to retreat away from the huts and up the hill into the wood.

'William must be near,' Rachel whispered as they reached a height where they could see the buildings again. But there was no one between the growling dog and the distant farm. Only empty scrub and boggy places.

Clouds covered the sun.

'You're shivering, Mum. Are you cold?'

No, it was terror at the thought of meeting that ruffian again. How could she have been so foolish?

Occasionally the dog stopped, head on one side, concentrating. Then it resumed creeping, creeping, herding its human flock of two until they were over the brow and the shadowy fir wood became an even murkier mix of pine, birch and rowan with thick understorey of scrub. And still the cur followed them.

At last, as if wearying of its task, it sat down and licked a rough patch on its black coat. Ears cocked it listened for a moment, then raced away, tail in air as if well pleased with itself.

'Will it come back?' Ben whispered, tightening his grip on her hand.

'I don't know.' She waited. Dogs are worse than wolves, she thought. Craftier.

'I think it's gone.'

'Hope so.' They waited a little longer then Rachel looked round her. 'D'you know where we are?'

'No idea.' Ben stared at the eight-foot high tangle of brambles under the trees. 'I think we're lost,' he said happily. 'We'll die of starvation and they'll find our bones and . . .'

'Shut it, Ben.'

He was right. They *were* lost. And she hadn't brought her yapp with her.

Mist closed in, its damp cloak enveloping and transforming the hill. Shapes of rock, hill and undergrowth shifted and melded into one another. Overcrowding trees stalked past them like ancient warriors intent on destroying Roman invaders. Every scrubby bush was in flux, morphing into mocking Old Ones, headless horses and treacherous spears. Creaking and groaning sounds muffled by cloud confused and frightened them.

Was that snarling? The sheepdog waiting to pounce out at them again? Or, even more terrifying, its master? The thug who bullied his own mother would treat them worse. Double trouble, he'd called Ben. They must get back to the house as soon as possible.

'That way.' She pointed. 'I think. But I'm not at all sure, Ben.'

'I'll climb a tree,' and he swung himself into the lower branches of a sycamore.

'Too foggy. Come on. We haven't come to any fences or walls so we're still on William's land. We must come to its boundary with the reserve somewhere.

'Then we can follow it till we're near the house. Cool.'

Unless they were going round in circles like lost people she'd read about who couldn't even distinguish uphill from down. She'd always thought, How stupid! Of course one can tell whether one's climbing or not. And now she found she couldn't. The sense of direction that had always been her pride was lost completely.

She was helpless in the dark and cold. Atavistic fear possessed her, but she walked blindly on. They went down a slope, then up another one. Damp scents of bruised plants accompanied their footsteps and the air became colder as a breeze shook raindrops dangling from wet twigs all over them.

Ben said, 'Didn't need another wash.'

'Won't harm you. Nor me.' Keep things light. Don't frighten him too.

The wood became more open and she stopped, sensing rather than seeing increasing darkness before her. 'Get back,' she ordered sharply, pushing the boy behind her.

The mist wavered aside for a moment.

They were on the edge of a steep cliff, whose depth she couldn't fathom until the rising wind started to blow the remaining cloud away.

'Arghh,' Ben exclaimed staring down into a steep valley. 'That's *close.*'

From their perch above the precipice they saw a mountain on their right rising above them, its side covered with rough screes that fell several hundred feet into the shadowy valley below. On their left sheer cliffs bordered a distant track leading down into the darkness. As the mist dissolved the valley opened onto an extensive plain bisected by a river.

Rachel recalled her map. 'That's not a river, it's the Menai Straits, a sea channel.'

The sun shone through a widening gap in the low cloud.

Ben said, 'The water shines so bright I can't look.'

'The flat island beyond it is Anglesey.'

'Mon the holy mother of Wales.'

'Who told you that?'

'School. Welsh stories.' He pointed above the cliffs on their left. 'Hey, Mum. Look at that.'

The mist was clearing fast over the scarp. The high moor Rachel had glimpsed previously stretched away into distant clouds. Previously it had looked bleak and frightening, but now the sun drew silver etchings of streamlets across it. Tumbled walls criss-crossed the heath, enclosing small green patches that had been sheep grazings before the new Reserve regulations came into force.

Rachel stared at a raptor quartering the moor. 'Too far away and too much sun for me to see the colour. I think it could be a hen harrier or a red kite. Out hunting small birds and mammals.'

As the clouds rolled further back Rachel saw to her amazement there were far greater mountains on the moor's horizon whose existence she'd never suspected before. Majestic monsters, far higher than the pigmy on her right. The sun lit savage peaks and emphasized shadowy valleys, hinting at treacherous overhangs and precipices. Why had she been so fearful of such an enchanted land? One day she'd cross the moor, its bogs and streams, bracken and boulders. She'd climb those mountain ranges, she'd . . .

Ben yanked at her sleeve. 'This is the very top of the pass and that track just below us is the old road down to the coast that the Bangor scientists use. If we can get down there it'll be easy to get home.' He investigated the edge of the precipice, untroubled by the drop. Super hero again. She pulled him back.

'No way. This brown rock's too crumbly. Frost shattered.' But she was delighted by his courage and sense of direction. 'It's back through the wood. We'll find our way easily now the mist's gone.'

Ben trotted behind her happily as they dodged the thorny scrub and passed into the darkness of thick woodland again. Small rises in the ground puzzled her, but she was sure the general direction was right. Then they mounted a ridge and saw the roofs of the house below.

'There's my bedroom window with the dinosaur cutouts,' Ben said.

'The window to the left belongs to William's bit of the house.'

Ragged and faded curtains hid anything inside.

'I can't see Annie's window.'

Rachel said, 'It's under yours. Hidden below the quarry face.'

'How do we get down?'

There was no obvious path to the house, only a slippery scree of broken stones held weakly together by roots of struggling ash and sycamore, mats of winter damaged nettles and straggling bramble. Those stones could carry them clanking and rattling down the incline and onto, probably through, the weak fence topping the yard wall.

'We can't get down this way,' Rachel told him, wrapping one arm round a tree trunk for safety. 'Those stones look too loose.'

'We'd fall into the back yard and break our legs,' Ben said graphically. He made an exploratory move, lost control and slipped forwards gathering speed. As he slithered past her on one knee Rachel grabbed at his jacket but it slid through her fingers. Then his foot jammed against a root and for a moment he teetered insecurely as it bent under his weight.

Still holding her tree, she eased forward until their hands met, hoping her tree would support both their weights. Its roots heaved, then settled as she slowly pulled him back up the scree where he could crawl to more stable ground. Stones landed with a clatter at the back of the house, but she was too scared to worry.

'Not the best way home,' she managed to joke.

'Thought I'd land in Annie's room and give her a surprise.' Ben rubbed a bruised elbow and inspected his bleeding knees.

'A heart attack.'

'Old witch.'

They retreated above the loose stones and surveyed the scene.

Rachel said, 'If we keep parallel to the house . . .'

'Got you. There's a gate between William's land and the garden somewhere in those bushes.'

Keeping to the top of the rise, they walked quietly past the back of the house. At last among the rhododendrons they reached the boundary fence.

And yes, Ben was right. A tall wooden gate, rotten and unlocked. They pushed their way through the shrubbery into the garden until they came to the lab and the covered walk leading to the house.

He giggled as she tickled his feet after dressing his knees. 'Give over, Mum.'

He was relaxed and happy. Now was the time to broach the school problem. 'Ben dear, how are you finding school?'

He stopped laughing and turned his head away. ''S all right,' he mumbled. Then he looked straight in her eyes. 'It's what Mrs Lloyd was saying to you yesterday, isn't it?'

'Yes, dear.'

He burst out. 'The kids don't like me. I'm older than them. They whisper at me in Welsh. They think I don't understand what they say but I do. *I do!*'

'Have you told your teacher?'

'*Her!*'

'If there's any bullying she can put a stop to it.'

'She's worse. She laughs at me. Because I don't speak Welsh proper.' There were tears in his eyes.

'That's dreadful. No teacher should behave like that. I'll speak to her on Monday.'

'No,' he said firmly. 'Don't you do that. They'll call me mummy's boy. And there's caning.'

'*Caning?*'

'I say words wrong and they tell on me. They say I swore. We're caned for that.'

Shocked, she hugged him. 'Caning's not permitted. I'll speak to Mrs Lloyd.'

He pushed her away. 'No. You'll make things worse.'

She changed the subject. 'Mrs Lloyd said your writing is behind. But you were doing so well in Coventry.'

'We write about where we grew up and they say go back to Coventry, and stop speaking to me.'

'And your maths?'

'It's baby stuff, Mum. I can't be bothered. And we just do nature, nothing about dinosaurs evolving into birds or space travel or how machines work. It's boring. Can I go now?' He drifted back to his room and shut the door firmly.

Chapter 6

James exclaimed, 'And what's that you're playing?'

Rachel jumped violently, raising her head from her hands to see him standing censoriously in the doorway.

It was the Tuesday afternoon after her discovery of the hens. She was sitting in the lounge waiting for Shuji, having requested a meeting to discuss the black market. She'd closed the olive velvet curtains against the winter evening and its dreary drizzle, wandered over to the music centre and decided on Tchaikovsky's Pathetique Symphony. Its cry of pain expressed the grief she could neither share with anyone nor articulate to herself. She buried her head in her hands.

And now James, his usually cheerful round face stern, interrupted her. When she told him he looked triumphant. 'I thought so. You know his works are forbidden.' He emphasised, 'Completely forbidden.'

'Why?'

He stared at her as if she was an imbecile. 'Don't you know anything about the man?'

'A bit.' But none of it seemed harmful.

'He's one of *those*.'

Of course! She'd checked out Eckstazia's website on gays as Alyson advised and been stunned by the invective of its videoblogs where Christians, their faces contorted with righteous anger, declared, 'Why do wars and famines increase year on year? What's the real cause of global warming? Why did Snaefell explode seven years ago, showering deadly volcanic dust and gases across the globe? Because God always intervenes when man descends into decadence, that's why!'

'Churches approve so-called marriage and church blessings for gays! Satan's last major piece in his game plan to cause universal moral corruption!'

'Politics boring, right? No, no and again no. This is a wakeup call for us in Eckstazia to stand for election. Together we'll return Christian laws to the statute books. Scriptural punishment for murderers, poofs, lezzies, muggers, crooks.'

'God curses those who break his holy law. So does Jesus. Death penalty for gays.'

A calmer note was injected into the blogs by a junior mentor. 'God loves us all, sinners as we are.' He raised his hand in blessing. 'He loves those who commit this odious sin, and so must we. We mustn't abuse them. Our duty is to open their eyes in kindness and lead them lovingly onto a better path. I've gently reminded many same sex couples that though they may walk down the aisle in a libertarian church to receive God's blessing, that same God will one day cast them into the lake of fire for their abomination.'

She repeated them to James, concluding, 'Completely over the top.'

'I agree they show little Christian charity.'

'I know several gay partnerships that are faithful and loving. And Christian.'

'Not Christian. They'll never be raptured.' He ran his fingers through his hair nervously.

'Really, James,' she said with displeasure. 'What's more important, one's sexual inclinations or loving God and our fellow humans?'

'If they loved God they'd keep his law.'

'Surely the Old Testament priests wrote down that law for their own time and society?'

He said conclusively, 'Written under God's guidance, true for all times and places.' Then with patient kindness, 'Surely you as a former teacher can see Tchaikovsky's influence would seduce our young people into thinking unlawful sexual orientations are optional?'

'If Tchaikovsky's as evil as that, why is his symphony recorded in our music centre?'

She assumed he didn't know because he didn't reply. Instead he retuned the centre to a soloist extolling the love and mercy of God to the strains of a poorly tuned Indian surmandal. 'This will suit you better. A positive message, not a whine about life's hardships. And well deserved hardships for *that* particular composer.' He paused. 'Or you could try Lament for a Dying Earth.' He looked at his damaged hand, reddening slightly as he said with hesitation, 'Something I composed myself a long time ago. But well received. Very well received. A string quartet.'

'Not my scene, I'm afraid.' Shuji had asked her to encourage James's musical talents, but why should she when the man had been so objectionable over her choice of composer? Anyway string quartets sounded like dying cats to her.

Seeking to mollify her he said, 'I'm sure Ben will settle down in school soon. *I've* never noticed any psychological problems.' Then, as she looked startled that he knew about her private concerns, he coughed awkwardly, turned and left the lounge.

*

Shuji arrived, followed by Annie with a tray of tea things.

'Now, Rachel, what's the problem?' He dunked a biscuit in his mug.

'There's a large black market being run from Penybwlch.'

He leaned forward in his armchair giving her his complete attention. 'That confirms what Annie. . .' He stopped quickly.

'*Annie* told you?' *Annie,* who was so deeply implicated?

He brushed it aside. 'It was nothing. Some complaint about William Parry which I ignored.'

She was not convinced but she continued, 'The pig that was illegally butchered on my first night here must have been a wild one from the reserve as there aren't any pigs on the farm. I'd have heard or smelt them. So William's trapping wild boar for sale locally. Annie asked me to pick up fish from the quay in an unmarked box. On my first Saturday Annie, William and another man loaded boxes into a van and...'

Shuji relaxed back into his chair, elbows on the plush arms and fingertips together. 'So you saw Annie and her husband borrowing Penybwlch equipment for use on their own farm. It's customary among farmers. You'll find local fishermen have licences. Wild boar need culling occasionally and no doubt William has a licence for that too. Yes, he chose a crazy time for butchering, but he's an odd guy at the best of times. And *we* benefit because we eat quality pork and bacon.'

'I've seen egg crates as well.' She was vexed by his indifference. 'And I was in my room when the government inspectors came. . .'

'A six monthly event, I'm told. It's important that everything should run correctly on the farm.' He offered her another biscuit, smiling. 'Really this all lies quite outside my remit.'

'They didn't inspect anything. I heard them talking in Ty Bach under my room the whole time. When they left they took crates of eggs, boxes and drums of some liquid with them. And William keeps hens. Ben told me . . . He was in the forbidden section. . . I know he shouldn't have been, and I did tell him not to . . .'

'Your young man isn't very obedient, is he? Annie has laid several complaints. I've had to tell him twice not to hang around the labs.'

She sprang to her son's defence. 'He's naturally curious. They are at that age.'

'And imaginative. He invented these hens perhaps.'

'No. He took me to see them on Saturday. I can show you . . .'

'Rachel, you really must *not* encourage your son to trespass,' Shuji commanded.

She had a strange feeling that his lack of interest in the trafficking was a sham. She emphasised, 'William Parry masterminds the trading.'

'Most unlikely. He's nearly as dull witted as his brother. Left school without any qualifications.' He spoke casually but he was certainly concentrating, leaning forward, his fingers clenched.

'It's completely illegal to keep livestock in this area. I checked the Welsh Assembly regs . . .'

He held up his hand to stop the flow of words. 'Yes, yes. I understand. And let me know if you spot any further irregularities. But at the end of the day it's a problem for Welsh officials. Not Eckstazia.'

She was stymied. He didn't have the same hatred for the shadow economy that she did. She'd seen first hand in Coventry how corrupt traders offered untraceable cash to the poor, giving small change for stolen goods they sold on at inflated prices to the rich. She knew from her more wayward pupils how their petty thefts lined the pockets of these jokers, and that once the youngsters had taken their first dishonest steps they were rarely able to escape the downward spiral. But it was useless to try and explain this to Shuji. He had no firsthand experience of the invisible tentacles of the black market octopus. Its sucker arms dragged the foolhardy into a vast underground market of blood diamonds, dodgy pharmaceuticals, money laundering, arms and drugs, where they were exploited, duffed up and sometimes murdered by the global criminal fraternity.

He broke into her thoughts. 'You look far more relaxed and happy than when you arrived, Rachel. And how's your young detective settling in at school?'

He looked so kindly that she burst out, 'I'm worried about him, Shuji.'

He said gently, 'That's the default position for parents, my dear.'

'His headmistress told me last Friday that he's sluggish. His medicine could be at fault. Some of these tranquillising drugs have only been tested on adults, not children.'

'There's no need to be concerned. Our practitioner is highly qualified in paediatrics and is well aware of such problems.'

She told him Ben was being put back yet another year and she had refused an educational assessment.

'These local schools have a poor name. Alyson and Eric often complain that Freya is having a very substandard education. If I were you I'd put him down for Eckstazia's Reality Academy in Bath as soon as possible.'

She hadn't heard of the place. 'Is it a private school? I could never afford it.'

'No worries. A recommendation from me will ensure you receive a grant. A very generous grant.'

'He's too young to board.'

'Nonsense. He'll soon be ten, won't he? The best possible age. Apron strings, my dear, apron strings. We don't want him tied to Mummy for life, do we?' He laughed softly.

'You're right.' Oh, it would be hard to see him go. Her cherished reminder of Daniel with the same endearing lock of hair falling defiantly over his forehead. Her only child whose every word and gesture was so delightful. But she must be strong. Unselfish. Do what was best for him.

'As for the educational assessment you've been offered, I'd advise you to think again. It'll indicate his strong and weak points and form a useful basis for your application to the Academy. He'll have first class tuition there as the Academy has excellent teachers, all qualified at one of the UK's Russell Group of universities.' He looked searchingly at her. 'Emmanuel also suggested you are overprotective of your son.'

'Ben comes first with me,' she said sharply, angry that Emmanuel had broken her confidentiality with both James and Shuji.

'No, Jesus must come first. Before all other commitments. Our reason for living is to bring delight to him, our Lord and Saviour. We serve him through our work and our relationships. Reassess your dealings with your son. Are you preventing his growth into independence because *you* need him to rely on you?'

She sat there silently wondering whether to broach the subject nearest her heart.

Shuji asked benignly, 'Is something else troubling you?'

She burst out, 'It's the Rapture, Shuji. What if I'm taken up and Ben's left behind? Who'd look after him?'

'You must trust the goodness of the Lord.' His voice was soothing. 'Why do you think he'd be one of the Left Behind?'

'He isn't interested in spiritual things.'

'Ah, you're referring to his behaviour in Llanfechan church.'

'Not only that. I pray with him every night – of course I do – but he's not at all responsive.'

Shuji cleared his throat. He looked sad but determined. 'This'll be painful for you, and I'm sorry to be the one to cause more unhappiness after all your trials, but it must be mentioned now. His father could be described as a doubter, I understand.'

'Dan was a philosopher first and foremost. He was cautious about all belief systems.'

'A highly intelligent young man. A great loss, a very sad loss both to his university and the wider world. Yet a man without any faith. A lapsed Jew. Now, Eckstazia's supported by many Jews. We're at unity with any faith that looks to the coming of a Messiah, a righteous judge. But Daniel denied his own inheritance as well as Christianity in a polemical article about Eckstazia. Our solicitors concluded it was libellous.'

She was shocked. Shuji was right that Dan hadn't been a religious man. He thought religions oppressive but, unlike some who claimed they were the root of all evil, he'd respected them for the learning of their philosophers. He hadn't been happy about the rapid spread of Eckstazia's influence worldwide, but had supported their charitable research and never objected to her employment in schemes part funded by them. She was still baffled why this tolerance had metamorphosed into loathing during the last months of his life, but even so she was surprised he'd been vitriolic in print.

She said, 'He never told me about any such article.'

'Sometimes we don't know as much about our loved ones as we think we do.'

'But how can this possibly affect Ben?'

'Our research, our very careful, well documented, well supported research, shows there's a genetic component to disbelief. No such thing as a gene for atheism, of course. But a tendency to doubt.'

'And you think Ben. . .'

'Has inherited such a bias from his father. Now I know that our little society here will have a beneficial effect, but I'm doubtful about the orientation of these narrow-minded local schools. The syllabus is not impressive. They support atheistic theories like evolution . . .'

He was watching her intently and for some incomprehensible reason she was uneasy. But she couldn't let that go. 'Why, Shuji, what's wrong with that? My research is founded on evolutionary concepts. So is yours. Evolution supports all pharmaceutical and epidemiological discoveries, all analyses of diet and food production, all environmental research. Geology, chemistry, physics all agree with these principles.'

'Not everyone would accept that.'

She smiled as she said, 'No, there are still wacko creationists who think that all the fossilised fishes were *drowned* in Noah's flood!' She thought she knew him well enough by now and that he'd laugh with her.

But she was wrong.

'It isn't amusing, Rachel. Great evil springs out of this atheistic creed. Social Darwinism destroyed millions in the Second World War because evolution claims humans are dispensable and only the strongest are worthy of survival.'

Her history wasn't good enough for her to argue the point.

He continued, '*All* the murdering godless regimes of the last century were based on evolution. The USSR and Stalin. Pol Pot's purifications in Cambodia. Mao Zedong in China where tens, maybe hundreds of millions died in his reforms and the ensuing famines. How can you support such a faith?'

'Of course I don't support pogroms. But evolutionary theory is a scientific concept. Not a faith.'

He frowned at her persistence, in sudden anger almost shouting at her. 'It's an atheistic creed. Its upholders are among Eckstazia's fiercest critics. Their aim is to let people die, the weakest people, the poorest and most sick. Then they, the strong and wealthy, will inherit all the world's resources.'

It was useless to reply so she said nothing and his normal composure quickly returned.

'So, Rachel, this is another reason why schooling in our Academy will be so beneficial. He'll learn the truth about God's creation of the world. You can be sure he'll be taught everything conducive to his salvation. And so you won't have to worry whether or not he'll be raptured with you when the Lord summons his faithful to meet him.' His voice soothed her doubts temporarily. 'Believe me, my dear, all sorrow and sighing will disappear in that day. We shall know that everything that has happened to us, everything whatsoever, has been for our good and to the glory of his name. I know you feel lonely at present, but that will soon pass. *We're* your family now. Eckstazia will care for you, as we always care for widows with children. Wherever you go in the world there are members who'll welcome you and support you. One day you may even find a closer relationship with one of our members.' He paused, then said meaningfully, 'I believe James took you and Ben out for the day recently. Most enjoyable, he said.'

So James's kindness was indeed due to more than a generous nature.

Shuji continued, 'I'll contact the Academy on Ben's behalf shortly. Emmanuel knows the headmaster well, so I'm sure it can be arranged with minimum fuss.' He stood up, bowed and left the room.

Afterwards she searched the web for Dan's polemical article but couldn't find a mention of his name. Nothing on the University website. His own personal site had evaporated into the ether. She sat bemused, fingering her necklace. It was as if he'd never existed.

She studied Reality Academy's prospectus. The biology syllabus was standard except for the inclusion of a discussion on the relative merits of evolution and intelligent design. No mention of an anti-evolution stance. And there were also competitive games with Eton and Harrow, canoeing on the Avon and mountaineering in Switzerland, strong grounding in all academic studies, a prefect and house scheme with supporting staff, matrons and everything an upper class parent could desire. Wonderful. Totally out of her sphere. Would Ben be acceptable among such superior pupils?

And James? She assessed her own feelings. Apart from today's fracas over Tchaikovsky she liked him very much. Not passionately. But she *wanted* a calm reliable friendship, didn't she? And most importantly, someone who'd be a good father to Ben.

*

Voicemail. So disguised and so thick a Welsh accent that Rachel couldn't tell whether it was male or female. 'Spy. We're watching you. We know where your son goes. Remember.'

William Parry? She listened again several times but was unsure. But who else could it be?

She dropped the yapp and looked round the woods in terror. It was a week since she'd told Shuji her suspicions and he must have cracked down on William. William, who had a dog that could deal with trespassers all on its own. A dog that might be following her even now.

She'd heard of dogs and their owners in such complete accord that they could read each other's minds. Don't be so superstitious, she told herself. That's an illusion, a trick like the horse that could count. Of course that cur can't communicate with Parry. But still she was scared for her son and herself.

She was on school rota. Before collecting Ben she bought him a mobile with money saved for a better jacket for herself. She warned him never to leave the school with anyone but herself or one of the scientists. If anyone else, anyone else *at all*, said they'd been asked to pick him up, he was to mobile her first.

'I'm not stupid, Mum,' he said sulkily. Then he burst out, 'I hate it. *Hate it! Hate it!*'

'Would you like to go to another school?'

He ignored this. 'I hate you too.' He stared out of the window at the dead bracken on the hillside, tears of rage in his eyes.

'Why, lovey?'

'You told Lloyd about the caning. She's furious. Called me a liar.'

'I'm so sorry. She told me they don't use the cane ever. Just have one in the classroom as deterrent. But how does she know it's never used?'

'She uses it herself.'

'Another school?' she suggested again.

'Where?'

'Rather a long way from here. You'd stay for the whole week and come back weekends.'

'Do they speak Welsh?'

'No. It's in Bath, in England.'

'P'raps I might.' He still refused to look at her and ignored Freya when Rachel picked her up from the high school.

Back at Penybwlch Rachel parked the car and followed Freya to the semidetached cottages where her family and the other scientists lived. These backed onto the yard buildings but had no access to it. They were Victorian, farm workers houses, nowhere near as grand as the main house with its two square towers. Each cottage had a central door with windows either side and corresponding windows above. Their bricks were an attractive shiny red with cornices over each window and a decorative string course between the two floors. Stout local slate covered the roofs. Alyson and Eric's cottage had a tiny paved area between door and gate while the Bangor scientists had an overgrown kitchen garden to one side with an apple tree suffering from canker and winter moth. A solitary blackbird pecked at a rotten apple and chattered off as they reached the door.

Freya ran in as her mother came to the door. 'Come in, Rachel. And Ben too,' she smiled as her daughter dashed upstairs. But Ben stalked away to the house, bashing his school bag against walls and railings.

'So what's the matter with him?'

'Misses his dad.'

'No way can you be both parents to him,' Alyson said frankly.

'Too right.'

Alyson's front door opened into a tiny hall with steep stairs at the far end. She looked embarrassed as she ushered Rachel into a sparsely furnished sitting room on the right. 'There's a broken spring on the settee so watch where you sit. I'm sorry it's all such a mess.' She went through the hall into the kitchen.

The carpet was threadbare where generations of people had walked. Cheap mats had been thrown over the worst bits. Rachel had never seen one of the old-fashioned woodstoves in use before, but Alyson's threw out plenty of heat combined with the scent of applewood. Even so the room was obviously damp for a musty smell overcame those sweeter scents. A fine old pitcher full of dried grasses, beech leaves and evergreens stood on the table, the falling leaves and needles accumulating on a rummage of papers and a couple of e-books. Several rows of shelves contained decrepit paper books, dusty from disuse. Family pictures flickered across an old wall-screen; baby Freya at the seaside, as a toddler playing ball with elderly people, probably grandparents, a young teenager dancing on a stony plateau with Eric and Alyson somewhere in Iceland. Alyson blanked the screen impatiently when she returned.

'Bryn Llawenydd they call this place. Hill of joy. How they came up with that I'll never know. Both cottages are two up, two down. Freya has her own room over the kitchen, and Eric and I are above this room. No windows or doors to the side or back, so the place never gets a through draught and it's always damp.' She passed tea to Rachel. 'Three of them next door, so they each have a room and share bathroom and kitchen. Walls like paper. Fortunately they don't have too many late nights and they're away weekends.' She looked intently at her guest. 'You're looking worried, Rachel.'

Rachel told her about this afternoon's voicemail threat, trembling with distress.

'Hey, come on,' Alyson said, putting her arms round her. She added a dollop of sugar to the tea. 'Delayed shock. If anyone tries kidnapping, you can trace him by his chip insert.'

'Can't. He hasn't got one. When he was born chip inserts were still experimental and Dan and I were worried about freedom of the individual. So he's got a wristband chip. It can easily be removed.'

'Who've you told about the threat?'

'Only Ben. And you.'

Alyson frowned, thinking hard. 'Tell everyone. Shuji can sort William. He isn't really . . don't get me wrong, Shuji's great in many ways, but he isn't really sympathetic. James'll be more help in keeping an eye out for Ben. He likes you. Admires the way you've brought Ben up on your own. And Eric, Freya and I'll take care of him as well. But why should William threaten him?'

Rachel explained about the black market.

'So Shuji's had William over the coals. Maybe he's also told the police and they're hammering William. That figures. I honestly don't think William will do anything because he'll be first suspect, won't he?'

'He's stupid enough not to realise that.'

'My advice is to leave the black market to Shuji. ' She hugged her friend and passed her a plate of honey covered bread rusks. 'Sorry about these. Can't afford biscuits even if there were some in the shops.'

Rachel was startled. 'Ben and I haven't had such good food since rationing started. Fish, lots of meat and veg. Yoghurts and fresh fruit. Eggs and cheese.' She licked her lips dramatically.

Alyson grimaced. '*We* have to buy our own food and the shops are appalling. Supermarket closed two years ago, so there's only local stores and you can never get anything fresh. They don't stock many lines. My car rota period is spent checking village shops. And the expense! They take more off your ration card than they should. You're very lucky in the main house. Living hush hush off William's black market, eh?'

'That worries me, much as I enjoy it. Shuji doesn't seem concerned where our food comes from.'

Alyson gave her another hug. 'So don't you worry either. Keep quiet and everything'll settle down.' She poured more tea. 'There's similar probs in Reykjavik. Last time we went home food was so pricey it went stale on the shelves while people queued outside waiting for reductions. They were fighting for mouldy cheese and cracked eggs. There's a flourishing black market but the authorities turn a blind eye. Just as well or no one would get enough to eat.' She moaned theatrically. 'Wish *we* could get a handle on *your* black market.'

Rachel thought, Doesn't anyone here dislike these crooks as much as I do?

Drumming vibrated through the cottage.

Alyson gestured upstairs. 'Freya's finished her homework.' She shouted, 'Turn it down.'

No response.

Sighing she left the room and a little later the volume was reduced.

'Wait till Ben gets the rhythm,' she said on her return. She pulled a comb out of her dark wispy hair and rolled it up more neatly. 'Bet you thought all Icelanders have fair or reddish hair like Eric and Freya.'

'I did wonder.'

'We've also Irish ancestors from the days when the Vikings raided the Irish coast for slaves. We're a regular mix. Freya's got a goddess's name.'

'Thor, Odin – that lot?'

'Yeah. Eckstazia folk, those that bother to know about Norse gods, don't approve. James for one. And Ashley the Bangor technician.'

'A name's only a name.'

Alyson smiled approval. 'For me and you. Not them. Never mind. What d'you think of James' sermons?'

Every Sunday evening since Rachel first attended the mountain church, James had spoken to the little group of scientists, though Hilary Barron had not joined them again.

'OK I suppose.' After Shuji's hint and Alyson's earlier comment she didn't want to sound too enthusiastic about James.

'Suppose! He's one of the best speakers I've ever heard. None of this wishy-washy liberal stuff like Tomos. Sock it to them, James, say I. Tell them like it is. If you're not for Jesus you're against him, and when he comes back you'll be on his left hand among the goats, with a very nasty future awaiting you.' Her fine eyes were bright with anticipation. A true Valkyrie who would joyfully carry the souls of sinners past Valhalla and dump them in perdition.

She was right of course. The world would be a wonderful place without thieves, murderers and warmongers. Yes, she was right. But Rachel thought of unbelieving Dan and was uneasy.

'James is a good guy,' Alyson continued. 'He may have gay tendencies but he's honest at heart. He'll overcome and settle down to a normal life.'

'Not easy to go against your inclinations.'

'We all have our fight against the temptations of the Evil One. But we've the resources of Jesus behind us. He overcame the Devil for us.'

'D'you really believe in a devil? Seems to me our probs stem from the conflict between our own needs and those of other people, not someone whispering evil in our spiritual ears.'

'Oh, Rachel, just look at the world! What other evidence do you need of a malicious power at work?'

Rachel didn't want to argue so she changed the subject and asked Alyson about the holy well of Llanfechan with its reputation for healing children. Without mentioning her hope it might help Ben in case Alyson laughed, she said, 'I've never seen the well because it's always dark and raining on Sunday evenings.'

'Haven't you seen Llanfechan from the moor?'

'Haven't been over the mountain yet. Too busy classifying in the woods because the stats are well out of date.'

'It's far nearer by the moor than by road. About an hour's walk from here on a bridle path. Go even further and you'll reach Bwlch y Ddeufaen.'

'Pass of the two stones?' William and the corrupt inspectors had mentioned Bwlch y Ddeufaen. 'A farm?'

'No, a Roman road between the mountains. Built to take their army from the Conwy valley to the coast so they could attack the druids on Anglesey. And there *are* two ancient standing stones, much older even than the Romans. I walked a short way along it when we first came here but it's a dreary place. Dangerous too.' She made fresh tea and as she poured it asked Rachel what she thought of Shuji. 'He's renaissance man. Worldwide experience, excellent publicist of Eckstazia's research, conscientious with good organisation skills. I'm not inspired by his art.'

Rachel grinned. 'He advised me to wear a widow ring. His daughter has a chastity one.'

'Really?' Alyson laughed, glancing at Rachel's hands. 'I hope you don't.'

'No, that's my wedding ring. The one next to it is the one I gave Dan.'

'Shuji's daughter didn't keep hers for long. Married someone Daddy approved and divorced two years later. She's his greatest disappointment.'

'And your rinderpest?'

Once Alyson got started on her research you couldn't stop her, Rachel found. She smiled as she listened. Over the top about cattle and their diseases. Barmy to outsiders. This was how researchers *should* feel. In a pause she said, 'You'll be pleased when the new lab's built.'

'Oh, the *rebuilding!*' Alyson laughed her harsh laugh. 'Eric and I were promised that before we came here.'

Rachel told her what Shuji had said. 'It's hardly an important building architecturally. Well hidden. Whose view will it spoil?'

Alyson shrugged. 'Welsh Assembly's a talking shop. So's the Snowdonia Reserve Committee. Eckstazia must get over those hurdles as well as jumping through all the other hoops designed to slow up progress. It'll still be just a sparkle in Shuji's eye this time next year, believe you me.' She returned to her own interests, describing the various laboratory procedures used in classifying the rinderpest virus. 'It doesn't affect humans and it doesn't persist in the environment. It's easily destroyed by heat and disinfectants. We've strictest security and sterilization procedures – showering, change of clothes and so on.'

'What does the disease look like?'

'The cattle get high fever, red patches round the eyes, discharges from nose and mouth, frothy saliva, reduced rumination, constipation and then diarrhoea followed by death in most cases. It spreads through contact and the incubation period lasts from three to fifteen days. The virus can still be found in the milk fortyfive days after recovery. *If* the cow recovers, that is. It kills cattle but sheep and goats sometimes develop clinical signs though they're rarely affected seriously. Deer and pigs generally don't show any symptoms even when infected so I'm not happy that William's killing pigs so close.'

'Highly dodgy.' Yet Shuji didn't seem concerned. 'How are the current problems in the Sudan and South America progressing?'

'South America's still a worry but the vaccine's being manufactured as a priority and the disease should be eradicated again within the year.

Devastated international trade in beef. That's why it's impossible to find it in our shops.'

'It's good for our beef farmers. Must be making a mint.' Rachel still blamed the British food crisis on greedy farmers. 'Why's Jenny's going out to the Middle East and India in April if the plague's eradicated?'

'Just precautionary. She doesn't say much, our Jenny. You won't put one over on *her*. Looks severe but that's just because she's worrying about rinderpest. Heart of gold really.' Alyson frowned. 'But it isn't the research I'm doing on the current strains in Sudan and South America that's my worry. No, it's the new strain Shuji, Jenny and James are developing, part of preventative research on mutations that *could* occur in the wild. Currently there's no vaccination for this one. It kills sheep, goats and pigs, the lot. It'd cause havoc world wide if it ever escaped. Seriously restrict mutton, venison, bacon and ham, also yoghurts and cheeses and all crops grown using ox power. Worldwide famine. Bioterrorists' dream virus.'

'They'd suffer too so who'd be crazy enough?'

'Militants on the periphery of legitimate groups. Some want to extend human rights to all animals. They say livestock shouldn't be treated as human property, so all domestic animals must be destroyed.'

'Hardly animal rights, let alone human!'

'Don't expect logic, Rach. There are fanatical vegans who want to force us all to live on their diet. Global warming extremists who want to destroy cattle because they fart methane. So lab security is exceptionally strict – that's why you aren't allowed access – and the robotic workers are all of the highest quality. Guaranteed to work safely with such a dangerous pathogen and destroy it in event of a bioterrorist attack on the building. But Eric and I still worry. It's impossible to enter the lab through the door alarms of course, but the external fabric is wood. The interior walls are security lined but I've seen several gaps in the lining. Outside intruders would have to know *where* to make a secretive entry, but it could be done. I just hope the robots are programmed to deal with a covert entry. Still, Jenny assures us the lab has the necessary certification and safety equipment.'

She stoked up the fire and in the pause Rachel asked, 'Have you heard of Eckstazia's Reality Academy?'

'The one in Bath? Of course. It's damned expensive. Everyone wants their kids to go there, but they only take the brightest. There's a scholarship exam but Freya failed it unfortunately.'

'Exam? Shuji didn't tell me that.' She frowned. 'He suggested I send Ben there. Said there wouldn't be a financial problem as Eckstazia will pay.'

Alyson stared at her in disbelief. 'I thought Ben wasn't very bright.'

Rachel protested, 'He's a lot better than his teachers acknowledge.'

'All right. Don't get aerated.' Alyson's face was pale with envy. 'I just find it hard to believe. You're *sure*?'

'He's going to recommend Ben himself.' She stood up to go as the door crashed open and Eric stormed in.

'We've no right, no right at all to do it.'

'What?' Alyson asked, alarmed.

'God has no hands but ours, James says. I know, I know. Jenny says it's for the good of the whole world. I believe that too. But *this* . . . Oh, hello, Rachel. I didn't see you.' He swallowed hard, trying to appear casual. 'How are you? Everything all right?'

She told him about the threat to Ben but he was barely listening, so making the excuse she must supervise Ben's homework, she departed, wondering about his sudden outburst.

*

Red letter Friday. Rachel sat comfortably in her favourite glade in the crook of a fallen tree, sheltered from the wind by surrounding shrubs. February was not yet past but the sun's warmth was considerable in the hollow.

She opened the connection to Emmanuel. His iconic face smiled from the small screen so the sun seemed more brilliant and scents of winter burgeoned with spring promise.

'Hi, Rachel. How're things with you?' Such calm, such peace.

'Wonderful. I love it here.'

The sky behind him was not as blue or as unfathomably deep as his eyes. 'And how is your young man? Shuji and I have thought hard how we may best help him.'

She forgave him then and there for communicating her private concerns to Shuji and James.

'James tells me there's a threat to Ben's safety. For now you and James must monitor his movements carefully. After Easter I've arranged for him to go to the Academy.'

She gasped with relief. 'But the entrance exam? An interview with the headmaster?'

'Those have been waived. You'll have plenty of opportunity to speak to the head when you take him at the beginning of term.'

'Uniform? I can't afford. . .'

'Supplied by the school. Plenty of second hand stock if you don't mind that.'

'Of course not.' She hesitated. How would Ben feel?

Emmanuel smiled again. 'Have you shown him the Academy website?'

She shook her head.

'The sooner he gets used to the idea, the better. He'll love it, Rachel. And I'll arrange a special child mentor exclusively for him. I went there myself and I enjoyed every minute. From your point of view it's not just the excellent academic record, important though that is. Nor the sports and social activities that help to develop a rounded personality. It's the knowledge that he's cared for, he's safe and above all he's happy.'

If only she didn't feel so upset at the thought of losing his daily companionship.

'Yes, it's hard on you,' Emmanuel said gently. 'Doubly hard because you're on your own. But believe me, Rachel, you're doing the right thing. One day you'll look back on this when he's a successful adult, and you'll rightly feel proud of your decision. My own mother suffered as you do, but we're closer than ever now because of the sacrifice she made for me.'

'I can't thank you enough, Emmanuel. You're a miracle worker.'

'No, don't thank me. I'm only a channel for the love of God. *I* need to thank you. You've courageously uncovered this illegal black market.'

'William Parry's the organiser. The police. . .'

'Not yet. Shuji isn't convinced William's capable of planning such a project. Together we're sorting out the man's considerable mental and social problems.'

His eyes were those of a man who'd resisted all the devil's wiles, who'd looked into the depths of human depravity and emerged untainted and full of compassion. He and Shuji would remonstrate with William and guide him tenderly into a worthier path.

Though, said her cynical side, they'd have their work cut out with that one.

'So keep your eyes open, Rachel. Try to discover the organizer and report to James. He has your welfare very much at heart. He's a good man and a faithful servant of our Lord.' Emmanuel's hair gleamed bronze, waving as the wind ruffled it. 'Is there anything else troubling you, my dear?'

His kindness overwhelmed her. 'Dan,' she whispered.

'I must be honest with you, dear Rachel. How could I be otherwise when I already admire your courage and fortitude so much?'

She was shocked to see tears trickle down his handsome face.

'You must already be aware that because he was an unbeliever you're unlikely to meet him again.'

'I pray nightly for his soul.'

Emmanuel shook his head. 'Our loving Lord teaches that the unrepentant soul who scorns God's love and salvation remains locked into sin for ever after death. No prayers of ours can soften such a hardened heart. Some churches have found this too difficult a truth so they compromise, but there's no scriptural foundation for purgatory.'

Those appalling medieval paintings. Torture and unending agony. Hellfire for ever and ever. Parched throats that will never feel the cooling draught of water again. Outstretched arms that no one in heaven can reach.

She choked back her sobs.

Emmanuel wiped his tears. 'Best not think about his fate.'

How can I *not* think about his suffering when I love him so dearly?

He continued, 'Instead thank God for his mercy and love in redeeming you for the beauty of heaven with himself.' Anticipation of that glory lit up his face.

It gave her no comfort, poor sinful soul.

Compassionately he said, 'My dear, put the past firmly behind you. Give any mementoes of Daniel to Shuji.'

'I've nothing but a photo and some letters.' His necklace was warm against her skin.

'Give those and your heart will find peace. Dear Rachel, you're very much one of *us*. We all respect you and want to make your life happier.' He smiled sweetly. 'You've been accessing my website on dealing with debt the Christian way.'

'Why, yes.'

'Eckstazia always helps its most promising members. We can offer you a loan to cover all your debts, a loan with minimal interest.'

Rachel gasped as a huge weight fell from her shoulders. 'I can't thank you enough, Emmanuel.'

'Never think I'm too busy to help you, Rachel.'

This great man had dipped into the well of his wisdom and offered her the eternal water that quenches spiritual thirst. He had singled her out. He shared her deepest suffering.

She was a special person.

She straightened her back proudly.

Chapter 7

'Why d'you and James bother me all the time?' Ben complained. 'I can look after myself.'

'Just for a while, dear. William will calm down if neither of us go near the farm buildings or his fields. No more snooping, eh?' Rachel smiled and he grimaced back as they went downstairs to take their Saturday walk in the woods.

As they crossed the hall Annie came towards them. She offered them two large pieces of chocolate cake with an ingratiating smile more deadly than her frown. What a change from their past brief and hardly courteous meetings.

'Great,' exclaimed Ben, grabbing the largest piece and munching with delight.

'Annie, that's lovely,' Rachel said, eating hers more politely. 'It's so long since we've eaten such a scrumptious cake. How kind of you.' Poor unhappy woman, she thought with her newfound compassion for lost souls. One should be gentle with such creatures in the hopes of showing them the path of salvation and joy.

Annie's smile was distorted by her twisted mouth. Two of her bottom teeth were missing and her upper teeth were badly stained. Ogreish. 'He's settling down now, isn't he?' She indicated Ben.

'Oh yes,' they both replied together.

'This is a good place for children. I brought up my two here. It was *my* farm till I was forced to sell to Snowdonia Reserve and rent back my own land. That's the way it goes.' She sighed and sat wearily on the oak bench, tears of self-pity in her eyes. 'I had five hundred sheep. Welsh cattle fattened for the speciality English market. All organic. All gone when the Reserve policy changed. No more farm animals. Wildcats and deer instead. I had to sell everything. Markets gone through the floor by then. No compensation, just "Your problem."'

Rachel replied robustly, 'It's certainly time farmers outside the Reserves got their act together and provided cheap food again. We're fed up with the expense, the rationing and paying grants to farmers as well.'

'Grants for growing weeds and butterflies and birds. Not farming. But the farm's William's headache now. And he does nothing. Why should I bother with wildlife, he says, if the government will pay me for just looking at the hills? He's an idle no-good, that one.' She shook her head sadly. 'My youngest, Huw, should be farmer here. He's on the roads, just a labourer.'

Why's she telling me this? She lied about William's van. She told Shuji about the black market. Why should I believe she ever owned the place? Annie, queen of this great house, landowner of all Penybwlch! Tell me another!

Annie was far away in her memories. 'It's been cold this month. And March will be as bad. Bad for the lambing. No grass for the ewes and the wind freezes the newborns. The crows'll have their eyes.'

And the beginning of March was indeed colder than it had been for years.

Rachel was happiest outdoors but even so on some days she'd have preferred her warm room, especially when the wind knifed through her old jacket. The earth was so iron hard the ruts cut your knees if you fell. Bare branches chattered with cold and heather humped itself into frozen mounds. Bracken crackled with frost. Even the gulls, ever wheeling, argumentative, snatching one another's food, had fallen silent.

She felt easier about Ben now he was behaving himself. He'd looked at the Academy website and his response was enthusiastic. Almost too enthusiastic, she regretted. As if he couldn't wait to get away from her. With some reluctance he agreed to see the school psychologist when she explained it would be useful for entry to the Academy. It would show just how talented he was and negate any adverse report by Mrs Lloyd.

She'd checked out the biblical quotations on Emmanuel's website and had to agree Dan's fate was dire. But she couldn't bear to tell Ben. She suggested an online mentor in the hopes a trained counsellor could break it to him gently, but her son pooh-poohed any such guide. Fortunately for her he never mentioned his father these days. Perhaps he was forgetting?

She strode through the woods towards the upper slopes to check out the vegetation in a shallow pond. She suspected there could be sundew growing there among the sphagnum moss come spring, a cute little plant with red sticky hairs on its leaves that trapped and digested insects.

She climbed a crumbling dry stone wall, dislodging a few top stones as she tumbled clumsily down the other side.

William and his dog were watching her.

'Shouldn't do that. There's gates, Mrs Kerem,' he said through the side of his twisted mouth. 'Pull the wall down, don't you? And *I* haven't time to be building it up again. Take me a full day.' His accent was more thickly Welsh than she remembered.

As she regained her balance he watched her steadily, gently swinging his shepherd's stick. His cur sat close to his leg, ears pricked, eyes staring at her, panting a little as it yearned for a word of command to worry her legs.

It was six weeks since the night of the pig slaughtering when she'd stood close enough to whiff his animal stench. Sweaty clothes, boots encrusted with bog, hen muck on his filthy hands. His jacket was foul with ancient mud, twine trailed out of its bulky pockets. The knees of his trousers were roughly patched and the patches themselves worn through. A few threads of dark hair escaped from his knitted hat, tangling with pieces of frayed black wool. His face was noncommittal, blank as granite, scored with deep creases round eyes and mouth. Roughshaven. A pale thin scar extended down his cheek from his distorted eye. His other eye stared at her as intently as his dog's. It was cold as frosted bracken, blood dark as their fronds.

She was mesmerised like rabbit with snake.

The wind whistled through gaps in the stone wall and soughed through the bare larch twigs causing last year's fircones to witter and patter. A sneering crow croaked warning.

'Seen enough, have you?' His mouth contorted like his mother's when she tried to smile. He was Grendel, descendent of Cain, outlaw with monstrous mother and tame dragon at foot.

She reached behind her for a loose stone from the wall.

He shook his head, grinning insanely. Ignoring her weapon he picked up a heavy spade and fork from the ground. She shrank back but he merely hoisted them onto his shoulder.

'Child abuser.' Her voice quavered but she stood her ground.

He stared at her, open mouth cockeyed.

'You threatened Ben,' she added more boldly.

He shrugged. 'Not me. I don't hurt kids. Now *you're* different.' He paused and a dribble of spit ran down the crease beside his chin. 'You spied on me. Told Akimoto, and he'll have me banged up if I don't do what he wants.'

'It's criminal to kill wild pigs . . .'

'Ignorant bitch.' He sneered and flicked his fingers at the dog. It jumped up, tail wagging, eyes on its master. He drooled through twisted lips, 'Hurry with your work. When the dog's tail shakes,' and he pointed to the cur, 'then the snow comes.'

'Yeah. I'll remember.' Plonker.

He strode away, left arm hooked round the clanging tools on his shoulder, right hand holding his stick. Lightly and swiftly he disappeared over a small brow. The dog looked back from the top and then vanished after his master.

She was trembling, aroused by strange feelings that she put down to fear. She was certain from his manner that he lied about the threat. He was an oaf, a vindictive one who'd attacked his defenceless mother. Shuji and Emmanuel were right. This guy was too stupid to coordinate a black market. So perhaps the business wasn't run from Penybwlch at all. The organizer could be any of those benighted peasants she'd seen in the town. Bucolic though they were, by the law of averages some must be intelligent.

She pulled herself up. She wasn't interested in the black market any more. No way. And was Shuji Akimoto attempting to convert William? William in heaven among the angels! Suddenly she was laughing till she cried.

Dog's tail shaking or no, it snowed. First a thin sleet under heavy purple skies that turned her back to the farm, her tasks unfinished. Then, long before she reached the house, snow feathers were frantically plucked from the clouds. They scurried before the chill wind, drifting into heaps along the walls and forming mounds over scrubby bushes.

Blessed snow! The first fall here for seven years. A sign that maybe efforts at carbon sequestration and banning of fossil fuels were working at last. Global warming was slowly, oh so slowly, being halted, perhaps reversed.

Tomorrow they'd be snowed in. Tomorrow she, Alyson, Freya and Ben would make snowballs and snow daleks, and slide down hills on plastic trays as she'd done in her childhood.

*

The snow lasted four days, then turned to slush by the end of the week. The sun rose red and early, stretching orange and gold clouds across the horizon as it yawned its way into morning. Today Rachel would cross the moors to the little church of Llanfechan and find the children's well. Holy water for Ben. No more medicine. Ancient remedies are best.

Her scientific training sneered: mere superstition of a foolish anxious mother. She didn't listen.

As she squatted in the cloakroom to tie up her boots a young woman ran in, jacket flying and rucksack bouncing on her back. She clutched Rachel's shoulder, jabbering in Welsh so quickly that Rachel could hardly understand her. 'Sow. Tree. Piglets.' Her breathing was heavy and uneven.

Rachel recognised the girl, a shy creature who worked in the house and scuttled away whenever she approached. She sat her down and put a comforting arm round her. 'What is it, dear?' she asked in English for her spoken Welsh was still poor. The girl hid her face and said nothing.

Rachel had once taught pupils as retiring as this. Patiently she winkled out that the girl had been treed by a wild sow with piglets on her way to work at Penybwlch. She looked beseechingly at Rachel with dull eyes. Her black hair was unkempt and she didn't wash between her legs.

Rachel asked her name.

'Janet Jones, missus. I help Annie.'

Annie bustled into the cloakroom and Janet's trembling increased. Annie's face was spiteful. She said in Welsh 'What d'you mean by coming so late, Janet Jones? Cleaners are two a penny, remember that.' She shooed the girl off to the kitchen. Assuming Rachel had not understood she gave her an ingratiating smile, saying in English, 'Thank you for helping the girl, Mrs Kerem.' She tapped her head meaningfully, 'She's simple. I'm training her up to get a good job.' She sighed at the heavy labour involved and her own worthiness.

Rachel thought, Poor kid. And I must warn Ben to keep well clear of the woods while the sows are farrowing.

She set off whistling old pop tunes. Skirting the woods she climbed up to the high moor, passing Penybwlch's boundary. The track had once been wide enough for farm vehicles, but now gorse grew down the centre and the ruts on either side were uneven enough to turn an unwary ankle.

She skipped over the rough ground, jogging to the top as she delighted in her increased fitness. Her working hours were long but who could object up here in the cold clear air? Eastwards beyond the river lay filthy cities of England with mounting garbage and unlit crime ridden streets. She didn't miss city amenities because she'd had no time to enjoy window-shopping or improving societies. At Penybwlch she was in the company of intelligent well-educated people.

Thinking of them her thoughts turned to James. She was more and more attracted to him. He wasn't handsome, as Dan had been. He didn't have Dan's fierce uncompromising intelligence; he was too stolid for that. She grinned as she remembered his clash with Jennifer the previous evening over the relationship between disease and God's punishment.

'God doesn't control bugs,' Jenny had said with decision. 'Any epidemiologist can tell you that.'

'Jesus and all his disciples healed the sick, as do holy men and women today. Doctors and nurses record that prayer helps patients recover. So God must be involved. I don't say ill health is due to sin in every case, but it often is.'

'Why do bacteriophages infect bacteria? And grasses get fungal rusts? God's punishing them for secret sins?' Jennifer snorted with laughter.

James protested, 'God created mild diseases easily curable by man to encourage him to explore and create. Then man disobeyed God, sin entered the world and diseases became virulent affecting the whole of creation. Humans get double the disease burden to alert them to their sins and return them to God.'

'Your evidence that humans have *more* diseases than other animals?'

'Just look around you. You can see we suffer more than animals.'

'That's a very anthropomorphic judgement. Diseases are necessary evils; they drive evolution.'

Rachel was amazed at her insouciance, for evolution was a red rag to Shuji. He entered the discussion with gusto but little respect for logic. Jennifer easily floored him and James together, but she never won a final victory over Shuji in any of her arguments. Eventually he would make a disparaging comment and leave the room.

All the same, James was kindly and loyal. Restful qualities she yearned for after the difficult years. And Ben seemed to like him.

Far away the sea sparkled in winter sunshine, and the Great Orme's sphinx-like headland melted mistily into the sky. On the banks of the estuary the windows of tiny box houses twinkled merrily in the sun and the towering castle had shrunk to a toy. A picture postcard scene from which all human aggravation and dirt had been erased.

A miniature launch lazed across the estuary, and she wondered whose it could be, for pleasure boating was the province of the super rich worldwide, from presidents to media moguls, industrial grandees to the godfathers of crime. The days had long since gone when ordinary folk could afford such hobbies. The launch turned out towards the sea to round the Great Orme. She decided to buy a model launch for Ben.

She stared down on Penybwlch's rough pastures, wondering why William Parry was never called to account for his slovenly care of the land. Countryside stewardship schemes provided his income, and for this he should cut down encroaching saplings and scrub to improve habitats for ground nesting birds and small mammals. He must maintain good quality haymeadows. He should monitor introduced mammals. Paths must be tended, waymarks conserved and bridges made across streams for holiday visitors from the cities. The latest National Agricultural Plan required all farm land to be returned to its state before the Second World War without fertilizers, pesticides or herbicides, and all field boundaries and gates to be properly maintained.

William couldn't be bothered. He took the money, maintained one fence to protect his illegal hen factory and bribed the farm inspectors.

Turning she faced the moor. The Snowdonia Reserve with its rented farms and its open moors stretched from the north coast to Brecon in the south. It was bounded on the east by the Conwy valley and on the west by Cardigan Bay. Before her stretched mile after mile of broken country with snow still lying in sheltered hollows. Heather and bilberry, bracken and furze. Few birds. Only the endlessly squabbling gulls, soaring on the rising wind. Solitary bees checked the heather and early blooming gorse for nectar. She laughed as a bee bumbled and tumbled its way out of a yellow flower.

Cutting sharply across the blue morning was her mountain, the one she'd seen with Ben a couple of weeks ago during their adventure in the woods. It was the first real mountain of the Snowdonia massif, far higher than the little ones that surrounded Penybwlch. Its snow covered top was brilliant in the sun and bare rocks shone knife-black against its purity.

The land of lost content. Can heaven itself be more beautiful?

That is a thought the Christian must not think.

A heaven without Dan.

But somehow her never-ending loss would be turned into joy. All she needed was faith. She clutched at the happiness she'd just felt but it was wayward as the mountain mists, dissolving as if it had never existed.

I believe. I *do* believe. Help my unbelief!

Emmanuel, guide me! Today's message, 'Charm misleads and beauty soon fades, but the obedient woman will always be honoured.'

Even the majesty of mountains wears away. Only God's laws are everlasting. Laws which no human save one ever kept.

James' text last Sunday, 'I count everything on earth as mere dung compared with knowing Jesus my Saviour.' Loving others more than God is idolatry.

In God's sweet paradise there'll be no regrets, no sorrow or sighing. I'll forget, unlike the blessed damozel leaning over the heavenly ramparts with stars in her hair and lilies in her hand, mourning and grieving for the one who will never come.

But sinner that I am, I know in my heart I don't really love God or desire his heaven. I want Dan, here on this moor, now, making love on the damp spring grasses among scratchy heather, laughing with sweet kisses.

I mustn't think like this.

She pulled her hair, punched her arm.

She'd think of Ben instead. But Ben was half his father, and Dan's eyes looked out of his.

It would indeed be wise to get rid of her mementoes of Dan.

A movement across an isolated patch of snow disturbed her. A large animal, no, several. Roe deer. She swung up her binocular glasses. Three pregnant females. Behind them, still a long way behind, a couple of wolves. Ever-watchful, ever-hungry predators, sensing future opportunity. She watched until the animals disappeared behind a bluff. Then she began to run again along the uneven trail towards the mountains. She dodged scrub and dead bracken fronds that tangled her feet. Reed clumps and tussock grass impeded her. Weary, she slowed to a fast walk. Even so the mountains came no nearer. Lost content indeed.

It was warm in the noonday sun and she took off her green jacket. Her red sweatshirt showed up brightly, but there was no one to see except the ever-circling surveillance satellites, and *they* wouldn't be interested in a casual walker. She started singing in a fairly tuneful soprano.

She paused by a fallen boulder. A circle of them surrounded an inner grassy area. Well over two thousand years old. Druids perhaps? These ancient folk had had no fears like hers. She envied them even while she pitied their ignorance of their sins and lack of a Saviour. Poor damned souls.

The path over the moor ran parallel to the river and when she looked back towards the sea the castle was still in view, part hidden by wooded hills. The river wound and weaved among mud banks on its way to the estuary, banks that would be covered with brackish water once the tide returned upstream. Low hills beyond lay fertile and smiling in the sun.

 Presently the moorland track led down towards a shallow stream gurgling and giggling around smooth stones and floating strands of weed. Split hoof marks of deer had left hollows in the mud where puddles collected. The water in the palm of Rachel's hand was colder than ice and she supped it gratefully.

The path rose again beyond the stream and as she mounted the bluff she saw she was nearing the foot of the mountain where it rose in rocky outcrops from the moor. But the path, if it was a path and not just a deer track, divided into numerous routes. Some meandered towards the mountain. One disappeared under a copse of crooked hawthorn forced to genuflect to the mountain by the prevailing wind. Another followed the line of the stream downhill then twisted up again towards deserted sheep pens. A wind turbine turned languidly beyond them and she knew she'd found the hidden church.

The walls of the pens hadn't yet tumbled to ruin. Inside them the ground was muddy, covered with old droppings and she was amazed how long these reminders of the past persisted. Beyond the pens, walls regulated the path, well built with upright capping stones. The smell of horse was strong here. Pony droppings lay among rush tussocks and hoofprints pitted the path wherever it was damp. So this was the way the wild ponies wandered to the churchyard.

Soon the path joined the road leading down into the valley. Car skid marks scarred the grassy clearing where the scientists parked their cars. The churchyard wall was too high to see over but at last she came to the gate.

The church looked even smaller in daytime. Like a scraggy ewe it hunkered down in a slight hollow, seeking shelter from the eternal wind. A few slates had fallen from the roof. The walls were deeply pitted between their stones and bright cushion mosses grew in the seeping damp. Plain buttresses supported its sides. The slate and granite gravestones were so deep in tussock grass that they could have been mountain outcrops but for the deeply scored names and Welsh texts. So many hill farmers and their families, century passing into century.

'May you sleep well,' she whispered.

She wandered round the building on a clearly defined path. Behind it a wooden shed was tucked into the L of the church, invisible from the porch. It was new, stoutly constructed with a tarred roof and supported on two sides by the church walls. No windows. Mud was thick round the door. She checked the padlock. Heavy, old construction, not possible to open electronically.

Dropping her jacket from her arm she fumbled in her rucksack for her pocket knife. Then she inserted the screwdriver attachment into the hasp screws. They were rusty, but still strong enough to be turned. As the screwdriver slipped she scratched bright marks across screwheads and hasp.

She unlatched the door and peered in.

It stank. She didn't recognise the greasy smell at first. Hessian sacks filled half the interior and she fingered the material thoughtfully. Jute was far too expensive to be shipped from tropical countries for mere sacking. Some local substitute. Retted nettle stems?

She poked a small hole in the weaving and recognised the stench. Sheep fleeces.

Sheep? Forbidden sheep on the mountains? And surely shearing time was long since past? It took place in early summer, the natural time for sheep to shed their winter coats. And why was it stored at a church?

She pulled a strand from the bale and popped it in her rucksack. Then she shut the door, screwed up the hasp and smeared mud over the marks she'd made. Picking up rucksack and jacket she looked round for the holy well.

The churchyard sloped down towards a rush filled corner some distance from the gate. Her boots squelched across bog grasses and buttercup leaves as she walked towards a tiny grotto surrounded by a high stone wall, its entrance hidden by tufts of rush. Under an open sky lay the smallest of dark pools, its square edges constrained by slate slabs humped from distant quarries centuries ago. A metal cup lay on top of a coiled chain clamped into the rock. Clumps of unfurling bracken growing from the surrounding walls gazed at their reflections. Grasses, last year's dying nettles, leaf rosettes of foxglove grew rank among the slabs.

She sat on a seat of slate and looked into the water. A cloud passed across it without disturbing its stillness. Motionless waterweeds disappeared into its shadowy depths. Eventually she took a plastic bottle from her rucksack and filled it. Debris of mud, weed and drowned insects floated in the cloudy water. No one in their right minds would drink this, however holy it was said to be. Its vaunted efficacy lay in the prayers of desperate parents of bygone ages who, lacking vaccinations against childhood ailments, believed the recovery of their child was due more to magic water than coincidence.

Slowly she tipped the water back into the sacred pool, watching the ripples disturb its calm surface. Still gazing she murmured, 'Dear God, please cure my son of his hyperactivity. Give him happiness and peace. Grant him true faith.'

As she wondered whether her prayer was just as superstitious as reliance on holy water, she became aware of chinking harness, a gruff voice swearing in Welsh and a slow thudding of hooves. They plodded along the other side of the churchyard wall towards its gate. More jangling, then the gate creaked open. Three men entered the churchyard. Her red sweatshirt was highly visible so she shrank back behind the grotto wall, hoping they wouldn't look her way. Their boots stomped along the church path then ceased. A few words, too distant for her to hear. A mobile phone rang.

She pulled her green jacket over her sweatshirt and peered out cautiously. They were out of sight behind the church. By the shed, she was certain. More illegal trading. She didn't want to know about it.

109

She estimated the distance to the gate across the open churchyard. No point in trying to hide. The men only had to step round the church to see her. Grabbing her rucksack she walked firmly but cautiously across the boggy patch, her mind full of possible reasons she could give them for her presence here.

She reached the gate without incident but it creaked as she slipped through. Two ponies stamped and hrrmphed at her, their leading reins wrapped round boulders. Surely the men would come running?

She ran along the track bending low beside the wall as it turned away from the path across a wet patch. The wall continued up a ridge where it was in such poor repair that she'd be able to peek through. Damn it, she *did* want to know what they were doing.

Concerned that her pale face would make her obvious she scrabbled in the mud and smeared her face liberally. Then she climbed up the ridge to watch the three men.

They leaned against the open shed, chatting desultorily. They were as disreputable as William, their jackets torn and patched and their trousers baggy. Their faces were gaunt, with deep eyes and sour mouths. They emanated corruption. One of them rolled a cigarette. The smallest, a hump backed goblin wearing a greasy cap, began to walk up the hill towards her hiding place.

She hunkered down, shivering.

Almost over her head he shouted 'That's him,' and the others puffed up the hill to join him.

She wriggled cautiously till she could look in the same direction.

Far away in the direction of Penybwlch a little figure galloped towards them, waving both arms and shouting incomprehensible words into the wind. The horse made a leap, stumbled and the rider lurched across its shoulder.

On the bank the men hooted. 'Ride 'em, cowboy.' They cheered as the rider righted himself and galloped on.

If only she could ride like that! She'd never ridden a horse in her life.

They came to the stream she'd crossed earlier and the rider slowed his horse as he disappeared into the dip. In a short while the pair trotted into view again, much closer.

William. Of course, who else?

His three confederates ambled away towards the churchyard gate while William led the horse along the track to join them.

He was just below her now. If he looked up . . . She held her breath

He stopped, fondled the pony's ears and rubbed the top of its head. It was a dun mare, larger than the other ponies, with dark legs and a long black tail, sweating badly. William pulled a cloth from his bulging pocket, rubbed the froth from her neck and wide belly and slackened her felt saddle. No stirrup leathers or irons.

So how did he stay on at a walk, let alone a gallop?

The mare nuzzled at his jacket. Suddenly she grabbed at its buttons with great yellow teeth and pulled. Smiling tenderly he stroked the white blaze on her nose and then gave her an apple from his pocket.

Rachel had never seen him smile before. He looked almost human.

He led the mare out of her sight towards the other ponies and his three accomplices. She followed till she could just see his animal's rump with long tail swishing impatiently. From here she could hear their conversation and she settled down among the hollows and boulders scattered across the broken landscape.

William's voice was clear and concise. No trace of the bumbling idiot. 'The mare was holed up at Ty Gwyn. Inspectors sticking their snouts in, chasing illegal animals.'

'What's up with them?'

'New guv. From Cardiff.'

The men swore with annoyance.

'We'll manage,' William said with authority. 'There's a new English woman with a kid at Penybwlch. Two snoopers. Told the Eckstazia boss about my hens so he hauled me over.'

'Thought you kept him sweet with all that food.'

'That's the previous boss. *He* never bothered his head where it came from. This new one wants something more for keeping quiet. Sheep for his experiments. Told him they're illegal here. There aren't any.'

They laughed and she lost the next few sentences.

Then she heard William answer a question, 'No. She thinks I'm daft. Fooled her completely.'

Someone mentioned pigs and he said, 'Said it was a wild one, didn't I? They don't know the difference. Slapped my wrist for cutting up a pig I'd found snared in the fence.'

They all sniggered.

Oh god! She wanted to sneeze. She swallowed hard but it spluttered up into her nostrils.

'What's that?'

She huddled down.

'Crow.'

William said, 'Don't put the mare back on the hill with the others when you finish with her. Leave her at Tanygraig and tell Dafydd I'll be over on. . .' But she couldn't hear which day.

Then he was running past her. If he turned his head he'd see her startled face, but he kept on down the track disappearing towards the stream. He reappeared on the far side loping easily across the moor more graceful than a stag. He was Bronze Age man, sure footed and at home among druid rings and hilltop forts and little fields millennia old. He was the Celtic runner warning of Roman encroachment, the heir of squabbling princelings who lost their land to English invaders. He was . . .

Botheration, she wasn't going to admire the man. She'd be able to run as fast as that herself before long.

Back in the churchyard the three men humped the woolsacks to the horses at a run. Once the ponies were loaded they brought three large pieces of cloth out of the back of the shed. At first Rachel thought these were merely hessian, but as they were unfolded she saw the underside was silvery. They covered the ponies from ears to tail. Each man collected a bulky stick and the first pony was led off towards the lower flanks of the mountain, soon disappearing over a rise.

The others waited, smoking idly. Then the second pair departed leaving William's mare. The third accomplice was the goblin, an old man, wiry and small with bow legs and hunched back.

She followed him at a discreet distance. As he reached the rise he fiddled with his stick. It opened into a brown umbrella with shiny underside and he raised it over his head. At last she realised why they travelled separately and why they covered themselves and their ponies so thoroughly.

High above them all the watchful satellites checked the whole country as they circled. Government posters announced, 'You're never alone. Ever.' How comforting if you were facing city muggers or your child was lost.

How threatening if you were involved in illegal trade.

A string of ponies all carrying loads. Easy to spot. Suspicious.

But these were individual animals wandering mountain tracks, their packs hidden from sight under brown sacking. The silvery material reflected body heat downwards to fool the satellite's infra red eye. The umbrellas performed the same function for their leaders. Simple but effective.

She was the only conspicuous one. A woman in green hooded jacket with muddy face, dodging behind boulders and walls.

Robotic checkers would alert their human counterparts. 'Something odd,' they'd buzz and the humans, all good citizens concerned with reducing crime, bored mindless from checking city streets, would turn to this innocent countryside with its mountains and moors, its cliffs of wild birds and its holiday beaches. From their swivel chairs they'd access her ID – 'carried for your own safety at all times.' Incorporating all her medical, financial and work details. And then?

Immediate email to Shuji.

Scalped for leaving the estate and taking time off work without permission.

She stood irresolute.

The troll vanished with William's mare into the hills. Bwlch y Ddeufaen lay that way, the pass through the mountains that led to the coast near Bangor. But she would go no further today.

She jogged back the way she'd come, hoping she appeared like a hill-walking tourist, too uninteresting for the robots to zoom on. As she ran she noticed how few marks the ponies had left. They were unshod. William had talked about putting the animals back on the hill. So they'd be hidden among the wild ponies that ranged the mountains. Who would suspect them?

She squatted near the little stream in a sheltered hollow warmed by the sun and munched her sandwiches. William was more than capable of orchestrating the black market and she both loathed and feared his cunning. She must be very cautious, for Ben's sake as well as her own. Shuji must be told about the wool trade, but warned to keep her out of the picture.

Then she dipped her sweatshirt sleeve in the water and scrubbed her camouflaged face clean, before jogging back to Penybwlch's estate. By the time she reached it she was trudging doggedly, knackered by her exertions. She checked out several wildlife sites and recorded them. Presently it grew colder as clouds, purple with foreboding, hid the winter sun. The wind whistled among dead grass stems and through scrubby heather and bilberry. She started to run home but the wind buffeted her and her legs were weary. She slipped and slithered down the last hillside, wind-driven rain whipping her back and penetrating her jacket. As she entered the woods the upper branches swayed violently against the livid sky.

The house was quiet when she pulled off her soaked boots and jacket and plodded upstairs to get a warm shower and find Ben. He wasn't in his room or any of the communal ones. She called. No answer. But of course! He must have stayed with Freya after school pickup. The soothing shower invited, but she pulled on shoes and wet coat again and went across to Alyson's. Eric opened the door.

'Is Ben here?'

'Alyson! Rachel wants Ben.'

Alyson came from the kitchen drying her hands. 'He went straight to the house. Didn't say anything all the way home in the car.'

'He isn't there.'

'He's hiding,' Eric guffawed, his gingery beard bouncing as he chuckled. 'Just like a lad.'

Yes, that must be it. Rachel ran back to the house through the storm and mobiled him but his handset was silent. Exasperated she accessed his wristband chip and it registered in his room. She found it hidden under his pillow.

She panicked. She yelled, begging him to stop playing but only the wind mewled round chimneys and turrets.

Annie stomped out of the kitchen. 'What's the matter with the boy now?'

'I don't know where he is.'

'He went out.' She turned away.

'Annie! Please!' Rachel clutched the old woman's arm. A sinewy arm, strong and unyielding. 'Out in the rain? The dark? Where?'

Annie pulled her arm away sharply. 'How should I know?' She stalked back to her work.

Then suddenly James was there, his arm round her shoulder, demanding to know what upset her.

She gabbled, 'Ben's lost. The reserve! The mad sow!' And then her worst fear, '*William!*'

Chapter 8

'Give him me! Open up!' Rachel screamed as she hammered the rain-splattered door of Ty Bach.

The door groaned back and William stood there in shirt sleeves and stocking feet, his face dour. 'What. . ?' he began , but she threw herself at him, grabbing at his collar, his neck and any other part she could reach.

'Give him back! *Ben! Where are you?*'

Her held both her wrists in one huge hand and forced her away, so she kicked at his groin. He swerved adroitly and twisted her round until her back was to him.

'Mad woman,' he muttered. 'Calm down, won't you.'

'Ben,' she snarled. 'Ben's here. You've kidnapped him.'

He was so surprised that he slackened his grip. She wriggled away and attacked him again landing a knuckle blow on his twisted mouth. 'I know he's here. *Ben! Ben!*'

He winced and rubbed his jaw, then backed off holding up both hands to ward off any more blows. 'He's not here. Never been here.'

'You threatened him.'

'I told you I don't hurt kids.'

'Let me see.' She tried to push past him but he held her back. 'Don't you molest me,' she shrieked. 'I've every right. . .'

'You haven't.'

'*Ben!*' she screamed, lunging at him again.

William took hold of her shoulders in a pincer grip so excruciating her eyes watered. He said firmly, 'Mrs Kerem. Ben is not here. *Not here.*' Then he released her. She took a deep breath and dropped her arms.

The driving rain splattered huge puddles on the uneven slate floor. Behind the house trees creaked and groaned on the steep hillside like savage animals about to spring on the humans below. In an inner room the wild dog howled and scratched at the closed door. Only Rachel and William were silent, staring at each other.

'You've checked his cell phone? His chip?'

'Of course.'

'So he's hiding. Or run away.' Then he said angrily, as if old memories had surfaced, 'Kids do at his age.' He looked beyond her into the stormy night. 'Search party?'

'James has called everyone. He's alerted the police.'

'Has he, now.' He was still staring into the dark. 'I'll come.' He took waterproofs from a peg.

'Don't bother,' she snorted.

William paused with one arm in his jacket. He looked at her oddly. If she hadn't known better she'd have thought he felt compassion for her. 'I know the woods better than you,' he said simply.

'Wolves. Sows are farrowing in the reserve. The cliff.' Tears streamed down her wet face.

He laced up his boots without comment. He opened the inner door and the waiting dog hurtled out, sniffed round Rachel's feet and dropped on its haunches at its master's light whistle.

As she ran towards the woods Rachel remembered what she'd said to the stricken people at the store on the quay. *They're far more frightened of us than we are of them. Stags never come near towns and wolves run away unless you corner them. So anyone who gets hurt has only themselves to blame.'*

How brash! How unfeeling!

Everything's different when it's your own son lost in the wind and rain, alone on a hillside where wild animals prowl.

He could be anywhere. Perhaps he'd stayed in the grounds of the house and not gone into the reserve after all. Though all the scientists from the main house and the two cottages were out searching, the woods were too dense for her to see their lights. Once a light glimmered and Freya called through the darkness, 'We'll find him, Rachel. God will help us. I'm praying ever so hard.' Her torchlight flickered and vanished.

What prayer could Rachel make? 'I was heartless, I see that now. Don't make him suffer for my sins. Because I know you punish children for their parents' faults. Please don't. Please, dear God, bountiful God, merciful and loving God.' And the final mantra, 'For Jesus' sake.'

Her yapp buzzed.

No, he hadn't been found, but James tried to be encouraging. The search was going well in spite of the weather and they'd finished combing the woods round the house. Now for the reserve.

She ran to the gate in the chainlink fence. Her feet slipped on wet mud and she tumbled to the ground wrenching her wrist. Ignoring the pain she pulled herself up by a treetrunk. What direction should she take? Could mother instinct lead her to him? She paused, trying to feel in her heart where he might be. Up the hill, surely. Towards the cliff and the black valley deep below it. She clambered upwards hysterically. Wind and rain obstructed her less under the flailing tree branches, but as soon as she came out of their shelter on the top she could barely stand. Buffets of wind unbalanced her and she grabbed at the nearest support. Gorse. Her hand stung with pain. 'Punish me, not him, God.' Would the pain in hand and wrist be enough to appease his just anger?

Regaining balance she flashed her storm light but it failed to penetrate the dense undergrowth. The infrared facility on her binocular glasses was useless in this storm of wind and rain. She called, and the wind flung back her words into her face.

The wolves, oh, the wolves were hungry in this cold season. They had followed the pregnant deer. How easily they'd follow her helpless child.

Calling and calling, her throat became too hoarse to shout. Tears of frustration and fear mingled with the rain on her cheeks. Her old jacket was soaked through and her clothes were clammy against her skin, but she didn't notice. She must carry on. She must keep going until she found him, cold, wet, leaf covered, bleeding from gashes made by angry sows. . . not dead. Please, not dead.

Eternity passed.

Her yapp buzzed again.

Ben was safe. Back at the house.

Exhausted by panic, the relief flooding her body drained her still further. She lurched down the hill, bruising herself on myriad obstructions, and panted into the hall, without registering the police car bumping up the drive.

Her son, still shivering from his experiences, sat on the hall bench wrapped in a rug. He clutched a warmer in one hand and with the other held onto the thick black mane of hair round the neck of William's dog. The dog made a happy rumbling sound in its throat.

She flung her arms round him calling his name incoherently, but he didn't respond.

'You're not hurt?'

He said nothing.

'Ben dearest. Ben, where were you? I was so frightened.'

He kept his face turned away from her.

From out of the shadows behind the boy came William's voice, accusing, angry. 'You told him you're sending him away because you don't want him.'

'I said nothing of the sort,' she retorted, furious at his interference.

'Yes, you did, Mum,' Ben said in a tiny voice.

She hugged him. 'Oh, darling. Of course I love you.'

117

'Toss found me.' Ben patted the dog and it gazed up at him with adoring eyes. 'William and Toss.'

Her eyes met William's. She must thank this disagreeable peasant. She struggled for words but was disturbed by noises behind her. Turning she realised the scientists were all in the hall watching her reunion and chatting about their part in the rescue. Jennifer, looking more disagreeable than ever, ran upstairs to get dry and Alyson and Eric shuffled Freya towards the door. Before they reached it three police marched into the hall, two with guns. The third man, an inspector, was tall, well-built to the point of plumpness and full of self assurance. He nodded to James who pointed to William, saying in a voice trembling with rage, 'Parry abducted the child, then pretended to find him once he realised he couldn't get away with it. . . .'

'He *did* find me!' Ben interrupted but the inspector said, 'We've had our eyes on this guy for a long time.' He ordered the constables to cuff William's hands.

Yet William was unfazed. He spoke rapidly to the inspector in Welsh, so that only Rachel of all the scientists present understood. Even so, their quick repartee, their contraction of local words and phrases and all the nuances of their shared histories made it impossible for her to comprehend fully.

To the fury of the inspector William threatened him with exposure, cool as a headmaster with a recalcitrant pupil. So were the local police tied into the black market along with the farm inspectors and God knows who else?

The mysterious Elwyn Isallt was mentioned several times. The inspector made a jeering reference to Parryboots. Something about him turning William from home years ago. William's father?

Rachel alone saw William's thighs trembling. He clenched his bound hands till the knuckles shone white. He couldn't wipe the spit from his deformed mouth and it dribbled down his chin onto his wet jacket collar.

Ben pulled at her encircling arm, crying so much she could barely understand him. 'Toss found me hiding from the wolves. Then William came.'

She spoke across the feuding males in a clear cold voice. 'Inspector, Mr Parry did *not* kidnap my son. He came on the search with the rest of us and was first to find him because he knows the woods.'

James turned on her. 'You told me he threatened Ben's abduction. I heard you accuse him in Ty Bach.'

'I was wrong. Ben wasn't there.' She said to the police, 'Leave Mr Parry alone. We should all be praising him for finding Ben.'

'He should be charged, missus,' the inspector said sternly. 'And the lad must be inspected by the police doctor.'

'No way,' she said firmly. Subject her frightened son to the sexual examination meted out to every abducted child since that dreadful porno ring was busted last year? Much as she disliked William she didn't believe he'd hurt Ben.

'I think you should take Inspector Jones's advice, Rachel,' James said kindly. 'Look at you, all bloody across the face and your hair full of thorns and leaves. You're not in a fit state to make wise decisions at the moment.'

Jones thrust out his manly chest. 'We'll prepare a statement for your signature, Mrs Kerem, and then we'll take him in for questioning.'

Gritting her teeth she refused the man's request as politely as possible. She turned to the farmer. 'Thank you, William. I can never thank you enough for saving Ben's life.'

There was a strange expression on his face. Surprise? Gratitude?

As James began to protest further, Shuji frowned at him. He took the inspector aside. A brief talk and the policeman nodded, 'Right, Dr Akimoto. I'll be in touch.' He gave a quick hostile glance towards Rachel, then motioned to his men to release William before departing.

Shuji said, 'Let's thank God for the little one's safe return to his mother.' The older scientist bowed their heads and the Bangor group sang a jazzy Alleluia praise the Lord.

James put his hand on Rachel's shoulder. 'A miracle. . . .'

Still annoyed by his attitude towards her she replied tartly, 'Miracles are merely events we don't yet understand. And I know exactly how Ben was found and who found him.'

She turned round, intending to ask William more. But he was no longer in the hall.

Ben was soon warm after a shower and he sat in bed sipping a warm drink

'I hunkered down in the leaves,' he said, almost ready to see the night's terrors as a big adventure. Rachel sat on the floor, one arm round him.

'It's very cold in the reserve, Mum.'

'I know, dear. People can be very ill, even die if they get too cold. I was ever so worried when you didn't answer your mobile.'

'The school kids pinched it. Said I shouldn't have one because their parents can't afford 'em.'

'How *rotten* of them. And never never take off your chip band again.'

'I was all right in the woods. Toss sniffed all round me like a wolf.'

119

'Scary!'

He wouldn't admit any fear of the animal. 'He's a terrific dog, Mum. He just licked me. He barked for William. I couldn't walk because my legs were all stiff, so William carried me a bit. He said, "You're too big to be carried all the way," so he made me walk and then I was all right. William stinks. I told him. But I like him.'

She hated being indebted to the man but she said, 'He was very kind. But remember he's also a most dishonest person.' She rested her head on his pillow. Every muscle ached. Her brain felt dead. 'Deary, why did you think I don't want you?'

'Freya said you were sending me away because I'm naughty.'

The cruelty of jealous children!

'I'd much rather have you near me, but your junior school is the pits. I thought you liked the sound of the Academy? It's a very good and happy place where pupils are well looked after. I wouldn't even think about sending you if I wasn't sure of that. It's horrid to be parted, but it's only for a few weeks at a time. And if you don't like it, well, we'll think of something else. But you must give it your best shot.'

He nodded. 'I'm not a baby, Mum.' He settled down under his quilt.

Her mind wandered hazily. Yes, she must thank God for answering her prayers. But, and this had always troubled her, how about all those mothers in similar situations who'd prayed just as hard and their child had died? No, it was sinful to feel such doubts. God might not answer her next time. She tried to feel properly grateful but she was too tired.

Ben said in a muffled voice, 'I thought the wolves would come and get me.'

She cuddled him and he clung closely to her. 'You're safe now. That's what matters. Did you ask Jesus to help you? I did.'

'No.'

'Why not, dear?'

'Jesus took Dad away to heaven. I want Dad here. With *me.*'

She tried to speak, but only stuttered, 'Jesus knows best.'

'No he doesn't. I hate him.' He turned over and fell asleep.

So he wasn't forgetting Dan as she'd hoped. How could she blame him for his anger against his Saviour when she herself was so troubled by doubt? What if he expressed his hatred of Jesus at the Academy? Would they expel him in case he infected other students? Ought she to mention his problems to someone at the school?

Yet it seemed God wasn't angry with her son. Hadn't he been kept safe in the woods? It *was* a miracle, and she'd been wrong to attack James. But why are God's messages so confusing? And somewhere a little niggling voice was saying, what a revolting god you worship. She suppressed it.

Ben's obvious liking for William troubled her deeply. The man was seducing her son.

*

She spoke to Shuji the following day. Risking reproval for her truancy she told him about the wool smuggling, but to her relief he listened eagerly without reprimanding her. She gave him her wool sample from the sack in Llanfechan's shed, emphasising William's involvement. She was already sorry she'd spoken on his behalf yesterday.

'Good, very good. Well done, Rachel. This information is most useful.'

She was sure now he had enough evidence to get rid of hateful William.

As he paused she wondered if he'd ask for her mementoes of Dan after Emmanuel's instructions to her. But he continued, 'Now to more pleasant matters. You've been with us nearly two months and I've had excellent reports on your work. I'm in the position where I can offer you another post more suited to your qualifications and more financially rewarding. It's my hope that with your expertise you'll feel inspired to join us.'

In her relief she sighed aloud. 'I'd be honoured, Shuji. I've always wanted to help the poor and needy. I have so much and. . .'

'Quite so. This new post won't be at Penybwlch, I'm afraid. In spite of our willingness to be flexible the Snowdonia Committee have stubbornly demanded such complexity of design that we've decided to forgo the new building here. It's time for us to move on and we've a designated site near Bristol. Work there should be completed by September and the new lab will be opened by the King in October.'

Bristol! England! Close to Ben and far away from Welsh crooks!

'Our exciting new Eckstazia team consists of personnel from teaching hospitals and UK universities, Cambridge, Imperial College London and others. They'll have connections with specialists in the States – Stanford's multidisciplinary Human Health Center, the University of California Los Angeles' Neuropsychiatric Institute and so on. We plan to develop a research project with a totally new approach.'

'What's that?' Rachel asked in excitement.

'You've heard of parasites which can brainwash their host?'

'Like the protozoan *Toxoplasma gondii* in rats? A parasite with two hosts, cats and rodents. Once it gets into a rodent brain it travels to the area dealing with conditioned responses and interferes with the animal's fear mechanism.'

'Yes, and very cleverly too. By brainwashing the rodent into liking the scent of cat urine, the rodents run from every hazard except cats. It was extensively studied at Stanford in the early years of the century.'

'So what's Eckstazia's approach?'

'Your life in Coventry was made miserable by street brawls and violence?'

'Yes, but I don't see. . .'

'The *Toxoplasma* parasite also infects humans and causes behavioural changes.'

'Increased risk taking and neuroticism, a possible cause of schizophrenia. You're not suggesting. . .?'

'No. We don't propose deliberately infecting the criminal with the current form of *Toxoplasma*. Our research will involve its modification so that the carrier will crave a particular calming drug. Our colleagues across the world will monitor and extend our findings. The Home Office is most interested in our project. Current attempts at medication as prescribed by the courts are bedevilled by the lack of co-operation among convicted criminals. This approach will ensure they're *addicted* to tranquillisers.'

'But . . .' she hesitated, 'isn't it, well, almost unethical? Altering minds permanently?'

'To make a thug less aggressive? Of the greatest benefit to society as a whole, I'd have thought. Especially as those left behind in the mayhem following the Rapture of the saints will have some partial protection from the criminals over-running Earth.

'My dear Rachel, members of the Eckstazia Research Council have the highest ethical credentials. The Home Secretary herself is an Honorary Member of Eckstazia's European Council. Professor Hilary Barron is Senior Ethical and Religious Advisor to the European Union. You can hardly think either would consent to anything amoral. And we all take mind-altering drugs these days quite legitimately. I myself take cognitive enhancers.'

One of the benefits of wealth; hardly possible for people of her status. She persisted, 'In the wrong hands . . .'

He said dismissively, 'That will never happen. We're not stupid, Rachel.' Then, more warmly, 'Emmanuel himself recommended you for this job. He told me how well you progress in your faith. He admires your conscientiousness in your work here and also how you did your duty towards your dependants in the past.'

It never seemed like a duty. If she didn't care for them, how would she live comfortably with herself?

*

A morning of intermittent sun followed the wet weekend. Rachel had noted down several mosses and liverworts and now she scraped a section of foliose lichen off an overhanging branch with her knife. She sat down on a rotten tree trunk, trying to ignore the damp seeping through her trousers as she studied the specimen with yapp magnifier. Grunting in satisfaction, she dropped it into a small box with several empty compartments. This she labelled with time, date, and situation and turned to another lichen.

Her mind wasn't wholly on her work. She was overjoyed at the thought of her new job. She wholly approved the project now she'd had time to consider it. Reducing crime on the streets and in the home, and reforming the prison population by making tranquillisers essential to convicted criminals. What could possibly be unethical about that? Didn't people of exemplary standing supervise the work?

And what about her relationship with James? Emmanuel frequently praised his integrity and consideration for others. His remarks on the night that Ben ran away no longer irritated her. She'd mistaken concern for condescension.

'You're very busy.'

She jumped. The man himself was standing the far side of the little clearing, his round face full of smiles. Delighted, she smiled in return and he came over, saying, 'I often walk here in my lunch break. I didn't expect to find the woodland dryad herself.' He sat down beside her on the slimy trunk.

She giggled to herself at the clumsy compliment. How like the dear man! 'Thank God the rain isn't shitting down as usual.'

'Really, Rachel. Be careful what you say.'

'What's wrong?'

'Surely . . .' He sighed at her ignorance before speechifying, 'Casual use of our Lord's name. Remember the Lord will not hold him guiltless who takes his name in vain. Combined with an unfortunate use of vulgar language.' He smiled to lessen the criticism. 'Let's forget it now.'

The scent of his aftershave lingered around them, waking her memories. She'd bought the same for Daniel's last birthday. He'd thanked her, kissing her warmly and that night their lovemaking had been so good, so much missed . . .

123

James' gentle voice dispelled her memories. 'I've been hoping to have a little chat with you ever since poor young Ben ran away.' He paused to emphasise his next words. 'Let me be frank, Rachel. I was very uneasy about William's involvement. I wondered why you refused the offer of medical help. Surely a mother is not the best person to . . . er . . .'

'Surely a mother *is* the best one to ensure her son's sexual safety. I'm quite certain William acted properly.'

'You're very good hearted, Rachel. Perhaps even a little innocent about these matters.' He sighed. 'I'm a trained counsellor and I've had to deal very frequently with the sad duplicity of the human soul . . . I think you should be very careful where William's concerned.'

'You can be sure of that.'

James moved a little nearer to her along the log. 'Shuji and I spoke to the scoundrel about the wool trading. He denied it until we showed him the wool you'd collected, not mentioning your name of course.'

She remembered William's comments about her to the other wool smugglers and two-faced Inspector Jones's hostility towards her when she refused to support William's arrest. 'I don't want any more to do with these Welsh thieves.'

'Of course you don't. We respect that. But you're quite right to report anything you overhear.'

'So William's to be sacked?'

Her hopes were dashed by his reply.

'Not yet. We came to an agreement very advantageous to completing our research here.' He smiled satisfaction and his dimple deepened. 'All the same I blame myself for approving his appointment by the Snowdonia Reserve. Since then I've found he's completely ignorant about farming and reserve management. He appeared the better of Annie's two sons at interview. Huw, her younger one, is stupid, almost imbecile. Yet Annie assured us he was the superior and maybe she was right, foolish though she is.'

'I'm sorry William's staying. He's full of low cunning.' She wasn't convinced about his ignorance. 'I've thought more about the wool trade. The carding and weaving must take place in Bangor and the coastal villages. Probably outwork in ordinary houses. The material's made up into clothes by lots of people with old sewing machines. Annie has one.'

James had lost interest. 'Congratulations on the new job. Shuji told me you'll be leaving us in a few months for the new centre in Bristol. I'll miss you . . . And Ben of course. He's a fine lad. A credit to you. But at his age he may be finding the lack of a father figure just a little . .

. er . . . disadvantageous,' he said carefully. 'Much as I love children, circumstances have been such that I haven't any myself. I'd be honoured if you'd let me become more involved with him.'

'That would be very kind.'

He put his arm round her shoulder. Its strength was a comfort to her. 'Does he enjoy football? There's a match in the town this Saturday.'

'He'd love that.' She leant more closely into his sheltering arm. 'Oh, James, he's struggling so. *Everything's* changed radically for him. A new language in a new school. Unfriendly staff. How can he make friends with seven year olds? The move to Bath can't come too soon.'

James said agreeably, 'You're very wise to accept the Academy's offer. It's got an excellent reputation, both academically and socially.'

'Emmanuel enjoyed his time there.'

'Emmanuel?' He drew back, smiling awkwardly into the distance. 'Oh, yes. Of course, of course. He went there, didn't he?'

She wondered at his hesitation.

He continued, 'I'd advise you to take up Emmanuel's offer of an Eckstazia loan as soon as possible. A very competitive rate of interest. . .'

She jumped up angrily. 'Emmanuel's been talking to you about my finances?'

He looked up at her in embarrassment. 'No. Of course not. Er, well, yes, I suppose so. Yes, certainly.' His plump face was red with distress. 'I'm sorry. Quite wrong of me. Concerned about you, you see.' He looked like a rebuked child as he twisted his regrown fingers with his good hand.

She was touched as well as annoyed. She took his damaged hand in hers and smiled forgiveness. He returned her smile, but doubtfully as if something further troubled him. But he said nothing other than he must return to work. She watched him go, convincing herself they could build a happy marriage together.

Two evenings later Rachel was resting in the dark after kissing Ben goodnight.

The dog barked from the room below. William growled back and Toss fell silent. The front door groaned and a woman spoke to William. He shut the door behind her.

Rachel rolled cautiously off her bed and peered through the edge of her curtain. Two men, one dumpy and the other taller with a rolling gait, strolled up the path and opened Ty Bach door. The dumpy man spoke softly to William and Rachel recognised both his voice and his bowlegged walk. He was the gnome who'd taken William's mare, loaded with wool, over the pass. His friend was a stranger to her.

She pulled back the carpet above the enlarged hole in the floorboards and put her cardboard cylinder to her ear. The conversation was distinct, though she still found some dialect words difficult.

The woman was saying, ' . . . poor quality. Aber weavers complaining of brambles and bracken in the fleeces. Especially yours, Prys.' She spoke clearly and with authority. The goblin answered too soft and low for Rachel to understand but now she knew his name.

William's harsh tones rang so clear that he must be almost directly below the hole. 'You didn't unload the launch?'

A new masculine voice, high in pitch and easy to hear, Prys's companion. 'Fuzz crawling everywhere in Liverpool docks. Jeffreys was fingered. Told them everything.'

Then Prys again. She strained hard to hear, 'Legalised torture,' and 'Last year's antiterrorist laws.'

'I know *that,*' said his friend. 'Not his fault. Anyone'd grass up.'

Then William. 'Does Hilary Barron suspect you, Dewi?'

'That I'm trading every time I ferry her between Plas Du and the university? God no. Got her mind on higher things.' Dewi paused, then, 'Now Jeffreys is banged up we've no one in Liverpool to disable the port spycams before we dock.'

So the launch Rachel had seen crossing the estuary eastwards towards Liverpool was almost certainly Hilary's and it was involved in sea trafficking.

The woman asked, 'Can we use any other small port along the coast?'

'Too risky, Marged. Spysats.'

The door bell rang.

'Who's that idiot?' said Marged. 'Woman up there'll hear that.'

William replied, 'No she won't. Nosey cow's knocking back port with the rest at the far end of the house.'

Captain Dewi agreed. 'No light in her window when we arrived.'

'Got everything she wants,' Marged said angrily. 'And she's got to mess up *our* lives. Who does she think she is?'

The new arrival greeted them all cheerfully and William laughed, a happy sound Rachel hadn't heard before.

The newcomer asked lightly, 'Is Parryboots on his way?'

Marged replied, 'He said he'd be late.'

So Parryboots who had once turned William from his house was now reconciled with him. Rachel looked forward to hearing him.

Glasses and crockery clanked.

'Here y'are, Elwyn,' William said and the new arrival thanked him.

Elwyn Isallt. Another much mentioned name. Isallt was probably his home. She'd key that into her area map later.

Conversation became too general for her to pick out any items. Chairs scraped noisily. Then the hum ceased as William said, 'Someone's shopped us. Akimoto got tough with me last Friday. Showed me a piece of wool from the shed at Llanfechan. Wouldn't say how he got it.'

'They're all at the church every Sunday, aren't they?' Elwyn said. 'One of them could've looked in the shed.'

'Tomos is sure they've never been round the back.'

So Tomos was involved too. Rachel felt let down. She liked the little priest and had assumed that someone in his position was honest. You just can't tell by looking at a man's face.

'That sneaking female upstairs?' Marged asked angrily.

'I watch her. She doesn't go outside Penybwlch boundary.'

So the ruffian was spying on her.

Elwyn used a word Rachel didn't know. *Berthau*.

'No way,' William replied.

The captain said. 'Everyone knows about the trade so anyone could be informing.'

Pryce said, 'Who'd benefit? We all stand to lose if it's fouled up.'

Marged asked, 'Does Akimoto know the wool route?'

'No. Only that there's illegal sheep somewhere on the reserve. He'll only keep quiet if I get sheep for him. Nearest flock . . .'

'Is mine.' Elwyn's voice. 'What for?'

'Their experiments. Trialling cures for cattle plague.'

'So why sheep?'

'How should I know?'

'What'll he pay for any deaths?'

'You're joking. "Payment" is not reporting us.'

'Can't have mine then.'

'Look. Fuzz are in on it, aren't they? Right. Jones daren't inform. But if Akimoto goes higher then he'll be ordered to haul us in. So we do what Akimoto says.'

Noisy chatter drowned the sound of a car driving up, but Rachel saw the lights cross her ceiling and she squirmed her way to the window and peered out. The driver was alone. He was a broad upright man who walked to the door with measured tread. She couldn't see his face but his gait showed him to be the oldest of the group. Parryboots for certain.

He entered and the buzz grew louder. She could distinguish a few words as the newcomer was brought up to date. Then William said clearly, 'I'm safe as long as I can get hold of sheep for their research. But it won't last.'

Parryboots' voice was deep and clear. 'We must move everything from here. Prys?'

The soft voice replied too low for Rachel to hear. Everyone started to talk together, so confusing that Rachel couldn't pick out more than a reference to Llewelyn the Great and the mountains of Snowdonia. Shuffling. Banging. Doors opening and boots on the path outside. She crept to the window and watched the five carry packages from the house to the yard. They were stowing Ty Bach's illegal goods in the sheds and she suspected they would then be distributed to hiding places round the district.

Once the job was complete the group returned.

'How much does that woman know?' Marged asked.

'Began snooping her first night here. I locked the yard gate after she saw me killing that pig.' William jeered, 'Woman's a fool. Thought it was a wild one. *'I saw you killing wild pigs illegally".'* They all sniggered as William's spoof falsetto sounded clearly through the floorboards.

Rachel blushed angrily in the dark.

'Never make a butcher, will you?' Elwyn laughed. 'Weapon of mass destruction you are.'

The others continued to josh William about his hamfisted killing.

'First time I did it, isn't it?' William was irritated.

'And the last, thank god, now Rhys is back.'

'Her sprog's the prob. He followed me. Then he showed her the hens.' William sounded very irate now. 'I saw 'em off with the dog. . .'

So he *had* seen her and Ben with the birds.

'. . . hoped that'd scare 'em silly. But no. She told Akimoto.'

Marged said, 'Jab her with a plague injection, William.'

They all laughed.

'Akimoto informed Jones Police. He was going to haul me in and interrogate me the night I rescued her brat. I reminded him he gets eggs and the old ladies when they've stopped laying. So he was stuck, wasn't he?' William laughed sarcastically. 'James Restall told him to lay off. Very helpful man, Restall. No idea Jones is a receiver.'

'Jones Police is in a difficult position,' Parryboots said. 'Can't trust him.'

Rachel strained to hear Prys. 'Jones Police is Eckstazia. See him in chapel with his wife.'

William said in a threatening voice, '*You* support Eckstazia, but you wouldn't inform. Would you?'

Prys protested in hurt tones. He continued to speak but Rachel could only catch a few phrases, none of which she understood. 'Catching the pony.' 'Red.' 'Near Cefn Llechen.' The following discussion made no sense either.

Never mind that William had rescued her son, she loathed the man. She despised them all for their greed and arrogance. She was so angry she forgot she'd decided to keep out of the whole business. She'd check out the goods in the yard next day and then tell Shuji and James. William would think the ensuing police inspection was Jones's personal decision. He'd never connect it with her.

Parryboots' voice was gruff and distinctive. 'You want to watch those farm inspectors.'

'Give it a rest, Dad,' William replied. 'They're OK. Keep them sweet, don't I?'

'Can't trust Jack Thomas,' continued the older man. 'Look what his grandfather did to my dad.'

'Don't you forget anything?'

'I'm telling you, William. I've known that family a lot longer than you have. His dad was a shifty guy.'

A confusing babble of chat from the rest of the group hid the remainder of the conversation. Rachel's attention wandered as the gossip flowed. As she moved stiffly to ease her legs she knocked the table and a pile of specimen boxes slid to the floor.

The voices went silent. Then someone whispered.

William replied in a normal tone. 'She can't understand us.'

'What if she's learning Welsh?'

'So? All these English scientists try to learn Welsh when they first come here but it soon wears off. No worries. She's too busy doing *my* job of classifying wildlife. I'm too thick, isn't it?' To Rachel's fury they all laughed.

As they chatted Rachel picked out Captain Dewi's high voice calling goodnight, followed by Parryboots asking Marged if she wanted a lift home. There was general mockery at that and then the noise of doors opening and boots down the path. The car drove away.

Silence.

Then glasses clinking. A female laugh. A very sexual laugh. William speaking in a low wheedling tone. Giggling and thumping noises.

Rachel replaced the carpet, but still the sounds echoed in her ears.

She shivered from cold and loneliness. Without bothering to wash she crept under her quilt and wept for Daniel's flesh against hers, her loss as sharp as the day he died. What comfort was masturbation, when heart as well as flesh was in anguish?

In the unforgiving dark she tried to forget. She forced her mind to remember Almighty God had chosen her, sinful as she was, to love and serve him. He had given her James. She must put aside everything else.

She thought her logical mind had won against bodily desire, and couldn't see it was already in retreat.

In her fretful dreams James smiled his dimpled and charming smile from a high seat on a standing stone. Mist swirled round him hiding the treacherous swamps of bodily desire, hiding the safe path leading to the coastlands of heaven's haven. Then it veiled James's face. Leaving a memory of a smile he faded like the Cheshire cat.

Chapter 9

Low cloud and damp drizzle accompanied the following morning, forming droplets on every twig and grey lichen tassel. They showered Rachel as she strode through the reserve woods but she barely noticed the water seeping through her ancient jacket. Nor, as she climbed from the woods to open country, did she give more than a passing glance at the bracken crosiers uncurling from their drowsing rootstocks.

She was immersed in thought.

Emmanuel and Shuji's plans of reform for William were codswallop. He would continue with his lucrative and illicit trade supported by most of the people in the district. Interesting that Annie wasn't present last night. And what exactly was Shuji planning to do with Elwyn's flock of sheep? Alyson had emphasised the dangerous potential of the current virus they were researching. No way would Shuji release such an organism into the outside world.

She looked up. If only the mist would clear. The faint sun, gold as a pirate's doubloon, gave no warmth. A cold breeze started up the valley.

Once the mist rose she'd be able to look down from this hillside into the yard and spot William's comings and goings. If he was watching her then she was certainly going to watch him. Eventually she'd see him leave and then she could enter the yard buildings before the contraband was removed, which was sure to happen very soon.

Slowly the louring cloud shredded and dissolved. The sun shone, birds sang louder greetings and Plas Du's black and sparkling roofs emerged from the mist. Penybwlch buildings were clear now and there was stick figure William, tiny dog at heel, moving sacks round the yard. She trained her yapp telescope on him, watching intently.

Suddenly she heard thudding. Horses cantering towards her the far side of the bluff. The bridle path was narrow so she climbed up the hillside out of their way and waited. The first rider appeared, yanking the reins back fiercely so the animal twisted its head round snorting in protest. It slowed to an amble then a walk as the pair slipped cautiously down the muddy incline towards the wood. A second rider reined in at the top of the slope, silhouetted against the low winter sun.

When the first rider saw Rachel, she jerked her horse to a standstill. It was Hilary Barron. She wore a camel coloured hacking jacket buttoned fashionably to the chin. Its gold embroidered collar and cuffs sparkled in the sun. Highly polished brown boots reached her calves and her tawny riding breeches showed off firm and muscular thighs. Her riding hat bore a jaunty blue feather and a few soft brown curls escaped from under the rim. She sat in the saddle with as much assurance as William on his gallop to Llanfechan.

Godiva, Rachel thought. Or that great Queen of the Iceni, Boudica. Her nervousness increased.

Since Rachel had retreated above the bridle path the two women were on the level. As they stared at each other Rachel noticed the passionate intensity of the professor's gaze, but this time she did not drop her own eyes. What long dark lashes the woman had. Such perfectly defined eyebrows. Her cheeks were slightly flushed with the exertion of her ride, smooth unwrinkled cheeks, yet she must be ten years older than Rachel. She smiled showing perfect teeth, and Rachel's tongue automatically probed the gaps in her own mouth.

'My dear Rachel. How delightful to meet you on this glorious morning. Do you often walk this way?' She glanced at the yapp in Rachel's hand. 'Of course, you're busy reclassifying the reserve plants. Such a wide area to cover alone. A mammoth task. But one we greatly appreciate. Shuji tells me he is most happy with your work. And also your ability to settle into his little community so easily.'

Rachel was charmed by her empathy.

The professor turned her horse round. 'Please walk with me a little way.'

To comply Rachel had to come down onto the path and now she must look up at Hilary. The horse skittered sideways playfully and Rachel shrank back. Hilary smiled and patted its glossy neck as it hrumphed through flaring nostrils. It danced a few more steps, arching its neck proudly and stepping lightly over the ruts and ridges. Its chestnut coat shone with good health and mane and tail were trimmed and tangle free.

Its rider said, 'You can't get good horseflesh around here so I had to buy him in the Midlands from a smallholder selling up. I detected breeding but he was in such poor condition that I forced the owner to practically give him away. Can you believe that such a fine animal would be treated so poorly? These farmers don't deserve decent livestock. Do you ride often?'

'Never been on a horse.'

'One day we must rectify that.' She looked intently at Rachel. 'I'll mention it to James. He's a reasonable rider himself.'

Rachel could feel her cheeks redden and hoped it wasn't obvious.

Hilary smiled knowingly. 'He thinks highly of you. He tells me he's taking your little boy to local football matches. Not that there's much quality play round here, but I suppose the locals do their best.'

Rachel was carefully noncommittal. 'He's being very kind.'

'An excellent man. His commitment to his work is beyond the call of duty. His discoveries in the field of rinderpest control have been widely acclaimed by his peers. He may even become a laureate of the World Food Prize, as was Walter Plowright.'

'Plowright?'

'Middle of last century. He produced a vaccine against the virus. A major contributor to the eradication of poverty and hunger in the tropics.'

'James said rinderpest control is still problematical.'

'So I read in his report. Eckstazia's committed to this cause and I've increased our funding into James' work.' Her eyes glittered. 'Emmanuel and I are convinced the results of his research will herald our dear Lord's return.'

What did rinderpest eradication have to do with *that*? Rachel wondered.

'Meanwhile we're investing the money from a large government grant in a well equipped laboratory near Bristol. When James' work here is completed he's the likely choice to head the complex.' Hilary stared down at Rachel. 'We're also collecting a team to study protozoa in the human brain with the aim of decreasing criminality.'

'Yes, Shuji told me.'

'Good. You've shown great resolution in uncovering this district's black market trade as well as labouring so hard at your current job. I'm sure our new behavioural project will be of interest to you. So are you with us, Rachel?'

'Certainly I am.'

'I'm personally very pleased with your response. To be frank I wasn't wholly happy with your appointment here. Although we didn't meet at Liverpool University when your husband was alive, I gained the impression from talking to your supervisors that you weren't completely dedicated to your research.'

'The baby . . .'

'Yes, yes, of course. Time consuming I've no doubt. Still, after Daniel died you changed career completely and taught in Coventry.'

'To be near my mother.'

'Yes, I appreciate that. But you must agree such a career move hardly shows the commitment to research we in Eckstazia expect. However, Shuji and James have made favourable reports of your work to date, and I accept I was mistaken in my initial opinion.' Hilary paused a moment, head bowed in thought. 'I only knew Daniel for a year, but his philosophical work was impressive. Very impressive,' she emphasised. 'Sadly his outlook became more negative. For some reason he was scathing towards Eckstazia's commitment to the welfare of the poor and suffering.'

She smiled compassionately and Rachel felt encouraged to say, 'He was bothered by Eckstazia's mission statement emphasising that Muslims are the antichrist. He thought that as Eckstazia is first and foremost an American creation then politicians committed to Eckstazia could force the world into war. That they even *wanted* war because Armageddon would lead to the return of Jesus.'

Hilary looked gently into Rachel's eyes. 'I'm afraid poor Daniel was well behind the times. We've evolved over the years and certainly don't advocate a jihad against other religions. In fact we've numerous associate members from among Muslims, Hindus, Buddhists and Jews. Even though they aren't Christian, there are many spiritual people among them looking for the return of a world saviour to put the world to rights.'

Disarmed by such sweet sympathy Rachel said 'Yes, I understand that now I've learnt more about Eckstazia.'

'Unfortunately Daniel's delusions were very wearisome for the other members of the philosophy department. He was . . . I hesitate to say it . . . becoming paranoid and I suggested he have a full psychiatric assessment. He refused. Quite intractable. In hindsight probably the effect of his failing heart, quite unknown to the rest of us.'

'It was very sudden.' Rachel choked.

'My dear, early death seems such a tragedy, but it's for a purpose. Seek for God and he'll reveal his deeper aims, far more satisfying and glorious than any of our earthly plans. Hold to your happy memories.'

'Not always happy.' He'd been continually angry, sometimes frenzied, in those final months up till the last few days when he gave her the necklace. She recalled her impatience with him and wished passionately and guiltily she'd understood both his mental and physical health were failing.

Hilary eyed her closely. 'I'm so sorry. Perhaps it's best just to forget. Put aside sad memories and get rid of any keepsakes you may have.'

'Yes. I'll do that.' Just the photo, the letters, but not the necklace warm between her breasts. It wasn't a lie, she reassured herself.

Hilary smiled kindly. 'Think positively of the future. Not just Ben's, though he's very important to you, but your own. You're young, highly intelligent. Spread your wings, Rachel.' Hilary reined in her gelding and opened her arms wide as the Angel of the North. '*You* can make a difference as you rise in your profession within Eckstazia. Our standing in the worldwide community gives us influence across the globe. We *can and will* encourage people to true faith in preparation for our dear Lord's return. And all those who seek to obstruct us will be crushed.' She composed herself and smiled down at her companion confidentially. 'I've been approached to take the position of the government's media tsar. A very influential post. Do you remember the Russian scandal three years ago?'

Even Rachel with her ignorance of politics had noticed this one. 'The Russian tycoon who bought up the UK newspaper websites?'

'That's her.'

'Didn't she boast her websites swung the electronic vote in the parliamentary election?'

'Correct. It was also said that when she threatened to withdraw media support the government cravenly gave in to her policy demands. That's why the post of media tsar was created to oversee all information given to the public. The current holder of the position retires shortly, so I'm in line for the position.'

'I wish you every success.'

'And I wish you success when the research team moves to Bristol.' She smiled warmly. 'But you'll be sorry to leave this beautiful place.' She waved her arm around the hills and the sunlit valley where a silver stream wound down to the river and the sea.

'Beautiful, certainly. But the people . . . D'you know what Dewi's doing?'

'Dewi?'

'Captain of your launch.'

'Oh, you mean David.'

'He stocks your launch with contraband. Trades between Liverpool and this coast.'

Hilary jerked on her horse's mouth. 'Are you sure?'

'I heard him talking to William Parry last night.'

'Parry?'

'The tenant farmer at Penybwlch.'

'That ugly man with the twisted eye?'

'That's the one.'

Hilary's face lost its calm and became distorted with anger.'Things are far more serious than I supposed. Using my launch indeed.' Before Rachel could describe the rest of the undercover committee meeting, Hilary dug her heels into the gelding's sides making him prance. The blue feather in her hat waved exuberantly as the pair galloped home towards Plas Du, followed by the ever watchful second rider.

Rachel raised both arms in the air and war-danced until she was out of breath. 'Yes! Yes!' She balled her fists. 'Goodbye Annie.

Goodbye callous Mrs Lloyd and your rotten school. Goodbye William and all your greedy friends. Especially Marged. The cheek of that moaning peasant! She should get herself an education instead of fucking William. I've worked hard and now I'm being rewarded. I'm special. One of the chosen. Respected and appreciated by the important people in Eckstazia. Everything works for good for those who love the Lord.'

Thankyou God, she said quickly, in case he thought she was ungrateful and withdrew his favours. And there was an uneasy niggle in the back of her mind. Had she betrayed Dan to Hilary? No, no. She had merely been honest.

She thrust her hands into the torn pockets of her dirty jacket. Goodness, she looked as tatterdemalion as William. This coat may have been a good buy on Coventry market, but now! What a shambles! She'd lost out when she spent her savings on Ben's mobile, now stolen, but soon she'd have enough to get something smart. Like the other scientists. Like James, so dapper in his Sunday gear.

James. Yes, James. The thought of him warmed her heart. So different from Daniel. Dan had been full of high spirits followed by bursts of depression. Together they'd been young and foolish, but in her maturity she wanted a quieter more ordered life. Security for herself and Ben.

She looked towards the farm. The yard was empty. William walked purposefully across the fields towards the woods and presently he and his dog disappeared in the trees. It was her opportunity.

She raced down the path, sure footed over the uneven and slippery ground.

'Hey ya! Slow down a minute!' James was marching towards her, his arms outstretched as she skidded into his hug. They both laughed as he released her.

'What's the hurry?'

Searching the yard could wait. 'I've just been talking to Hilary Barron.'

'A lady of the greatest integrity.'

'She told me about the eventual team transfer to Bristol and your forthcoming - and well deserved - promotion.'

'Maybe. Maybe. Nothing's decided finally.'

She spilled out her hopes of working with the new research team. 'But I studied the diseases of ticks that cause lyme disease, James. I'm not at all qualified in protozoa. . .'

'You've shown us how flexible you can be.'

'It's wonderful! I'll be near Ben at the Academy in Bath. And though I'll miss these mountains I find the people detestable.'

'Both secretive and dishonest,' he agreed. The friendly scent of his aftershave allured her as he put his arms round her again and drew her close. He bent his face down and she returned his kiss with similar gentleness. His sensuous lips were warm but flaccid. She kissed him more fiercely as her body responded to the comfort of his embrace.

He drew back a little. 'Let's be patient, my dear.' He looked at her tenderly. 'Everything must be done in order and simplicity. We're the Lord's children; we must honour him with our bodies as well as our thoughts.'

A sincere man. A kind and honest one.

She smiled lovingly at him.

'Dearest Rachel. You wear the imperishable jewel in your heart which God values above all things. A gentle, quiet and obedient spirit.' He held her firmly, smoothing her wind-tangled hair with tender fingers. 'So darling, will you marry me?'

'Of course,' she said. It was so long since she'd felt such comfort. 'But there's Ben. He must be happy to have you as stepfather first.'

'Of course. Will you tell him today?'

She thought for a moment. 'Day after tomorrow he's going with you to the football. I'll tell him after that.'

He frowned a little. 'No sooner?' When she shook her head he smiled and said proudly, 'And then we can let everyone know that I'm going to marry the dearest and best woman in the world. They'll all be very pleased.'

Arm in arm they walked back towards the farm, parting before the other scientists could see them.

*

To Rachel's annoyance it was impossible for her to visit the yard unseen as Alyson and Annie were drinking tea in the suntrap between the two towers in front of the house. So, elated by her engagement to James, she collected a plate of Annie's lunchtime sandwiches and joined them in the warmth. Relaxing there she realised she'd forgotten to tell James about the meeting in Ty Bach last night. It could wait till she'd scouted round the yard.

Annie sat with thin legs wide apart, her skirt riding up above her knees. Her face was sour as ever as she said to Alyson, 'William's never here when you need him. You'll have to sort it yourself.'

Alyson shrugged and turned to Rachel. 'Hi. You look cheerful. Been up the hill? I envy you. Better than our stuffy lab. The bikes have had flats for weeks and William can't be bothered to repair them.'

Annie adjusted a wisp of grey hair escaping from her bun. 'He's an idle good-for-nothing.'

Rachel and Alyson said nothing.

'Now, my Huw. There's a clever man. *He'd* show them all how to run a farm.' Annie continued grumbling as her elder son came whistling up the drive. His dog disturbed a dozing cat and chased it into the yard.

Just as well I didn't go straight to the sheds, Rachel thought.

Alyson demanded William mend the bike tyres. He stared at her insolently as his mother remonstrated in Welsh. His face was rough and unshaven but he didn't smell as rank as usual. Perhaps Ben's criticism had had a good effect.

Rachel didn't bother to listen to their argument. Soon she'd be leaving behind all their petty quarrels.

And then William turned to her, smiling cynically. 'Did you enjoy your walk in the woods? Such a pleasant companion you had.'

What piercing eyes, what a strong physical presence. How pallid James seemed in comparison. Hastily Rachel airbrushed the disloyal comparison from her thoughts.

But how had the man seen them? Rachel muttered something inaudible, well aware of Alyson's fervid interest.

'I know these woods well. Don't I, Mam?' He glared at Annie with such hostility that Alyson moved to protect the old woman.

But Annie was unafraid. She spat an incomprehensible curse.

'No need for that, Mam. I shan't tell on you.'

Annie pulled her skirt down over her blotchy legs and stalked into the house.

He grinned like a fox in a hen run as he turned back to Rachel. 'Ben's going to the Bangor football match with Restall, isn't he?'

'Dr Restall has kindly offered to take him on Saturday,' Rachel replied haughtily, cursing herself for the blush that spread over her face. How had he found that out?

Alyson was obviously following the exchange with increasing curiosity.

William, clearly enjoying Rachel's discomfort, took a whistle out of his pocket and blew. Silently. In answer to the high note the farm dog appeared at a gallop, tongue hanging out and tail wagging. He squatted at William's feet, gazing up at him eagerly.

'Did you hear the whistle, Mrs Gunnarsson?' William asked Alyson.

'Silent as the grave.'

'Toss obeys me when I'm out of his sight but not his hearing. People are amazed to see him gather up animals when no one's around. They don't know I'm controlling him. Watching.' He tossed the whistle idly from one muddy hand to the other. His smile was full of hatred. 'Isn't that so, Mrs Kerem?'

'I'm sure your dog is a very intelligent animal,' she said icily.

'He can herd any animal. Hens, goats, cattle, sheep as well as any humans who stray into private places. By the way, you don't catch hens by chasing them. You walk up to them softly softly like this,' and he held his big hand out over the lawn. 'Over their heads. They think your hand's a bird of prey and they crouch down. Then you,' and both women jumped as he shouted '*grab 'em.*'

The dog yawned.

'Look at those lovely teeth, ladies. Slashing teeth. Not like bulldogs that don't let go, but just as lethal. There was a guy illegally exercising his dog on my hill last week. Dog won't ever come back, will he, Toss?' William nodded at them both and strode off to the yard, Toss at heel.

'Was that to do with the black market?' Alyson asked.

Rachel told her about Toss herding her with Ben into the woods until they were lost. 'We never set eyes on William,' she admitted. 'Thinking back, Ben heard the whistle. His young ears can pick out higher tones than I can.'

'Shuji and James were talking about black market sheep the other day. Concerning experiments to do with rinderpest carriers.'

'I'm really not interested.' Though she was, but the fewer people who knew her involvement, the less likely William was to pin any reprisal on her and Ben. She changed the subject quickly. 'Have you heard about the new lab in Bristol?'

Alyson said excitedly, 'Shuji told us this morning. Now our work's nearly complete Eric and I will be going there shortly. Thank God. We may have superb equipment in this lab, but the building's falling down, fire's a constant hazard and Freya's suffering from the rubbish education. Shuji, Jenny and James are staying, helped by the Bangor students until their research on the new virus strain is finalised.' She frowned and whispered, 'Now you're coming on the team I can tell you Eric and I are seriously worried about this one. It's so much more dangerous than the strain *we* dealt with. And that talk of experimenting with Welsh sheep. Eric doesn't think they're taking proper safety precautions. And . . . No, I'm sure he misunderstood . . . ' She paused before continuing, 'But I'll miss the hills. Remind me of Iceland.' She stared hard at Rachel. 'And so you're coming too. Once he relocates you'll be working with *James*.'

Again Rachel blushed.

'You and James . . . I did wonder. He's always praising you to the skies.'

'There's nothing between us . . . Well, yes, there is, but Ben doesn't know and of course it depends on him liking James and it's early days and I'd rather you . . . '

'Kept it under my hat? Of course, Rach.' She lent back and looked her friend up and down. 'You make a handsome pair. You look so much better than when I first met you from the bus. Weighed down with trouble, permanent frown, complexion an utter mess. And you could barely struggle up a hill, could you?'

Rachel laughed. 'Life's opened up for me since then.'

'But Rach. I've known James a lot longer than you have and I ought to warn you . . . '

'Gay tendencies? Does he even admit them to himself?'

'I don't think so. But he must be harbouring some deep-seated anxiety because he's so vitriolic about gays.'

Rachel said drily, 'I had noticed.'

'And he and Shuji go walking together most weekends.'

'Friendship.'

'Naturally.' Alyson sounded cynical. 'Anyway he's got two options. Remain single and chaste or marry someone of the opposite sex and be faithful to her.'

'I'm just there to provide respectability? I'm sure there's more to his love than that.' Rachel smiled. 'But I must think of Ben first.'

'Ben will grow up and leave. Once he's boarding at the Academy you'll lose him. A husband's for life. So what do you really want for yourself?'

'James can give me everything I want.'

'The other thing is his attitude towards women. Keep quiet and do as we're told by our men folk.'

'Does he try that approach on Hilary Barron?' Rachel laughed, but recalled the jewel of obedience he claimed she wore in her heart.

'Absolutely not. But he's a bad influence on Eric.' She looked so uneasy that Rachel sensed marital disharmony on this point. 'It's the surrendered wives syndrome.'

'The what?'

'A good Christian wife doesn't argue with her man. She listens to his woes – that's called companionship. She doesn't tell him about her own troubles – that's grumbling. She cooks and cleans and bears his children, rearing them in the fear and love of the Lord without complaint. She . . . '

'I get the picture. It won't be a problem.'

'It won't?' Alyson sounded disbelieving. 'I've never thought of you as a doormat.'

'Thanks for your advice, Ally,' Rachel said sarcastically. 'But I can always talk to Emmanuel.'

Alyson stared at her in disbelief. '*Emmanuel?* That android!'

'Android! He's real.'

Alyson laughed. 'Come on, Rach. Who's met him in the flesh?'

'Lots of people. Archbishops, senior Hindus like Prem Mishra, the Islamic scholar Shaykh Yassin. . . .'

'The Buddhist nun. And so on. I can see you've studied his website. I bet they only ever speak to him over the internet. Just like you and anyone else he mentors. But he's programmed through and through.'

'Where's your proof?'

'I've been doubtful for years. Somehow he never seemed real. Not really real if you get me. Then James said something to Jenny the other day and I was sure they think he's an android too.'

Rachel remembered James' strange hesitations when talking about Emmanuel. She hadn't told anyone but Emmanuel about her debts but James had found out. So either Emmanuel was leaky or . . . ? An android? Controlled by another mentor? Why would anyone want to do that? Ridiculous. No, he was real.

Alyson said jokingly, 'Emmanuel's a popular resource for all those poor guys who can't sleep at night and need someone to boost their confidence.' Then more seriously, 'You're not a kid, Rach. Make your own mind up. That's my advice. Though I can see you don't want it.'

Rachel held back an angry retort.

'Back to it.' Alyson finished her third mug of tea and got up. 'Boring life in the lab. Jenny, lucky devil, is only interested in her coming advisory tour to agricultural departments in India, Pakistan, Afghanistan and Australia. Holiday trip, more like. At least she's not as sour as usual. She's been soreheaded since Shuji got the top job here after the previous director left. She's senior to James so thought it was a shoo in.'

So that was the reason for Jennifer goading Shuji so often during evening discussions.

As Rachel finished her lunch she heard the farm van croak into life. William disappeared down the drive in a cloud of exhaust. Why the traffic police didn't impound the vehicle, Rachel couldn't imagine. They were probably hand in glove with him like everyone else.

Now was her opportunity. A rapid check of the farm buildings.

Cautiously she climbed the padlocked yard gate. Once inside the yard she was invisible from Annie in the house.

She hadn't seen the yard in daylight. It was roughly square, surrounded by buildings on all sides. Its concrete surface was hollowed and chipped, while primeval dung rotted in the cracks. To her right a couple of sheds abutted against the back of the cottages. Their doors were bolted but not padlocked. Obvious storage places. At right angles to these stood a row of pigsties smelling fustily of their long departed inhabitants. Broken buckets, a split wellington boot, rusty nails and paper sacks dotted with rat droppings occupied the empty pens. Nothing illegal. Between the sties and the far right hand corner there was a gap leading to the fields. If she heard the van return she'd escape that way.

In front of her a long open shed held a rusty harrow, an outdated horse rake and a heavy roller and, of far more interest, a very large stack of wooden boxes. On her left were substantial two storey buildings. She opened the door of the nearest one. It stank of biofuel. Drums and jerry cans of the stuff crammed tight to the roof. The next building had open double doors and she recognised the garage she'd peeped into on her first night at Penybwlch. It was stacked with sacks and barrels. No room for the van. And hanging on the wall as she'd long suspected was an illegal rifle with a night vision scope attached. Adjoining the garage and extending into the corner of the square was another building with rusting metal window frames as old as those on the laboratory building. A little concrete slope extended down from the door, and yes, she identified the pig butchering room at once. Checking round her in case Annie had left the house, she crossed the yard and opened its door.

It was certainly the same room, but there was no sign that any animal had been slaughtered here. The place smelt of dust not blood. The rough stone walls were grey with cobweb curtains. A stack of large paper sacks took up most of the space, reaching almost to the tie beams. She made a small slit in one with her knife. White powder. Looked and smelt like flour. Gingerly she touched it with the tip of her tongue. Yes, flour. Where did it come from? From Liverpool in Hilary's launch? From Anglesey, once the breadbasket of North Wales, essential for all those warring princes in their endless battles?

Wooden egg crates were stockpiled alongside. Surely they couldn't all come from William's hens? How often did hens lay eggs? Once a day? A week? Twenty or so a year like some wild birds? Her ignorance of the provenance of her food was as profound as most urbanites.

The slate shelf that had held the butchery tools was now packed high with large cardboard boxes and she opened one. Smaller green boxes inside were labelled 'Classic Impact. 12g:1 1/16 oz. Paper case. Biodegradable wad. All types of game and general purpose.' She made a hole. Orange shotgun cartridges. Other boxes held metallic rimfire cartridges.

Stunned she counted the number of boxes on the shelf. Calculated the number of cartridges. So the black market wasn't just illegal food trading. It was more extensive and more dangerous.

She knew little about weapons. She'd met Dan on a university rally to ban firearms after a spate of city crime. People power ensured the government enacted a ban on all shooting, including wild game and now only the police and the armed forces were allowed firearms.

So what was the Welsh gang's strategy? Banditry? They had a history of raiding across the borders. Taffy was a Welshman, went the nursery rhyme, a thief who stole my leg of beef. But shotguns and rifles would never be a match for police firearms.

Then she recalled last night's puzzling reference to Snowdonia and Llewelyn the Great. Were these mad people planning one of their irrational uprisings like their conquered ancestors?

The room grew darker as the sun vanished.

She must inform James immediately. She slid a cartridge into her pocket and turned to leave.

The darkness was the silhouette of a man.

William.

He said very softly, 'I knew you'd come. You were spying on us from your window last night.'

Outside a robin sang of freedom. Gulls screamed. The surrounding trees whispered and creaked as the moment extended eternally.

Her mouth was too dry for her to ask what he would do.

He walked towards her and took her gently by the shoulders.

There was massive strength under that pretended gentleness.

'Now,' he said grimly, his cold eyes staring bleakly into hers, 'how do we treat spies?' His grip dug into her flesh. 'You could have an accident in the reserve. The wild sows would find you. The foxes and carrion crows. Crawling munching maggots.'

She shivered and a look of sheer pleasure crossed his face.

'Who would mind? Ben would cry for you. That cold wet slob James might squeeze out a little tear. No one else.'

Her eyes were wide with fear.

143

'Lost your claws today, pussy? Nothing but trouble, isn't it? Before *you* came everything worked fine. *You* told Akimoto to report us.'

'So did Annie,' she muttered.

He snorted derisively. 'Liar. My mother may be a snake but even she wouldn't betray us.' He released her. 'What's in it for you? Promotion, is it? And the chance to send your son to a private school? Too proud for a Welsh school, are you?'

His angry sweat was pungent and earthy. His uneven eyes implacable as mountain rock. 'So now our trade's disrupted and people starve because of you.'

'Starve?' she whimpered. 'Because of me?'

'You're well fed. *I* see to that. *You're* privileged.' His thin scar grew livid with his rage.

'I'm not privileged,' she bleated. 'I work as hard as anyone.'

'You've never done a day's hard labour in your life.'

He put the fingers of one massive hand very carefully round her throat. She shook uncontrollably as his touch sent electric shivers through her body.

'Stop that,' he growled, but she trembled even more. Feelings suppressed for many years swamped her good sense and her moral code. A tsunami of shameful lust rose up to overwhelm her.

His voice became deceptively mild. 'There was a sick pigeon. It shook all over when I picked it up. Poor bird. So frightened of me . . . ' He glared at her. '*And I killed it just the same.*'

She quavered, 'What good will it do anyone if you kill me?'

'Rid the world of a troublemaker. But you're right. There're better ways of silencing you.' He was holding her so closely that she could feel the hardness of his body. To her chagrin her own body gave in to him, melting against him in the sudden force of her own desire and need. He thrust her back painfully against the boxes.

'Horny, aren't you,' he sneered triumphantly. 'James can't satisfy you? What a surprise!'

'He's a gentleman.'

'That's a new name for it. Your lot condemn gays out of hand, don't you? Based on a law invented by crazy priests three thousand years ago.'

'God's law.'

He sniggered.

'You'll end in hell.'

He said calmly and sardonically, 'There's terror, isn't it?'

She was scared by his swift changes in mood but now she said firmly enough, 'What are you going to do with me?'

144

'Let you go. Unharmed.' He stood back from her. 'But you won't tell anyone about what you've found. Because if you do you won't see Ben again. He'll be reared by strangers and that's the worst thing that can happen to any kid.' He spoke with feeling. 'He'll live the same life as we do. Poor and hard. And he'll know it's your fault. If ever he meets you again he'll hate you. So keep your mouth shut, Rachel Kerem.'

Chapter 10

It was no idle threat. Nor were the gun cartridges.

She must inform someone. She dare not inform.

The monster knew her too well.

How rash to scout round the yard before informing Shuji of the illegal goods, just because she wanted his praise for her initiative.

And she was obsessed by the strength of sexual desire that had haunted her ever since Daniel died. Masturbation wasn't the answer. She needed a man. And from the wicked way her body had responded to William, any man. How had she fallen this low, into the morass of sin and wantonness that was sucking her into perdition?

Who could help her? Emmanuel?

Ashamed of her feelings she stopped contacting her mentor directly. Instead she browsed his pages on sex. Pray without ceasing. The devil is attacking your newly redeemed soul. Put on the armour God has provided so you may stand firm against the wiles of the devil. The great shield of faith will quench his flaming arrows, wear Jesus' salvation as your helmet and make the word of God your sword. Persevere.

Once or twice he sent a message missing their weekly chats and asking how she was. She said she was very busy and things were difficult and would he pray for a miracle to help her? He referred her to James, praising his kindness to Ben.

At first James was a comfort. She admitted tearfully and guiltily that she'd been wrong about William and the ruffian was a danger to her son and herself. James caressed her, promising his help. She was relieved she didn't feel the same degree of sinful sexual arousal with him – proof that she was overcoming her lust. She was also grateful he was taking on the role of father for her lonely boy and keeping him out of William's orbit. There were one or two teething problems, as was natural. When the pair returned from the Saturday football match, James complained to her Ben joked about going up into heaven to be with Jesus. 'It *is* a strange idea,' she said, but James was indignant. It was God's promise so Ben should believe it. And the boy continually made lavatorial puns. 'Just his age,' she said smiling. James was insistent she discipline him. She didn't. Instead she asked Ben how he'd enjoyed himself.

'Orl rite.'

He was often noncommittal, so she was happy that he and James were bonding. Then she mentioned a trip to Anglesey planned for all three of them. He said he wasn't going anywhere with that man. He refused to say why.

James asked, 'Have you told him of our engagement?'

She told him what the boy had said. 'I can't tell him yet. We mustn't get engaged until he accepts you.'

'I'm not marrying *him*,' he told her crossly. 'You're his mother. Sort him out.'

'It isn't as easy as that, James. Boys don't see things the way we do. Give him time.'

She insisted she and James keep apart for Ben's sake.

Worse, Ben wanted to help William with his hens. He'd taken a shine to the farmer and his dog since the rescue in the woods. Rachel forbad him. 'He's dangerous, two-faced,' she said, and told him William had threatened abduction.

He sulked.

She was afraid he didn't believe her.

In a few weeks he'd leave for the Academy, out of harm's way. But if she delayed telling Shuji about her discoveries till then, everything, including the ammunition, would be spread among the insurgents. William would certainly make her prior knowledge public and she'd be considered their accomplice. A prison sentence. Ben would be taken into care by the Social Services. Forced adoption; lost for ever.

Even if the worst didn't happen, she'd still lose her job. How would she repay Eckstazia's loan? And if she didn't keep up payments she'd lose her credit status. Become a nonperson, a society misfit without access to any financial backing. Reliant on cash, the ever-diminishing pound and pence coins, the torn and tattered paper notes.

She kept mum with the scientists and dodged William as she would a mad dog. She snapped at Annie. Every night she tossed and turned, fretting at her indecision. She berated herself for the cowardice of motherhood, for putting one child's welfare before that of many. But still she kept silent until it was too late.

Other doubts surfaced.

On Sunday evening James preached on the love between David, future king of Israel and Jonathon, prince of the ruling house. Didn't Jonathon love David as his own soul?

He and Shuji exchanged looks.

How passionately David kissed his friend when they were parted by the King's jealousy. When Jonathon died in battle, David wept. 'Your love for me was greater than love for women.'

What *did* that mean? Rachel wondered.

James continued, 'Such brotherhood is rare, precious and approved by God. Men are capable of a depth of love incomprehensible to women. Sisterly friendships are more superficial.' Here he smiled at Rachel compassionately. 'We know too well the sin of gossip is common among women. Nor is this a modern sin. St Paul's letters continually warn the female members of his congregations about backbiting.'

Rachel looked quickly at Alyson but her head was bowed and eyes closed. Jennifer was out of her range of sight, and Rachel wondered what both women thought. Young Ashley was trying not to giggle as Martin dug her in the ribs.

'Same sex friendship must be pure as well as deep,' James reminded them. 'We must beware of falling into sexual sin. There are so-called Christians who lead the flock astray, and their punishment will be the heavier when the Lord comes. We in Eckstazia can be proud of our record. Our demonstrations and petitions last year resulted in the banning of same-sex marriages and blessings in UK churches. Yes, we were reviled by the secular media but we stood firm. Men, and here I include women, become alienated from God when they indulge in sex outside marriage and homosexual unions. They trample on the redeeming blood of his Son Jesus. But we must not condemn because we ourselves are frail. Instead we offer the hand of friendship in Christ to all sinners. In costly love, simplicity of heart and humility.'

When Penybwlch closed, both Shuji and James would relocate to Bristol and join her at the new facility. Might this David and Jonathon take precedence over Rachel and James?

And in the back of her mind the nagging worry about Dan gnawed away. She ought not to leave it to the Academy counsellors to explain his fate to Ben. It was her duty, however painful, to tell him as gently as possible. But how could she, when she couldn't face the sorrow of eternal bereavement herself?

She felt she was approaching meltdown as she tussled alone with her fears.

A week after her meeting with William she was wearily tidying Ben's cupboard before he returned from school. Clothes and toys spilt onto the floor and he'd refused to sort it. He wouldn't be pleased with her, but then he'd been in an odd mood all week. Was it something at that unsympathetic school? Or her own anxieties affecting him? She hoped he'd get over his antipathy to James by the weekend when it was planned to take him round the castle.

The sash window was open and at first she was too engrossed by her worries to notice voices outside. Then she recognised an attractive female voice talking to Annie. Jealous Marged, William's girl.

She went to the window and squinted down into the narrow passage between house and retaining wall. All she could see was long fair hair tied roughly round the top of the girl's head. She said, 'Jackets. Size ten and eleven. Cut close.'

'I always do.'

'Trousers ready?'

'Hmph.'

As Rachel had suspected Annie was one of the cloth outworkers.

Marged said, 'Your boss has reported the wool trade to Jones Police.'

'Not personally he didn't. Too sly for that. He told Restall he promised William he'd keep mum, but it was necessary to warn Jones just the same.'

'So Restall told Jones? And Akimoto kept his conscience clean?' Marged's voice was scornful.

'Thick as thieves, those two.'

Marged sniggered.

Annie said harshly, 'Jones won't do anything.'

'He's checked out the shed at Llanfechan.'

Rachel almost clapped her hands for joy.

'Anything there?'

'The stink. Tomos couldn't hide *that*.' Marged laughed then said angrily, 'We daren't carry the wool from Colwyn over the bwlch this year.'

'Jones'll sit on it now. He'll report there's nothing in the shed and that'll be it. He needs the trade as much as anyone.'

'Don't trust him,' Marged said. 'You find out who snitched to your boss.'

'I'm sure that woman's behind it.'

'Kerem?'

Annie snorted, 'She's hitched to Restall.'

'Is she now? William says she's stupid. She'll do anything for that boy, and William can handle *him*.'

'I know.'

'William's clever,' Marged said admiringly.

That evening Annie told Rachel triumphantly that she didn't have any spare bread. The ham was cooked specially for Shuji, not for little boys. Butter? Rachel was joking. Milk was sour. Except for Shuji's portion. Rachel had used up this week's egg ration. Baked *beans*? Junk tinned food. Of course there weren't any. Though Rachel had seen a stack of tins in the store cupboard before Annie locked it.

Rachel looked desperately at the scraps she'd wheedled for Ben's dinner. Never enough for a growing boy. How he hated being consigned to a solitary early meal. And where was he?

When he finally returned after dusk, he scorned the food she'd prepared and stomped off, rudely refusing to do his homework.

The scientists arrived for their dinner and Jennifer began one of her interminable graces. 'Bless our meal, Lord Jesus, as we await your return . . . '

'You've bloody untidied my cupboard and I can't bloody find anything,' Ben yelled from the landing.

Shocked briefly into silence, Jennifer started again. As Rachel fled upstairs to remonstrate with her son the scientist's voice came clear and firm, 'Keep us from vulgar language and contemptuous treatment of our seniors . . . '

'Bloody crap,' Ben shouted from the top of the stairs. Rachel slapped his leg. 'Get to your room,' she ordered fiercely.

He hesitated, not quite sure whether he dare disobey. Then he walked defiantly to his room and slammed the door.

It wouldn't be long before she'd lose all control.

James lifted his prayerful head as she panted back to her chair. He raised his eyebrows, whether in disapproval of Ben or displeasure at her shortcomings at discipline, Rachel was uncertain.

'Even so, come, Lord Jesus. Amen,' the scientists said in unison. They drew back their chairs and sat down to await Annie, a sweetly smiling Annie with her trolley of succulent ham, pasta in a creamy mushroom sauce and a melange of French beans and peas. The New Zealand wine was excellent and exclusive. How many could afford its airmile taxation?

Starvation. Was William lying? The Welsh were thin, but that was no longer unusual. As food prices had risen the days of gross overconsumption just faded away. The kids at the schools? Weedier and paler than the ones she'd taught in Coventry, but wasn't that due to parental ignorance about diet?

James said, 'D'you know Ben went to see Parry straight after school?'

'I've told him not to hang out with William,' she replied coldly, watching Annie observe the exchange with pretended indifference.

'The man's hardly the best role model for your son. Ben's appalling outburst stems directly from this association. It must be nipped in the bud.'

She was furious with him for criticising her so publicly and in front of the housekeeper. James clearly didn't understand how much Ben rebelled against unhappy schooling, his lack of friends and loss of his father. And all that anger he turned on her, resenting that she, his prime carer, couldn't ease his aching heart. Growing up is hard. Punishment not always the answer.

'I'll deal with it my way, James.'

'I hope you will. Spare the metaphorical rod, Rachel, and spoil the child.' He thanked Annie as she served him another portion of ham.

Strangely the excellent food seemed tasteless and the conversation insipid. Yes, they were all good honest people here, concerned for the welfare of the poor in other countries, but did they have to be so self-assured, so blind to what went on around them?

Through her fog of anxiety she heard Shuji mention Emmanuel's name.

'Alyson says he's an android,' she said lightly.

Shuji, James and Jennifer stopped eating and stared at her.

'Explain yourself,' Shuji said icily.

Bewildered by their hostility and wishing she'd kept her stupid mouth shut, she stuttered, 'No one's ever seen him off screen.'

'You'd hardly expect him to turn up on your doorstep, would you?' Jennifer asked with heavy sarcasm.

'Alyson said how could anyone know he's not just a program? She's right. Androids look and talk just like people.'

Shuji said, 'She's accusing Eckstazia of the grossest duplicity.'

'I'm sure she didn't mean. . .' Rachel tailed off as he glared at her.

'Don't repeat this slander anywhere, Rachel. That's both first and final warning.'

*

The wind on the hills the following day was dry and sour as only March winds can be. Heavy clouds tumbled across the sky and out on the grey sea, gusts whipped wavecaps into a snow-white frenzy. Birds hid among the heather and even the ubiquitous gulls deserted the skies to flatfoot their way among creeping thistle and dead grasses in untended fields.

Rachel's cheeks were chapped by the cold and her eyes streamed with the force of the wind. She trudged up the mountain above the farm, weary from sleepless anxious nights. Part way up she paused and stared unseeingly across the valley, her thoughts as incoherent and bitter as the chaotic skies.

A fellow traveller marched towards her down the hill. He stumbled against the wind, his long black coat wrapped tight around him, so he looked more like a child's lumpy Guy Fawkes than a man. As he came nearer she recognised Tomos, the dishonest priest of Llanfechan. They greeted each other and she would have gone on but he inquired after Ben. Whether or not he knew about William's threat to kidnap her son, his inquiry inflamed her suppressed anger and fear.

'Don't you dare raise a finger against him!'

Amazed the young priest protested, 'Of course I won't harm the boy.'

'William's going to take him away from me.' She started to sob.

Tomos said firmly, 'He will not.'

His face was so kind that she stuttered, 'How can I tell him?' Her tears fell faster.

'Tell him what?'

'His father's in hell.'

Shocked, Tomos asked, '*Who* told you that?'

'It's true. It's in the Bible.' She collapsed in the heather almost choking in the paroxysm of her grief. She stammered, 'Dan was the best part of me. My anchor in life. He loved me in spite of what my father said.'

The priest sat down beside her. 'What did your father say?' His voice was very gentle.

'It was because of me he left us. He took my little brother as well. Because I'd corrupt him, he said. My mother told me.'

'How old were you?'

'Twelve.'

The priest said simply, 'Poor child.'

Surrounded by his compassionate understanding she suddenly saw the sad history from a stranger's point of view. A family spat, words said foolishly in anger, a deserted wife aiming to turn her young daughter against her father. Her long concealed guilt at the past dwindled, sighed and faded away like a ghost at cockcrow.

'And why do you think your kind husband is in hell?'

'Unbelievers are damned.'

'Poof,' said Tomos in unpriestly tones. 'If you believe that you'll believe anything. And you *can* believe anything if you pick bits out of the Bible. You can believe God calls us to ethnically cleanse other nations. Or that you should stone people to death who offend against the sexual laws of an ancient Palestinian society. And you can justify slavery.'

'Jesus said. . .'

152

'Other people wrote many years after Jesus died that he had said this or that. We have to make allowances for their personal bias.'

'But what do I say to Ben?'

'Tell him his father is with God.' He smiled peaceably, his eyes as calm as Emmanuel's. 'In heaven. Which isn't a particular spot in the universe but anywhere where God's love is, and there's no place without God. No hell. God's the movement of love between us all. That love you feel for your husband and your son is God in you.'

'I can't *see* that.'

The priest stood up stiffly and opened his arms wide. His tattered coat blew out in the gale. Underneath, his thin black trousers had worn grey with age and the holes in his brick red jumper were darned with navy thread. 'See the hills surrounding us like God's love. Listen. Listen. Can't you hear the voice of God in the wind?'

'Nothing. It means nothing.' She bowed her head on her knees.

The scarecrow stared down at her, troubled by her inability to understand. 'You're a biologist, aren't you? Tell me then, what's the greatest miracle in the universe?'

'*I* don't know.' She was exasperated.

He squatted beside her again, saying carefully, 'This universe is self-conscious through us. In our brains, in this conglomeration of Big Bang atoms, we meditate on the universe that makes us. We ask it questions. Tell me, how is it possible that a cluster of non-living atoms can become self-aware?

'Another miracle. Where does love come from? Not from God-far-away. Love evolves out of care for others. The stickleback's care of his babies, the dinosaur fossilised as it guards its eggs, the lapwing protecting its chicks and all the concern and care between humans. Love is a law of the universe more ancient, more basic than gravity. Part of God-in-all-things. God giving Godself to everything that is.'

She looked up and met his clear blue eyes. All his strength was concentrated in them as he willed her to understand.

But he was a hypocrite and a thief. She said bitterly, 'So God is love, everything's right with the world, and you can grub after money as much as you like.'

'Money? I'm hardly rich.' He stuck his thumb through a hole in his coat.

'You racketeers keep animals inside the reserve. Sell sheep, pigs, hens. Manufacture clothes and God knows what else. All for yourselves. While bribing officials to keep their mouths shut. Evading taxes that should support people who are too poor to buy decent food.'

'Our people are unemployed and starving.'

'Does that justify your swindles?' she asked in a rage.

The wind blew Tomos' cap off his near bald pate and he raced to jump on it. His ginger fringe of hair was risible.

'We provide food and clothes for our poor,' he said proudly, waving his cap to emphasize his words. 'William's a good man, though a wild one. He and his cousin Elwyn work hard to relieve poverty. There's no one better at programming than Elwyn, yet he risks his career by working with us. As for William, did you know that the blood of Llewelyn the Great runs through his veins from his mother's side?'

'So what? Probably everyone in this benighted country is related to some ancient princeling or other,' she said sarcastically. 'He's an evil man.'

She jumped to her feet, despising his sophistry. Running uphill with the wind behind her she didn't look back until she stood at the top. Down below the priest had reached the woods and soon he disappeared in the direction of Penybwlch.

Dishonest little man, limited by his introverted Welsh world. William the Great indeed! Hadn't the conspirators in Ty Bach talked about Llewelyn and the mountains of Snowdonia? Did these idiots really think they could hole up in the hills like a medieval prince and see off the forces of law and order with their popguns? As for William's cousin Elwyn, a shepherd who was a top notch computer expert! Tell me another!

She turned to look across the moors to the further mountains, long since clear of snow. The wind gusted round her in this exposed spot and for a moment she heard, felt and perceived the love that is God permeating everything that existed. She was most deeply understood and forgiven, as if a kindly voice silenced her internal critic and a friendly hand was stretched out to her in encouragement.

How could there be a hell? A place where love is not?

She stood on the threshold of comprehension but she did not go through the open door.

The moment faded.

She knew Emmanuel would explain it as a delusion of the devil who can appear to us in angel's clothing.

*

'Heh Mum. Grab this.'

Rachel went into Ben's room where he was supposed to be doing his homework. Water cascaded from the broken gutter down the outside of his window and into the yard beneath. The trees rocked and creaked as their branches waved. Rain and wind, the eternal rain and wind. Drowning thought, sweeping away beliefs.

'I thought your Welsh composition had to be handwritten,' she began as he pointed to something on the yapp screen.

'Hate writing.'

'Everyone has to learn how to write.'

'They don't. William can't.'

'You don't want to grow up illiterate like him.'

He pouted. 'But look what I've logged into, Mum.'

Rachel gave in and looked. And stared.

Hilary was finishing a sentence, then the screen switched to Shuji.

'How d'you access their e-phone?'

'Fiddling around.'

'We shouldn't listen. It's private.' She faded the sound.

'They're talking about Dad.'

She upped the sound.

'It was horrid. They said . . . '

'Shut up, Ben,' she said, grabbing the yapp from him. He held onto it and they tussled, shouting at each other. She smacked his hand sharply, swearing. He cursed her in Welsh as he let go, but she ignored him and ran back to her room, shutting the door firmly. He banged on the door but she ignored him until eventually he stopped.

She aligned the yapp with her wall screen and a huge Shuji stared into her eyes. Automatically she turned her head away though she knew she was invisible to him. She reduced the picture to manageable proportions.

He was saying, ' . . . but it wasn't right.'

Hilary's face appeared, frowning. 'How can you doubt the Inner Council? He would have destroyed everything. Remember in the day of glory *we* shall judge the angels. The coming reign of peace and love justifies anything we do to hasten the Lord's return.'

Shuji passive face appeared. He nodded agreement before changing the subject. 'Jenny found nothing. I'm sure she hasn't got it.'

'I agree. Do we really need to keep her on board now?'

They were talking about *her*. Rachel felt cold. So her room *had* been searched last month. What had Jenny been looking for? How different was Hilary's contemptuous tone from that sparkling praise out on the hill a week ago!

'She's no high flier,' Shuji replied, 'but she's hard working and competent in her field. Amenable. Keen to learn Christian doctrine. And there's James.'

'Ah yes. She told me her first marriage was unhappy.'

155

How dare the woman!

'It'll be good for James too.' Shuji smiled obsequiously at his superior.

'I'm concerned Alyson might tell her.'

'That's sorted. I spoke to Eric this morning.'

Rachel resolved to question Alyson at the first opportunity.

Hilary turned to the smuggling. 'I've sacked my captain and the University will find me an English captain instead. The priest?'

'Reported to his bishop, an Eckstazia supporter. I told her that Tomos preaches liberal doctrine explaining away Jesus is merely human and salvation is universal.'

'In spite of my continual remonstrations. How will people repent and turn away from their sin if they think they'll be welcomed into heaven whatever they do?'

'I also told the Bishop the priest coordinates the black market. She was horrified.'

Hilary smiled. 'So it'll collapse quietly. Unless Parry?'

Shuji said contemptuously. 'A stupid oaf. He can't even sign his name. He's useful to me, and he'll do as he's told, so I shan't sack him yet.'

Hilary's attractive face quivered on the screen. 'Everything's co-ordinated this end. Jennifer Beard's ready?'

Sections of the screen blanked out so Rachel couldn't see Shuji's face but his few words were clear enough. 'Easter, as we planned. But. . .' Again there was unusual uncertainty in his voice.

'Doubts, Shuji? We've been into this before. No doubts. The Rapture is coming. Jesus . . . ' and then the whole screen went dark and silent. Hard though she tried Rachel couldn't make contact again.

'Ben!' she called, hurrying to his room. He was sitting on his bed scribbling in a notebook which he shut hastily. He looked up at her, his face a blotchy red. 'What did they say about Dad?'

'Can't remember.'

'It's important. Do try.'

'Get lost.' He stared at the window, the wall. Anywhere but her.

Only now did she think just how unpleasant she'd been to him. 'I was over the top,' she apologised.

'Like yesterday.'

He was right. She was always edgy these days. 'I shouldn't have sworn at you. And don't you use bad language either, dear. Don't copy William.' She sat beside him and reached out her arm but he moved away. Hiding his face he told her, 'They said Dad was a horrible man.'

'Dad was a dear man. Clever. Kind.'

'And something about tubers.'

'*Tubers? And Dad?*'

'Yeah. Doesn't make sense. And he'd something they wanted rid of. They searched his files after he died and couldn't find it.'

'They searched . . . ?' She couldn't believe it. Those kind Eckstazia friends who'd helped her sort his belongings before encouraging her to bin the lot? Those carers who'd taken turns to nurse her ailing mother so tenderly while Rachel was teaching? Plenty of opportunity to scour the flat. 'Anything else?'

'*You* came in then.' He was aggrieved.

'They're wrong. Dad didn't have anything about Eckstazia. I'd know, wouldn't I?' She fingered the pendant on her necklace then put her arm round him and this time he didn't move away. 'Don't worry about it, dear. Let's look to the future. It's the weekend and you'll love the castle tomorrow. It's a wonderful place, they say, full of dungeons and towers. Real ones.'

'Not going.'

'Why ever not?'

'Dad's in hell.'

In spite of all Eckstazia's teaching she cried out, 'Of course he isn't. Who said that? William?'

'Course not. William doesn't say things like that. James said.'

She couldn't believe James would be so cruel. 'What did he say?'

'Dad was an unbeliever and unbelievers don't go to heaven when they die.'

'Jesus loves him as much as we do. Even more. He was a *good* man.'

'James said I must forget about him because soon I'll have a new dad. Are you going to marry him?'

'Yes. No. Oh, I just don't know, dear. He's very fond of you.'

'Hate him.' He snuggled closer. 'Where's heaven, Mum? I don't want heaven if Dad's not there.'

'Nor me,' she sighed. They wept together for a while for their shared loss.

He recovered first. '*I'll* look after you, Mum. You don't need James.'

'Thank you, my love,' she said softly. After a pause she continued, 'I don't want you to see William, dear.'

'He's wicked.'

'The *bad* sort of wicked.'

'And I like Toss.'

'He's not a good man. He's running an illegal business.'

'I know *that*,' Ben said scornfully. 'He's very angry about Tomos.'

'Tomos?'

'I like Tomos. He makes me laugh in church. He's going away.'

'Going where?'

'He came to see William this morning.'

So that was where the priest was heading when she met him on the mountain.

Ben continued, 'He's been sacked. Sent a long way away. Why do nice people always go away, Mum?'

'That's how it is sometimes. Other nice ones come.'

He wasn't listening. 'William says he's a really good man. The reason he's so thin is because he eats the same food as poor people. He gives them his rations. D'you know William's friend has a boy my age who died of hunger?'

'Don't believe everything William tells you. People don't die of starvation in Britain.'

'Tomos hid wool for people's clothes in a shed,' Ben said excitedly. 'It's behind our church where we go every Sunday. I'm going to look next time.'

'It's empty now. The police are watching it.'

'William says he'll. . .' and Ben drew his finger across his throat and gurgled convincingly. 'If ever he finds out who snitched on Tomos.'

'William has a bad temper. Remember he's threatened to take you away from me.'

He began to cry but he ordered her to go away when she tried to comfort him. How could she protect him from the heartaches of life? She was terrified by William's hold over him and furious about James's heavy handling.

She ran downstairs and burst into the lounge. 'James, I must speak with you.'

James and Shuji looked up in amazement at her flushed red face.

Shuji said, 'The avenging angel herself! Whatever is the matter, Rachel?'

'Shuji and I are very busy at the moment,' James said a little reprovingly. 'Give us an hour.'

'No, no. Get it over and done with, James, and then we can continue our discussion. I'm sure what Rachel has to say is of greater importance.' Shuji stared at her expectantly.

'In private, James,' she insisted.

'You can hardly expect Shuji to leave the room.'

'We can talk in the dining room.'

James sighed and heaved himself out of his comfortable chair.

As they crossed the hall he said amiably, 'Now the evenings are getting longer I'll have to teach you to ride. You'll love it over the moors.'

But she ignored him and burst out, 'How dare you tell Ben his father's in hell suffering torment for ever and ever?'

James sighed. He sat heavily on one of the upright chairs, lent his elbows on the polished table top and stared at her. 'Of course I didn't, Rachel. Do you really think I'd be so crass? I merely told him very gently his father hadn't accepted Jesus as his Saviour, so he wouldn't be in heaven.'

'So where is he then if he isn't in heaven? In purgatory?'

'Pugatory's just make believe. There's nothing in the bible about such a place.'

'So where does that leave Dan? Ben isn't a fool. He knew what you meant.'

'My dear Rachel, we just don't know where he is. Blotted out of existence perhaps.'

'Eternal bereavement,' she cried out. 'Is that what God demands of us?'

He patted her shoulder in bewilderment. 'Do calm yourself. It's not your problem. Your husband made his own decision not to believe, so leave the matter in God's good hands and stop worrying. These speculations can send people mad, and we don't want *that*, do we?' As she sat silently, head bowed, he continued, 'In this life we must live in faith that all will be well. In heaven all our tears will be wiped away and we'll know everything was for the best. There you'll forget all about Daniel.'

'*Forget? Forget?* If I'm to forget those I love what's been the use of living? They're part of me. Without them I'm only a fraction of a person.' She hesitated before crying out, 'Surely you understand I'd rather spend eternity suffering with my dear husband than be in heaven with a God who's condemned my beloved?'

'What an extraordinary outburst! And where does that leave *me?*'

She rubbed her eyes with her hand. 'I'm sorry,' she whimpered. 'I don't know. I can't work it out. I. . .'

He handed her his handkerchief. 'You're making your face very blotchy. Now I'll be quite honest with you, Rachel. For your own happiness, because you aren't happy are you?'

She shook her head, staring blindly at her dark uneven reflection on the table top. Patterns from its long dead tree were etched eerily across her image and unconsciously she counted the lines. Far away James' voice floated over her head.

159

'Please believe me when I say I find this whole matter very distressing, my dear. But however painful it may be, we must be open with each other.' He cleared his throat and she jerked to attention. 'It's for the best that Ben knows the truth. That you must agree. It's important for his future, for his relationships with others and the whole orientation of his life.'

She thought of her son's stricken face. 'You'll make him hate Jesus.'

'No, *you're* causing that by your rebellious attitude. Think carefully about your duty to the boy. You've been entrusted with the awesome responsibility of bringing him up to love the Lord, yet you're infecting him with your own doubts. Be your own sternest critic. Isn't your behaviour self-indulgent? Doesn't it show dereliction of care? Ben has a precious soul. You're answerable for the way you nurture it.'

She answered sadly, 'He's most upset. He refuses to go with us to the castle tomorrow.'

'Then you must change his mind. We already missed last Sunday's trip because of him. He has to get over these whims before we marry.'

'If he doesn't. . . ?'

'Really, Rachel, will you let our future together be decided by the fancies of a little boy? Take control of your own life, for goodness sake. Read Emmanuel's site on good parenting. Now I must continue my discussion with Shuji. You can keep the hanky.'

160

Chapter 11

Rachel dropped her yapp on the table. What use would it be on her trip to the castle with Ben? The town was so small and quiet it was impossible to get lost or to be in danger. And the wretched thing reminded her of work. Today was holiday.

They called at Alyson's cottage, but Freya said Mum was busy at the moment. Some other time. Alyson's secret remained hidden for the moment.

William still hadn't repaired the bicycles.

'We can't go,' Ben whined. 'Can't you mend them, Mum?'

'I could if I had inner-tube patches. We'll see if we can get some at a garage in town but we'll have to walk there.' She sighed. There wouldn't be this problem if Ben had agreed to include James in the party. They'd have travelled in comfort in James' car instead of walking down the winding road in a drizzle of rain.

Ben broke into her thoughts. 'William told me there's a quick way to town across the hillside past Plas Du. I know where the path starts.'

As they walked on the springy turf the sun shimmered through the watery sky. It would be fine soon. Rachel's heart lifted as she told Ben, 'James is going to teach me to ride. Would you like to learn too?'

'Dunno.'

'Like Hereward Swordhand?' He was the current boys' hero, one eyed rider of an eight legged horse and saviour of the planet Serebos circling Tau Ceti eleven light years away.

Ben didn't reply and they walked on in friendly silence.

During the night Rachel had tussled with her doubts and reluctantly accepted James was right. Dan had made his own choice and she must leave her distress over his eternal suffering in God's hands. James had certainly been heavy-handed with Ben, but on the whole his involvement was good for her son, not least because of the contrast with crass and treacherous William. Now she must help her son overcome his natural indignation with James.

As her father had once told her, it was a woman's job to keep the peace. A job, he said with a sneer, at which his own wife had patently failed. Rachel had decided then and there to be one who turns conflict into harmony, unlike her mother. Privately she blamed her for the family break-up and this poorly hidden contempt had marred their final years together. Once the older woman said with the liberty and insight of the dying, 'You've never loved me, have you?' Rachel had protested loudly to hide her confusion. Today, briefly remembering her mother she brushed any uneasiness aside. Of course she had loved her. Hadn't she given up her research work in Liverpool to care for her in her final years? Hadn't she accepted the older woman's many faults? Deep down she felt blind and savage resentment against her internal critic. Unacknowledged anger and therefore dangerous.

She shifted her rucksack of sandwiches and water more comfortably on her shoulders as they climbed a stile by a locked gate.

'We're crossing Plas Du's land now,' Ben said.

The hillside was sheltered from the perpetual wind by tall shrubs of gorse that blocked their view until they reached a bracken clearing. As the sun came out fully it lit up the house. It was merely a couple of hundred yards away and from this angle they could see it was built on a slight eminence, not into the hillside like Penybwlch. Cultivated varieties of early azalea in crimson, cream and yellow flower nestled against it. The terraces stretched down towards the curving drive but none of the fountains was working. Rachel noticed a grassy helicopter pad some distance from the house. There's luxury, she sighed.

Yet for all its beauty and opulence there was something ominous about the place. Plas Du, Black Mansion. She shivered.

'The back roofs slope right into the ground and they're covered in grass,' Ben said, peering through his mother's binoculars.

'It's zero carbon designed. Makes its own energy. Doesn't need wind power.'

They both turned to look back at Penybwlch's large white wind pump circling its arms in the wind.

'There's William,' Ben said. 'And Toss. Near the woods. D'you think he can see us?'

'He'll have us spotted.' Rachel suppressed a shudder.

The path continued towards the house until they were brought to a halt by a six foot fence of chainlink with barbed wire along the top. Beyond it was a second lower fence.

'Surveillance wired,' Ben said. 'Touch it and you trigger cameras relayed to the house. William told me.'

The public path had once gone past the house, but was now reangled to run parallel to the fence in both directions.

Ben said. 'I vote we go up.'

'Agreed. Down will take us back to the road.'

'Plas Du means black house.'

'That's because the front roof is black.'

'Solar tiles. Who lives there, Mum?'

'Professor Hilary Barron when she's not at Liverpool University or advising government or chairing Elstazia's Central Council.'

'Is she very posh?'

'You met her once. That smart woman in the church on our first visit.'

Ben wrinkled his nose. 'Can't remember.'

'She e-foned Shuji yesterday.'

'That woman was Hilary? She was horrid about Dad.'

'She ran me down too, though when I met her a week ago she was full of sweet talk.' Rachel's anger at Hilary was all the more intense because of guilt. Why had she told the woman that she and Dan hadn't been happy? Tacitly agreed he was mentally sick in those last weeks? Hilary's charm seduced the unwary into confidences that should be kept private. No wonder the woman was so successful.

She was furious that Jennifer had searched her room. She'd tried but failed to reset the key code so her room remained open to any of her colleagues who wanted to spy. And how dared her Eckstazia friends search Dan's belongings? Pretending kindness and concern to fool her. How that hurt. And all for nothing, because there was nothing to find.

So why were Eckstazia still so concerned? Shuji, Emmanuel and Hilary had all told her to get rid of Dan's remaining possessions, so obviously they feared something to the discredit of the movement. Yet as far as she was aware Dan's increasing contempt for Eckstazia in the last month of his life wasn't based on any evidence. She'd searched extensively for the polemical article Shuji had claimed Dan published but as it hadn't turned up she doubted its existence.

Probably the whole thing was an over-reaction to some minor criticism. Like Shuji's anger when she'd joked Emmanuel could be an android. Eckstazia members were so very concerned to display an impeccable image to the world of sinners. 'So that some may be saved when they see our good works,' one of her Coventry helpers had quoted biblically when she asked why they were being so kind to her, a stranger. She'd been impressed by their selflessness at the time. Easily encouraged to join an organisation that did so much good in the world.

As for Shuji's anxieties so quickly contradicted by Hilary ... What was all that about?

Barking disturbed her. A couple of Alsatians raced through the long grass and leapt up onto the inner fence snarling, ears back. As mother and son set off up the hill the dogs ran parallel, growling inhospitably until they grew bored and trotted back towards the building.

'Don't think the Prof likes visitors,' Ben remarked.

Soon they came to the end of Plas Du's estate, climbed another stile and were out onto the open hillside. Rachel stopped to inspect some strange grassy hollows at one point. 'Iron age village, I guess. The hills are full of old structures. There's a druid circle on the high moor.' She pointed across the valley towards the far mountains, covered in their usual cloud. 'I'll take you one day. And Ben, whenever you're walking in a new place look back over your shoulder from time to time. Memorize the route. Then you'll always find the way home.'

The bridle path turned towards the town and soon they were looking down over the eight towers of the castle. The Dis-Union Jack flag had been replaced by a black flag with a golden cross but the dragon flew as proudly as ever. Sunlight flickered over the grey-brown walls as cloud shadows raced across it and momentarily darkened the wooded hillsides beyond.

Ben stared long and hard through the binoculars. 'The Welsh must be very clever to build that. How old is it?'

'I've no idea. James said it would be open by eleven so let's go straight there.'

The newer houses and gardens spread out well beyond the town walls. As they wandered through suburban streets she forgot her own injunction to look back and memorize the way they'd come. They stared into weed filled gardens with garden sheds and greenhouses rotted and collapsing.

'What a mess.' Ben stared at the houses critically. 'Slates missing. Wood bare and cracked. Windows stuffed with cloth.'

'It looked far better from a distance,' she agreed. 'People are certainly poor here. As bad as the worst bits of Coventry.'

'Why don't they grow vegetables if they're so short of food?'

'They're inside the restricted zone.'

'What's that?'

'Too close to the reserve. Domestic plants can escape into the wild and destroy the natural vegetation we're trying to recover. Like rhododendrons brought from the Far East did two centuries ago.'

'Penybwlch's got masses of those.'

'It's one of William's jobs to destroy them, but he can't be bothered.'

Ben said thoughtfully, 'So has Plas Du. And a vegetable garden.'

'I wondered about those too.'

They walked along the main road where grass grew in clumps through bulging tarmac. Eventually they entered the old town through its medieval archway. Here the houses had no gardens, only small yards at the back. Buildings were neglected. Sticky tape held cracked glass together. Fissures penetrated the denatured wood of unpainted sills, doors and window frames and yellowing plastic frames bowed dangerously.

Apart from a few scavenging dogs and some dirty children playing round a central statue in the square, the place seemed as deserted as on their first visit. The statue itself was so damaged its pedigree was uncertain. Papers and plastic bags drifted around it, blocking its disused water bowl.

Rachel and Ben stumbled across trendy cobbles laid a few years ago in expectation of continuing tourism, now pitted where the stones had loosened in substandard mortar.

She had visited the shops a few times and was unimpressed by the goods on offer and the sullen service. Spring was almost here yet no one was painting or tidying up for the approaching summer. No one anticipated droves of wealthy tourists. Behind the glass frontages of once busy teashops lay heaps of unanswered and unwanted mail.

The castle glowered over them, clutching at the sky with its four turrets atop the main towers. The stones were massive, the rock foundations impenetrable to sappers.

Its entrance lobby was unmanned and locked. They thumped a bell, called out. Only the circling ravens answered. Then, slowly with a decrepitude in keeping with the ancient fortress, an old man shuffled across the empty car park, unlocked the kiosk and supported himself on its counter. He demanded entrance money and asked if the young man was interested in a plastic kit of the castle.

The young man was. He handed over his pocket money.

'Built in the late 1200s,' Rachel read in the flyspotted leaflet the keeper gave her. 'And it was an English colonial town, not Welsh at all. The Welsh weren't even allowed to live in it. Part of Edward the First's iron ring of castles to keep the Welsh under control.'

'I know him. He fought with Llewelyn ap Gruffydd, Llewelyn the last, prince of all Wales who married Elinor who was daughter of Simon de Montfort who was an enemy of Henry the Third who was Edward's father,' Ben said in one breath.

Rachel laughed. 'They've taught you something at school then.' She read aloud, 'Today the statue of Llewelyn the Great stands proudly in the town square.' So that was Annie and William's ancestor. Crumbling and undistinguished. Very apt.

The old man spoke from behind them in singsong tones, 'Here is the Great Hall. Unique. Bowshaped because it follows the curve of the rock outcrop beneath.'

As she could read in the leaflet for herself. But no doubt he'd hold out his hand for a tip as they left. He could certainly do with money to buy some decent clothes. She wondered at a tourist industry that allowed its employees to look such ragamuffins. She wrinkled her nose. Unwashed as well.

Ben looked up at the flags and the custodian said, 'Both are flags of Wales, young man. We fly the black and gold of St David for a month after his holy day. We aren't included on your flag. It only represents Northern Ireland and England.' He sounded angry.

Rachel was watching some people working at the base of one of the towers in the outer ward and Ben took the leaflet. 'That's the Prison Tower. Dungeons,' and he started to make his way there.

'Can't go there, young man,' said the custodian. 'Not safe.'

'It says *here* I can,' Ben pointed out.

'Leaflet's wrong. Tourist board don't spend anything these days on upkeep. Roof collapse.'

'But those people there are going in and out,' the boy persisted angrily. 'They haven't got hard hats or anything like that.'

'That's the rules,' the man said nonchalantly, but he nodded at the workers and a man with broad shoulders marched towards them. He stood in front of them quietly with his hands by his sides, but every line of his body was threatening.

Rachel pulled Ben's hand and they crossed the drawbridge into the inner ward and the private apartments of the king.

'Edward was besieged here,' she said to him, leaflet in hand. 'But the castle stood firm against the Welsh.'

'Owain Glyndwr captured it once.' He ran up the spiral staircase in one of the towers and she followed him.

The view made them gasp. The castle stood guard above three bridges crossing a turbulent river cramped into a narrow passage by a long cob of land. The cob jutted out from the further shore of the estuary and along it ran a road and a disused railway. These crossed the river and disappeared below them. On the far side of the estuary low hills were covered with houses as far as the eye could see.

Rachel pointed to them. 'That's the town we visited with James. It's got much better shops than this one, but too far without bikes.'

'Shush, Mum. What are they doing down by the dungeons?'

A man entered the main gate with an empty industrial trolley and others stacked it with boxes and packages from the dungeon. Meanwhile the custodian remonstrated with them, pointing towards the inner ward as if reminding them Rachel and Ben might be watching. The group stood still for a moment, arguing.

'William's little helpers,' she said.

Ben was serious. 'I thought you said the black market's disbanded.'

'I thought it was. It's more widespread than we thought. Is anyone *not* involved in it?'

By the time Rachel and Ben left the castle the men had disappeared except for the bruiser who watched them truculently, arms akimbo, legs apart. His stare unnerved them and they scuttled out past the custodian, slapping a small coin in his cupped hand, and hurried down to the quay. Here in the shelter of the town wall they unpacked their sandwiches, disturbed only by hungry seagulls.

'The store's closed,' Ben said, pointing to the brick building where they'd collected fish for Annie on their first day at Penybwlch. It looked even more dilapidated now. Grass grew out of the broken guttering and groundsel flourished in the cracked paving in front of the two great doors. The smaller entrance door was padlocked.

'Where's that riot truck going?' Ben watched it drive across the cob of land, over one of the bridges and vanish beneath the castle walls.

'Trouble somewhere along the coast,' Rachel said.

She watched an elderly man approach them along the deserted quay. There was something familiar about the steady confidence of his gait as if time and space both belonged to him. Like all local people he was poorly dressed. Well-worn trousers, scuffed down-at-heel shoes, a jacket mossgreen with age and its lining hanging out. His hair was granite grey and his face craggy with age.

'Mrs Kerem,' he said and his voice was familiar too. 'It will be best if you and Ben leave the town by the harbour gateway as soon as possible.'

Ben interrupted him excitedly. 'I know who you are. You're Parryboots, William's Dad.'

Of course. She'd heard him in Ty Bach with the other conspirators and glimpsed him from her window. William certainly didn't favour his father. He had his mother's thin cruel features.

'Why boots?' Ben asked

Parryboots' face softened. 'I started work as a lad in a shoe shop, delivering orders to villages and farms. So Boots it was, and the name's stuck with me.' Then he turned back to Rachel, staring at her with hostile eyes.

'And why can't we go through the town?' she asked aggressively.

He raised one bristly grey eyebrow. 'Please, Mrs Kerem. Think a little. You're known to have passed information on illegal trading to Dr Akimoto, causing us no end of problems. You're unwelcome here on market day.'

Market day? So the men in the castle were shifting illegal goods in preparation.

'You're unsafe. People hate you.'

'Because I'm honest? Because I dislike you getting rich at the expense of everyone else?'

The old man hrrmphed in disbelief. 'William told me how ignorant you are.' From his pocket he took his plastic ration card and waved it at her. '*You* say this system's fair. But it doesn't work out that way. The total quantity of food and clothing's so reduced that it's barely more than in wartime Britain ninety years ago. Cities riot for a return to the cheap abundance that's gone for ever. To calm them down part of our share is sent to Cardiff and Swansea and English cities. Yes, we have ration cards. But we don't have the food or the clothes. We're only a country area so the Welsh Assembly ignores our calls for help and Westminster are merely concerned with the escalating riots in English cities. So we run small bartering markets in towns and villages. We ask around and people gladly give what they can so we can distribute to the very poor. Farmers give food, wool, and hides. . . .'

'Surely the agricultural department notices the discrepancies?'

'We're adept at adding a little here, subtracting a little there. Hiding bits in the paperwork.'

'And keeping animals illegally on the reserve!' she attacked. She hadn't been treated to such a lecture since she was a schoolgirl.

'Wales is a poor country so we've chosen to accept European grants and cover much of our land in these reserves, mistakenly in my view. No wonder people here hate them because they deprive us of food.'

Rachel protested, 'But our wildlife flourishes. And it's better to trade more fairly and buy our food from countries producing it more cheaply than we can.'

'Things have changed. World-wide people want the same standard of living we've enjoyed in the west. Higher wages for a start. The Chinese have improved their diets and so have less food to export. The Americans suffer from climate change and no longer export wheat. Old colonial countries sense opportunity in our ever-increasing need for their crops. They raise their prices because aren't they merely getting back some of the profit we made from them in the past?

'So we're highly taxed and debts are huge. Supermarkets collapse because their customers can no longer afford rapidly rising prices. And things won't get better. Population increases above sustainable levels. Don't forget global warming. Every year more good agricultural land world-wide is blighted. Lowland is flooded by the rising sea. Deserts expand in central China, Australia and huge areas of Russia.'

Angered by his domineering tone she railed, 'None of this excuses your profiteering.'

Parryboots said bitterly, 'You don't even see us as human, do you, Mrs Kerem? We're just ignorant Welsh proles to you and your friends.'

'I wish I'd never found out what's going on. But I *do* know now. And I won't be an accomplice to fraud and tax evasion.'

'And your own organisation, Mrs Kerem? Is Eckstazia totally honest? You and your fellow scientists don't rely on ration cards alone, do you? You feed far better than anyone else in this area. Oranges! Bananas!' He made a sound of disgust.

Ben stared from one to the other. 'I *like* bananas.'

They ignored him.

'Do as you wish, Mrs Kerem. You've had plenty of warnings.' Parryboots turned his back on them and strode away.

'Why's William's Dad so angry with us?' Ben asked.

'He's an ignorant moron,' Rachel shouted, and her son shrank away. Her boiling rage engulfed her so completely that she ignored Ben's fear of her anger. How dare the Welshman harangue her so! He reminded her of . . . she struggled to dredge the memory up from her subconscious. It was surely her overbearing father and his criticisms of her. Though she had felt herself forgiven when on the mountain with Tomos, she was unable to extend the same to her disparaging parent. This fuelled her anger against Parryboots.

'I'm not being intimidated by *him*,' she said through clenched teeth. 'Come on,' and she stalked off in the direction Parryboots had taken.

'He told us to go *that* way, Mum.' Ben trotted after her, pointing away from the town towards the lower harbour gate.

'*You* can go that way if you want.'

He hesitated, obviously afraid, then scurried after her.

Behind them screeching gulls tore apart the remnants of their sandwiches.

*

After a short distance Rachel stopped. 'Listen,' she said.

Cart wheels rumbling over uneven ground. A subdued chatter of Welsh voices. Then hurrying footsteps. A woman appeared from a quayside cottage with a sack over her shoulder. She exclaimed on seeing Ben and Rachel and scurried away.

As the pair followed her they saw the high street was now crowded with trestles where men and women worked among them hefting sacks and boxes. Farm produce stalls were packed with eager purchasers, mainly women in headscarves with shopping trolleys and bags. Root vegetables recently lifted from clamps were still encrusted with earth.

Among bundles of early greens grown in cold frames and greenhouses lay eggs brown with hen shit. Flour was ladled into customers' bags from paper sacks similar to those William had stored at Penybwlch. Other trestles were loaded with old tools, spades, picks, chipped chisels, screwdrivers and hammers. Compartments of shallow wooden boxes were filled with rusting nails, screws and washers of different gauges, assorted window fastenings and boiler maintenance kits in unsealed bags. Men hunted for vehicle spare parts from radiators to tractor transmission belts. Women squabbled over second-hand clothes and cut offs of coarse local cloth. Unsurprisingly no ammunition or shotguns were on display but Rachel was convinced trading in those was going on behind the scenes.

'So this is where the men in the dungeons were bringing their goods,' Ben whispered, because it was striking just how quiet the whole operation was. Rachel and Ben were used to the lively street markets in Coventry where traders sang out their wares. But here, though the street was clogged with trestles, goods and shoppers, everyone bargained in undertones, elbowing anxiously from one stall to the next as they proffered their own goods.

Something was strange about the whole business and after a moment Rachel realised what it was. Little cash was changing hands.

She wasn't surprised that nobody used a finance card to pay for goods. Far too incriminating. The European Union now regulated all personal finance cards, ensuring they were issued to every citizen. Cards were fairer, they announced. Tax credits could be added more efficiently guaranteeing the poorest never went without. The underlying reason was that surveillance police could monitor all transactions. But though paper and coin had fallen into disuse they were still in circulation for occasional dealings between small shops and traders. And, because cash is untraceable, for black market goods. Yet here shoppers bartered in kind. Potatoes for cloth, a shovel for eggs, fresh milk for a pint of beer.

Rachel was amazed by the orderly exchanges made so quietly. Then she realised an ominous silence was spreading through the market as the townspeople turned from their muted chatter to stare at them. Then menacing whispers shivered through the crowd.

'What's the matter?' Ben said in his shrill treble.

Rachel hushed him, putting her arm round him as the crowd opened as if to entrap them. Remembering the intimidation she had encountered occasionally in Coventry from feral youths, she turned nervously to make a retreat, but already a row of men stood behind them watching her coldly.

So the pair walked slowly forward. A woman spat in front of them and Rachel thought she recognised her from the shop on the quay. The crowd muttered more loudly and now she picked out the Welsh words.

'That's horrid.' Ben understood them too. He returned a few of them in Welsh and a woman stepped out and slapped his cheek, calling him a wicked boy. He cried out angrily and made a fist at the woman.

Rachel grabbed him and hissed, 'Keep going.'

'But Mum, she said . . . '

Rachel squeezed his arm savagely.

'Ouch, you hurt.' Angry tears filled his eyes.

They were three quarters way up the street when a loudhailer crackled gibberish at full volume. Police whistles screeched. Sirens howled. Riot police approached in a fixed line from the far end of the street and when Rachel turned she saw more penning them in at the other end. Their mailed fists held combat shotguns. Their shock shields, black and shining as a dor beetle's carapace, could throw off any attacker with brute electric pulses. Rows of gigantic warrior ants, all alike in goggles and helmets, incapable of human compassion, impregnable.

Rachel had seen riot control in both Liverpool and Coventry. Before the first teargas canister was fired she seized Ben's arm even more fiercely and dragged the terrified boy towards a nearby alley.

By now helicopters roared overhead. Pilots shouted incomprehensible orders. All around traders and shoppers panicked, obstructing every exit. Some tried to pack their wares away before the approaching police kicked the trestles over. Vegetables, tools, crockery clattered and smashed to the ground. Flour rose in white choking clouds mingling with the stench of sweaty fear and the reek of spilt biofuels and broken beer casks. Coughing and spluttering increased as tear gas spread. Shoppers rubbed smarting eyes, ran in wild disorientation or collapsed among the debris.

A large man tried to protect a woman who was scrabbling at her smashed eggs, bright yellow yolk dribbling through mudbrown fingers. Suddenly he leapt into the air, his shriek nonhuman in its intensity. As he convulsed to the ground Rachel recognised him as the man who'd threatened them at the castle. She also spotted the policeman who'd floored him. He was aiming his pulsed energy projectile launcher in her direction.

In a frenzy she bulldozed her way down the alley entrance, hitting out wildly at equally hysterical people, treading on fallen goods and possibly bodies, lugging Ben after her. But her grip failed and he ran back into the melee and away from her, disappearing in the chaos.

Hysterical now, she tried to follow him but a surge in the crowd carried her in the opposite direction through the alley and into a broad churchyard full of terrified people. She had no idea where she was. Again she attempted to force her way back, screaming in panic for Ben, but the mass of fleeing folk crushed her against a gravestone, winding her. Then she was jerked savagely to her feet and kicked on the shin and her arms forced upwards behind her back in excruciating pain.

'Got you.' A rough male voice, speaking Welsh.

He slackened his grip and she turned to stare into the young malevolent face of a complete stranger. Another yob yanked her hair, swearing words so filthy she didn't know them. Two or three others joined them grinning at her evilly, enjoying her terror.

They pulled her across the cemetery, discussing in English what they'd do to her. Rape was the mildest punishment.

'And your brat. We've got him.'

She bit her captor's arm and he yelled, packing his punch towards her eye. She twisted her head away and he caught her ear, deafening her. Then he rammed a dirty rag into her mouth, tying it fiercely behind her head. Her arms were twisted, her foot trodden on and her ribs punched.

Together they forced her into a quiet corner. They pulled off her jacket and ripped her blouse so her breasts were naked. One lout fondled them, leering.

They argued among themselves, one fumbling at her trousers and demanding to have a go at her then and there. The leader demurred. He was for public shaming and he won the day.

They propelled her down several streets till they reached a place she knew, the central square, full of terrified people. Here they pushed her upright against the shabby statue of the great Llewelyn, so everyone could see her half-nakedness.

Those nearest hooted at her and the threatening crowd increased, hatred in every eye. Someone tore up a loose cobble and she flinched, waiting for the pain, but the stone missed. Others followed suit and she knew her end was near. She collapsed, unable to display the courage of fabled martyrs.

But the stones didn't come.

Instead she heard a woman remonstrating in Welsh, but she was too stressed to cope with translation. Some of the crowd argued with the woman, and Rachel caught the name Olwen . . . but still no stones. Then the bandage was wrenched from her mouth and she was hauled, none too gently, to her feet. She slumped against the statue base as one of the louts patted her shoulder and whispered derisively, 'We'll keep an eye open for you.' Then her captors swaggered off.

The once-hostile crowd turned away to face the black riot vehicles now standing guard around banks and public buildings. A police line held weapons at the ready, their heavy masks hiding contemptuous eyes as they observing the trembling riffraff. Some fool-hardy souls chucked the loose cobbles intended for Rachel at the police. They were immediately half-stunned and thrust into the waiting vehicles.

Rachel was alone with a stern elderly woman, angular as Annie, who looked contemptuously at her. 'He told you to go. Now go.'

Rachel quavered, 'Ben. *Ben.*'

But Olwen left her, making her way through the crowd to the upper end of the square where she joined a figure Rachel recognised. Parryboots. Directing people, easing the panic. He did not even glance in her direction, but she knew in her humiliation that he'd saved her.

Pulling her torn clothes round her, head down, limping, she staggered across the square and back to the medieval archway she and Ben had entered so happily a few hours ago. Once outside the old town she leaned on some railings and tried to collect her scattered thoughts.

Where was Ben? If she dared go back to hunt for him the hostile Welsh would surround her again. Perhaps the riot police rescued him? Surely they'd be kind to him? He was only a little boy. How could he be a threat to anyone?

She wiped her mouth and there was blood on her hand. She shook her head to combat the deafness in her left ear and then she heard shouts of 'Fire! Fire!'

People panicked again, rushing out through the archway past Rachel. They pointed hysterically back towards the market where evil black smoke billowed up from spilt fuels. The air was filling with the stench of rotted houses burning along with their contents.

If Ben was back there . . .?

A fire engine siren shrilled and dopplered into the town, scattering the fleeing crowd. Then another.

Above the chaos Rachel heard a high voice calling '*Mummy! Mummy!*' She was back in her nightmare trial that first night in Wales, the abduction of her son, the loss of all she held dear. Then she realised with a leap of hope that it was Ben himself calling her and a moment later his dear arms were round her and they clutched each other as if they would never let go.

'Did they hurt you?' Rachel whispered.

'Course not. Parryboots helped me.' And that was all he'd tell her. 'Come on. Let's get home.'

173

She swayed away from the supporting rails.

'Mum, what's happened? Your clothes? Your mouth?'

'I fell in the rush. Then some louts hurt me.' The pain in shin and ankle was hardly bearable.

'Did the police kill the man helping that woman?'

'I hope not.' How could she possibly know the amount of pain a body can stand before it pegs out? She knew the electromagnetic pulse caused maximum pain and temporary paralysis and was used as part of a strategy for non-lethal crowd control. But records of any ensuing deaths or permanent nervous debilitation were unavailable to the public since the passing of new anti-riot laws.

'We must go. Quickly,' she said, starting to shuffle away from the town.

'Not that way.'

'I can't remember.'

'I can. I looked back like you told me.'

She was so very slow. He said, 'Ring James. He'll bring the car.'

'I left the yapp at home.'

He led her through the streets outside the town and back to the mountain path. Wearily they climbed the hill, stopping frequently for Rachel to rest.

Ben said, 'That was scary.'

'You did well. I'm proud of you. But we must be careful. These people hate us.'

'Will you be safe, Mum?'

'Don't worry. I'll be OK.' But she couldn't convince herself of that. The mountains were full of hideyholes, of unsuspected hollows, crags, tumbled walls and occasional scrubby trees. Too easy for William or one of his friends to trace her lonely journeys. Rifles. Plenty of ammunition. Even if William kept his promise not to murder her there were plenty who would. Those fierce young thugs. The palpable hatred of the crowd.

They were crazy people, these Welsh. Tomos the priest had seemed decent enough but his ideas were way out. As for Parryboots and his starving poor, how bizarre was that.

Then she thought again of the thin pale children at Ben and Freya's schools. Lethargic dull children who didn't rush round the playground when school finished but trudged wearily home in small quiet groups. And *all* the people at the market looked so old. Thin hair, sunk cheeks, deepset eyes. Cadaverous. Had she ever seen healthy looking Welsh apart from the Bangor students who shared good lunches with the other scientists? Perhaps she'd been wrong. Perhaps . . . The idea nagged at her.

And another niggle surfaced. Parryboots had a point. Eckstazia certainly wasn't honest in its dealings with her. She must speak to Alyson as soon as possible.

Ben stopped suddenly. 'It's still smoking.'

From their vantage point on the hill they looked back at the town. The smoke rose lazily and thinly into the cold air. It was grey now not black, household grey, people's belongings. Embers.

He said, 'Someone lit the biofuel. Why?'

'Just happened. So much commotion.'

'No, Mum. I mean I *saw* someone light it. Policeman.'

She wanted to say they wouldn't do such a thing but she remembered the stony face of the man with the stun gun.

As she struggled over Penybwlch stile Ben gave a deep sigh.

'What's the matter?' she asked.

'I've lost my castle model. And we didn't get the puncture repair kit for the bikes.'

*

Rachel examined her wounds and bruises as she showered. Ribs, breasts and arms bruised. Shin and foot almost too painful to stand on. Mouth swollen and a tooth loosened. With Ben's help she went slowly downstairs to find the first aid. James accosted them in the hall.

'I hope you both enjoyed your trip to the castle,' he said in a tone showing he wished the opposite. He stood with arms folded across his broad chest. His face was unyielding.

Rachel collapsed onto the hall bench, hiding her bruised face.

'I was frightened,' Ben said. 'But I was brave, wasn't I Mum?'

James said, 'You don't need to be frightened of holes in the ground.'

'Holes?' they both asked.

'Dungeons.'

'It wasn't them frighted me.'

'Frightened,' Rachel corrected automatically through swollen lips.

James was unobservant. 'Whatever. You must learn to be strong in Jesus. Then you'll find the threatening things shrink into proportion and become of no consequence.'

'In this case he was right to be afraid,' Rachel defended him. 'But he acted with courage.'

'Your mother sees many excellent qualities in you, Ben. Quite right that a mother should. But she is somewhat overindulgent.'

175

'Overwhat?' Ben looked up at Rachel.

'Too soft with you.'

He looked puzzled. 'You jolly well hurt my arm.' He pulled back his sleeve and showed the fading squeeze marks.

'I'm glad to know she disciplines you occasionally. But your visit to the castle today . . . ' James frowned. 'You run off and play, Ben. I want to speak to your mother alone.'

Ben took a swift look at James's stern face and raced to the yard.

'No,' Rachel called. 'Come back.'

He scampered on.

James said, 'Let him go.'

'He's off to find William. Surely you don't approve?'

'There are a number of things that don't meet my approval. He's a stubborn and wayward young man. I regret to say this, Rachel, but it seems we're coming to the point where you must choose between having a loving stepfather for Ben who'll gently teach him discipline or . . . ' He hesitated.

'Yes, James?' But he didn't register the chill in her voice, or if he did he ignored it.

' . . . or rearing him on your own. I don't want to be unkind but I think you should ask yourself whether you're capable of combining the role of both parents. Whether you, a young and inexperienced woman, have the qualities necessary to rear Ben so he becomes a responsible and reliable citizen, a lover of the truth in Jesus.'

'I do my best . . . '

'I'm sure you try, but you need to let your mind be remade by the Spirit of God as St Paul tells us.' He paused to let his words sink in. 'I've every affection for you, dear. Indeed it's *because* you're so dear to me, it's my duty to warn you you're too easily deluded by our permissive society. What kind of adult will Ben become if you indulge his passing fancies and never teach him self control?'

She felt too weary to argue the point in spite of her anger.

'Give me your reasons for taking the boy on a treat when he refused to go with *me*.' James sounded hurt. 'I specifically said he must get over his whims, and here you are, rewarding him.'

She rubbed her ribs gingerly with her sound arm. 'I'm sorry it upsets you. But please consider his point of view. You insulted his father, so naturally he wouldn't want you to take him to the castle. But why should he miss out on a treat because he defended his father's memory? And he's my son, James, so if I want to take him on an outing I can.' She looked up at him.

At last he saw and he cried out, 'What's happened to your face?'

She told him about the riot and showed him her ankle. He exclaimed in horror once he saw the swelling. Helping her to her feet he took her to the first aid cupboard and wrapped her ankle and leg in a mediboot. Its soothing medication and electrical currents would soon ease the pain and reduce puffiness. But even as it soothed her she remembered the poor and wounded townspeople and their limited access to such luxuries.

He also bandaged her arm, saying he'd take her for a check up with Eckstazia's doctor. This she refused. Leaning against him she told him about her fears for her safety and Ben's.

He promised to contact the police inspector and advised her to suspend her monitoring of sites on Penybwlch's mountain until security could be arranged.

Gently he continued, 'I won't mention Ben's father to him again, my dear, since it upsets him so. And I'm getting quiet ponies for you both to learn to ride. You'll enjoy that once you're better. I've arranged a dispensation so we're allowed to graze them on the farm here.'

She thanked him but was so overwhelmed by the day's troubles she forgot her intention to question Alyson until it was too late.

Chapter 12

The beetle ambled round inside the pink bell of an early bilberry flower. It was unaware its body had collected pollen grains that it would dust on another flower's stigma, causing the growth of a new seed. Its legs were finer than a hair. Its feelers flickered as they collected information about its mini universe. Giant Rachel was far too huge to be comprehensible to its midget consciousness. So small and ignorant a life. So easily crushed by a careless giant.

Blind courage. Life coursing through insect blood and muscle, nerves and pinhead brain. Similar consciousness informed her too of warmth and cold, danger and food, mate and stranger. But the human range of choices was far wider and included the burden of self-awareness. To find her truth she must dissect her motives like the peeling of an onion, down to the inmost heart.

She lay on a heather bank, the spring sun warm on her back. Early solitary bees chuntered happily among the first flowers. Selfheal and bedstraw wove through mountain grasses. Trefoil rosettes of tormentil extended downy stems. On the lower mountain slopes silver birch thrust out baby leaves on delicate twigs and beneath them bluebell leaves grew rank, protecting developing flowers. Larch branches propelled delicate needles of bright green into the spring exuberance. Distantly a robin sang, but other birds were conspicuously absent. She hadn't seen wheatears returning to breed or heard the twittering of stonechats and 'zre,zre' of pipits. Plover, lapwing and curlew shunned any open fields and moors scanned by sparrowhawks and quartered by lynx. Only strident gulls soared far overhead where the restless wind troubled the clouds.

None of it reached her heart. She was as tormented as clouds, as agitated as gliding gulls. Yes, she'd promised James two days ago she'd restrict her monitoring to the woodland sites, but the hillside was warm in spring sunshine. So she'd weaved and ducked along the bridle path, searched the mountains long and hard with her binoculars and finally settled in this most isolated of hollows.

And still she was very afraid.

Paranoia. Was this how it started? Overwhelming fear becoming fixed in the mind until it can never be shaken off?

She prayed for safety with every fibre of her being, but lacked assurance that God would ward off any mad Welsh gunmen. Why should he protect such a sinner? Half waking this morning she'd dreamt vividly of James making love to her. Her sexual cries of satisfaction

178

had woken her to miserable loneliness. Was it sin to want sex? Was it OK if she dreamt of James like this? Emmanuel's website spoke of purity of thought. Lustful desires must be controlled. Under the circumstances she couldn't rely on God's protection. He certainly hadn't been in evidence during the riot.

She massaged her ribs. Not so sore now the healing bandage had done its work. Her hearing had returned and she was barely limping. James had been attentive and kind all Sunday and helped Ben clear out an old shed so he could build his models there. Yes, he would surely be a good stepfather to her unhappy son.

But there was Alyson. She'd visited her friend's cottage yesterday and Eric had refused admittance. Alyson was too busy just at the moment, he'd said with obvious awkwardness. She remembered Shuji had told Hilary he'd spoken to Eric about Alyson's secret. So what was going on?

A short distance up the hill the dead bracken rustled.

Somehow she must steer Ben away from William.

A snuffling noise at her ear and a wet tongue on her cheek made her jump with a squeak.

A sheepdog. Toss.

Even as she leaped up in dread she heard someone whistling tunelessly on the hill above her, and the dog's master bounded into view like a lusty ram at the autumn roundup.

'Sleeping on the job?' William skidded to a halt beside her.

Oh God, did he have a gun? She stammered, 'Looking at beetles. It *is* my job.'

'Show me.'

In her confusion she'd lost the flower and all the other beetles had gone into hiding. At last she said, 'Here's one.'

He uprooted the twig with his great paw.

He could strangle her with those hands and who would ever know? But she was not afraid of him, no, she was not.

He stared at the infinitesimal creature. 'So small. So delicate.'

She couldn't control a flash of camaraderie. 'Most people think I'm mad to like them.'

He gave a noncommittal snort, dropped the twig and squatted on his haunches beside her. His smell, though agricultural, was definitely less rank. But against her will his proximity caused an electric thrill through her body.

He said roughly, 'Be thankful no one died on Saturday. There's lots of injured. And everyone blames you. Eleven houses uninhabitable and many others smoke damaged. People have had to leave the town and find shelter with friends and relatives after losing all their belongings. Aren't we poor enough, Rachel Kerem?' He sounded like his father.

She tried to say it wasn't her fault but he wasn't listening.

'Shuji Akimoto told the Chief Constable of North Wales Police. A row of local police with batons'd be enough to disrupt the market but the Chief decided our force can't be trusted.'

'He's right there.'

'Jones was severely reprimanded and kept in the dark about the raid. We'd have cancelled the market if we'd known the Chief was sending the riot squad. Overkill.' He looked away, swallowing hard. 'We're rationed at starvation levels. We exist on the public because there's no jobs. And every year the dole buys less and less, so there's never enough for decent food for our children. And you . . . and you . . . What do *you* care?'

Around them bees shimmied through the heather. A magpie called from the woods below where the trees rustled their branches in the perpetual wind. The dog raised its sleepy head from its paws, stared round and dropped back into a doze.

His uneven eyes were dark and secretive like his father's. 'Remember what I said about your son? And you still told Akimoto there'd be a market on Saturday.'

'*I* didn't know. One of your lot informed.'

'How likely is that!'

'Someone who hates you.'

'Blaming my Mam again, are you?' And now he grinned. A grandmother is going to gobble you up grin. And there's no protective woodcutter on duty.

'Keep away from Ben!'

'It's our insurance against your informing, isn't it?' His harsh voice had lost its English precision. He was Welsh; his thoughts, his beliefs, his culture all totally alien to her.

'I've another *cynllun*,' he leered.

The meaning of the unknown word was plain and she snarled, 'Do you really think you'll go free if you attack or murder me?'

'That wasn't what I had in mind.'

'Your pathetic ammo! Will your madmen hold up food lorries? Hole yourselves up in Snowdonia like some medieval princeling and his followers and escape reprisals?'

To her surprise he laughed. Rolled back on the heather and guffawed long and loud. Between tears of delight he stuttered in Welsh she understood, 'Idiot woman! Elwyn'll love that.' Then still chuckling, he resumed his English, 'No, I promise I won't hide in the mountains with my guns, Rachel Kerem. Or Dick Turpin any lorries.'

And she realised how hysterical and foolish she'd become. The ammunition was for local farmers like himself who'd hidden their guns when the new laws came out. They'd bag a deer or wild pig, rabbit, pigeons, anything edible. Nod, wink and a little gift to the Reserve rangers.

He picked a stick of heather, fiddled with it, tapped his teeth with it as he reflected. 'Rachel,' he said at last. His voice was calm, even gentle.

'Yes?' She was wary. She knew how swiftly his moods changed.

'This rinderpest. Akimoto's researching cures, isn't he?'

He was pumping her for certain. Or did he know more and was just testing to find out how much she knew? Either way she couldn't see that it mattered if she told him about Eckstazia's research. She praised Shuji Akimoto's perspicuity. 'Before the recent plague epidemic he was in Kenya close to the border with Sudan and then he organised foot and mouth control in the Argentine . . .'

'Plague follows that guy round.'

If only her voice wasn't so quavery. She said as boldly as she could, 'So he's well versed in the spread of cattle diseases in those areas and the best methods of control. He heads the current research here into new mutations of rinderpest so when they occur they can be eradicated quickly. He's dealing with a very virulent new strain not yet present in the wild.'

'How does he know in advance it's going to mutate that particular way?'

She hadn't thought of that before. 'Computer simulation I guess.'

He grunted and picked at his teeth with the twig again. 'If it escaped . . . Only affects cattle doesn't it?'

'This one affects similar animals too. Pigs maybe. Goats . . .'

'Sheep.'

'Yeh, sheep.' She watched for his reaction as she said, 'But no worries as there aren't any near the reserves.'

He hesitated, very briefly. '*Aberthau*.''

The word Elwyn had used. She'd heard '*berthau*'; no wonder she couldn't find it on the yapp dictionary. 'What's that?' she asked, intrigued.

'Sacrificial flock, reared quite legally in Anglesey, well outside the reserve, but they're brought to Penybwlch in the winter. I take some up to the moor. Didn't you hear them calling in January when you were skulking in the woods?'

'I thought I was mistaken.' So he wasn't going to mention Elwyn Isallt's sheep that were surely hidden inside the reserve somewhere.

'Reserve rangers say it stops the wolves killing too many deer or scavenging in the town. *They* don't care. It's just *nature, wrr.*' He was angry now, but not with her. He said in Welsh, '*We* can starve but wolves must have their easy dinner. And I'm responsible for the poor creatures being torn to pieces. I dream about them. Crying, crying and then they gasp and choke as the wolves tear out their woolly throats. They shake and jump as they die. The living ones run mad. They've never known the cruelty of nature. They've been reared soft and kind and now they cry like frightened children for the protection of men. And I walk away.'

Rachel wasn't impressed. 'So d'you dream about the pig you killed?'

Then she wished she'd bitten her tongue.

'You understand Welsh very well. Exceptionally well,' William said thoughtfully. He broke the stick he held into little pieces and threw them into the heather. The dog jumped up and sniffed at them before sighing and settling down again with his back to the humans.

She met the farmer's stare, his snakelike mesmerising look that had so often terrified her. She would not be intimidated this time. She would suppress all sexual desire. She stared back, putting as much contempt in her gaze as she could, forgetting it was foolish to stare at a hostile male animal.

Some say that eyes are windows of the soul. His were gloomy as bog pools on the moor and just as treacherous. Her body quivered, fear mingled with desire, at the smell of his sweat mingled with dog and poultry and the scents of heather, bilberry and bog myrtle. He commandeered her senses, sucking her down a tunnel of darkness like the funnelling spider's flytrap. Somewhere in that night she saw his empty soul and was appalled, before the heat of lust overwhelmed her. She was unable to withdraw her gaze or her pity but was eventually forced to shut her eyes because of the proximity of his face.

His lips were cold as the hill wind, his tongue fierce and hot as flame. His hands cradled her face, her arms, her breasts. She was barely aware that she helped him remove her trousers. She did not even want to control her body's response to his thrusting.

He was slow and thorough.

He was experienced in the needs of women.

And then he was pulling up his trousers, smiling with self-congratulation. 'I'm good, aren't I?'

Oh yes, but she wasn't going to say so. Her momentary exhilaration dissolved like mist.

'You aren't too bad yourself,' he said.

She shifted uneasily on the heather bed. Such praise was abominable.

'You needn't worry about pregnancy. I've had the snip. Too many in the world already. Too many rotten lives.'

He sat looking down on her as she shielded her face with her arm.

He said, 'Cat got your tongue? Don't pretend it's rape. It's what you wanted.'

No, I didn't, she wanted to say. I've betrayed myself. But he'd laugh.

All the same he knew her thoughts, because he laughed as he said, 'Conscience troubling you?', and the drowsy dog looked up and flicked its ears before yawning and resting head on paws again. It was so indifferent to them that she was sure it had witnessed this scene many times.

She sat up and rearranged her clothes. Dan's necklace flashed in the sunlight.

'What's that?' William asked.

She hid it in her hand as he stretched his own towards it.

'Let me see.'

It was futile to refuse. He traced the intertwining curves with his finger as she'd so often done herself. 'Almost Celtic,' he said quietly, turning it over. 'Double sided too, but the work on the other side is poorer. D'you know what it is?'

'A pendant of course. My husband gave it me.'

'He worked with that professor woman, didn't he? What did he think of her?'

'None of your business.' How did he know?

I think it's . . . Elwyn'll know.' He dropped it back between her breasts, smiling the smile of a man who owns a football team or a world class company. Or a compliant woman.

She turned her head away. 'I've done wrong.'

'God, you religious people. What's wrong with fucking when you need it? A bit of pleasure in a sad world,' and he waved his arms to take in the whole universe. 'Look at all this. Spring. Full of fucking creatures. Does your God hate them too?'

'It's sin for humans outside of marriage. We're made in the image of God.'

'Sin, pouf. Get real, woman. Image of God? Look at yourself and don't be so presumptuous. Why do religious folk bang on about sin and the need for repentance? Because if you believe them you're theirs for life. *They'll* tell you what's right and wrong and how to live your life. *They'll* tell you you're running from the only true love in the universe if you don't obey them and their dumb-ass books. It's power, that's what it's called. Hidden manipulative power.'

She could imagine Daniel making the same robust point.

He said thoughtfully. 'That red jumper you're wearing under your jacket. Someone in red was seen walking the moors when we moved wool. I think it was you. You gave us away.'

She cursed both her inability to lie and the telltale flush on her cheeks.

'Yes!' He clenched his fists and shook them in the air. '*You* betrayed us. I was afraid it might be one of us, but it was *you*.' He grabbed her arm. 'How?'

There was no point in denying so she told him of her journey to the little church in the mountains and her hiding place by the well. 'I wasn't spying. I went to get . . .' She was too embarrassed to tell him she'd superstitiously been collecting holy water for Ben.

'What?'

'Nothing. Just exploring.'

'You're no good at lying, are you? And you told Akimoto, didn't you?'

She remembered Ben's graphic description of William's anger at Tomos' dismissal only too well. She jumped to her feet ready to run. William watched her scornfully. He snapped his finger at Toss and the animal leapt up.

Rachel got the point. She sat down again. So did Toss, but his eyes were fixed on her.

'I can't manage without Tomos,' William railed. 'He knows which people most need help. He lives among them, eats only what they ate and wears the same poor clothes. He takes away their misery with his kindness.' He thumped the heather with an angry fist. '*His* God is good. If I believed in a God, it'd be his.'

She remembered how Tomos's compassion had dissolved her sad memories and how, for a moment, she'd seen a gentle God who wasn't a threatening judge after all.

William continued, 'He's gone to some priest's hangout near Cardiff. His bishop's going to arrange a new posting in England somewhere.' He groaned. 'He's wise. Good. He's my guide. I'm a better man when I'm with Tomos. How shall I talk to him when he's in England?'

'There's plenty of electronic systems.'

184

'Are you crazy? The police have a handle on them all. We never ever use them.'

'How do you communicate then?'

'Sly, aren't you. Of course I won't tell you.' He stared across the valley. The sun went behind a cloud and immediately the breeze was colder. The dog got up, stretched and snuffled at its master's hand. William patted it unconsciously.

She was tense with the dread of another of his sudden rages. But he merely said quietly, 'It isn't the rogues we have to fear, it's the empty headed fools like you.'

He stood up and started down the hill without looking at her again. He shouted as he went, 'Will *you* tell James I was first to get in, or shall I?'

A crow cawed overhead. It stared with stone cold eyes at her supine body on the heath, hoping for carrion.

Rachel stared back.

The bird croaked, 'Bitch on heat.

Flesh is filth.

Death disinfects.'

It soared away on an uprising wind, free, sinless as the breeze sighing through the heather, 'Whore. Whore.'

The saints warned, Beware lechery; beware the seduction of irresponsible and easy sex leading so sweetly and easily into total degradation.

She thought, A few days ago I stood on top of this very hill and felt that God is the love undergirding the universe, filling eternity so that hell itself becomes part of heaven. An understanding love that never condemns, that encourages us to learn from our mistakes.

Lies, lies, porky pies, zizzed the bees.

She cried out, 'I was wrong. Tomos is wrong. I hate God because I can't live up to his demands. I can't love him more than Dan or Ben. How can God forgive that? Will he or my fellow Christians forgive me for my lust? James' huffs and inflexibility are nothing compared to my sin, my liaison with a grubby peasant who's so illiterate he can't even sign his own name. There *is* a hell and it's here and now. Hell is the place where there can never be forgiveness from God or humans.

'Idiot! Lunatic! I'm totally in William's power. Lying, cheating, deceitful William with his tarts and casual sex. He hangs the dual threats of kidnapping Ben and informing James like an executioner's noose over my head.'

She beat her hands on the spiky heather twigs, despising herself utterly. Her hands bled, and still she punished her body as if somehow this would alleviate her guilt.

It didn't.

She looked at her hands remembering a sixthform friend who'd taken to self harming with a biology scalpel. Blood poisoning had almost finished her off.

This was not the way to die.

Far away the crow landed heavily on a twisted hawthorn. It cawed her name.

She stood up, licking the blood from her palms as the bird's cry drew her inexorably to the cliffs over the pass. Not far away was the exact spot where she and Ben had stood a few weeks ago, gazing down on the coastal villages and at Anglesey across the Menai. How long ago. How innocent she'd been.

She dislodged a stone.

Bump, bounce, bump, bounce, bump. Gone forever into the peaceful depths of the valley.

A beetle voice in the heather scrub clacked, 'My larvae will eat away your sinful body.'

A fly hummed, 'So will mine, so will mine. A slut's flesh can't poison us.'

She thought, All die. Tree and buzzard. Human and marsh thistle. Back into the earth that fed them.

'Respect the dust,' called the gulls. 'Our grave and our cradle. You whose multitudes overrun the world, who have taken so much from the good earth, why do you greedily demand resurrection of your dust?'

Death is nothing. Merely the recycling of earth's resources.

The wind chilled the cliffs and whistled through the clattering twigs of a stunted birch,

'Atom and molecule, I carry free
round the fair earth; small drifting particles
binding to rain, bonding in leaves,
sugar and protein, growth for the children,
bread for the living, food for death's maggots.
Dissolving in rain dust circles again.
Atom and molecule I carry free.'

She shook her head to free it of the voices. One part of her recognised they were her own thoughts. Another part heard the song of the earth with its wisdom based on billions of years of teeming life, far more ancient than the meditations of sages and saints.

The void below sucked her towards eternal rest.

She stretched one foot out over the abyss.

No one would be harmed by her death. It would be best for Ben to be rid of his slag of a mother.

'Don't be a fool.' She heard Dan as sharp and clear as if he stood beside her. 'Our son needs your love now more than ever.'

She stepped back.

But choosing life entailed bearing the burden of her sin.

'God, I beg you,' she said aloud. 'Shame me as I deserve but don't punish me by harming Ben, I entreat you, God. For Jesus' sake. For Jesus' sake.' But the Jesus mantra no longer eased her soul. God hadn't hesitated to crucify his own son. What would he do to her, lost sinner as she was? But she'd fight God all the way. She'd protect Ben from every possible danger. She'd . . .

The madness receded.

She'd learn by her mistakes. Start over.

Short term. She'd rush back to Penybwlch, find Shuji, tell him William had raped her. Police swabs would confirm. William would be jailed. Her relationship with James would be safe.

Only one problem. It wasn't true. He didn't rape her. He was gentle, not rough. She hadn't resisted. And in the past she and Daniel had lambasted those women who invented date rape to get even on a man.

She'd tell James straight. No, she baulked at the total humiliation involved. But would William have any such qualms? She'd tell James they weren't suited. He'd almost suggested a break-up after her trip to the castle, hadn't he?

Long term. She and Ben were in danger. Some local was probably watching her even now. She'd ask Shuji for immediate transfer to somewhere safe, well away from Wales. Elstazia had connections all over the globe. And, great relief, no one would ever find out she'd kept silent about the ammunition cache.

But she wasn't even sure she wanted to continue working for Eckstazia. They were all fine dedicated people, no doubt about it, but she couldn't live up to their Christian standards. She'd find a teaching job back in England. References? Her previous head thought highly of her. Eckstazia would cancel Ben's schooling at the Academy, but there were plenty of good state schools. Eckstazia's loan? Interest was generous, one point above the Bank of England rate. Manageable on teacher's pay.

*

Ben stroked his mother's head. She lay on her bed with papers scattered round her. She'd missed dinner, missed sorting Ben's food.

'Is that better?' His small warm fingers tickled more than they soothed, but his love was a better medicine than any painkiller.

She managed a smile. 'Much better, dear.' She hadn't felt this rotten since her own mother's death and funeral.

'You must be more careful.'

He sounded just like his father. What if William told him he'd fucked his mother today?

Her son picked up her scarred hands. 'Don't fall down again, will you Mum?'

It was only a white lie. How else could she explain her cuts?

The boy continued, 'Alyson was funny when she collected me from school today. Funny weird I mean. Cross. Told me to tell you she knows what a rat you are. That's horrid, isn't it?'

Rachel regretted her automatic frown because pain stabbed her temple. 'I'll see her tomorrow and we'll sort it out then. You do your homework.'

He sat down with the yapp and she picked up the documents and studied them again. Quite clear. She must revise her options. Her trial period was over and her recent agreement with Eckstazia meant she must complete a year in research, so she couldn't return to teaching immediately. Worse, the small print stated her loan would be called in when she left Eckstazia. She was tied into them indefinitely.

There was a knock at the door and she groaned.

Ben called, 'Who is it?'

'Dr Beard. I want to speak to your mother.'

'She's poorly,' Ben said protectively, but Rachel called, 'Come in, Jennifer.' Then because she was still angry with the woman she said, 'Take another good look round. You won't find anything of my husband's.'

Jennifer barely hesitated. 'What *are* you talking about?' She smiled coldly at the sick woman. 'A bit delirious after your fall this afternoon? Shuji said you refused to go to hospital.'

'I didn't hit my head. I've got a stress migraine.'

Jennifer indicated her bloodied hands. 'Quite the Lady Macbeth.'

Yes, thank you Jennifer, she thought, I know *that* reference. 'Real blood, not imaginary.'

'We're all sorry you had to miss dinner.' The scientist seated herself gracefully in the easy chair and looked across at Ben. 'Surely you aren't playing with your mother's expensive yapp?'

'Homework.'

'Doesn't your school provide suitably indestructible computers?'

'They're bollocks.'

Jennifer gave a horrified snort and turned to Rachel. But Rachel was already rebuking her son for his language.

Jennifer said to him, 'I hope you aren't planning any more jaunts into the reserve during storms, young man. I don't recall you apologising for the trouble you caused us all.'

Outraged, Ben looked at his mother and she made a calming motion with her hand.

'Sorry,' he muttered rebelliously.

'That's better.' Jennifer looked at her watch. 'Bedtime, surely.'

'Not for . . .'

Rachel interrupted hastily, 'Pop along, dear. Finish your homework in your own room.' She winked at him surreptitiously, and he grinned in reply.

With excessive politeness he said, 'Good night, Dr Beard,' and left, yapp in hand.

Jennifer said, 'Yapps don't grow on trees. You won't get another one if he ruins it.'

Rachel shrugged and immediately winced.

'James sent me. He's very upset . . .'

Oh God. Had William told him already?

' . . . that you're refusing to see him.'

Rachel sighed with relief. 'I'm just too tired . . . ' she said lamely.

'Of course I'm very pleased you and he have an agreement. But I've known him a lot longer than you and I can read him like a book. I'm very concerned for him. You aren't making him happy, Rachel.' She paused but Rachel said nothing. 'I don't want to know anything about your relationship with him. That's your private domain.'

The woman's tongue was almost hanging out in her desperation to know. Had she once had an affair with James? Or hoped for one? Rachel wished her brain felt less addled. 'Thanks for telling me,' she managed, hoping the scientist would now leave her in peace.

'Ben's completely out of your control, isn't he? He needs a male figure in his life and James will make an excellent father and mentor for the boy. As trustworthy as Odysseus' friend.' Jennifer's mouth curled in a smile that didn't reach her eyes. 'I admire your ambition and your skill in getting what you want . . .'

The cheek of it! James had shown interest in her long before *she'd* started to consider remarriage.

'A true Clytemnestra.'

'Clite?' Bother, she should have let the reference pass.

'A clever woman who got what she wanted. Until the final curtain.' Jennifer waited for this to sink in. 'Even James thought your behaviour sneaky.'

So Jennifer wasn't referring to James' attachment to her. 'What behaviour?'

'*I* saw through you straight away. I've come to tell you to take over the cottage at Bryn Llawenydd on Saturday after Annie's cleaned it.'

'Cottage?'

'That's what you planned, wasn't it? I thought you handled it very cleverly. Telling Shuji about Alyson.'

'What did I say? I can't remember anything bad.'

Impatiently Jennifer reminded her, 'You told Shuji last Thursday she denies Emmanuel's existence.'

'But that's hardly . . .'

'Emmanuel is one of the most saintly people I've ever met. When the Rapture comes, he'll be the first to rise in the air to meet our Lord. You wait and see.'

'But Alyson . . .'

'Shuji is pretty weak and ineffectual when dealing with personnel probs, but he spoke firmly to Eric the following day, demanding he put her right. I don't know what Eric said to her, but Alyson marched up to Shuji today and was most rude. He rightly dismissed her immediately and the family go tomorrow. Our work is too important to allow disaffected employees to remain on the premises.'

So that was why Alyson refused to see her yesterday and called her a rat today. Her dear friend was leaving in anger and Rachel tried in vain to suppress a sob.

Jennifer said, 'You may have succeeded in getting their house but don't think you'll take their place in my lab. You aren't a patch on Alyson.' She ran her hand through her hair in exasperation, 'It's all very inconvenient. I'll be rushed to complete everything before my trip after Eckstazia's London conference.' Then she straightened her back and took on a determined look. 'The wiles of the devil can't scupper God's plans. We'll finish anyone who's against us – against the Lord. We'll win in the end. The day of reckoning is almost here when Jesus' righteous judgement will prevail and sinners'll perish forever. Praise him!' She stood up. 'You're a crafty woman, Rachel. But ambition isn't everything. Don't forget love and compassion for others.' She paused with her hand on the door lever. 'Oh, you're to see Shuji tomorrow morning first thing.'

Chapter 13

Rachel gave a hesitant knock on Shuji's office door. She shivered in anticipation. Once Shuji realised her life was in danger he'd surely find her another placement. When she proved to him what a liar William was she'd be safe from any claims the oaf might make about their sexual liaison. The man would be hauled in over the black market, eventually imprisoned.

She knocked again more loudly.

'Come.' Shuji stood in front of his desk, arms folded. His pale face was lit by morning sunlight, his white sweatshirt and trousers dazzled like angel's garments. Behind him his painting glowed and its flame coloured creatures rose into glory. She had never felt so intimidated by his presence.

He bowed his magnificent head. 'Please sit down.' He walked past her to the tower window. Staring down the valley so his face was hidden from her, he said, 'You were in town during Saturday's riot.'

'A terrifying experience for both me and Ben. We were bullied. My life's. . .'

'Talking to a known dissident.' His voice was cold.

'William Parry's father. He threatened . . .'

'Recorded on camera, together with your conversation.' He turned round, his eyes bulging with anger. 'Who do you think you are? These people are dishonest and you consort with them. They lie and cheat and you treat them as your friends.' He marched back to his desk, clenching and unclenching his fists. 'Yet again I've had to make excuses for you to the police. Thanks to me you're not slammed up. This is the last time, Rachel. I shan't support you again.'

'Parryboots . . .'

He banged his hand on the desk so she jumped. 'There, you see, you call him by his nickname like a friend. What possessed you to take your son to an illegal market?'

'Shuji! Please listen to me.'

'Well?' He was still severe.

'Whatever you've been told, my conversation with Mr Parry was highly critical of the illegal market.' In her memory she had trounced the man thoroughly. 'He threatened me. You know I was set on by louts. Ben was taken from me. We escaped . . .'

'Why didn't you take the yapp? You could have contacted us.'

'How d'you know . . .?'

He frowned. 'I track your whereabouts. Of course.'

Light dawned. 'It monitors my position and pulses the data back here.'

'Every five minutes.' He turned on his wall screen and a map of the estate appeared. He enlarged a section. 'Here you are.' He jabbed his finger along a red zigzag. 'Yesterday, Monday twenty fourth of March, out on the mountain, in spite of James' warning. Later by the cliffs. That's where you fell, see the long pause. Then you returned here.'

So he must have known about her trip to the little church before she told him. What else did he know? The incriminating pulse couldn't tell him she'd had sex with William.

'It's for your own safety.' He shut the screen down.

'William Parry threatens to abduct Ben and I know my life's in danger.' She hesitated, then burst out, 'They've got guns. Ammunition's been stored in the farm sheds. . . . Please. Help me find another post with Eckstazia. Anywhere outside this barbaric country. Somewhere we can feel safe.'

To her surprise he didn't question her on the ammunition. Instead he stared at her with his heavy lidded eyes, and she couldn't read their expression. His slim manicured fingers drummed nervously on the desk and she couldn't help comparing them with other hands, rough large farm hands that could be surprisingly gentle. She groaned at the bitter memory but Shuji didn't hear her. He walked to the window again, his back to her.

'Yes, yes, you're right. We can't risk another death.'

Another death? What was he talking about, this formidable man who used the black market for his own purposes?

But even as she looked his back sagged. He leaned against the mullion for support, his head sinking between his shoulders. He was shrinking before her eyes like poorly rooted mountain grass growing in a boulder crack shrivels under the heat of noonday sun.

He spoke, and she couldn't recognise his trembling voice. Softly, as if to himself, cracking with emotion, he said, 'People dying of starvation before my eyes. Holding out hands. So many hands. So large at the end of their stick arms. Children with huge terrified eyes. The wailing. Groaning. Then the shocking silence because there is no food and never will be any. The stink of the dying and the unburied dead. Little bodies wrapped in torn cloth, their dying parents grieving over them.'

His voice sank so low she couldn't grasp the words. His strong legs that had easily carried him over the mountains with James were buckling like straws. His clothes were white as a shroud. She was terrified at his collapse, but as she got up to summon help he forced himself upright and said loudly, 'It can't be right. Jesus, it can't be right. We shouldn't use tuberine. Whatever Hilary claims. As for rinderpest . . . I can't agree. James and Jenny say many will be saved. But nobody's seen what I have. Too high a price, Lord. Why do you command your servants to let loose such pain?' He sighed deeply as if his burden was too great to bear. 'But you commanded us and you've promised salvation out of all this suffering. If God is for us, who can condemn us?' He banged on the window with his fist. 'All the same, I'll argue my case again in London at the Conference this weekend. It's not too late for Council to cancel.'

He turned round and jumped when he saw her. 'Still here? Get off with you.' And then in a kindlier but dismissive tone, 'Yes, I'll sort out a transfer immediately. Be more careful. We're very concerned for you and the boy. We need to know where you are at all times, Rachel. Take James' advice. He'll look after you. Both of you.'

*

The following weekend Ben dumped his final load of model planes and trucks on the settee with the broken springs. 'What's the matter, Mum? Don't you like it here?'

Rachel sat at the cottage table head in hands.'I tried to mobile Alyson but she wouldn't answer. I never wanted her cottage.' She'd not even seen her friends being driven away to the bus station by Martin last Tuesday, as she was with Shuji at the time.

Rain, the eternal Welsh rain, drummed on the windows and trickled onto the inner sills.

'House stinks.' Ben wrinkled his nose. 'Worse than hens.' He'd scarpered earlier to help William clean out food hoppers and the memory was still strong.

'It's the damp.' She told him Alyson's theory about the lack of through draught. 'And I bet they were built before there were proper damp courses.' She opened the woodstove doors and stared gloomily at cold ashes. 'Never tried to light one of these old things before.'

She went into the kitchen for the kindling and matches she'd spotted earlier. Bags and boxes lay scattered on the floor where James had helped dump them. He, Shuji and Jennifer were doing overtime at the lab all weekend, though he'd arranged a break tomorrow, Sunday, to take Rachel and Ben riding for the first time. He also promised to bring crockery, cutlery and kitchen utensils from the main house since there was nothing in the cottage's drawers and cupboards. All that was left in the fridge was a cracked jug of fresh milk along with mouldy unrecognisable items that Rachel dumped immediately. In one cupboard Ben had unearthed a half-full coffee jar, a chipped cup holding sugar, an opened packet of soft water biscuits and a scattering of tea bags.

During the week Rachel had scoured the local shops for food. But as Alyson had warned her, it was poor quality and expensive. After her ration card was swiped in the last shop, the assistant returned it with a frown, telling her she had so few points he'd been forced to take next week's as well. She tried to argue against this illegality, but he was adamant. 'Don't come back then,' he said. This morning William had given Ben a dozen eggs in a paper bag. She blessed the farmer. For the first and only time.

She knelt by the stove with her kindling as Ben took his models upstairs. 'Hey Mum,' he shouted. 'There's a cat on my bed. Ginger stripy. Skinny.' He came down cradling the mewling animal.

'It's pretty.' She stroked it gently but it didn't purr. 'D'you think it was Freya's? I'll find it some food.' She opened a precious tin of meat, tore a piece of cardboard from a box in lieu of a dish and spooned out some food with her fingers. The cat drew back. 'It's shy. It'll eat some when we aren't watching. What will you call it?'

'Bryn. Because this house is called Bryn Llawenydd.'

'That's nice.'

'My room's cold. The carpet's *tiny*. Doesn't cover the floorboards.' He stared at the thread of smoke in the stove as a baby ember sparked and died. 'That's not going to keep us warm'

'Alyson had an electric fire.' She couldn't see it anywhere. Perhaps she'd taken it. The electric kettle was missing too. And the wall screen in the living room. The family must have been loaded down with boxes when they left.

Fortunately there was an electric cooker. The environmentally unfriendly sort that had gone out of fashion in Rachel's childhood. She switched it on, left the door open and continued unpacking.

Smoke crept out of the oven. Greasy choking smoke.

'Phew,' Ben said. 'Trying to burn the house down?' He slammed the door and turned the appliance off. 'I thought Annie cleaned everything after Alyson left?'

'You know Annie. Everything of the finest for Shuji. *We* don't count.' She looked at her meagre purchases. 'We shan't eat as well as we did in the main house.'

'*You* did, you mean.' Ben shuffled his feet on the slate floor. 'Shan't have to go back next term, shall I?'

'Told you. Academy's settled.'

194

'Can I leave now? There's only three weeks before Easter break.'

'What's happened?' He hadn't talked about school all week and she'd been too busy with her own troubles to question him.

His face was full of misery as he turned to her. 'Us in town last Saturday. The kids know we messed up the market. They hate me. Spit and piss in my dinner because we have lots of good food and they're hungry.'

'How dare they! How can the staff allow it!'

'They say they haven't seen anything. Tell me I'm privileged so I shouldn't moan and not to rat on my friends because no one likes sneaks. And, Mum.'

'Yes?'

'The kids know I'm seeing the shrink on Monday. They call me mad. And other things.'

'Mrs Lloyd should've kept it quiet.' She was furious.

'Do I *have* to see the shrink?'

'I'm coming too. She'll give you a good report which we'll send to the Academy, because I suspect Mrs.Lloyd's review will be prejudiced and inaccurate. Then you can stay home. But you're not to spend time with William.'

'OK. Great.' He started stacking dry food in the cupboard under the stairs. 'It's huge,' he said as he vanished inside. 'Goes right back . . . Hey, Mum. There's a door.'

'D'you know where the light's packed?'

Ben rushed away and rummaged around. He flashed the light stick at her and pushed back into the cupboard. 'Bolts at top and bottom. I can't shift them.'

She winkled away at the rust with her pocket screwdriver until the bolts were free. Ben pulled them back and leant his shoulder against the door. 'Won't budge.'

'Let me see.' She passed the light up and down and located an old fashioned hasp, also rusted in place. She freed it, but the door remained fixed. 'Fastened the other side,' she said, rattling it in vain.

'Bet it goes into the yard.'

'Sure to. These cottages were built for farm workers, so you'd expect an exit directly to the yard rather than having to go all the way round.'

'Alyson didn't know about it. Bet William does. He'll open it for us then I can meet him easy.'

'More easily,' she corrected. 'But no way.' She shot the bolts.

'Why not?' he wailed.

'We don't need a back entrance.'

'Yes we do. You *said*. The draught'll stop the damp. I *hate* the stink.'

'No.'

'*Why?*'

'It's remaining shut, Ben. That's my final word.'

He stormed off to his new room, muttering under his breath.

She was certain he'd disobey and William was sure to encourage him, so she searched for a strip of wood to screw across door and frame. But she couldn't find screws or nails.

All night her fear of William and her insecurity nagged at her. On Sunday James gave her and Ben their first riding lessons. Ben's little grey pony stood quiet as a mouse when James helped him up. It walked decorously round the field, James at its side. He pulled it into a trot and Ben bounced uncomfortably.

'Rise and fall,' James shouted to Rachel's horror. 'Rise and fall!'

Then, as her son easily got into the rhythm, she realised the command was not to fall off the animal.

For her the experience was less successful. Her brown pony was bigger than Ben's and friskier. James heaved her up into the saddle, then made her raise her leg while he tightened the girth. She slipped off the other side.

'Sorry about that,' James said. 'You'll soon get the hang of balancing. And you're a proper rider when you've fallen off seven times. So there's only six to go.'

She refused to trot. Walking was scary enough. She managed one circuit of the field with James at her side, then he insisted she try on her own while he and Ben stood by the gate with the other pony. When they were furthest away the mare rolled her eyes, pulled at the slack rein and decided to return to her companion as fast as possible. This time Rachel bent forward and grabbed the coarse black mane for dear life. Knees flapping, she bumped crazily up and down as the mare trotted through the grass.

'That's it! Well done!' called James. 'Hold tighter with your knees and rise up and down.'

How impossible! She slid gratefully to the ground on her arrival, knees trembling at the ordeal, and refused to mount again.

'Soon get the hang of it, my dear.'

How likely was that when she had no intention of mounting the beast again!

She recalled William's mad ride over the moors without a saddle. Not an enjoyable memory.

When James kissed her she emphasised what a liar the farmer was. James agreed evidence was stacked against the man and he was sure he'd be charged with his crimes before long. Meanwhile she must keep Ben away from him. Yes, it was time the boy left the unsavoury local school. He could easily work at home. And Shuji was investigating her immediate transfer to a safer venue. He said, 'I'll miss you, dear. But it won't be for long.'

At evening church she watched Shuji surreptitiously. He looked perfectly normal. She dismissed his earlier ramblings as another example of Eckstazia's creedal excesses.

The senior scientists were all spending next weekend at Eckstazia's annual London Conference. She didn't envy them. It would be full of arguments between those claiming the Rapture would take place before the seven year tribulation, those who claimed scripture referred to a post tribulation Rapture and others determined the Rapture would be mid tribulation. Each group would heatedly contend that the others were trapped in delusions of the devil's making. Shuji was doubtless caught up in a similar interminable row. She congratulated herself on her own more liberal views. As for Shuji tracking her movements, well that was just for her own safety, wasn't it?

On Sunday night she woke sharply at midnight, wondering what had disturbed her. The curtains were open to a full moon shining ghostly grey light over her unaccustomed surroundings. She crept out of bed, shivering, and pulled on a jumper.

She peeped into Ben's room. His arms were flung out in childish abandon and in the moonlight she could see him smile. Sweeter dreams than her own, thank God. He'd covered his quilt with the small carpet and Rachel's bare feet were chilled by draughts coming up through exposed floorboards.

The stairs entered directly into the living room. She'd managed to get the wood burner going at last but without coal to bank it up it had expired in the night. The thin carpet couldn't prevent cold rising from the stone floor beneath. Probably it was laid directly onto earth. She stood on one leg and ran her foot up and down her calf to warm it a little. Then she did the same for the other foot. She turned on the kitchen light and padded over the slates to her trainers before switching on her recent acquisition, a kettle from the main house. She smiled. Annie would have a fit when she came back from her weekend at home to find so many utensils missing from her kitchen. James' prob, not hers, thank God. As for this wilderness cottage! Why, her mother's council flat in Coventry had had more modern equipment. She never thought she'd miss that cramped flat.

As she poured the water over her tea there was a grinding noise in the cupboard. She jumped, almost scalding herself. Then laughed. A mouse. But rather an odd one, surely? She put the kettle down to investigate.

The noise became louder. A rat?

She opened the door cautiously but nothing ran out.

Then a voice she knew only too well whispered from beyond the bolted door, 'Hey, Rachel. Open up, will you.'

'No. Of course not. Get lost, William.'

'It's urgent.'

'Stuff it.'

'Really important. Not sex.'

Quite so, she thought bitterly. *Any*thing else is more important to him.

'*Please,* Rachel, I won't touch you, I promise.'

As if a William promise was worth anything. She remained silent, expecting one of his rages, but he said, 'Rachel, it's sheep. We need your help.'

'Oh, yeh.' She was intrigued, but not daft enough to open the door.

'Honest, Rachel.' William shook the outer door gently.

'In the middle of the night?' She slammed the cupboard door and picked up her stewing tea.

The stairs creaked. Ben came into the kitchen, shivering in his night gear. 'Who's here?' He stared round. 'I heard voices.'

'Nothing,' Rachel said as William thumped the door shouting, 'It's me, Ben. It's William.'

'No,' Rachel ordered as her son squeezed into the cupboard and pulled at the bolts. Then she hesitated. She was sure William wouldn't try anything on if Ben was around, and she was very curious about Eckstazia's activities at Isallt. But she wasn't stupid. She hid a kitchen knife behind the kettle.

'God, it's like a morgue in here. Where's the electric fire?' William asked.

'Alyson took it.' Rachel was mesmerized by the naked carcase of a hen he was holding by its dirty feet.

'No she didn't. It was here when I brought some things for you the day before you moved in.. . .'

Rachel certainly wasn't going to thank him for the food and firewood.

'If that woman took it I'll . . .'

He meant Annie.

He swung the hen by its feet. 'Just plucked it. She's too fat to come back into lay this spring, so you two can have her. Catch.' He pretended to throw it at Ben who ducked. William grinned.

'I don't know how to prepare it.' Rachel was bemused by this sudden friendliness.

William found the hidden knife and smirked at Rachel before cutting off a scaly leg. He pulled the tendons so the toes curled as if to grab Ben and the boy snatched it and threatened his mother, laughing.

William informed her, 'Then chop off the neck, like this. Use it for soup. Then put your hand up its bum and pull everything out. Save the heart and liver, take the stones from the gizzard and dump the rest. She's old so you must boil her. With all these bits and a few onions. Here.' He fished in his bulky pocket and pulled out a strand of twine, pocket knife and two onions. Hen feathers floated to the floor. Followed by a jangling bunch of keys.

Rachel thought over what he'd said. 'Are those the cottage keys?'

'Sure thing.' He winked at her. 'Spare lot. That's how I got in on Friday.' He threw them on the table. 'There you go. Safer for me to come through your back door. Then no one knows.'

No way! She'd fix that door tomorrow.

Rachel had cleaned the oven so now she turned the heat on and opened its door. The room slowly warmed as she poured Ben a juice and made tea for William. It was surreal, sitting at the table at midnight with the man and treating him as a guest.

A tiny mew came from the back door and the cat oozed into the room. It shunned William and curled itself round Ben's legs. He picked it up.

William said, 'So this is where the farm cat's hid herself. Fleas and all.' He stretched out his hand but she slunk deeper into Ben's arms and hissed. He shrugged.

He leered at Rachel.

She blushed angrily.

He smirked and gulped his tea, then wiped his sleeve across a dribble escaping the drooping corner of his mouth. 'Enjoy your ride today, did you? I got you the animals and the licence to keep them here. Ben's little pony Iago is quiet but he's got character. You've got my mare, Bronwen.'

A horse was a horse was a horse to her. Four legs at each corner all best avoided and a head mobile as a snake's with massive teeth. She hadn't even recognised the dun mare that William had ridden to the church.

'Great,' Ben said.

'Never getting up on one of those things again,' said his mother at the same time.

Ben went on, 'James is teaching us.'

'The good and holy James,' William said.

Rachel shot out, 'You always have to sneer at people better than yourself, don't you?'

They glared at each other with mutual hostility.

'What d'you want?' Rachel asked. 'Just tell me and then go.'

He heated more water and made himself another mug of tea. Leaning casually on the worktop he said, 'Your pendant.'

She automatically clutched it.

'Elwyn reckons it's a data chip. Fits your yapp.'

Ben jumped up, dropping the astonished cat and rushed to the living room. He thrust the yapp at her. 'Try it, Mum. Quick. I bet Dad left us a message.'

Her hands trembled as she tried to fit the pendant. Nothing worked. Ben couldn't fix it either. She set them down on the table, still shaking. So it was *this* that contained Dan's article and maybe other information. It was *this* Eckstazia wanted destroyed.

'I'm sure I'm right,' William said. He checked them again. 'Elwyn has adapter cables. I'll take them both to him.'

'No, you won't.' She grabbed both necklace and yapp.

'Oh, OK. You come too. It's not far, just over the hill. I want you to check out his sheep. One's sick.' He paused. 'Of course, you don't know. Akimoto told me he'd support me if I provide . . . '

' . . . Elwyn's sheep for his experiments.'

She was pleased to see his surprise even while she wondered what support Shuji was offering the rogue.

He raised one eyebrow and his forehead wrinkled expressively, reminding her of Parryboots. 'You knew about his sheep all along, didn't you? Yeh. Well. Jennifer Beard made him inject some of 'em last Tuesday.'

That interview with Shuji. Were his strange words connected in any way?

William said, 'We want to know what's going on. I can't access Penybwlch on my yapp. It's inferior to yours.'

So he'd kept the Reserve yapp he'd been issued with before she arrived.

'I'm allowed access.' She brought up the website on the small screen.

William scanned it.

Ben said, 'So you *can* read.' He sounded disappointed.

'Suits me that people think I'm stupid, Ben. Never let on just how much you know. Not even to your nearest and dearest. Always keep a bit up your sleeve. Copy your mother. Very secretive woman.'

He leered at her.

She shivered with fury. 'Finish reading and go. Just go.'

He said, 'It doesn't say more than you've already told me. You're researching a highly dangerous pathogen. Is Beard infecting Elwyn's sheep with that particular strain? We must know because there aren't any precautions in place. Elwyn told her deer and wild pigs come close to the yards. She said it didn't matter.'

'Then it doesn't. No way would a dedicated scientist like Jennifer Beard run that sort of risk. I don't know anything about this experiment. They haven't told me.'

'There must be details in the lab. Check it out.'

She related the heavy security.

'What are your mob playing at?'

'Nothing underhand. Eckstazia is a highly respected worldwide organisation. It's got research centres in major countries and supports research in many others.'

'Blah, blah, blah. Who pays your wages, my girl? I've searched the science reviews and can't find any mention of the research at Penybwlch.'

'That's not unusual.'

Ben squiggled his legs until he was kneeling on his seat and leaning on the table. '*I* know.'

Rachel smiled at him. 'No you don't, dear.'

'Yes I do. It was James and Jennifer. They met when James brought me back from football and he told me to run along so I did. Then I hid in the bushes. They thought I was a blackbird or a squirrel,' he said proudly. 'I'm good, aren't I, William?'

'Proper little spy.'

'And?' Rachel asked.

Ben wrinkled his forehead. 'James said, "We've got the sheep. Are you ready?" And she said in a week. Then he asked her about biosecurity and she said it didn't matter because it would be just before Easter. Then they said something about Emmanuel and going up in the air and all that crap.'

William said, 'Don't swear in front of your mother.'

'*You* swear.'

'That's different.'

'Why?'

For the first time since she'd known him William was floored. 'Weeell. You're younger than me.'

Ben frowned. 'I'm ten now. Just because you're ancient . . .'

William tried to protest.

' . . . you do what you like.'

William dithered. 'It's not like that.'

'So?'

William stuttered.

Rachel started to laugh. He glared at her then grinned sheepishly. She said to Ben, 'Are you sure you're right? Jennifer said biosecurity doesn't matter? It doesn't make sense.'

He thought hard. 'Yeh. That's what she said. I'm sure.'

'Well done, dear.' They smiled at each other.

William observed, 'You've got a good mother, Ben. Look after her.'

'I do, don't I, Mum?'

'Very well, love.'

How wretched William looked. What kind of upbringing had he had with canny Annie?

He said to her, 'You know far more about this little beastie than Elwyn and I do. You'll come to Isallt tomorrow?'

'It's tomorrow now.' Ben was looking at his watch.

She deliberated. Yes, she must access Dan's final message as soon as possible. Equally important she must check this experiment at Isallt. But - 'I've an appointment at Ben's school.'

'The shrink, isn't it? Take no notice of him, Ben.'

How did the man know? 'Tuesday I'll come.'

Ben asked, 'And me.'

'No,' William said. 'Too far. We're walking. Can't take the van; the spysats'll watch it. There's special jobs you can do for me.'

Ben looked proud.

'He's too young to be left by himself.' She wanted Ben there. She didn't want to be alone with William again. And yet she no longer felt that electricity between them. Something in her had died when she stood on the cliff edge. Was it her youth?

William studied her face. 'You'd be quite good looking if you hadn't lost that tooth.'

'And you'd look better if you didn't have that scar and squinty eye.'

He leapt up and his chair clattered against the wall. He kicked it away, clicked up the door latch into the barn and slammed the door behind him. Rachel and Ben heard him slide the outside bolts and then there was silence.

'Phew,' Ben said. 'He's touchy about his face, isn't he?'

*

The school psychologist was a small dark haired woman with the hint of a moustache. She had the troubled look of someone used to abuse from parents whose perfectly mannered genius child she'd assessed as a trouble-maker of under average intelligence. She scrolled through her report distractedly while sheltering herself behind the Head's large desk.

'Please make yourself comfortable, Mrs Kerem.' The Head indicated the low easy chair. She was smartly dressed as always in cream silk blouse and maroon wool suit. Her lips smiled. Her eyes triumphed. 'Our psychologist Miss Lewis has investigated your son and is in a position to give you advice on handling him.'

Rachel's hackles rose, but she greeted them both politely.

Mrs Lloyd sat in a higher chair and stared down on Rachel. 'I have to tell you some good news.' Her mouth turned down. 'Ben has been making better progress in a couple of areas recently.' She almost smiled, 'Though there are numerous problems we must discuss with you.'

The psychologist coughed, shuffling some papers. Rachel could see they had Ben's writing and drawing on them and wondered what information the woman had managed to winkle out of her son.

'Mrs. Kerem.' The psychologist's voice was low and soft but determined. 'Your son presents as a ten-year-old of good average intelligence. This level of intelligence is not reflected in his schoolwork. In part this is due to his poor command of Welsh and his very recent arrival in the district, so if he applies himself more rigorously it should right itself as he matures. It has been necessary meanwhile to place him in a lower class than his age and intelligence would normally expect. He finds making friends difficult, in part because of the difference in age, but also due to a certain negativity in his character. It is this that gives rise to our concern.'

Mrs Lloyd interjected, 'The staff and I have found him uncooperative and stubborn. There's always disruption in the playground when Ben appears.'

Rachel protested, 'Due to bullying by other children.'

'We've a very strict policy in place. Any bullying is reported by the children themselves and quickly punished,' said the Head.

The psychologist supported her. 'This is one of the most caring schools in the district. There are never any complaints to my department in Caernarvon. Sadly Benjamin evinces an aggressive manner that acts against his acceptance by his peers. Do you, Mrs Kerem, know of any friends? ' She peered over her glasses.

'No,' Rachel admitted.

The psychologist brought up a document as she continued, 'Tests and my own observations reliably demonstrate he suffers from attention deficit hyperactivity disorder. This assessment is supported by discussions with Mrs Lloyd and your son's teacher. I understand he receives medication for this condition?'

Rachel hesitated. It was a long time since he had taken his dose.

'Perhaps an increased dosage is necessary. I'll report my findings to our child psychiatrist who deals with medical affairs.' She tapped in a reminder. 'I've studied his psychological profile from his former school. We're concerned at the apparent deterioration in his behaviour since he was in Coventry, although there were worrying indicators even then.'

'His teachers always told me he was doing well. That he's bright and well behaved. What exactly *are* these indicators?'

The psychologist scrolled down the report. 'He comes from a one parent family.'

'Widowhood is hardly a life choice.'

'No, Mrs Kerem, of course not. Single parenting is merely one of several government indicators for picking out children that may be at risk of offending in later years. Another one is the home environment. I understand you had no home of your own but lived in your mother's council flat?'

'I cared for her while she was dying.'

'Very commendable. But the flat was situated in one of the most rundown areas of the city.'

'It wasn't like that when my mother first moved in.'

'The effect on a young child's future behaviour is considerable.'

'Few children in deprived areas become criminals.'

'Maybe so. But statistically the proportion is higher, so the government requires we monitor children from such backgrounds with especial care. Currently you're not a home owner and live in tied accommodation. If you lose your job your home vanishes too. This is hardly a stable situation for a young child. Equally serious was the parental refusal to have an identification chip inserted at birth. This lack of access to his life circumstances made it far more difficult for me to assess him as fully as I should.'

'Neither his father nor I wanted chip insertion when Ben was born. We felt it was an unwarranted intrusion into a child's life and open to misuse since it can't be removed. And it was still optional in those days.'

'Optional but strongly recommended for all concerned parents. Am I right in thinking his father died when he was five? Such an event has a very profound effect on a young child. Especially boys of his age.'

'Naturally I'm fully aware of that. I do my best to counter any problem arising.'

'Then there's his truancy.'

'Truancy? He's brought to school and collected every day.'

The Head said, 'He absconds. Lunchbreaks especially.'

'The other children urinate in his school dinner.'

The Head was outraged. 'Impossible, Mrs Kerem. Nothing like that has ever happened here. My staff are eagle eyed. They would report any such misdemeanour to me and I would deal with it immediately.'

'My son is not a liar.'

The psychologist checked her screen. 'His score on the Male Child Deceit Indicator is worryingly high.'

'Precisely,' Mrs Lloyd agreed.

Before Rachel could protest the psychologist said, 'I've placed him on the At Risk Register.'

'*At Risk?* On the possible offenders list . . .?'

'At Risks have been monitored since the early years of this century. I have to say the results have been most promising in pinpointing future criminals.'

' . . . *My son! Possible criminal!'* Rachel was on her feet, leaning across the desk. '*Added without my permission!'* She banged her fist down.

Mrs Lloyd jumped up to protect the shrinking psychologist. She placed a finger on her call buzzer, breathing heavily. 'If you threaten us I'll request assistance. You don't help your son by such behaviour.' Rachel swallowed and stood back and the psychologist breathed a sigh of relief. 'Frankly you have no say in the matter. But here's a leaflet advising you on the course of action to take should you disagree.'

The psychologist tapped a comment into her report murmuring, 'Parent excessively antagonistic to psychological assistance.'

Mrs Lloyd continued, 'This is for your son's good, Mrs. Kerem. There are health issues associated with children at risk which require continual monitoring.'

Rachel forced herself to appear calm. 'He's perfectly healthy.'

'Somewhat small and underweight for his age. We *are* concerned.' The Head smiled. It was not conciliatory.

The psychologist said, 'Research shows that children who engage in antisocial behaviour and suffer from attention deficit hyperactivity disorder are far more likely to contract gum disease, chronic bronchitis and heart disease as they grow older.' She hesitated. 'There's another marker we must consider. May I inquire whether there's a history of alcoholism in his family?'

'Of course not!' An aunt in Dan's family, a cousin in hers. Don't even think of mentioning them!

'Good.' The psychologist tapped some more.

Rachel turned to the Head. 'Your school completely lacks sympathy for a child who's recently been bereaved and then uprooted from his home. I always understood that Wales is a friendly part of Britain, but both he and I have been treated like unwelcome strangers.'

'Spying, Mrs Kerem.' Mrs Lloyd was self righteously pompous. 'My staff and I and all the children are perfectly aware of your son's involvement.' She lost cool, spitting out, 'And yours.'

The psychologist looked questioningly at both woman, but neither enlightened her.

Rachel picked up her shoulder bag. 'I am withdrawing my son from this school as of now. He's been accepted . . .'

'At Eckstazia's Reality Academy.'

How did everyone in this damn place know her private business? Rachel continued, 'An excellent private school in England where he'll be treated with dignity, kindness and respect.'

The psychologist started up angrily. 'I hope you understand, Mrs Kerem, that my full report and his listing on the At Risk database will both be made available to the head of any school your son attends.'

That evening Rachel's anxieties were partially relieved by James's visit.

Ben said to him, ' I took Bryn to see my pony this afternoon. He let her sit on his back.'

'Bryn?'

Ben ran into the kitchen and picked the cat off its blanket.

'Hold her legs, not just her body,' Rachel said. 'She's not comfy like that.'

The boy cradled the little cat on his knees as James fondled it. 'What a pretty puss.' The cat purred.

'Bryn likes you. She doesn't purr much.' Ben kissed her fluffy crown as he opened the door and let her run out into the night. 'She's only a farm cat. But she'll go to heaven just the same.'

'I'm afraid not,' James said. 'Eternal life is only for humans.'

'I want her there with me.'

Rachel joined his protest. 'There's room in heaven for animals, James.'

'My dear Rachel, that's wishy-washy liberal thinking. There's nothing in the bible about animals being saved.'

'Lion lying down with the lamb on God's holy mountain?'

'That's merely poetic imagery.' He put his hand on hers. 'Accept things, dear. Don't question everything.'

'I'm a scientist. Debating is my nature.'

'You don't doubt the laws of gravity. God's Word is more certain than they are.' He shook his head, smiling. Then he became serious. 'I'm afraid you've caught Alyson's infection. That's why she was dismissed. Too many questions about our work.'

'Your work in the lab? I thought it was because she said Emmanuel is an android.'

'Er . . . Yes, yes, of course.'

As she wondered at his confusion, Ben broke in, 'I'm going to ride Iago tomorrow. I left school today and I'm not going back. And Mum's given me stacks of homework.'

James dimpled. 'You'll be ahead of everyone at the Academy next term.'

'Will I like it?'

'Yes, of course you will. It takes time to settle down but there'll be other new boys like you.'

James' cheery smile always made Rachel feel warm inside. As she prepared coffee in the kitchen she hummed to herself. Yes, her two men were bonding well. She and James would never agree on everything. Why should they? But they'd learnt a lot about each other in the past few days and teething problems were over. She'd ask about the sheep research once Ben was in bed. Both Alyson and Eric had been concerned about it.

Ben lying . . . She tapped on the worktop unconsciously with a spoon. Could the Head be right? Kids go through these phases. Perhaps Ben had made up some of the bullying. She must watch him. Nip it in the bud.

She was still concerned about her projected job move. Much as she hated this country, she disliked uprooting herself and Ben again. Would she be located far away from his new school? And from James? It was for the best, she told herself, shuddering as an image of William on the mountain flashed across her mind. *That* contretemps was over. She'd confessed abjectly to Jesus and was confident she'd received pardon for that and her momentary hatred of God. All that was behind her now.

207

Confident she could sort William, she'd warned Ben to keep mum about tomorrow's trip. It would be a one off, essential because she had to find out what message Dan had left her.

Oh, Dan, lost Dan. No, she mustn't think of that and she must never ever mention her distress at his damnation to James again. No, she wasn't distressed about it any more. She really wasn't. All her worries were laid on Jesus. She was happy.

Ben and James sat close together separating the parts of a model Hereward Swordhand and his horse that James had brought with him. Ben ran upstairs to fetch more glue.

While he was gone Rachel told James about her ill-fated morning with the psychologist. 'So this dreadful report will go to the Academy and ditch his chances.'

James put his arm round her. 'A state school assessment by a second rate Welsh psychologist? They'll dismiss it. Or reassess him themselves with a first class man.'

Ben arrived at the bottom of the stairs. 'You two getting married?'

'Only if you're pleased with it too.' James's dimple deepened as his smile lit up his face. 'Your Mum and I think we'll make a very happy couple, but you're just as important. How would you like to have me as your Dad? I think we get on fine, but you must be sure too.'

'Yeh. OK.'

'Good. I'm really pleased.'

'I'll glue the horse's head on. Look, Mum, he's got eight legs. D'you think he gets them tangled up ever?'

She laughed. 'Sometimes he might. But Hereward sorts him out. He's a champion rider.'

Sudden gunshots made them all jump. Loud, close. From the woods beyond the farm buildings. They rushed to the door and stared at the woods, dark, forbidding under a bright moonlit sky.

Ben screamed, 'They'll shoot Bryn!'

'Stay here, both of you,' James ordered but the boy shot off towards the woods followed by Rachel yelling at him to stop.

Chapter 14

A tiny rustle in the shrubs. A shuffle of young leaves in the night breeze. Rachel stood quite still, straining her ears. Thank God, no more gunfire. No trampling poachers. But no noisy child either, calling for his lost cat. And it was dark as a cave, the moon's light hidden by pine, fir and head high bramble.

She yelled Ben's name again and again as she stumbled through the damp undergrowth. Rotten leaves stank decay. Roots tripped her. Brambles trapped her legs, ripped her bare arms. She ignored them. Called and called in vain for her son.

No reply. Nothing at all.

So Shuji had confronted William about the ammunition stored in Penybwlch and now William was taking his revenge on her. Hadn't he boasted previously how well he knew the woods? Hadn't he hidden in them himself from his hag of a mother when he was a boy?

William had found him. The poachers had abducted him.

She would never see Ben again.

Sickness rose in her throat. Her knees felt liquid. She clung to the scaly trunk of a pine, slithered down it till she was on her knees. Then she pulled herself together.

Curse them all. They won't win, she swore. Where's James? Together we'll scour the whole of this rotten country till we find him.

Distant rumbling built rapidly into a cacophony, jarring her ears. The noise reverberated round the hills, growling and clattering. A whirring of blades.

James had called the police. They'd sent an autocopter. Unmanned, and monitored from the base in Caernarfon. Capable of picking human sound out of any racket. Night vision. It would spot Ben and his captors straight away.

But why hadn't they just sent a police car like last time he was lost? Why the autocopter? It carried non-lethal weapons and was normally used in situations dangerous to riot police. Against mobs, *armed* mobs.

She screamed vainly at the hovering shadow overhead. 'Get lost! He's only a little boy!' As she yelled she heard exploding canisters spraying tear gas into the woods. The whirling monster had pinpointed her. Heat ray gun, immobilising its victim by toasting the skin to 54°C? Or pulsed energy? And she saw in her mind the man shot into the air at the town riot, emptying his bowels, vomiting, totally disorientated.

The robotic raptor homed in on her. Hearing her. Seeing her.

She ran. Anywhere as long as it was away. Her terror momentarily overwhelmed her mother instinct.

But the autocopter controllers were merciful. Perhaps they could see she held no rifle, so they didn't unleash the full force of weaponry on the frightened woman. Instead it was the gas that immobilised her. It forced her burning eyes to squeeze tight shut. Her nose ran with mucus and she coughed and spluttered. She stood quite still, unable even to think, trying in vain to shield her face with arms and hands.

She staggered downhill, falling frequently. By luck she reached the gate into the garden and stumbled into James' arms.

He held her tight, murmuring endearments. Supported her through the house to the warm lounge with its comforting log fire where he wrapped her in a rug. He wiped her eyes and nose. Her coughing subsided.

'Ben,' she whispered. *'Ben.'*

'The police've come. They stopped me searching, too dangerous, but I told them about Ben.'

'William. . . the poachers have got him.'

'They'll find him. Everything's under control.'

It wasn't, but she was shattered. She shut her itching eyes and heard through a half conscious haze the voices of Jennifer and Shuji questioning James. They were angry with her. Why had she rushed so foolishly into the woods? James explained and Jennifer exploded with rage over uncontrollable Ben.

Shuji said coldly, 'So now the police must split their forces and search for that wretched boy as well as the terrorists.'

What terrorists? Rachel didn't have to speculate for long.

Shuji continued, *'She* told me William Parry is hoarding ammunition on the farm.'

The other two scientists exclaimed in horror.

'He's useful to me and I haven't reported it to the police. That was a mistake.'

James said, 'So he's supplying the terrorists.'

'Indubitably.'

'And how did they discover our research labs?' Jenny asked. 'Parry again?'

'Certainly. Our security relies heavily on our concealment in this unlikely venue. Only a select few know our location.'

'We know the man's a criminal,' James said. 'The terrorists would pay him well.'

Rachel was overcome with coughing and didn't hear the reply. As she recovered a little she heard James leave the room saying he'd make her a drink to soothe her throat.

Jennifer and Shuji continued their talk in hushed voices.

'We can blame the terrorists for the local outbreak,' Jennifer said.

'Truly all things work together for good for those who love the Lord. And in a few weeks' time there'll be too much commotion for anyone to trouble about Snowdonia.' His voice trembled with excitement.

'If they *had* broken in . . .!'

'Then security robots would have destroyed all our work. But Jesus protected it.'

'Praise his name!' Jenny too was on a high. 'His return is imminent.'

'Without a doubt. And we, his chosen, are blessed to assist his coming.'

And as Rachel strained to understand them, James returned with Inspector Jones.

'*Ben?*' Rachel croaked, her chest tight and painful.

The inspector's voice was cold. 'You were the only person discovered in the woods, Mrs Kerem. We're still looking.'

Shuji broke in. 'William Parry stores ammunition in the farm sheds. Mrs Kerem has just informed me . . .'

Liar, she thought angrily. Breaker of promises.

'Somehow he discovered the nature of our work here . . .'

She remembered her conversation with William on the mountain.

' . . . and informed his terrorist friends.'

Jones nodded grimly. 'We'll find him.' He turned to a thin policewoman hidden behind his bulky body. 'Test her hands.'

The woman grasped Rachel's muddy hands and inspected them before passing a small sensor over both back and front. An X-ray fluorescence molecular sensor. Gunpowder check.

'Test positive, sir.'

'Can't be,' Rachel whispered.

'Her house,' Jones barked. 'And the farm sheds.'

The policewoman marched off smartly.

The inspector turned to Rachel. 'Now. Explain.'

She said hoarsely, 'Policewoman . . . held . . . my hands. Has she touched ammunition?'

Jones frowned. 'We're always careful to avoid contamination.' But as he didn't press further, Rachel could see she'd scored a point. Instead he accused her of warning the terrorists. His frustration at his failure to capture even one was exacerbated by his superior's recent reprimand .

'I didn't see anyone in the woods,' Rachel retorted as both her voice and head began to clear. 'How can they be terrorists? Would terrorists fire shots to let everyone know they were coming? Poachers, I bet.'

'So you know them?'

'No. But I know they've got my son.' She started to weep inconsolably. James knelt beside her, arms round her.

Jones fired further questions at her. 'Explain why you were at the illegal market consorting with a known dissident, Geraint Parry, known as Parryboots. You're involved in this fracas tonight, warning terrorists. Where did they go?'

Shuji interrupted. 'Mrs Kerem isn't in a fit state at present to answer all your questions, Inspector, but she's been very frank with me and with Dr Restall, her fiancé. We can reassure you on all the points you've raised with such admirable clarity. For instance, she spent the evening with Dr Restall in her cottage and didn't leave until the shooting started. Now it's important you find the boy.'

'The autocopter controllers saw no one but her. It's been withdrawn. Far too expensive to use for a civilian search. Mrs. Kerem, you were in the woods with them, so again, where did they go?'

At that moment the policewoman returned. 'Sir.'

He nodded.

'Sir, no ammo in the sheds but definite traces. The house is clean. The boy's fast asleep in bed. Sir.'

The room spun as Rachel collapsed in relief. Her stomach went into spasm. She retched. She lost control all over the chair, the rug James had put round her and the carpet. Through a haze she was aware of their concern mingled with irritation at the stench. Grumbling, Jenny cleaned her up, spending most time on disinfecting the carpet and chair. James supported her to the cottage past a blur of police. Jenny half carried her upstairs, removed her clothes without hiding her disgust and helped her into bed.

When she woke next morning, Ben stood by the bed, shamefaced.

'Cup of tea, Mum?'

Rachel rolled over and groaned. The early spring sun lit up her room, dazzling her sore eyes. It must be very late. She stretched out her hand for the tea.

'What's that mess on your arm?' Ben worried.

The scratched skin was red and swollen. No wonder it was throbbing.

'I caught myself on brambles last night.' Blood poisoning? Then she remembered. 'Tear gas. It affects raw skin.' She struggled upright and the room swayed slightly. Cautiously she got out of bed. She was OK. Just about. She padded to the bathroom for soothing lotion and plastered it over her arms. Her stomach heaved. No, she wasn't OK. She crept back into bed.

'Thanks for the tea, Ben, but water's all I can manage.'

He sat on the bed. 'Sorry, Mum,' and burst into tears.

She put her arm round him gingerly because his jumper aggravated her broken skin. 'Twice is twice too many, young man.'

'Won't run off again. Promise.' He brightened. 'The policewoman thought I was asleep. I fooled her.'

'So you did, you wretch. Wouldn't have fooled me.'

'Bryn hadn't gone far. I caught her by the gate to the house. She slept with me all night.'

Rachel coughed and sipped some water.

'The poachers got away, didn't they? William . . .'

'Yes, he was there with his friends. If you'd gone into the woods they'd have mistaken you for game in the dark.' Then she buried her head in her pillow saying in a muffled voice, 'I thought they'd kidnapped you.'

'William wouldn't do that.'

'You don't know him like I do. He's threatened to.' Thank God the police would take him in now. But, and it was a big but, she needed him so she could get to Elwyn's and find what was hidden in her pendant. And then there was Jenny's experiment and those odd references to a local outbreak followed by a great commotion.

'William's got night goggles.'

Raising her head from the pillow she replied, 'I'm sure he has. I put nothing past that man,' she said. 'That doesn't alter the fact he could have shot you.'

'Or you.' He began crying again.

'We're both fine,' she comforted him. Then she read him a lecture on the perfidy of William and his fellow conspirators, the evils of poaching and the sanctity of wild life. 'All the same,' she concluded, 'people round here *are* short of food.'

'That's what Parryboots said.' He thought for a minute. 'Will you go with William to his cousin's?'

'I must. Dad's message to us.'

He nodded sagely.

She continued, 'Tomorrow. I can't manage it today.'

'I'll go and tell William.'

She wasn't happy, but she said, 'Warn him the police are after him. And tell him what I said about poaching.'

He stood at the door, his face solemn and adult. 'Will you be all right on your own?'

She smiled. 'Yes, dear. Quite all right.' Then, more seriously, 'But I don't want you hanging round with William. And you've got that homework I downloaded . . .'

He fled.

Eventually she dressed and ensconced herself on the settee. She felt distinctly better, even managing some toast. James arrived, hidden behind a large bunch of daffodils and catkins he'd picked from the sheltered garden. He arranged it with a designer's flair in a jug he found in the kitchen.

He was full of solicitude and distressed to see her inflamed arms, but in a hurry to start work. He'd be back later, she must rest, be quiet, read something improving from Emmanuel's website. It was full of good things, couldn't go wrong if she followed her mentor's explanations of God's word.

After he rushed off she looked at the flowers for a long time, admiring the golden trumpets among the dangling lamb tails and pale unfolding leaves. If only she could live for the moment like birds and beetles. Enjoy this beauty and forget her troubles. She rearranged her cushions to pad the broken spring on the settee and dozed.

The doorknocker roused her. Annie, scowling as usual but carrying a plate of scones. 'Heard you're off sick,' she said briskly. 'So I made *pice bach*.'

Rachel thanked her in surprise. 'I haven't forgotten that lovely chocolate cake you made us, Annie.'

'These'll do you good,' Annie said, turning on her heel and striding back to the house, her black skirt flapping against her stick legs.

Rachel put the plate on the kitchen work surface to share with Ben later.

She'd barely settled down again when James returned. No, thank you, he wouldn't try Annie's scones because he'd just eaten lunch. He seemed uneasy. He went to the window and stared out at the sunlit drive beyond her tiny front yard, his back hunched. 'You've been in the wars continually this past two weeks. Attacked in the town, falling on the hillside and now suffering from tear gas. God has his reasons for permitting this pain and punishment. Perhaps you've something to tell me.'

She held her breath. Had William told him?

'Since your arrival I've often noticed how unhappy you look. Is there something from your past life you need to confess before you can feel fully guilt-free? If you feel unable to trust *me*,' and his voice was full of sadness, 'then speak to Emmanuel. We both want to help you lead a full and happy life.'

'No misspent youth,' she smiled, hoping to lighten the mood in her relief he hadn't found out about William.

He turned round and stared at her, persisting, 'Your marriage to an unbeliever?'

'Why does everyone run Daniel down? He was a good man, honest and upright.'

'The devil can disguise himself as an angel of light to confound the saved.'

'Take that back this minute, James.'

'I didn't mean your late husband . . .'

'Eckstazia has been less than honest with me over Dan. In Liverpool and Coventry they pretended friendship so they could worm their way into my home and search everything. And here too. Jennifer Beard has gone through my private belongings.'

He looked hugely embarrassed. 'No, she wouldn't . . . We don't do that kind of thing.'

'What do they want?'

'I really don't know anything about all that.' He was apologetic, almost shaken. He changed the subject, poached an egg for her lunch. He was tender, caring. Oughtn't she to ask the doctor to check her arms?

When he left Ben came back. 'William found dead piglets in the woods. Tear gas done it. He was very angry because the sow was unhappy and mad. He had to shoot her. He wasn't with the poachers. He's angry with them too. He told them not to shoot round Penybwlch because Shuji would report them, but they came anyway because there's lots of animals in our woods this time of year. He says you *must* come to Elwyn's tomorrow because it's serious with the sheep. Oh, and he said not to worry about the police. Jones don't dare do more than threaten. It's just for show.'

She must get to Isallt tomorrow. She was certain by now that her pendent contained the missing information about Eckstazia. Whatever it was, it was vitally important to them. So much so they wanted it destroyed, even four years after Dan recorded it. Shuji and Hilary had both mentioned it. Odd that James didn't know about it. She groaned, remembering police weapons and electronic equipment could well have corrupted the files over the past few weeks.

Restlessly she watched world bulletins on her yapp. The European Society for the Welfare of Wildlife was cock-a-hoop that woodland and wetland across the Union were increasing. Farming too was making progress along organic lines. A bill to enforce changes in land use and the banning of all pesticides was due to come into force in 2030. Insect life would begin to recover at last. More butterflies, dragonflies, pollinating beetles and bees. Following this report a Chinese landowner in Tanzania described his move there. The market back home was excellent. Labour in Tanzania cheap. The interviewer asked was he underpaying? Of course not, his workers got higher wages than any other employees in the district. A Tanzanian factory manager extolled his value-added foods, chilled and shipped to the China at huge profit. Trade was booming everywhere but here.

And Rachel remembered her conversation with Parryboots, and felt ashamed that she with her postgraduate degree knew less about the world than a Welsh tradesman.

*

Rachel was woken in the night by Ben complaining of tummy ache. He was sick before he reached the bathroom. She mopped him up, helped him wash out his mouth and put a warm jumper on him because he was shivering. Cleaning the floor made her nauseous, and she too was sick. Then she had stomach cramps and retched again and again until nothing came up but a thin watery chyme. Diarrhoea followed. Ben joined her and they were wretched together.

She stoked up the wood burner and they sat in stinking misery and pain on the sofa. Sometimes they sweated. At other times they were chilled. Occasionally one or other would get up and struggle back to the bathroom. Afraid of dehydration she made sure they frequently sipped salted sugar water.

Gradually the wish to die passed.

'Food poisoning,' she said, thinking back over the day's menu. Ben's ground beef? She'd cooked it thoroughly and, still feeling unwell from the previous night, she hadn't had any herself. Soil bacteria from organic vegetables? All washed and properly cooked.

'Lots of kids were off school sick last week,' Ben said helpfully.

She felt thoroughly miserable. Perhaps this sickness was more of God's punishment for her liaison with William. And God had even included poor Ben in his wrath. She left a message for James not to visit until they were clear of possible infection. James texted a comforting reply without further comments.

William was less courteous. He swore as he shouted through the locked back door, 'If this is a joke it isn't funny. You've *got* tc come to Elwyn's, Rachel. It's *urgent*.'

She didn't reply.

Ben went to bed early without complaining, leaving Rachel so low-spirited and feeble that she contacted Emmanuel on line.

He was in a church. Not a little peasant chapel like Llanfechan but a soaring cathedral where sunlight spilt bright colours from medieval glass across the stone floor. He knelt with his back to her, facing a stone altar with medieval carvings. Its surface was covered with a white cloth embroidered with gold, but his hair shone more brightly than the thread. The cross was solid silver, intricately carved with Celtic interweavings. Her pendant's ornamentation was tawdry by comparison.

Only distant organ music sounded in that place of peace. The sanctuary of saints. The house of prayer and praise. In her weakness she almost wept as her anxieties dropped away one by one and she shared its holiness.

At last he turned to face her. His face glowed and she remembered being told how the faces of saints shone as they spoke to God. 'Let me tell you a mystery. Very shortly this world will come to an end. But we shan't all perish. No, some of us will be raised to greet the Lord in the heavens without passing through death and decay. Like Elijah, swept up in a fiery chariot. Like Jesus, raptured into heaven forty days after his resurrection.' He raised his arms to the heavens, 'Even so, come Lord Jesus. As once you departed from this sinful world so unworthy of your love, come again and judge the sinner, punish the wicked, bring righteousness, love and peace over all the earth.'

She was humbled by his companionship with the Holy.

He gazed directly into her eyes. 'I think perhaps there's something you need to tell me.'

How had he guessed? Had God spoken to him directly?

His voice was serene as the music. 'Sometimes the Lord allows us to suffer in order to remind us of past sins unredeemed. Perhaps Daniel . . . ?'

She was puzzled and exclaimed, 'Oh not him. William.'

With sublime tenderness he coaxed her to tell him of her sexual encounter. She said how disgusted she'd been with herself.

'That's the prompting of the Lord,' Emmanuel said gently. 'How dreadful if you'd enjoyed fornication, Rachel.'

She tried to meet his eyes firmly, while squashing into oblivion a little insubordinate voice whispering, 'But I did enjoy it at the time.'

217

'We can remove William. But have you told James?'

She shook her head.

'Don't you think you *should* confess? Throw yourself on his mercy?'

'It'd cause him too much hurt and it won't happen again.'

Emmanuel shook his head and looked sad. 'Be open and honest in all your dealings with your husband to be, my dear.'

'I must make my own decision on this, Emmanuel.'

'As you think best. And I respect your current decision, while not agreeing with it. I'll pray for you.' He turned towards the altar again, communing with a spirit far holier than any human soul.

She felt a rat. A rebellious one, refusing to go quietly through the Eckstazia maze. Shouldn't she do as Emmanuel advised? He was so much closer to God than she was. She watched, mesmerized, as gradually the scene in the cathedral faded and she was left looking at today's message on his webpage. 'Jesus said, "Nation will make war upon nation, kingdom upon kingdom; there will be famines in many places. With all these things the birth-pangs of the New Age begin." Even so, come, Lord Jesus.'

*

Thud. Thud.

William banged early next morning on the back door.

Ben was making tea for his mother. 'She can't come. She's way too poorly. I'm poorly too.'

William griped at this feeble behaviour. Wasn't Elwyn's problem far more urgent than a bit of belly ache? 'Tomorrow then?'

'Only if she's OK.'

'Useless women,' he muttered loud enough to penetrate the door.

'I'm hardly Hereward Swordhand,' Rachel said when Ben relayed the message. 'He's up and about straight after a massive headwound.'

Ben giggled. 'Unreal, Mum.'

James sent a text message. He needed to talk to her on a matter of grave urgency. Late afternoon.

As she OK'd this, Ben ran sobbing from the little front garden with a mass of black feathers in his hands.

'The cat,' Rachel said, about to give him a simple lesson on predators and prey.

The boy shook his head. 'He hasn't been mauled. He's all in one piece.' The blackbird was in full spring plumage, and his beak was a brilliant yellow. 'I always hear him singing and this morning I didn't.'

She took the tiny body gently. 'I liked to listen to him too.'

'He's got a nest in next door's bushes.'

Any other male that moves in will sort the fledglings out, she thought sadly, but didn't tell her son.

'I fed him yesterday. Bits of Annie's scones.'

Annie's scones!

She and Ben had both eaten them two nights ago. Surely the woman wouldn't have poisoned them? But she remembered something else. 'Didn't you give some to Bryn?'

Little Bryn was fit and well, washing herself in the sunshine on top of the garden wall. She purred as Ben stroked her. 'She sniffed at them, but she wouldn't eat them. And she eats most anything.'

'Cats are the wariest of animals. Are there any scones left?'

He shook his head.

'Not even crumbs?'

'No, Mum.' He looked up at her. 'Was there something nasty in them?'

She hesitated. She had suspicions, no proof. She could ask her doctor to send their stool samples to the path lab, but it might be too late now. Would they check out the bird?

'I don't know,' she said. 'But I can find out.' She put the bird in a cardboard box and called the doctor. He was out on his rounds, said his receptionist. Snowed under with calls. The current flu epidemic. If it wasn't really urgent. . . Surely Mrs Kerem could come to the surgery herself? Appointment – let me see – nothing left this week, but next Thursday? Oh dear, it's really urgent is it? Well, I'll let him know as soon as possible.

To pass the time Rachel checked out Penybwlch research citations. She was sure William was wrong when he told her there was nothing. He was an impatient man. His search would have been less than thorough.

But he was right.

Eckstazia's Chinese research into hazardous pesticides on cotton was mentioned. Work in India on diseases in jute, now widely grown as biofuel. Potato blight studied in the Russian facility. Development of renewable energy resources across the world.

Nothing on rinderpest.

She idled through Eckstazia's website.

Though Eckstazia had been an important body worldwide before Dan's death, its influence had mushroomed since. As she had predicted, Hilary Barron had recently been appointed media tsar. World-wide Eckstazia controlled the Republicans in the US and were strong in the

European parliament and United Nations. Their financial and spiritual assistance to African churches had united many of these disparate groups into a Holy Alliance awaiting Christ's imminent return. South American churches were strongly supportive.

So many people admired Eckstazia and supported its projects. How could anything dishonest stay hidden? No one doubted them. Except Dan. Thinking of him something clicked in her mind. Tubers. Ben said Hilary and Shuji were talking about Dan and tubers. And there was that time when Shuji was so distressed and he'd said, 'It can't be right, Jesus. We shouldn't use tuber-something.'

She voiced close-sounding words to the yapp.

She came up with tuberine. A neuromuscular paralysant. Can be lethal in small doses. Normal use – open heart surgery. Has been used by some regimes to assassinate prisoners when mixed with scoline and administered as an injection. Gives appearance of heart attack with hypotension and respiratory failure.

Dan had died of a heart attack at the surgery of the University Hospital dentist. And Eckstazia funded the hospital personnel.

No, Ektazia wouldn't murder someone.

Wouldn't they? In order to facilitate Jesus' return? Hilary had told her that anyone obstructing Elstazia would be crushed. She said to Shuji, 'The coming reign of peace and love justifies anything we do to hasten the Lord's return.' James often quoted St Paul's claim that Eckstazia members would judge those who tried to delay his return and punish them. Jenny had used that odd sentence – we'll *finish* anyone who's against the Lord. Did she mean finish as in physically terminated?

Or were their words mere Eckstazia-talk?

She had no evidence.

Only speculation as improbable as her earlier notion that William and his gang were going to hide away in Snowdonia fastnesses.

She looked for the doctor from her window, admiring the snowy unfolding petals of a giant magnolia by the carpark. Eventually she saw Jennifer Beard getting into her car. She staggered over.

'Good heavens, Rachel, you're white as the magnolia. Nothing serious, I hope?'

Rachel cautiously replied she was almost better from food poisoning, thank you. 'Are you going to Isallt to check the rinderpest experiment?'

Jennifer eyed her thoughtfully, the dark crease between her eyes deepening. 'James told you, did he? Yes, unscheduled visit. Keeps the guy on his toes.'

'Are you testing the new strain? The highly lethal one?'

Jennifer started the engine before replying. 'No, of course not. God, Rachel, we'd never get permission to do field trials with that one. This experiment uses improved vaccination against the new strain of lineage one that erupted eighteen months ago in Sudan and the Argentine. It's under control there now but there were rumours it killed sheep as well as cattle. So I'm checking. All perfectly proper and above board.' She looked at her watch nervously. 'Lot to do before next week's trip to India. Wretched conference in London this weekend too. We're all going. Hilary's orders. Some other time, eh?'

That's never, thought Rachel as she watched the scientist tear off down the drive. But she was relieved at the clarification of the research.

The day dragged on. She made supper, leaving Ben to watch for the doctor.

'He's come,' he called. 'James is talking to him. He's not getting out of his car. He's driving away.'

By the time Rachel opened the front door the doctor had vanished and James was on his way to the cottage. His normally cheerful face was grim.

'I told him you were greatly recovered and didn't need a visit. Really Rachel, he's a very busy man and you shouldn't call him out unnecessarily.'

She gaped at him. 'You sent the doctor away without asking me?'

'I watched you talking to Jenny earlier. You're obviously better.'

How *dare* he? In her fury she shut the door in his face, but he kept his foot in it. 'Rachel, we need to speak.'

Reluctantly she let him in.

'Go upstairs, Ben. What I have to say to your mother is private.'

His face was red with suppressed rage, the delightful dimple wholly eclipsed. He swallowed several times then burst out, 'You and that bloody peasant.'

'William's been lying to you?' Curse the man. May he rot in hell.

'Parry? I never speak to the man if I can help it.'

Her flesh crawled. '*Emmanuel?*'

'Of course, of course.' He was breathing as heavily as a marathon runner approaching the finishing line.

'You and he talk about *me*?'

'Don't be obtuse. I *control* him.'

'So he is an android,' she snarled.

'What does it matter? I help you, don't I? I rescued you from the hold your wicked husband had over you.'

'How dare you!'

221

'I never meant to fall in love. What a fool I've been.' His cheeks and neck were as scarlet as a turkey's wattles.

'An *android*! You liar!'

'*Me?* It's you and Parry. How could you sink so low? How could you be so deceitful after all I've done for you?'

Her belly and chest were iceblocks. She would never be warm again.

'Rape?' He took her silence for assent. 'That scoundrel raped you? Thank heaven for that!'

Outraged she spat, 'No. It wasn't rape. I was lonely.'

His eyes protruded, his face grew purple. He lunged at her and she jumped behind the settee.

Words slipped from her mouth unbidden. '*Eckstazia's stooges* murdered Dan with tuberine.'

'*How did you find out?* He was evil. Satan's agent. '

So all her doubts were resolved.

He picked Ben's Hereward Swordhand from the table and threw it wildly in her direction. It smashed against the stove and fell into the hearth.

They glared at each other across the settee. He was panting. She was shivering. In the momentary silence she thought inconsequentially that his fire could never melt her ice nor her coldness ever quench his flaming anger.

'You'd better go,' she said at last, her voice high and constricted.

He struggled to control his rage. 'Eckstazia don't accept fornicators among their employees. Remember that.' Then he swallowed hard, clenching and unclenching his fingers. 'You're a wicked woman, Rachel. I'm disappointed, deeply disappointed in you. You're dishonest and untrustworthy.'

She knew he wasn't a violent man by nature. But neither would he forgive and forget.

He opened the door. With his back to her he said in a strange croaking voice, 'I loved you. I wanted Emmanuel to bring you to happiness in our Saviour.'

To her great relief he left quietly, merely slamming the door.

She turned to see Ben at the foot of the stairs.

He was trembling. 'Dad? Dad was murdered?'

She nodded, speechless.

He picked up the shattered model with tender care. His voice was tiny, broken like the toy. 'I can't mend it.'

No, nothing could be mended now.

'Mum. Aren't you getting married after all?'

The ice of James's betrayals filled her throat.
'Mum. *Mum*. Won't the doctor test my blackbird?'

Chapter 15

'I don't fuck women unless they ask for it,' William said in a friendly way as he and Rachel climbed through the woods from the cottage.

Rachel said nothing. Emmanuel – no, *James* - had threatened to remove William yesterday. At the time she thought he merely meant to sack him. Now, knowing James's poisonous hatred and Eckstazia's capacity for murder, should she warn the odious man of his danger?

William jogged so fast she panted to keep up, out of condition after her sickness. Toss bounced ahead, snuffling at the grasses and bushes, happy in the spring sun. Wood grasses grew rank under budding oak and ash. Great clumps of bluebell leaves and buds would soon turn the woodland into a blue sea. Here and there sweet chestnut and lime had been planted by long dead Victorian hands and now their bright tender leaves were pushing out of protective winter buds. Banks of spreading rhododendrons would soon be in royal purple flower, overhung with golden pendants of laburnum. Blackbirds and robins sang with abandon from bush and tree claiming their nest territories.

Rachel was blind to it all as she thought, the world would be a better place without William Parry.

Near the hill top William pointed out the remains of a dead fox half under some brambles. 'Lynx,' he said. 'Must've been disturbed cos lynx always drag their kill away.'

How full of cruelty life is, she thought.

They reached a high stone wall at the top of the woods. Broken glass and rusted barbed wire ran along the top. William pushed aside a clutch of nettles and briar rose and unpadlocked a wooden door. She followed the dog through and was immediately on open mountain. Hill and hidden valley, rocky outcrop, heather and sleeping bracken. The endless moor, broken only by sentinel mountains guarding Bwlch y Ddeufaen and the Roman Pass. Exposed and bleak in its late winter dress, but not as desolate as her heart.

'Best time of year,' William said. 'Lambing almost over. Long hours. Late at night, up before dawn. Hard work but rewarding.'

William working?

'I'm at Elwyn's all through the lambing,' he said as if reading her thoughts. Then, grumbling, 'The ewe's died. You should've come earlier.' He pointed across the moor to a smallholding isolated among a clutch of trees on the flank of a distant hill. 'That's Elwyn's. I grew up there.' He stared at her and raised the eyebrow of his damaged eye. 'What's that retard done?'

She shrugged.

'Annie said he was in a champion strop last night.'

'It's nothing.'

He took a small black walkie talkie from his pocket and tapped. Static blurred the reply, and he repeated his taps. He nodded with satisfaction at the second reply.

'Letting Elwyn know we're coming?' Rachel asked.

'Correct.' He grinned at her. 'Coded. Very secure.'

'Morse,' she said.

'You're the first person I've met in years who knows anything about Morse.'

'We used it as kids at school.' She couldn't remember it well enough to interpret his taps, but she wouldn't let him know that.

She plodded on, head down.

Murdered. Dan murdered. Even now she could hardly believe it. She thought, 'I believed in Emmanuel. Lived out the life he taught me. Tried to copy his saintliness. Told him everything. No, I told *James* - and God knows who else. Fool, I never suspected. I should have known. I *do* know android conversation is indistinguishable from human's. I was duped because I'm too trusting. I wanted so much to be part of Eckstazia's family. Their friendliness – all fake. Trying to find out what Dan had on them. Even William's better. He never pretends to be kind.' She fingered her pendant. 'Today I'll find out. What then? I'm on my own. Completely.'

She tried to blank her erratic thoughts to everything but the miles ahead along the uneven track. Round gorsebushes and obstructing boulders, through boggy patches and across chuckling rills, on and on. Toss trotted in front, enjoying the myriad well-loved scents, plumed tail held out behind. The warm sun woke bees and beetles. It couldn't reach the chill round her heart.

'Hey, let's have your glasses,' William called. 'Our ravens.' He pointed to two distant birds wheeling and diving, flying on their backs. Together they watched the pair soar towards the sun and swoop down again, somersaulting as they came. 'Bigger 'n crows. Wedge shaped tails.'

She thought, if only I was a bird. Gliding on thermals. No cares except food and chicks. No heaven, no hell. No need for salvation.

'Not many birds on the moors now.'

'No. I haven't heard any plovers or stonechats.'

'Not permitted to kill their predators, isn't it? Weasels, rats, ferrets, crows and foxes take out the ground nesters. Even hen harriers are disappearing because they nest on the ground too. And now we've got wildcat the tree nesters'll go in time. And the woods are losing bluebells to the pigs.' He paused, pretending not to watch her but obviously concerned for her, to her surprise. 'I'll take you to see the deer calve one day soon. Bit of a walk so you'll have to get fit.'

She tramped on towards Isallt.

'Not that way, Rachel. Quaky bog. Not up to the neck, but hard to get out of all the same. When sheep grazed these hills they used to die there. Deer calves and foals still do.'

He took her a roundabout route, down a steep incline where a stream blocked their way. The water ran peatbrown and little clouds of early midges hovered over it.

'Used to be a bridge here.' As he splashed through the shallow water his walkie talkie bleeped. 'Right. Spysat's due over in ten minutes.'

'That's Elwyn?'

'His computer checks satellite times and it's linked to his radio. There's not many places to shelter this time of year. Too early for bracken.' He pointed to a wall above the stream. 'We'll hunker down by that. It's been warmed by the sun, so with luck our temperature will be close enough not to stand out. Keep your hands and face out of sight. Our clothes are dark enough to meld with the heather. Dog's a damn nuisance; too much belly white.'

Toss started to whine. He stared back the way they'd come, wagging his tail softly and giving little wuffs of welcome.

William groaned. 'Ten to one that's Ben following us. Couldn't have timed it worse. You get over to the stones and wait. Toss 'n I'll sort him out.' The dog gave a happy bark and raced William back over the stream and up the valley side.

She reached the wall and peered over. It was the sidewall of a ruined farmhouse, nettles and rowan saplings growing rank inside and a gap where the door had been. It had faced across the moor to the distant sea, a dream of a view.

She squatted where William had pointed out, head on knees. How had they lived, those distant people? An impoverished existence here on this barren moor. Sheep, a cow perhaps, a pig. Walking daily to work in the granite quarry over the hill. Breathing in the rock dust. No compensation for the hacking cough that slowly, inevitably killed the breadwinner.

She'd spent the night sitting immobile on the settee, unable to sleep after James had left. It was warm by the stones. Snoozy.

Next she knew, Toss's wet nose was nuzzling her hand and Ben was scrambling up the bank of the stream holding out her yapp. 'You forgot it. You need it for Dad's data chip.'

'*No*! It tracks every five minutes.'

'Can't you dismantle the pulse?'

She shook her head.

Ben's mouth turned down.

'No worries, we'll use Elwyn's,' William said. 'We're still inside Penybwlch's boundary. Quite legitimate for you to be here, Rachel, checking out your bugs.' He thrust the yapp into the tumbled wall. 'Pick it up on the way back.'

'You all right, Mum?'

'Yeh. Fine,' she told him.

'Don't you worry about what James said.' He squeezed her hand. 'He's pits. *I* love you.'

'Thanks, guy.'

'They're haters.'

'Yeh. Sure.' She gave a weak grin.

He and William strode on together with Toss leading the way happily.

She heard Ben say, 'I'm on the At Risk list.'

'Which is?'

'I might turn into a criminal. I truant, start fights. . .'

'Good man. So did I.'

It wasn't what she wanted Ben to hear. Or was William's fiercely independent view better than James' reproofs?

Ben told William about the blackbird and scones. 'Annie wouldn't put something nasty in them, would she?'

'Screwy old witch. She might. Mad as a blowfly in a sheep's arse. She farmed Penybwlch when I was a kid. . .'

So Annie did sometimes tell the truth.

'. . . she knows where all the poisonous plants grow. There's bryony berries. Celandine gives you a bad turn. I never eat any of her cooking unless she eats it too.'

'She's evil,' Ben said firmly.

'Steer clear of the old bat, that's my advice.'

She trudged after them, getting ever further behind.

They waited for her at the boundary wall between Isallt and Penybwlch. Both faces showed anxiety. She forced her mouth into a confident smile as she climbed the stile.

William said, 'He told me about Dan.' He looked shocked.

Even then she didn't warn him.

In front of them Isallt farm buildings sheltered in a small hollow. Beyond the hillfarm the land started to slope down again towards the coast and a little town. A few roof tops were visible, a chapel frontage, a Welsh flag limp in the quiet air and the tops of some trees. Further still lay blue sea and the entrance to the Menai Straits. Close to the farm were sheep pens as secretly constructed as William's hen sheds. Woodland and gorse scrub half circled them. Invisible unless you knew what to look for.

Elwyn was stockier than William. His brown face was equally lined and his clothes smelt of sheep dung. He pulled his greasy cap more firmly onto his head, spat on his palms and hauled a carcase from behind one of the pens. 'Is that it?' he asked Rachel.

The poor corpse was stiff and cold.

She turned its head upwards. Already maggots burrowed round dirty nose and mouth.

'Dribbles and frothing?'

'Yes,' Elwyn said.

She checked the eyes. 'Cattle get red patches but she hasn't got those.'

The shepherd's face was full of anxiety as he jerked the stiff back legs apart.

'Phorr!' William exclaimed. Dried faeces caked the swollen udder and the wool round the anus.

Ben held his nose. 'Gross.'

She asked, 'Diarrhoea?'

Elwyn nodded.

Alyson had described rinderpest symptoms to her and yesterday she'd checked pictures on the internet, but she wasn't a vet, so how could she be certain? 'I think so,' she said. 'But cattle plague may present differently in sheep. Any others?'

Elwyn took off his cap and scratched his head. His hair was lighter brown than William's, receding at the forehead and with a touch of grey down the sides. There was a white line across his forehead where his cap had protected it from the sun. His English wasn't as fluent as William's and he reverted to a slow and gentle Welsh. 'Yesterday a lamb died with the same symptoms. I told Beard when she visited. She was odd. Like she expected it. Almost pleased.'

William spat contempt.

'Told me to leave it with the dead ewe but I buried it. There's thirteen more ewes down with fever, not eating, no milk.' He indicated the small pens adjoining the nearest covered yard. 'Three of their lambs I've put to ewes that had stillbirths and the others we bottle feed. In this yard there's the treated ewes.' Then he pointed to a second yard. 'They're controls.'

'How many Welsh ewes in all?' Rachel asked in English.

'Not *Welsh*,' William jeered. 'Think our sheep'd stand being penned up like this? They'd be over the hurdles and up the mountains before you spit. No, these are stupid lowlander ewes. Four hundred of them.'

'Will all the sick ewes die?' Elwyn's kindly face was screwed up tight. 'The lambs as well?'

'It spreads when they lick the newborns,' she replied gently. Then, puzzled, 'It doesn't make sense. Tell me again, Elwyn. You injected all the sheep in the first pen with the Sudan virus?'

'No, only five of them.'

'Ah. So then you injected all the other sheep with this new vaccine to prevent them catching the virus?'

'No.'

'None of them?'

'None.'

'Jenny told me she was testing two things. A rumour that some sheep as well as cattle died in Sudan and Argentina last year and an improved vaccine developed in our lab. It doesn't add up.'

'She promised they wouldn't suffer. What can I do?'

'Nothing for the ones that are sick. Make sure they don't contaminate the controls.' She explained the precautions he must take.

'Beard didn't tell me any of that. Perhaps I've spread it to them too,' he growled as he walked away from them, head averted.

'Girl's blouse,' Ben said. '*I* wouldn't cry over sheep.'

'You're a dummy.' William's voice was cold. To Rachel he said, 'Deer live in these woods. Will they be infected?'

'No.' And then, 'I really don't know.'

The stench of damp sheep and bedding drowned in urine and faeces combined with screeching and bleating of lambs and ewes was overwhelming. She moved up the hill.

Elwyn and William were made of sterner stuff. They leant on the metal hurdles talking rapidly to each other, occasionally rubbing the head of an inquisitive ewe. The animals were restless, eyeing Toss with suspicion as he lay pointing his nose towards them.

Rachel reached the shelter of the tree belt where she'd be hidden from the ever-circling spysat. She was indescribably weary. Her legs felt so weak she collapsed on the turf. But this field experiment nagged her.

Too casual by far. Yes, the Sudan virus was controllable, but no one in their right mind would be so laid back about it. No vaccine? That's mad. Unless Elwyn had misunderstood? But he wasn't stupid, any more than William. She thought back to the night she was so ill with gas poisoning and overheard Jenny's conversation with Shuji. What had they said? Something about blaming terrorists for an outbreak of rinderpest in Snowdonia? If only she could remember exactly, but her mind had been on Ben's disappearance. And something at the end of Shuji and Hilary's phone call niggled her. Also Shuji had used the android episode to destroy her friendship with Alyson so she shouldn't tell me . . . what? None of it added up.

'Here, Rachel,' William shouted.

She ignored him. Elwyn strode up to her. His smelly jacket was smeared with yellow, black and purple splodges of animal medications. Broken zip, tied round the waist with twine. Baggy trousers pushed into muddy wellingtons. Distress had reddened his weather beaten face but couldn't hide that air of freedom she'd first met in Tomos and Parryboots. He had an inner certainty and reliability William lacked. Where William was frenetic, Elwyn was calm.

He held out his hand. 'Your data chip.'

She passed it over trustingly.

He turned it in his scarred hands, exploring its carved faces with a broken nail. His fingers were thickened from manual work and she marvelled that he could manipulate minute electronic equipment.

'No.' He looked up, his face full of disappointment. 'I need a different connection. I'll make one up if you leave it with me.'

She held out her hand. 'No way.'

He nodded as he returned it. 'Then I'll send you one tomorrow,' and he demonstrated how she should connect it. 'Let us know its contents. I think your husband knew more about Eckstazia than they wished. But *murder* . . .'

'I thought they were *good* people,' she moaned. 'Obedient to God, always seeking his will.'

He shrugged. 'They reduce God to a set of rules from a holy book. You can defend any behaviour from the Bible.'

'Then what is *God*?'

'A way of life, Tomos says. Learning sympathy even for those we don't like. Always searching.'

'No certainty?'

He smiled, and she was deeply touched by the sweetness of his weather beaten face. He spread his arms to the hills around them. 'Here I find God.'

'In all the bloody struggle for survival?'

'In the mystery. The silence.'

How strange, she thought, that somehow he found a loving God in these mountains, while she with the same human eyes saw nothing but indifference in rock and grass and the overarching sky.

As they stood together in friendly quiet watching Ben play with Toss, she realised her antipathy to the black market was fading fast. She trusted Tomos, she respected Parryboots, even though she disliked his diatribes, and she liked Elwyn.

Elwyn said, 'William told me about Annie's scones. She's a cruel woman. She almost blinded him when he was ten.'

'That scar?'

'She beat him for cheeking her. That was her excuse. So William came here to Isallt to my mother, Parryboot's sister.'

'So we must condone his behaviour? Poor upbringing's no defence for *that*.'

'We suspect Annie beat up William's half brother when he was little. Said he fell downstairs and naturally there weren't any witnesses. Huw never recovered his wits.' Elwyn smiled grimly. 'Her second husband is boss over her. You speak to him if you've any problems.'

He was uneasy, frequently staring down the narrow valley towards the seaside village. He asked to borrow her binoculars, shouted, 'Get moving!' and bounded down the slope to William and Ben.

'Beard's on her way. Into the woods all of you.'

As they squatted beneath an overhanging birch Rachel asked William how Elwyn knew.

He winked. 'Another secret, my dear.' Then he relented. 'A friend of ours, Dewi, used to be captain of the Prof's launch. He's got a flag in his garden in the town. Beard has to drive here along the coast road and Dewi knows her car.'

'So I bet he pulls the flag down when he sees her,' Ben said.

'Got it in one, young man.'

Her conscience nagged her. Kindness to those we don't like, Elwyn said.

She said, 'William, you're in danger,' and explained her fears of James's revenge.

He shrugged. 'So what?'

After a long wait Elwyn called them out of the wood. 'I reminded her she'd told me none of my sheep would show symptoms and asked would any more die? Perhaps, she said, and had I seen any dead deer or wild boar. I said no and that she'd told me before we ran the experiment they wouldn't be infected no more than the sheep. And she said it's just a precaution, of course they won't.'

'And you trust her?' William asked.

'No. She thinks I'm a Welsh oaf.'

A very frightening idea had come into Rachel's mind. She said, 'You're right, Elwyn, we shouldn't believe her.'

William gave her one of his expressive looks. 'You've changed your tune.'

She ignored him. 'Can you move the infected sheep where the deer can't get near the pens?'

Elwyn said, 'The deer take no notice of our walls and there's no land fenced high enough to keep them out. Can't take the sheep to Penybwlch now Akimoto's ordered police surveillance for the lab.'

William snorted. 'Ordered, yeh. Not being deployed till next week. But you're right. Too much bleating.'

The two men discussed other possibilities, employing so many of those abbreviations common to longtime friends Rachel couldn't understand.

Then Ben whistled to them from the edge of the woods. He waved his arms and half a dozen crows flew up behind him cackling angrily. The men paid no attention but Rachel trotted up to her son.

'Wha' you found?' she puffed.

He led her behind a stunted hawthorn to a deer scraping. A pregnant roe deer lay there, her open guts spilling onto the earth. Her eyes had been torn out. Her black moustache and white chin were matted with drool and blood. Flies buzzed furiously round her torn anus and her rump patch was brown with diarrhoea. She stank.

A little way off a pair of crows squabbled over a length of intestine.

*

'Leave the yapp here,' Ben ordered. He demanded a detour as he and Rachel made their way home from Elwyn's.

His mother fixed the instrument in the branches of a solitary rowan. 'Now where?'

'William said I must show you his hideout just in case.' Ben stepped gingerly onto a disused sheep track running across a steep slope. 'Careful across this scree. William says he runs down it. Two minutes forty three seconds top to bottom.'

She imagined him riding the moving stones, leaning back nonchalantly, digging in heels at every stride. In the valley the cottage chimneys and their wooded gardens appeared very far away. A dog stared up and barked, but no one came out. Nervously she looked down at the ever-narrowing path.

'You'll die if you fall,' Ben said cheerfully. 'Roly poly and crunch right to the bottom.' He negotiated a steep rise followed by bare rock.

It wasn't so bad once she got used to it, but she was happier once she reached firmer ground where low gorse and heather roots held the loose pebbles together.

She stared across to the moors. High fluffy clouds driven by a cold wind raced across the sun, patterning the moors with moving light and shade. Isallt woods were a distant dark speck. By now Elwyn and William were burning the roe deer and the dead ewe, separating out the sick sheep, taking as many precautions as practicable. All the way across the moor she told herself Jenny couldn't be testing the highly lethal new strain of rinderpest. The one that had never been out of the lab. The one so powerful it killed not merely cattle but sheep, deer, pigs and goats. No, it was *impossible*. But Eric and Alyson had been so concerned about its containment. What *had* Alyson found out?

She tripped on a heather root. Righted herself and paid more attention to where she put her feet, hoping she'd never have to cross this mountain in an emergency or at night.

'Not far now,' Ben called over his shoulder.

He trotted downhill a little way to a straggle of oak, rowan and birch in a damp hollow. Here it was warm enough to shed her jacket, though her internal chill remained. A trickle of water flowed through the dell down a zigzag gully, quickly vanishing among impregnable bramble and bracken, nettle and scrubby trees.

Ben had disappeared.

She pushed through the branches, crawled round a large boulder and found him at the entrance to a cave.

'They were looking for granite years ago,' her son informed her. 'They made this hollow and found a spring of water. Then they dug in a long way.'

She followed him into the cave.

It didn't go so very far and it certainly wasn't roomy. Together they blocked most incoming light but she could see boxes and gas bottles stored at the far end.

'William says no one knows about it but him and Elwyn. They found it when they were kids. It's really safe.' As they left he said, 'I asked William is it a hideout for Eckstazia's time of tribulation. He says the Rapture's barking.'

'He isn't a Christian.' Not that that seemed a guarantee of probity any more.

When they reached the main path back to Penybwlch she collapsed exhausted under the mountain ash. The ankle she'd strained on the day of the town riot was giving her gip. Ben watched her with concern.

She said, 'I'm going to lose my job.'

'Like Alyson and Eric?'

'Just like them.'

'I don't mind except for the pony. I hate James. I'm not going to their school.'

She shook her head.

'What will you do?'

'It's not easy to get a job. Lots of people are unemployed.'

'We can go on the dole like the parents of school kids do,' he said cheerfully.

'Eckstazia'll turn us out of the cottage and the social won't cover lodgings, let alone food.'

'We'll manage, Mum. We always do. Let's go home now.'

She wished she had his optimism. She wished she wasn't tied to her Eckstazia loan. The penalty clause for non-payment would certainly be enforced. These days bankruptcy was the worst option as swingeing penalties followed bankrupts for five years.

As they came down through the woods towards the buildings he said, 'You could marry William.'

'No way!' She almost laughed.

'What about Elwyn? He lives with his Mum. I like him.'

'I don't know the man.'

As they went inside the cottage he asked, 'Did you really fuck William?'

Chapter 16

Janet Jones, Annie's helper, stood patiently at the cottage door the following morning. She looked as anxious and as uncared for as ever and she shook her head when Rachel invited her inside. Instead she held out a small package. Elwyn's yapp connection.

Rachel thanked her, smiled gently and asked how she was.

The girl looked up, her thin face pinched and spotty with malnutrition. Annie certainly wasn't generous with food scraps from the scientists' table.

'Please.' Janet's Welsh was so soft Rachel could barely understand it. 'Annie hates you, missus. She made *pice bach* with poison berries. Megan helped. You be careful.' She scuttled away before Rachel could reply.

Why Megan? Was she jealous of Rachel's association with William? Crazy but possible.

Except for the old Skoda the car park was empty, as all the scientists were at the London conference. The Bangor crowd was away for the weekend, as was Annie. Ben was feeding William's hens. She was alone.

She connected Dan's data chip and brought up four files. One was a recorded message. The second referred to automents, the third to rinderpest and the fourth was a copy of his lost article on Eckstazia. She opened the first.

'Dearest love . .'

The sound of his voice undid her. She groaned, her chest heaving with the pain of loss. Her time had been so filled with the effort of coping that she'd bottled all the grief inside her and now it threatened to drown her. Those problems she'd had with Dan, how minor they were! Why had she ever thought James could fill the gap he'd left?

As the recording finished she recovered. She replayed it and listened more carefully.

After his greetings to her and Ben he apologised for giving her the pendant.

'Its information is dangerous for you.

'And I'm sure that if you're listening to this then I'm no longer around. Either disappeared or dead. I know how Eckstazia works and they won't allow me freedom much longer. If you doubt this, check on the following. They uncovered too much as well.' He supplied a list of three names.

'You must pass on this information. I wish I didn't have to put you in danger, but I know I can trust you. No one else believes me. It's *essential* you show these files to someone in authority. But be extremely careful. Eckstazia has followers everywhere.'

Yes, she knew that only too well.

Daniel repeated his warnings throughout his appeal to her. He gave her an access key to Eckstazia's most secret website. But first she must read the data files he'd copied.

The Automents report began with fulsome praise of God and Jesus and a demand to the Holy Spirit to guide us all into the way of Truth. Come, oh Judge and send the wicked into the place of eternal punishment. Bring peace to those who love you.

It described the system of automatic mentors as it pertained five years ago. Originally set up by a US pastor to help answer religious questions, it morphed from a page of script into an android, as people preferred a talking head answering their questions directly. Automents became a teaching phenomenon. One trained counsellor could monitor fifty enquirers by judicious control of his or her android. Quite quickly the mentors became accepted as real people. The novices invented histories for them and claimed miraculous powers for their own mentor, trends the Eckstazia counsellors did nothing to discourage.

How open to abuse, Rachel thought angrily.

Then some bright spark came up with the idea of combining the automents with the Rapture to bring about mass conversions. This vision was the nub of the report.

Jesus' return is imminent, it said. He is coming like a thief in the night and naturally he expects active assistance from his faithful. Automents will be coordinated from a central committee in South Carolina, US, with subcommittees in other countries. Trained counsellors and their androids will be multiplied worldwide and used to educate all the faithful. Meanwhile the central committee will monitor the situation. It will chose a suitable moment, say the Christian festival of Easter which celebrates Jesus rising from the dead. On that date all androids will go offline forever. Raptured into the arms of Jesus. We suggest a program be devised showing the mentors actually floating up into golden clouds.

True, unbelievers will mock. They always do. Let them continue on their way to perdition unchastened. Many more humble souls will convert in terror of this evidence of approaching judgement.

Who could fault such a strategy?

Rachel said aloud with great bitterness, 'Who indeed? Only the sane.' She turned to Dan's copied file on rinderpest.

Again this opened with praise of God and prayers for heavenly guidance. It emphasised the obligation of believers to hasten on the day of the Lord by whatever means available.

The time is nearly here. Look at the state of the world – abortions, immorality, homosexuality, mass murders, drugs, wars, terrorism, earthquakes, tsunamis, hurricanes, global warming – the list is endless. God is unleashing his great and terrible time of tribulation, when two thirds of the human race will perish. Our new monthly journal Blood Bath, The Coming Endtime is going to highlight distress and pain but emphasise that starvation, disease and war are no longer our enemies. They are welcome signs of the coming of the Lord when he will create a new holy heaven and earth, and sorrow and sighing will flee away forever.

Then the file proceeded to relate the state of rinderpest world-wide four years earlier. Eradicated. Research establishments turning to other problems.

It continued: As we decided earlier, Eckstazia will continue funding its own rinderpest research in the UK, explaining this is a precautionary measure we are willing to fund for the good of mankind. The organisation will seek out a quiet location and not publicise this work in any way. The scientific community will soon forget us.

Once we have mutated a more virulent virus we will charge suitable personnel with the task of infecting cattle, say in Ethiopia, where cattle plague was once endemic. Perhaps an area where the disease has never been recorded? South America would be interesting. Already vaccination stocks have run low and maximum panic will ensue as food and transport are affected worldwide. This strategy will be timed to coincide with the automent Rapture. Come, Lord Jesus, Amen.

Deliberately infect cattle with a dreadful disease? *Spread* famine with its related epidemics and wars worldwide? Eckstazia, whom the world's leaders praised as saviours of mankind?

Rachel frowned as she thought back over the past months. This is what Alyson found out. This is why Shuji made sure she was disgraced. No one will believe her.

No one will believe *me*. It's all too crazy.

What had William said about Shuji Akimoto's travels? *'Plague follows that guy round.'* And so it had, from the Sudan to the Argentine.

Eckstazia had spread rinderpest eighteen months ago. And failed. Thank God the virus had been controlled before many starved.

But people *had* starved and Shuji had watched them die. He had protested to Hilary and she castigated him for his doubts. And he'd said in his office, *'Too high a price.'* Then he changed his mind. *'But we act in your name, Lord. Salvation comes after suffering.'* And finally, still unsure, he talked about the Eckstazia conference where he now was, as of this very minute. *'It's not too late for them to cancel.'* But would he stand up to the Central Committee? Outwardly he was tough, but inside mere marshmallow.

Oh yes, she thought, now I'm certain Jenny has infected Elwyn's sheep with this new strain, and there's no antidote. Jenny, Shuji and James return from the London conference tomorrow night. Jenny collects the lethal virus and goes on her merry way to Afghanistan, Pakistan, India and Australia. The multikiller. The bringer of war and famine and disease.

Two weeks to Easter. The best day for the androids to vanish into heaven. The beginning of the end.

This time Eckstazia's left nothing to chance.

Rachel banged her head with her hand.

If Eckstazia approved the starvation of millions then she and Ben were in serious danger.

Ben bounded in from collecting the morning's eggs. 'William isn't back from Elwyn's yet, Mum.' Then, seeing the data chip attached to the yapp he cried out, 'Has Dad left me a message? Has he, Mum? Let me hear.'

She played the recording of his father's voice. A loving message telling him to grow up honest and kind so Rachel would be proud of him. 'Take care of your mother. Look after yourselves. Love you both forever and ever.'

'Doesn't sound like Dad's voice.' Ben was disappointed.

'Memory's a tricky thing, my dear. It *is* Dad.' She wiped her eyes. She knew now why Dan had been so disturbed those last few months of his life.

Ben put his arm round her and they sat in silence for a while. Then he asked what else she'd found out and she said she feared the virus infecting Elwyn's sheep was truly evil.

'As soon as William returns we'll decide what to do.'

But William didn't return.

And Dan's access code to Eckstazia's Central Council was out of date. She spoke the three names Dan had given her, but was told there was no record of such people. She tried to send Dan's documents to websites run by humanist scientists. Her state-of-the-art yapp didn't permit access to those sorts of sites. A double-edged sword indeed.

It was three o'clock and soon it would be evening. The police wouldn't set a watch on the lab till Monday.

'William's still not back,' Ben said, putting his head round the door. 'I'm going to feed and water the hens and collect the evening eggs.'

'Righteo.'

He'd be gone an hour or more. There was no one to watch her. If only she didn't feel so cold inside. Like she'd never be warm again.

She pulled on her jacket and boots and went to the yard. Sledgehammer, lump hammer, a pick. She carried them across the drive, up the steps, through the gate into the garden and round the side of the house to the lab.

Hesitantly she smashed a window with the lump hammer. The glass crashed and then tinkled to the ground. A bird chattered, but nothing else noticed her vandalism. She'd never done anything so bad in her life. She'd always been law abiding.

Don't be so gutless, she told herself.

She put her arm through the gap and fingered the safety cladding that covered the inside of the lab completely. It was solid, strange and slippery, impervious to her probing. Both Alyson and Jennifer had said that if the seal was broken by terrorists the internal security robots would destroy everything inside the building. It shouldn't take long. She swung the heavy sledgehammer at the curious material. No impression at all. She tried again. And again. She slammed the pointed end of the pick against the cladding and felt a dent with her fingers. She swung the pick several more times and thought she'd pierced it, but couldn't be sure.

There had been no rain for days and everything was dry.

There were jerry cans in the fuel shed.

She filled the wheelbarrow with as many as she could manage, then wheeled them back across the drive. She dragged the wheelbarrow backwards up the steps, stopping to reset her load as the cans slipped on the slope. Then she returned for a second load.

How long ago now, her first night here when she and Ben had braved the dark and rain and struggled down this path to rescue a dying pig. So innocent she'd been. So stupidly blind.

It was getting dark. She'd have to chance the blaze being seen by some of the valley farmers. With luck they'd ignore it. Didn't they hate the arrogant people at Penybwlch? What about her near neighbour at Plas Du? Hilary Barron was in London but her staff would be there.

She must take the risk.

There was no wind, only the scent of coming rain in the still air.

She doused the building and laid a trail of fuel. She threw a match and fled to safety. The flame galloped down the line of fuel, leapt, whooshed and roared into the air, surrounding the lab with a black halo of destruction and the stink of burning fuel. In between the planks of the rotten wooden structure little flames appeared, dancing marionettes. Surrounding laurels crackled and hissed. The pungent scent of singed firtree wafted through the air. Smoke spired upwards like an evil genie.

Then she smelt another stench. A choking and penetrating stink as the cladding melted, collapsing inwards, smothering anything that remained.

Relief flooded through her, and excitement combined with wild joy. She danced round the blazing lab, warm for the first time since her conflict with James. She laughed like a harridan, hoping the flames would spread to the house and burn down the whole fucking lot.

Then she tripped, twisting her strained ankle again. It didn't faze her. Instead she sat on the lawn, watching the flames die down while the first drops of rain splashed cool against her skin.

Ben came running through the garden, calling 'Mum! Mum! There's a fire in the lab!' Then he saw her. '*You* lit it, didn't you?'

'It's finished. The virus is dead,' she said. 'Rain'll douse the embers.'

'But Elwyn's sick sheep?'

'When William gets back I'll tell him they must all be destroyed. Burnt.'

*

Ben bounded into the living room followed by a wet but jubilant Toss.

'He's back, Mum.'

The dog shook raindrops all over her as she struggled upright. Even after resting her ankle all night and morning it was still swollen. Ben sat on the floor, his arms round Toss who licked his face enthusiastically.

Then William himself, filling the little room with the reek of oil and damp dirty sheep wool. 'What've you done now?'

Gingerly she placed her swollen foot on the ground. 'Tripped over last night.'

'Plonker. Just when I need all the help I can get,' William said, looking exhausted. 'We're taking the sheep down to the village playing field where there's no contact with deer. Spreading like fuck. Infected some of the control batch. They're shitting blood. We walked as many as we could to the village, but we've got to truck the rest.' He put water in the kettle. 'God, I'm dry.' After a mouthful of tea he continued, 'Elwyn's truck broke down. Spent last night trying to fix it. I've walked back for mine. They'll record me driving on the coast road but it can't be helped. We've assistance from the village but we need more. I sent Megan to bring Parryboots and his mates. Ben, you'll come back with me.'

'Sure thing.' The boy grabbed his wet gear and started for the door.

As William turned to go he said, 'What's that stink of fire?'

'I burnt the lab down last night. Every evil thing in it destroyed.'

He gaped at her, struggling for words as realisation dawned. 'What was on the data chip?'

She told him coldly and succinctly, concluding by handing him a memory stick. 'Two copies are better than one. Keep it safe.'

He put it carefully into an inner pocket. 'Mad. They're *mad*. Jesus' return? Stark raving bonkers.'

Rachel said sombrely, 'Jennifer's overseas plans are stymied now the lab viruses are destroyed. But it can spread like bushfire from Isallt's sheep. If that deer died of it it'll spread into the reserve. Then across the UK.'

'Eckstazia'll be implicated. It's their research.'

'They'll be up in the clouds with Jesus by then,' Ben said with a laugh.

'Who'll check?' asked Rachel. 'Everyone will panic. They'll try to find a vaccine and contain the outbreaks. They'll need to bury heaps of dead animals and find other sources of food. Britain will be isolated. No one out or in. But Eckstazia will isolate the virus from an infected animal and export it.'

'So all Elwyn's sheep must be destroyed immediately.' William sat down and drummed on the table with his thick fingers. 'You say the lethal bug affects pigs as well. There are lots of illegal backyard pigs in the village. We must slaughter and bury Elwyn's sheep and lambs. I can get a digger but we need a livestock carrier to take them to a suitable burying ground. Jack Thomas. . .'

'The farm inspector?'

'Yeh. Him.' He was too anxious even to note surprise at her knowledge. 'His dad has a couple of trucks and drivers. Lives along the coast near Bangor. He'll be at home today, it's Sunday. Phone calls all recorded so I can't contact him.'

'You can drive there,' Ben said.

'No. Too many spycams on that road. Incriminate him. If you hadn't been such a pillock, Rachel, *you* could walk the mountain road over Bwlch y Ddeufaen.' He frowned at her bandaged foot. Then he brightened. 'That's it. Bronwen.'

'I'm not getting on that animal ever again.'

'Come on,' he wheedled. 'She's quiet. She knows the road like the back of her hand.'

'Hoof,' corrected Ben.

So shortly she was balanced precariously on the mare's back.

William put his hand on her thigh. A warm hand. Comforting, though she wouldn't admit that even to herself. He looked up at her but didn't speak.

Why on earth should she feel pleased at the approval in the man's eyes?

She pulled her waterproof close, bent over and adjusted her damaged foot in the stirrup. She gathered up the reins in a meaningful fashion.

Ben stood on the bottom bar of the open gate swinging to and fro. He wailed, 'I really want to come. Iago's a great goer.'

'I've said no. That's it.' To William she said, 'Take good care of him.'

'Of course. Wish you hadn't used so much biofuel.'

'In a good cause.'

'I'll be short. Elwyn's low too.' He stroked the mare's neck and she pushed her head against him. He whispered into her ear and ran his fingers through her tangled mane. 'When you canter sit down like you're in an armchair.'

'*Canter?* You're joking.'

'She's safe.'

'*I'm* not.'

'Be sure to keep to the path once you reach the Bwlch. There's boggy places where Bronwen could stick fast. She panics in the quags. Keep between the two big stones. You're through the pass once you reach an old stone wall with a gap where the mountain gate used to be. Downhill the track is good again.'

They shut the gate to the woods behind her.

The rain was constant. Down her neck, dripping off the bottom of her jacket, drenching her trousers, filling her boots.

Apart from blackbirds clattering their warnings, the breeze in the trees and the pattering of rain everything was quiet and peaceful. The mare's unshod feet sucked and plopped on the wet grass track. Eventually they came out of the woods onto open mountain and the steep climb up to the moor. Normally Rachel would have rejoiced in the sights of spring and the fresh clean scents of burgeoning growth. But there was no pleasure balancing on Bronwen's back with a good two hours of hell ahead.

The mare plodded up hill resolutely, ears flicking back and forwards, occasionally shaking her head against the rain. Rachel tightened her thighs against the firm belly and gripped the pommel of the saddle for fear of slipping off over Bronwen's tail. The reins fell slack on the mare's neck but the animal kept on steadily and calmly.

The path up was interrupted frequently by steep dips downwards. Rachel clutched the back of the saddle and moaned as she slid towards those twitching ears. She righted herself as the track sloped up again. Bronwen snorted and stepped faster.

If the animal trotted! Horror! Rachel gathered the reins again hoping to thwart any such notion in the mare's head.

They reached the top. Beyond them stretched the moor for miles and far away the mountains guarded the pass of the two stones.

Only they didn't.

Today the drizzling clouds sat so low that visibility was only a few dozen yards. The track meandered, split into several smaller paths, wandered around and became a bridle path again. Bronwen walked steadily on. How well *did* the animal know her way? Might she be confused by the mist? Go round in a circle like humans do? The only advantage of this weather was that no wild Welshman would be able to take a potshot at her. Spysats would be confused too.

It was early afternoon. They wouldn't reach the pass before dusk at this rate. She pressed her knees into the mare's sides, collected the reins and called, 'Chuck chuck.'

Bronwen flicked back a contemptuous ear and trogged on.

Rachel tried 'Get on' in Welsh.

Perhaps the mare understood Welsh better than English or maybe she was bored with her slow pace, because she broke into an easy amble. Easy for her that is. Rachel bounced. Her legs shook, her arms jiggled, her breasts wobbled and her bum felt as if it was being pounded by a malevolent masseur. Gradually she settled to the pace. Still painful but not likely to fling her off into the heather.

The mare slowed as she picked her way down the bed of a stream.

Was it the one Rachel had waded on her way to Llanfechan church to fetch holy water? It didn't look very similar.

Then the mist lifted a smidgen. The mare was spot on. They had reached the junction where one track led to the little church, hidden behind its hill, and the other to Bwlch y Ddeufaen taken by the wool traders.

Bronwen headed for the church.

Rachel pulled her head round.

The mare skittered, refusing to take the road to the pass. She had had enough of rain and a stupid rider. She knew how great a distance lay past the standing stones and down to the Bangor coast.

Rachel swore at her.

Bronwen hrrmphed and shook her head up and down, scattering droplets from her mane.

Rachel kicked her heels into the warm wet flanks.

Bronwen blew out a great sigh of resignation and turned up the pass road.

Rachel heaved an equally great sigh of relief.

The clouds settled down again, shrouding landscape, blurring distances. Wreaths of pale mist coiled like the veils of a houri's dance, revealing nothing, tantalising.

They trudged between two tall thin stones. Were they on the pass?

No, they were only the remains of old gateposts with tumbled walls stretching away either side of the gap. Surely they hadn't reached the walls William had spoken of on the far side of the pass? There were no way marks in this fog, and the passing of time was equally confusing.

Then they came into darkness and a cold wind that seared away the mist. Gloom stretched either side where bleak mountains soared away into the clouds. In front of them the murk of Hades. Someone weeping 'Cor *lii*, Cor *lii*.' A lost soul, a sick Roman deserted by his cohort and dying alone, a stone age woman mourning her child. Or only a lonely curlew flying low across the rushes.

Clouds descended again over black bog and wet whin bushes. The mare snuffled at the raw air, hesitating for the first time over the plethora of winding paths leading everywhere and nowhere.

Rachel shivered. Not only from the chill wind piercing her wet clothes but from rank fear. Completely lost among peat hags and quaking bog.

Then Bronwen's ears flicked. She sidled and danced a few steps, decided her route, plodded on.

The first way-stone loomed up on Rachel's left. She'd never seen anything like it before. Massive, higher than her, pointing a threatening finger into the clouds. Its foot was hidden in mountain tussock grass and heather. Grey lichen blotched it and the pockmarks of age disfigured it. Beyond it lay the quagmires and the one safe route between the two boulders.

Whoever raised it here thousands of years ago had felt similar dread to hers. Had sacrificed to their unknown gods for safe journey through morass and confusing mist. What oblation could she make to this monster for her own succour?

Only the horse comforted her with its warmth and energy in this land of death.

Once she dared look behind her, fearing to see the mountain erl-king beckon with a seductiveness no mortal can refuse, or to find snuffling hell hounds galloping silently after her, faster than the whirling mist. She pressed her knees into the mare's flanks, forcing her on, careless of the treacherous ground, forgetful of William's warnings.

A hundred yards on and the horse shied nervously. Rachel swayed over the mare's shoulder for a desperate moment and then righted herself. Bronwen had been jinxed by the second way-stone suddenly rearing out of the mist. It was square and stout as a small house. Black lichen streaked it like solidified tears. It mocked her little life with its longevity.

They jogged past, and now the path was firmer. Shortly they reached the gap in the broken wall that marked the end of the quags. The path became stony as they headed down hill. The mist paled and lower hills and coastline emerged dimly in the evening light. The mare stepped out, ears flicking, tail swishing, eager for home at the end of the long slope down to Jack Thomas's village.

*

Rachel dozed. Lurched awake as her head banged against the truck side window. Rain slashed across the headlight beam and obliterated potholes and cracks in the coast road back to Isallt. Behind them the lights of the following truck dazzled her in the wing mirror. Windscreen wipers moaned steadily, sloshing the rain either side. The engine hummed, drowning the conversation between Jack Thomas and his father. Jack sat in the middle seat, legs straddling the gear lever. A small man, wiry, short legs. He smelt of tobacco and livestock. His father was hunkier, dark haired and wide bulging eyes. He drove intently, fast but careful.

Jack was a quick intelligent man who'd grasped Elwyn and William's problem immediately and ordered his father to bring both trucks over, including shot for slaughter. He was on his mobile now, arranging a burial site far from any susceptible animals, precautions against police interception put aside in the urgency of the situation.

Wedged behind her was a pair of metal crutches Jack's father had begged or borrowed from a neighbour. It wasn't just her ankle that was sore. Her whole body ached and she understood why jockeys have bowlegs.

She shifted uneasily as the truck cornered a roundabout and turned uphill to the little town below Elwyn's farm and the playing field where the sheep were gathered. A man rushed into the road, gesticulating wildly in the truck headlights. Jack's father crunched on the brakes and jumped down, followed by Jack. Behind them the second truck squealed to a standstill and its driver joined the group of shadowy figures.

Eventually Jack came to Rachel's window.

'Trouble, Rachel. Deep trouble, Dewi says. Three men from Plas Du. Stun guns and coshes. Dog went for them. William smashed their car lights. In the dark they couldn't use their guns. Big fight. When help came from the village they made off with your son. William. . .'

'Ben! They've got Ben? Take me to Plas Du *now*!'

He hesitated. 'The sheep. . .'

'Forget the sheep.'

His look was compassionate. 'OK.' He swung into the driver's seat, shouted a few words to his father and Dewi and set off back to the coast road. 'Parryboots never showed. William's badly hurt and Elwyn's taken him to their hideout. I don't know where it is.'

'I do.'

'I don't want to know. Dewi said they kicked William when he was down. The dog's dead.'

She mourned silently for Toss, the bouncing cheerful dog that Ben loved so well. For William she felt a little compunction.

Chapter 17

The rain slackened and clouds cleared as the empty truck bounced along the coast road until they reached the town, passed the castle and turned up the mountain road towards Plas Du and Penybwlch. As they rounded the last corner Jack turned off the lights and drove very slowly by moonlight towards Plas Du's forbidding gates.

'Can you manage the rest, Rachel? I don't want those buggers to recognise Dad's truck out here where it shouldn't be. He could lose his license.'

'I'll cope.' She shook his warm hand.

'God, woman, you're cold.'

'I'm OK.' She struggled with the crutches, limped to the gate and contacted its intercom as Jack turned the truck and drove back down the pass.

The gate swung open. Lights came on along the side of the drive. It wound uphill, deep among trees and shrubs. She adjusted the crutches on her arms and took a few tentative steps. Not good. Snails travel faster and with far less pain.

As she staggered up the steps to the glass atrium the doors slid open and a porter in navy suit and pale blue shirt welcomed her by name. She was taken to a room without windows in the heart of Plas Du. Small but comfortable. Thick beige carpet on the floor, two easy chairs and a table with three upright chairs. Strange instruments hung from the walls. Hidden lighting changed colour gradually so the walls and floor glowed now with amber hues, now palest green, now the blue of the sky at zenith, now subdued purples and reds.

An empty room.

'Where's Ben,' she said to the porter. 'Bring him and we'll go.'

'Fiona's coming,' said the man.

'Fiona? Who's that? I want my son. You've no right . . . '

'Fiona will be here soon.' The door clicked behind the porter and there was no door handle. Rachel passed her hands over the wall but couldn't find the key.

She sat by the table nervously. In front of her was a grandfather clock with an intricately designed face but lacking a minute hand. Useless.

Even as she stared at it the door opened and a dour woman entered. Rachel recognised her as Hilary's companion both at church and when out riding. She was a formidable woman in a black sleeveless shirt revealing heavy rounded muscles. Her trousers hung baggily from her thick waist. Her boots were polished as a guardsman's.

But no Ben.

'Where is he?'

Fiona sat down lightly opposite Rachel. Chunky she might be, but she was also fit and strong.

'You've no right to hold him from me!'

When the woman spoke her voice was high and clear. 'You've come to thank us for rescuing him from that riffraff, I hope. He told us you'd left him to go for a ride over the hills. It seems the Welsh mob carried him off to use as hostage. If I may say so, Rachel, - and I'm certainly not criticising the way you rear your son, he *is* your child after all - surely it was a little irresponsible to neglect him and ride off to enjoy yourself?'

'What *are* you talking about?'

'Now he's resting. He's very tired after all the excitement. I hope you don't mind waiting, Rachel? I'm looking forward to a little chat with you before you leave.' She wrinkled her nose. 'Horse is *so* pervasive. I suggest a shower at your earliest opportunity.'

The door opened and the porter brought a tray of coffee and sweet biscuits. Fiona poured a cup and handed it to Rachel. 'I see you've noticed the Professor's clock. European. Twentyfour hours on the face. A geocentric pre-Copernican solar system with the sun as a gold sphere rotating round the earth.' Her voice was monotonous as a guide round a stately home. 'She was given it by a colleague at Oxford University as a daily reminder of the fallibility of science. What is true today is overturned tomorrow. Only the Word of God is unchanging.'

'Just bring Ben and we'll go.'

A circular metallic ring full of intricate designs hung on a sidewall. It mesmerised her as it twinkled in the changing lights.

'Ah, the Professor's astrolabe. An ancient instrument used by astronomers to predict the position of heavenly bodies. Persian, thirteenth century. Given her in grateful appreciation by the senior Lady Mujtahideh. . .' Fiona swallowed her coffee in a gulp and poured herself another. 'As you know, the female ayatollah. She's steeped in Islamic law and also a physicist of international standing.'

'Stop playing with me! I demand to see Professor Barron.'

'Demand, Rachel? Really you have no such rights. The Professor has left everything to me. She's far too busy a person to deal with minor matters like these. And she's not due to return from London till midday tomorrow. By which time you'll have left the district. With or without Ben. That depends on your co-operation.'

'I'm not leaving my son.'

Fiona's tone changed as she leaned towards Rachel. Her mouth wrinkled in an effort at a smile. The cat playing with the mouse knows it has invincible power in its paws.

'One of Parry's mistresses contacted me late this afternoon. She said Parry and his rabble are intent on scuppering Eckstazia's vital research into rinderpest.'

Megan? Janet Jones said she was dangerous, but would she really put her dear William's life at risk? And William had sent her to fetch Parryboots and his friends but they hadn't showed. Had Megan betrayed them all?

'And, even more seriously, that you're involved.' She thrust two biscuits into her mouth and crunched them with strong white teeth. 'You're a clever woman and you must realise you're in a difficult position. But the Professor has your welfare at heart. You can rely on me to help you.' She smiled again, more tiger than cat. 'Megan's an ignorant woman. *We* know, don't we, that it's far more serious than that. With your help Parry's mob decided to gain control of the virus and use it as a bargaining tool, holding the world to ransom for their greed. They've stolen the experimental sheep and now hold stocks of a very lethal virus. Fortunately they're amateurs. We've haven't found any connections with key bioterrorists.'

'What an insane story! No one will believe it.'

Fiona smiled. 'The media doesn't deal in logic, my dear, only in shocking stories. And *we* control it.'

Music played, a male voice sang 'La donna è mobile'. Fiona strode to a floral decoration on the wall, saying, 'Yes?' She reduced the sound and listened carefully to the caller, nodding. 'Good. Well done. Yes, I'll let you know shortly.'

Then she turned back to Rachel. 'The gang have just been rounded up by the police as they were burying Elwyn Robert's sheep. Interestingly there's a farm inspector among them. But no Parry or Roberts.'

Rachel clutched her necklace as if Dan's memory could give her inspiration.

'What's that in your hand?' Fiona held out her hand for the necklace. When Rachel refused she twisted her arm till her eyes watered. Then she yanked the trinket over her head and examined it. 'Ah, so that's it.'

She took a yapp out of an inner pocket and inserted the pendant without need for any connection. The contents came up on the wall.

'So that's where you hid it. Ingenious. We scrubbed every reference to Daniel Kerem's article and here it is in full. Along with the other files we suspected were held somewhere. Well, well. As we feared. Daniel's spy in our camp.'

'Hardly. I didn't read it till yesterday.'

'You expect us to believe that?' She put the pendant in her pocket. 'The Professor will be very interested.' Then she turned angrily on Rachel. 'James told us you're another of Parry's mistresses. You've destroyed a good man who loved you far more deeply than you deserved. Have you no remorse?'

'He spied on me using his android. I hate his deception.' Anger grew in her, but she must keep her cool. Only careful negotiation would release Ben and she had yet to find out what bargaining chips she possessed.

Fiona raised an eyebrow. 'You're hardly in a position to denounce him. You've already delayed our Lord's return. Eckstazia has set back the rapture because of your interference.'

Rapture! Rachel thought, suppressing her contempt. Merely online androids vanishing into a spurious background of brilliant light.

'The signs of the coming tribulation are plain. Increasing war and famine. Rampant infectious diseases. Evil triumphant. Yes, the Antichrist has many supporters, some as stupid as you and your friends but tiresome just the same. Jesus *will* return whatever you do. Justice, peace and mercy *will* flow down from the skies. Love and harmony *will* reign. *You can't win.*' Fiona's eyes sparkled in anticipation of the glory to come. She continued, 'Your husband's reports are worth nothing. No one believes them.'

'*I* do.'

Fiona frowned. Then she said coolly, ''But you aren't going to say anything to anyone, my dear. Because you're lost eternally. If you once accept Jesus' pardon and then deny him, your damnation is sure. The dog returns to its vomit and gobbles it up. The washed sow rolls in the dirt again,' Fiona quoted, her face twisted in righteous anger. 'There is no *second* salvation, Rachel. God can no longer forgive your sin.'

Rachel held back a nervous giggle. Had she really once believed in Eckstazia's weird doctrines? All down the ages people had hoped war and famine and plague were signs of Jesus' return. Always they were disappointed. No, it was people of courage and compassion who must save the world. Aloud she said, 'Then bring Ben and let us go.'

'With *you?* The mother who leaves her son in the hands of a scoundrel like Parry? Come, come, Rachel. Children are taken from their parents for less. He's already on the At Risk register. A word from me . . . '

They were both totally in Eckstazia's power. 'What do you want?'

'Where are Parry and Roberts holed up?'

Hoping to save both her son and the wounded men she said firmly, 'I don't know.'

Fiona tapped impatiently on the table. 'I think you do.'

'No. Why would they tell me their secrets?'

Fiona spoke into her yapp. They heard heavy footsteps echo along some distant corridor, coming closer. The door opened. Another of Hilary's servants stood there supporting Ben. He nodded to Fiona and retired.

Ben's face was white and streaked with tears. When he saw his mother he ran screaming to her, one arm outstretched. The other, wrapped in a bandage, hung by his side. She gathered him to her and they held each other for a long moment, hearts beating fit to break.

'What've they done to you?' she whispered.

He clung to her, too traumatised to reply.

'What've you done?' she demanded.

'The bandage covers a minor operation to insert an identity chip so you can find him whenever he runs off again. Just give him normal painkillers when the anaesthetic wears off.'

'How dare you! You've no right. . .'

'You should thank me. It's something you should have done long ago, then his wild escapades wouldn't have caused so much havoc at Penybwlch.' She paused to pop another biscuit in her mouth. When she offered the plate to Ben he huddled further away from her. She said sweetly, 'Before you go – and you needn't worry, I shall let you go quite freely – I must ask you again where Parry and Roberts are hiding.'

'Don't tell them,' Ben whispered.

Fiona smiled in satisfaction. 'Thank you, Ben. I was sure your mother knew. Now please, Rachel.'

Ben curled up on the chair beside her. He was trembling and she soothed him as best she could, tenderly holding his arm. She heard him mutter Toss's name and whisper, 'He's dead,' and she was filled with burning hatred.

Eckstazia could easily take Ben from her permanently. She must get them both away from this evil place now, this minute. As for William and Elwyn, she'd done her best to protect them.

'A map,' she said, and when Fiona shone it on the wall Rachel got up stiffly. 'It's a cave on that hill. Difficult to reach.'

'We have dogs.' Fiona pinpointed the site on her yapp and sent its details to her henchmen.

Ben burst out, 'You mustn't hurt William.'

'What makes you think I will?'

'Mum, he was crying. William was *crying*. They punched and kicked him.' His face contorted at the memory.

'Now, Rachel. One or two points. You appreciate all your son's records are indelibly contained on his chip. His truanting. His At Risk status. His appalling psychological report. And *we* can track your son as well as you. We'll always know your whereabouts through him. If you think of having it removed . . . You've heard of the so-called zombie drug?'

Rachel nodded, her mouth dry with fear.

'Ben's chip contains a minute amount. Concentrated and highly potent. Don't be alarmed, it won't leak. Unless you try to remove it. Or if we hear you're attempting to traduce Eckstazia. The Professor has complete control and she'll certainly activate it if necessary. He'll be mentally damaged permanently and it will be your fault.' She said confidentially, 'It's experimental of course. The first time the zombie drug's been used in a human subject. You must let me know just how it affects him if . . . '

Forgetting all pains in the heat of her fury Rachel leapt up, her arms outstretched to throttle the woman opposite her. Ben's legs entangled hers. The table was in her way. Fiona easily pinioned her arms back and forced her ferociously down into her seat.

'Why don't you simply murder us like Dan?' she burst out.

Rattled, Fiona exclaimed, 'He was Christ's enemy.' She stumbled, trying to cover her admission. 'Eckstazia never murder people. We work for the ultimate good of the whole world.'

'Cattle plague across the globe? *Not murder?*'

'The Welsh gangsters will pay dearly for their threats to disrupt the world with their stolen virus. Details of their ultimatum will shortly be made public. Eckstazia's name is clear. Everyone knows how much good we do for humanity.' She paused, her face contorted with suppressed rage. 'Jennifer's trip will go ahead. We are under Jesus' protection and we won't fail. Jesus will return in spite of all the Antichrist's stratagems.' She banged her fist on her palm, emphasising her piety. Then, with righteous malice, 'As for *you*. You're without a job. Unable to pay back your loan from us. Eckstazia will declare you bankrupt and you'll be without credit for the next five years. A nonperson financially. I will personally see to it that your teaching reputation is destroyed. You are unemployable. And your details are already incorporated on the Police Records website at my request. Available to everyone. Now be off with you both.'

As Rachel and Ben stood up she said finally, 'Collect your gear from the cottage and leave before morning. No, there's no transport available.' She indicated Rachel's crutches with a thin smile. 'You must walk.'

Rachel limped through the door, her arm round Ben. 'Don't mind them,' she whispered to him with fierce joy. 'We've won.' If her ankle wasn't so painful she'd dance in triumph. 'They don't know yet I've destroyed the virus and all the records. The sheep are buried. The world is safe from animal plague.' And then reality broke in. 'There are other diseases they can research. We've won the battle against madmen, not the war.'

Ben wriggled away from her grasp as they crossed the hall. ''Why did you shop William?' His eyes, so like Dan's, were dark with contempt.

'You're free. We're both safe.'

'That's what Judas did to Jesus. They'll kill him and Elwyn like Dad.' He stared at her with loathing and she watched his childhood flooding away in the knowledge of human treachery.

He marched off down the drive into the darkness of the night.

Rachel shuffled down the drive as fast as she could, calling 'Wait, Ben, wait.'

He waited in the shadows at the gates, sobbing harsh tears, which he tried to hide as she approached. He turned his back on her.

'What else could I do?'

He shook her arm off his shoulder.

'If I lied and told them a made-up hiding place they'd haul us in as soon as they found out.'

'And activate the zombie drug.' He turned to her then and she hugged his slight frame to her heart. He whispered, 'They can find us *anywhere*. Will you still look after me, Mum?'

'Always. *Al*ways.' She held him tight.

'P'raps the zombie drug's a lie.'

'They lie all the time. We'll check it out,' she said firmly while knowing it wouldn't be that easy.

As they reached Penybwlch gates they heard a car engine approaching from the valley.

'Scientists coming home,' Rachel whispered, and they stepped back into the bushes as a car paused at the gates for verification.

The driver looked towards them.

James.

Could he see them? She shuddered and felt her body clench as if a cold hand squeezed her heart.

But the car drove on, its tail-lights growing closer together as the distance increased. The black gates swung smoothly together, giving a final jerk as they clanged shut and hid the car from view.

Momentarily she remembered his last broken-hearted words to her and was filled with pity and guilt. Then she thought, he cares only for his own hurt pride while plotting without remorse to bring suffering to millions.

Ben whispered, 'He'll see the lab's burnt down.'

'We daren't go back to the cottage.' If only she didn't feel so sick, so feeble.

'Bryn. I must find Bryn.'

'Where can we go?'

Ben opened the pedestrian gate and started up the drive towards the cottage.

'*No, Ben!*'

Then a miaow from the bushes and the little cat rubbed itself against the boy's legs. He gathered her up in his good arm and turned back. '*Now* we can go. I know where. Lean on me, Mum.'

So supporting each other and without a backward look at their home, they hobbled down the valley towards the town.

*

After what seemed like eternity Ben guided Rachel down a sideroad to a terrace of ancient stone cottages. A middle-aged woman was getting into a medical car parked at the roadside. She seemed familiar.

Then a man of similar age came out of the cottage, someone Rachel definitely knew – too well. Parryboots. William's father.

'Olwen,' he called, holding out a bag. She took it and drove off, and by this time Rachel had remembered where she'd seen the woman before. Olwen had rescued her from the thugs on the day of the market raid.

This was one place she didn't want to be, and she turned to go as Ben whispered, 'That's his wife.' Then he called out to Parryboots, who recognised them in amazement.

'You got away from that place! But what's happened to you both? Come in, come in.' He called out to someone inside, 'Janet, stretch out the soup for two more.'

The front door opened straight into the main room, a small square room with a log fire, a small settee and an upright chair. A thin cotton carpet partly covered worn red quarry tiles, and was augmented by a sheepskin rug with bald patches in front of the slumbering fire. There was a table with three chairs in one corner and a steep flight of stairs facing the front door. Opposite that another door led into a kitchen, which emitted delicious cooking smells.

When had she and Ben last eaten? She couldn't remember.

'And a cat too,' said Parryboots, putting a couple more logs on the fire.

Bryn snuggled closer into Ben's protective arm.

'Sit down, sit down. You look exhausted. Olwen – she's a GP you know - she's gone to collect William and take him to Bangor hospital.'

'No!' Rachel exclaimed. 'She's not safe. Plas Du thugs will be there.'

'They don't know where he is.'

Shamefaced she admitted that knowledge of his hideout was the price of her and Ben's release. To her surprise he gave a sigh of relief. 'They aren't there. They're both in a safe house in the village.'

Ben asked, 'Who'll take care of the hens?'

Parryboot's worried expression relaxed into a smile. 'Good man. Care of animals is important in any crisis, isn't it? Annie and her husband are feeding them.' He frowned again. 'William's badly hurt. Local nurse said his heart stopped briefly and she suspects skull fracture as well as broken pelvis, collarbone and ribs. The thugs aimed particularly for him. Elwyn's hurt but not so badly. They concussed his Mam.'

Ben gave a little moan. 'Poor William.' He clutched Bryn so tightly that she miaowed, and Rachel put her arm round him, drawing him closer.

Janet, Annie's helper, came in with the soup. She looked as downtrodden as ever, but she'd lost some of her shyness. Handing steaming bowls to Rachel and Ben on the settee, she said, 'Police took Elwyn's Mam to hospital. They're everywhere on the coast road. They gave me a lift some of the way and then I ran here with news of the fight.'

'Best and fastest messenger we have. No one suspects Janet,' Parryboots said. 'Olwen should be safe too as long as the police don't stop her on the way to hospital and recognise William.' He drummed his fingers on his knee, and Rachel recalled his son making a similar gesture in her cottage earlier in the day.

He went on, 'Jones Police daren't let this go. He'll have to report Elwyn's illegal sheep, *and* the illegal burying even though there was a farm inspector present.'

She put Ben's bowl on the floor as he slumped against her, eyes shut and face white and pinched. She stroked his hair off his forehead. Both were wet with sweat, but he was shivering, though the fire was warm and little Bryn nestled beside him like a purring hotwater bottle.

Parryboots got up and found him a hand-knitted rug. 'We learnt where you two were when Jack Thomas called in on his way back from Plas Du – well-named Black Mansion. What happened to Ben's arm?'

When she told him about the chip he growled, 'What evil people they are!'

'They know we're here. We aren't safe anywhere.' She kept her voice low in the hope Ben wouldn't hear.

'I'll stop the transmission.' He took a metal-mesh armband from a shelf and handed it to Rachel. 'Faraday cage,' he said. 'Interrupts transmission. We've used them for years.'

'But the zombie drug!'

'Eckstazia can't reach him, can they? We'll check it out at the hospital. If they haven't got the equipment, we've friends in Manchester. Let him sleep now, poor exhausted boy.' His voice was low and tender, and to her chagrin Rachel burst into tears.

Janet knelt beside the settee, her arms round Rachel, soothing her, and Rachel sobbed until she could cry no more. In a daze of weariness – when had she last slept well? – she felt Janet settle her comfortably among the cushions and then she was blessedly unconscious.

Occasionally she woke with a start, thinking she was incarcerated in Plas Du and Ben was lost forever. Then with indescribable relief she realised he was sleeping peacefully in her arms on the settee and Parryboots was dozing close by in the other chair.

She woke when a car drove up and through a haze of sleep she felt a rush of cold air as the outside door opened.

'Not good, but he'll make it.' Olwen's voice, weary and troubled.

'Shh. They're asleep,' Parryboots whispered.

'Lost a lot of blood from a knife wound to his back. Minor skull fracture. Brain scan OK but his good eye was hit with something hard. A boot probably. They hope to save its sight. Bruising everywhere especially ribs with two breakages. Other suspected breaks are dislocations.'

In the following silence Rachel's thoughts echoed Ben's earlier distress. Poor man indeed, though she still found him obnoxious.

Then Parryboots asked quietly, 'And Elwyn? His Mam?'

'She's unconscious still. Oxygen. She's been poor physically for years and she may not get through.'

'Devils.'

Rachel lay there silently, listening to someone making tea.

'Elwyn's the best of the three. Mainly bruising and minor wounds.' Olwen paused, then said, '*She's* OK?'

Rachel knew Olwen referred to her.

Parryboots listed her problems succinctly and continued, 'She did well. Recognised the sheep virus and worked out it was the new vicious variety. Destroyed the lab and its contents. Fetched Thomas and the trucks.'

'Rode over Bwlch y Ddeufaen. *I* wouldn't ride that way on such a bad day.'

'And she rescued Ben from the fangs of Eckstazia.'

'Is it true they murdered her husband?'

'It's true.' Parryboots sounded grim. There was a pause while the mugs clinked and then he said, 'So, Megan informed Eckstazia about the sheep burial.'

'I can't believe it.'

'We have to. Janet confirmed Rachel's claim that Megan was sent to call me to help. She never came.'

'But why would she do such a thing? It doesn't make sense.'

'No. Impossible to understand.' Again a pause before Parryboots asked, 'Police?'

'All over the place. I was stopped three times coming home. Jack Thomas and his Dad are in for questioning along with Dewi. And they've discovered the burnt out lab at Penybwlch.'

'We must keep a low profile till it blows over. Are all the sheep dead and buried?'

'Confirmed.' A long sigh from Olwen. 'I'll get back to the village surgery. A number of people with minor wounds. Then I'll go on to the hospital again. Try and prevent police taking Elwyn in till he's rested. Keep an eye on William. I'll let you know any developments. Keep cheerful.'

'And you.'

The breeze from the open door wafted round Rachel's head again. She began to drift back to sleep. For the first time for years she felt at peace. Not out of danger. Uncertain of her future and Ben's. But warm and comforted. Accepted. Among friends.